He slipped... and g... close in his arms!

"I don't want to go back to that lonely bed downstairs. I want to sleep with you in my arms every night for the rest of my life."

"You just want to hold me?" Mara asked.

"Hold you, kiss you, make you mine forever."

"But . . . I am yours."

"Not the way I want you to be," he whispered hoarsely. "I want us to be man and woman in all the ways there are. I want to share my life and dreams with you. If I stay now, there'll be no going back. It'll be this way from now on."

She pressed against him as innocently as any young female animal that responds by instinct to the male. She lifted her face to meet his kiss, her lips parting as his mouth possessed hers. His hand slid down her back, holding her hips more tightly against him. She pressed warm lips to his cheek. "I want you to touch me," she said.

Also by Dorothy Garlock

Annie Lash

Dream River

Lonesome River

Restless Wind

Wayward Wind

Wild Sweet Wilderness

Wind of Promise

River of Tomorrow

Published by
WARNER BOOKS

MIDNIGHT BLUE

DOROTHY GARLOCK

WARNER BOOKS

A Time Warner Company

For my grandsons,
Adam and Amos Mix
who give me love and, at times,
a pain in the neck

WARNER BOOKS EDITION

Copyright © 1989 by Dorothy Garlock
All rights reserved.

Cover illustration by Sharon Spiak

Warner Books, Inc.
1271 Avenue of the Americas
New York, N.Y. 10020

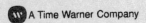 A Time Warner Company

Printed in the United States of America

First Printing: July, 1989

10 9 8

Chapter
ONE

"H'yaw! H'yaw! Move, ya bastards! Hightail it, ya dang-busted, mangy, worthless, sonsabitches! Yore lazy meat ain't fit fer buzzard bait!"

The long, thin leather cracked over the backs of the straining team, and insults spewed from the mouth of the stage driver on the box. He whipped the horses into a full gallop as they raced toward a group of small, weathered buildings nesting amid a grove of aspens. Above the steady sound of wheels and iron-shod hooves, a stream of profanity came from the man wielding the whip.

"He always does that." The traveling salesman with the side whiskers slapped his chubby palms on his knees and smiled at the young woman facing him on the opposite seat.

"Why?" she asked with a questioning lift of her brows.

"I think it's called making an entrance. Sometimes passengers are waiting to go to Cheyenne. You should hear him when he gets to Cheyenne. He puts on such a show that everyone in town comes out to see the stage come in." He made an airy gesture toward the window, but his admiring glance stayed on the girl's face.

She merely regarded him, not answering; then, deliberately, she turned her head and gave her attention to the ramshackle buildings they were approaching.

"Do you live near here, miss?"

The question got the drummer no more than a cold stare from emerald green eyes; but, for whatever the reason, it was by now all he had come to expect. He could count on one hand the number of words she had spoken since he had boarded the stage at the mid-morning stop. She wasn't the type of woman who usually traveled alone. He looked her over, a deliberate inspection that she chose to ignore.

She was pretty—kind of, the drummer decided. Of course, he was comparing her to the painted women who served the spirits he sold to the saloon owners. She was much too prim for his taste, but he had to admit there was something about her that brought out the protective nature in a man. She sat as straight on the seat as if she were sitting in a church pew. At the last stop, when she had gotten out of the coach for a few minutes, he noticed that she was of medium height for a woman and had a small waist, generous breasts, and rounded hips. The drummer had seen the yard man look at them. Behind her back he had held out his hands, palms up, and had drawn up his fingers while giving the drummer a knowing, wolfish grin.

No, she was not beautiful, but she had something more than beauty. The fat man watched as a worried frown drew her dark brows closer together. She brushed the hair back from her face before she straightened the straw hat on her head and jabbed the hatpin in place to hold it there. Damp from the humidity, her thick dark auburn hair curled and escaped in springy tendrils from the pins that held it coiled to the back of her head. She mopped her face, looked with disgust at the dirt left on the wisp of white handkerchief, tucked it into her sleeve at her wrist, and pulled on her soft white gloves that showed a slight soil on the fingertips.

The drummer concluded that she was fastidious, and not suited to this rough country. Her skin was very white and soft. The heat inside the coach had brought a touch of pink to her cheeks and moisture to her temples, but her emerald green eyes could turn the air frosty, as they had done when he tried to start a conversation. They had shown anger at the profanity used by the driver and laughter when a bird had flown alongside the window of the coach. Since the whiskey salesman considered himself an authority on women, he marveled that this one could be so distant and so seductive at the same time. She had a body made for love! Just looking at her affected him in such a way that he removed his hat and placed it on his lap to hide the sudden bulge that appeared there.

What was this innocent, proper miss doing traveling alone and stopping off at a remote, run-down place like Sheffield Station? She caught him looking at her and lifted her small pointed chin haughtily while pressing her mouth into a line of disapproval at his close scrutiny.

"Shef . . . field Sta . . . tion!"

The driver expressed his displeasure with the team by issuing another stream of obscenities and tramped on his brake. The coach rocked as the split reins curbed the horses to a stand. He swung easily down from his box, opened the door and waited to help the woman take the long step to the ground.

"Ten minutes," he said curtly to the drummer.

Mara Shannon McCall graciously accepted the driver's help, then quickly removed her hand. She looked anxiously around. Not a buckboard or a wagon was in sight. A feeling of uneasiness began to close in on her.

The old man bringing up the fresh team gave her the briefest of glances as she stood waiting for the driver to unload her trunks. Her knees shook and her breath locked in her chest. In all her nineteen years she had never seemed so alone. She fought nervousness and tried to settle her breathing. Feeling vulnerable and scared, she slid her hand down the side of her dress to touch the comforting shape of the little pistol in her pocket, and silently thanked her friend, Lars, for insisting that she bring it. No sign of her stress showed on the face she presented to the stage driver when he piled her trunk and carpetbags on the ground at her feet.

"Somebody meetin' ya, miss?" The driver was a string-bean of a man with straggling whiskers and a tremendous wad of tobacco that seemed permanently lodged in one cheek.

"Oh, yes. They'll be along." She turned away, then back to the driver. "I was told the McCall holdings are five miles north of this place."

"More likely six or seven." He took off his hat and scratched his head. This one was a puzzle. Laced up tighter than a drum in a corset, wearing lacy gloves, and going to *that* place. Hell and shitfire! He was paid to drive the stage, not stand around worrying about silly women.

"There ain't nobody here but old Jim, miss. He be no danger to ya or to nobody else. No help neither," he added dryly. "I can't be waitin' for somebody to fetch ya. I got a schedule to keep." He screwed his hat down tight on his head. "Yo're sure somebody's comin'?"

"I never expected you to wait," she said, disregarding the question, and went to sit on the bench beside the door lest the driver feel encouraged to ask something more personal.

He completed a final meticulous check on the harnessing of the fresh team, then swung easily up the hub of the big front wheel to his place. He booted off the brake and a yell sent the team surging into their collars. The drummer waved as the stage took to the road in a cloud of dust.

The air was hot and still. Black flies buzzed around Mara as she sat impatiently on the bench in front of the station and removed her gloves. She lifted off her hat, fanned her face with the stiff brim, and wondered if she should have gone on to Cheyenne to wait for Cousin Aubrey to come for her.

Minutes passed. The station keeper had disappeared with the tired team. The door of the shack stood ajar, and Mara went to it and called out. There was no answer. Under her hand the door opened wider, and she spoke inquiringly into the room. It was empty. She viewed it with disgust. A chair was turned over, scraps of food lay on the floor, and the bed was unmade. The headmistress at the school she had recently left would have had plenty to say about that! What a shocking thing, not to have the bed made in the middle of the day. Not only was the room a shambles, but there were dark stains on the floor. Someone had either bled here or, more than likely, the slovenly occupant had brought a small animal he had killed into the shack to dress it. She wrinkled her nose at the foul odor and turned away. She was thirsty, but not thirsty enough to drink from anything in that place.

Mara walked out to the edge of the hard-packed yard and looked beyond the road to the wide empty land with its waving grass and the sky over it. She thought of a remark her Irish immigrant father had made when she was just a child. *All that land,* he had said, *and not a potato planted.* He and her mother had come to America to escape the famine in Ireland. He had worked his way to Colorado and had made a gold strike. His dream had been to own land, not a hole in the side of a mountain. He sold his mine for a tidy sum and invested his money in Wyoming land, planted a field of potatoes, and built his wife and daughter a fine house. Colleen McCall enjoyed their prosperity for five years before the smothering sickness took her life. Heartbroken, Shannon McCall had taken his eleven-year-old daughter to Denver and placed her in Miss Fillamore's School for Young Ladies because it had been her mother's fondest wish that her daughter receive the education she had never had.

Five years before she had come to terms with her father's death and had accepted the loss. Miss Fillamore had impressed upon her that she was an orphan and the school would be her home.

How extremely fortunate for you, Miss Fillamore had said. *You will have a position and will be able to teach other young ladies as you have been taught.*

Fortunate? Mara had found herself gradually becoming a replica of Miss Fillamore, a woman who had no interest outside the school. Then, quite suddenly, Mara became homesick, realizing that she was not ready to devote her life to other women's daughters. She had a home and land in Wyoming. Her father had left it to her. She wanted to go there, to the place he had built and where he and her mother were buried.

Mara thought of Cousin Aubrey and his wife, Brita. She had seen them only once, when they had come to Denver to tell her of her father's death. Aubrey McCall was her closest relative now that her father was gone. Therefore he was her guardian. He assured her that he and Brita would take care of her inheritance until she came of age. Brita was a gentle, motherly type of woman just as Mara's own mother had been. She had liked her immediately. Cousin Aubrey was a handsome, strutting man with a glib tongue. He had taken over her affairs and continued to pay for her schooling. Now and then he had also put a nice little sum in her account at the bank, so that she was able to dress as fashionably as the other girls. Mara was grateful to him and Brita, but she was of age now and capable of tending to her own affairs.

Aubrey McCall had a son, Cullen, by his first wife. By his second, Brita, he had twin sons. They must be fifteen by now, Mara mused. She had not met them, but she had met Brita McCall's son by her previous marriage, Pack Gallagher, when he came to the school with her father. Brita and Mara's mother had been childhood friends, and it was through Mara's mother that Brita had met Aubrey McCall after Pack's father had died.

Mara remembered now that her father had been fond of Pack Gallagher, had considered him the son he had never had. He had talked to her about the boy, telling her how he came to have the name Pack. Because of trouble between him and his stepfather, Pack had moved out on his own. His real name was Jack, but it was converted to Pack since, as a strapping fourteen-year-old, he had begun packing supplies over the mountains to the miners in the gold fields who paid him with gold nuggets.

Shannon McCall had brought Pack to the school on his last visit before the accident that took his life. He was a dark, brooding young man with a mop of blue-black hair and dark blue eyes. If not for the deep blue eyes and the curl in his hair, he could have been taken for an Indian. Black Irish, her father had teasingly called him. Pack had merely grinned and acted as if he would rather be anywhere in the world than sitting on a bench in front of a fancy girls' school. He had been dressed in the rough clothes of a teamster, and Miss

Fillamore had been indignant about his being there, although nothing was said until after he and her father had left.

Mara had not heard another word about Pack Gallagher since that day so long ago and had not given him a thought until today. Since he didn't get along with Cousin Aubrey, she presumed he had left this part of the country by now.

When an hour had passed, Mara began to pace up and down in front of the shack. There was silence, utter silence, except for a bird, a meadowlark. His song was a fine sound, but not the sound for which she was listening. Once again she shaded her eyes with her hand so she could see against the glare of the sun. Nothing moved. She was not only angry at being stranded here, she was uneasy too, and it irritated her that the station keeper had disappeared.

Suddenly the man came from the back of the station. He was leading a horse that was hitched to a light, rickety wagon; the boards in the bed of the wagon were loose and rumbled as it approached. Mara stood and waited for the station keeper to speak. He went straight to the hitching rail and looped the reins over the bar.

"Mister?" Mara asked in exasperation, walking toward him. He went past her as if not seeing her and lifted her carpetbags, one in each hand, and put them in the back of the wagon. "Did someone come for me?" she asked when he carried her trunk and slid it in alongside the bags.

"You go," he said, not looking at her.

"Go? Where? I don't know the way to the McCall farm. I've been away for almost seven years."

"That way." He pointed to a trail that turned off the main road and headed northwest.

"Is the farm on that trail?"

"Yep." He untied the horse and stood waiting for her to climb up to the seat.

"Whose rig is this?"

There was no answer. The old man lifted his shoulders in a noncommittal gesture. Mara waited to see if he would say something more; and when he didn't, she climbed up to the seat, placed her hat beside her, and reached for the reins. She looked down to thank him, but he shoved the reins into her hands and hurried into the shack.

"Thank you," she called. The only answer she received was the slamming of the door. "I think he's glad to be rid of us, horse." When she slapped the reins against the swayed back, the animal moved so suddenly that she lurched backward. Righting herself, she spoke again to the horse. "We're not in that big a hurry."

The horse was not the kind of slick, well-trained animal she had driven in Denver, but she knew about horses. Every girl who graduated from Miss Fillamore's school knew how to ride and how to drive. Mara had loved that part of her education and had spent many hours talking to Lars Neishem, the groom who cared for the horses at the school. It was Lars who had insisted that she take the pistol when she told him she was leaving the school and going back to her home in Wyoming.

Ah, miss, he had said. *Ye ort a be on yer land.* Although Lars was Norwegian, he had the same love of the land the Irish had. *The land will be here forever. Do not give up a foot of it. There be more to life than bein' stuffed in a corset and seein' to spoiled, rich girls. Ye should be havin' a family of yer own.*

The day was suddenly beautiful. Out on the road the sky seemed clearer, bluer, the air sweeter. There was a slight breeze but no dust. Mara began to feel elated. It was going to be all right after all. She was going home!

The mare plodded along without any coaxing, giving Mara time to think of the home she had not seen for years. She could see in her mind's eye the white house on the hill, looking down on the potato fields. She remembered how proud her mother had been of the oval glass in the front door and the elaborate fretwork decorating the porch that stretched across the front of the house and partially down one side. The house was not large when compared to some in Denver, but it was spacious and luxurious beyond anything Colleen McCall had ever dreamed of having. She delighted in calling it McCall Manor after the big estates in Ireland.

Mara thought of the day she had left her home to go to the

school in Denver. She had looked back one last time to see the shining windows, the flowers growing along the walk, the latticework at the bottom of the porch her father had so painstakingly made. Mara had imagined her mother was watching from the upstairs window. The image was so vivid that she had waved to her, then turned back to her father who sat on the wagon seat, his shoulders slumped, his face haggard with grief.

"Dear Mama and Papa," she said aloud. "It's been a long time, but I'm coming home!"

The trail curved up and over the summit of a grassy ridge. The scene below was colorful and quiet and stirred a memory in Mara. Cottonwoods and willows showed bright green along a stream that ran parallel with the trail. The Wyoming hills hid many valleys among the bare, grassy ridges that sloped up toward the foothills. Mara's home was in one of those valleys, and out beyond the ridges stretched an unlimited expanse of prairie land.

Something was lying in the road ahead. At first Mara thought it was an animal. Then, to her surprise, a man pushed himself erect and stood swaying on widespread legs. Every once in a while he took a determined step forward. Mara pulled up on the reins and stopped the horse. The man appeared to be very drunk. She watched him fall, push himself to his feet, take a few steps, and fall again. She decided that a man in his condition posed no threat to her. She would simply drive around him.

As she drew closer, she could see that his face was as black as his hair. His clothes were mere rags and he wore no boots. He held his hand against his side as he staggered, making little progress forward. Was he an Indian or a Negro? Mara looked at him with disgust. How in the world did a man this drunk get out here barefoot? She had just begun the swing around him when she saw that the hand against his side was covered with blood. At the moment of her discovery, he fell again.

Mara stopped the horse, wound the reins securely around the brake handle, and sat looking at the man. His feet and ankles, although bloody, were white. His face was blue-black as if a layer of coal dust had settled on it. His eyes were swollen almost shut. What was left of a buckskin shirt hung in tatters on his large frame. Mara could see blood ooze from a hundred cuts on his shoulders and arms. He was badly hurt. Realizing this startled her. She could not simply drive away and leave him. Without hesitation, she climbed down off the wagon seat.

Mara had never seen such a bloody sight. For an instant her sensitive nature rebelled against it, and she turned her face away. He had not received such injuries from falling off a horse, she was sure of that. He was a big, strong man with massive shoulders and evidently a strong heart to have suffered such injury and still be on his feet. He had coal black hair and a stubble of dark beard on his cheeks. One eye was swollen completely shut, and the other opened a mere crack. He had been horribly beaten about the face, his nose broken, and it was beyond her reasoning to even guess what had happened to inflict the wounds on the rest of him. Then, knowing that she was all the help the man was going to have, she knelt down beside him.

His split lips parted and he whispered, "Help me."

"Mister, I'll help you if I can," she murmured. When he seemed not to hear, she repeated the words louder.

The wounded man muttered unintelligibly. Then he lifted his head and tried to see her.

"I'll help you," she repeated.

"Shef. . . field."

If Mara had not just come from there, she would not have been able to make out the word. There was no point in telling the man she was not going back to the station.

"All right," she said soothingly. "We've got to get you into the wagon."

Mara looked around. Water from a recent rain stood in a puddle beside the trail. If she got some, it might revive him long enough to get him into the wagon. She went to her trunk and pulled out a towel she had decorated with tatted lace and embroidery. Not exactly designed for the purpose at hand, but it would serve. Now for something to hold water. She dug about and found an old garden hat. It could be reblocked afterward.

When she returned to the road, the man was lying in the same spot. She set the hat full of water on the ground and placed the wet towel on his face. He pushed himself up into a sitting position.

"Stay still a moment." Her voice was as stern as if she were speaking to an errant child.

His hand fell away from his side and blood oozed from a wound. She suddenly realized he had been shot! And more than one time if the wound in his thigh was a bullet hole. Oh, the poor man! If she could get him into the wagon and get him home, Cousin Brita would know what to do for him.

"Can you drink?"

He didn't answer and Mara looked at him helplessly. He was such a big man that she could not possibly get him into the wagon without his helping. One thing she had to do was wrap something about his thigh and his middle to help staunch the flow of blood. She hurried back to the trunk.

Her hands were bloody and the skirt of her travel dress was soiled by the time she had finished the bandaging. An old petticoat was wrapped securely about his middle, holding a towel against the wound, and a wool scarf was tied about his thigh. She dampened the towel once again and wiped her hands.

"You've got to help me get you up. I'll bring the wagon up so all you'll have to do is take a few steps to reach it."

She led the horse forward until the back of the wagon was even with him.

"Listen to me, man. I can't do it by myself."

Knowing she had to shock him into helping her, she took the hat by the brim and threw the remaining water in his face. It seemed not to faze him. Mara got behind him and placed her hands beneath his arms and lifted. It was useless. All she could manage was to raise his massive shoulders no matter how hard she tried.

Mara looked down at his dark head. Despite the dirt and

twigs in his hair, she could see that it was fine and black as coal. He was a working man in the prime of life. His arms and shoulders bulged with muscles, but he was not using any of them now, and she was wearing herself out. It made her angry, and her Irish temper flared.

"Help me, you damn, stupid dolt!" she shouted. "What kind of man are you to sit there like a stubborn jackass and not try to help yourself?" She gave him a rebellious glance and wished she could remember some of the swear words the stage driver had used. Suddenly she did. "Hell and damnation!" The words came easily and she enjoyed the thought of what Miss Fillamore would have said about that. "Get on your feet, you ugly, worthless hunk of buzzard bait," she commanded. "Get in that wagon, or—or—by granny, I'll put a rope around you and drag you along behind it!"

She looked at his poor feet and almost cried for the agony it would cause him when he stood on them, but she hardened her heart against his pain and knelt down until her face was even with his.

"You are gutless!" she shouted. "You're a gutless man. Do you hear me? You're going to die out here because you don't have the guts to help me and you'll be on my conscience for the rest of my life, damn you!"

His response was only a flicker of dark lashes. She was almost sure he couldn't even see her now, but he could hear. His swollen lips parted and his tongue came out to lick the water she had thrown in his face.

"Help . . . me."

"I'm trying to. Can't you see that I'm trying to do just that?" she pleaded. "Mister, I want to help you, but I can't lift you. Please try to get on your feet. I'll help as much as I can."

Slowly he began to roll over onto his knees, supporting himself with one hand on the ground. His head hung down as if it weighed a ton. The hand he had used to cover the wound in his side was pressed close against him.

"Oh, my Lord! Oh, sweet Jesus!" The words came from Mara's mouth in a rush when she saw the injury to that hand. His thumb was cut to the bone.

The man managed to get his feet under him while making little grunting sounds. Mara got in front of him, speaking words of encouragement, and lifted with all her strength regardless of having to come in contact with his bloody body. When he was standing, her head came to beneath his chin, reaffirming her earlier guess that he was a big, tall man.

"Take a few steps," she urged. "Good! Good! A few more and you can sit down on the back of the wagon." He backed to the wagon and sat down heavily. She climbed up into the wagon, took a quilt from her trunk and spread it over the rough boards. "Move back just a little and you can lie down."

The moans of pain that came from him when he moved were like those of an animal caught in a trap and in terrible agony. The sounds cut into her, filling her heart with pity. She realized he was using all the strength he possessed to obey her. He managed to move back, and she eased him down onto the quilt. His knees came to the edge of the wagon bed and his feet hung down to within a foot of the ground, but Mara decided there was nothing she could do about that. She could, however, put something under his wounded thigh to support it. Once again she went to the trunk. He mumbled when she lifted his leg to place a folded skirt beneath it, and she leaned over to hear what he was saying.

"Sheffield . . . Station. Please . . . lady."

"There, there. Lie still and don't worry. Everything will be all right now."

Mara climbed up on the wagon seat and urged the horse on down the road. She looked back at the man lying on her quilt. His head rolled from side to side, and he was holding his wound now with his good hand. Oh, dear, she thought, the rough ride could kill him and he would die without anyone knowing his name or what had happened to him.

Her joy in coming home had turned to anxiety for the man who lay in the back of the wagon. She had done what she could. It was as simple as that. She drove at a gait that was easy for the horse pulling the rumbling wagon, trying to avoid the jarring holes and ruts in the road. She watched an eagle soar through the sky until it sailed into the distance and she could no longer see it. The ride was cruel on her bottom and back, making her aware of the agony the man must be suffering.

They crossed another grassy summit, and below it yawned a valley, long and narrow, with the faint, white line of a trail running through it. On a rise overlooking the fields below was the McCall homestead. The late afternoon sun glinted on the glass windows of the house just as it had done the day Mara had left. Tears came to her eyes and she blinked rapidly to clear them. When she could see again, she saw that more buildings had been added to the compound: unpainted log buildings, and a railed fence where horses were penned. Oh, it had changed so much! The house was not nearly as large or as grand as she remembered it, but the peaked roof and wraparound porch were dearly familiar. She didn't remember the trees being so thick or so big.

The trail rounded a bend and the house was lost from sight for a short while. *Home! Home!* The word kept repeating itself in Mara's mind. She had no doubt of the welcome she would receive. The letter she had sent was probably still waiting for Cousin Aubrey in Laramie or he would have been at Sheffield Station to meet her. How surprised everyone would be to see her! She placed her straw hat on her head, giggling at having to hold the reins between her knees while she shoved the hat pin through the crown to hold it. Her dress was bloodstained and her shoes were muddy. She hated to arrive home in such an untidy state, but there was no help for it.

Mara resisted putting the horse to a faster pace because of the injured man, but she had no control over her heart. It was beating faster. She could hardly wait to call out to Cousin Brita that she was home.

A column of blue smoke curled lazily from the cobblestone chimney until, catching the wind high up, it was swept away. Mara could smell it now. It smelled of pine and reminded her of the pine chips her mother used in the trunk to keep the bedding smelling fresh. Her eyes, shining with happiness, were glued to the homestead. The only activity was centered around the long low building at the back. Several horses were tied to a rail fence that penned more horses.

Suddenly Mara realized that a sea of waving grass covered the land her father had plowed and planted. That thought was swept away immediately as her attention was drawn to the house. The shape of it was the same, yet somehow it was different. She was soon near enough to see bare ground in front where there used to be flowers and green bushes. The picket fence and the swinging gate were no longer there. Each turn of the wagon wheels brought new revelations, each more dismal than the one before. A front window was boarded up with flat weathered plank, and the front door was folded back and propped open with a wash tub. Firewood was piled on the veranda where the porch swing used to hang. Several large logs lay on the porch, an ax head buried in one of them. The beautiful latticework was gone from around the bottom of the veranda, and the cornices and fancy fretwork no longer decorated the eaves of the porch.

Mara watched with a sick feeling in the pit of her stomach as a dog raced out from beneath the porch to nip at the heels of the horse as it pulled the wagon up the rutted drive to the front of the house.

Mara was stunned with disbelief.

A man in a black coat came from inside the house and stood on the veranda as she approached. While he waited, he smoothed his gray hair back with the palms of his hands. Mara stopped the horse and stared at him.

"What ye be doin' here, miss?" he demanded in a deep Irish brogue.

Mars was so astonished she was unable to speak. Her eyes widened, her breath quickened, and for an instant his face was a blur. The man looked so much like her father it was uncanny, yet she had never seen her father look so disreputable. A rough stubble of whiskers covered the man's face, the front of his shirt was dirty, his face was bloated, and his eyes were watery. He leaned against the porch post, rubbing a trembling hand across his mouth. He was an older, unkempt version of the man who had come to Denver five years

before. He was Cousin Aubrey, and he didn't even know who
she was.

"Who be ye?" he asked again, squinting his eyes to get a
better look at her.

His harsh voice jarred Mara out of her stunned state of
mind. She was tired, dirty and frightened. She had a dying
man in the back of the wagon. Her temper ignited and flared.
"I am Mara Shannon McCall and I live here!"

Chapter
TWO

"Who did ye say ye be?"

Mara stared at Aubrey for a full minute while her mind accepted the fact that this was reality and not the homecoming she had dreamed about during the long journey from Denver. A small dart of panic shot through her but was overridden by a hot flush of anger.

"You heard me. I am Mara Shannon McCall, Cousin Aubrey. I've come home!" She wrapped the reins around the brake and climbed down from the wagon seat.

"Ah, Jesus! Ah, Godamighty! Sure 'n 'tis Mara Shannon, herself. Why'd ye go 'n come here fer?"

"Because I wanted to!" she retorted sharply. Anger and disappointment were keeping tears from her eyes.

"Cullen . . . ain't goin' ter like it none a'tall."

"Cullen? What's he got to do with it?" Mara pushed at the straw hat that had slipped to one side of her head and looked beyond Aubrey to the boy who came out onto the veranda.

"Who is she, Pa?" He had the McCalls' dark hair and eyes and he was not much taller than Mara.

" 'Tis Mara Shannon."

"Cousin Mara? Now ain't that a corker! Ma'll be plumb—"

"Hush yer blatherin'," his father said crossly. "Go tell Cullen."

"He rode off a while ago," he snapped back at his father, and then smiled at Mara. "So you're Cousin Mara. I'm Trellis."

"One of the twins?"

"Yup."

"Is your mother here? There's an injured man in the wagon, and we'll need help getting him into the house."

"Ma's not . . . well. She can't move about." The boy went down the steps and looked over the side of the wagon. "Hellfire! What happened to *him?*"

"I don't know. He's in terrible pain—"

"Not now. He's dead to the world."

"Dead? Oh, he can't be!" Mara went quickly to the end of the wagon.

"I don't mean dead, dead. He's unconscious."

"Oh, thank heavens! He was so courageous. I found him on the road, and he helped me as much as he could while I was getting him into the wagon."

Aubrey walked down the steps, stared at the unconscious man, and froze. His face turned a bright red and his arms flopped against his sides. He looked like a crowing rooster.

"The devil take ye! Ye'll not be bringin' the likes a him in *my* house. Get rid a him!"

"But, Pa," Trellis protested, "ya can't—"

"I can," Aubrey roared. "Get him gone."

"Be reasonable, Pa. We've got to help him!"

"Reasonable, ye say! Ye be traitor to yer own pa? Ye got nothin' to say here. Nothin' a'tall!"

"But I do! I've got plenty to say." Mara spoke up firmly, her face flaming with anger. "I think you're forgetting that this is *my* house. The man is injured and needs help. Trellis, where is your mother?"

"Ma's sick. She can't get up no more. I been doin' what I can."

"I'm sorry about Cousin Brita. But we can't let this man lie out here and die!"

"And why not?" Aubrey demanded.

"Pa, ya know why not," Trellis said patiently. "I'll go get someone to help get him into the house."

"He'll not be comin' in!" Aubrey shouted.

"He is a human being and he will go into the house where I can look after him." Mara didn't know where her courage came from, but she was grateful for it.

"So that's the way it be, eh?"

"Yes! That's the way it is! I may have been away for a long time, but I'm back now and I have a say here. You'd better understand that right now!"

"Ye ungrateful snippet—"

"Aubrey! Trellis! Who's here?" The woman's voice came from deep inside the house.

"I'll go tell her." Trellis turned to Mara. "And I'll get someone to help get, ah, him into the house."

Mara was reluctant to leave the injured man alone with Aubrey. He stood glaring, first at her, and then at the man in the wagon. She could see the hatred in his eyes. It was a strange and unexpected situation she found herself in. There was no time to grieve over her unfriendly welcome. She would see this man into *her* house and do what she could for him. If he died, at least her conscience would be clear.

When Trellis came back out to the veranda, Mara stood at the end of the wagon as if she expected Aubrey to attack the injured man.

"I told Ma."

"Sure 'n ye would," Aubrey sneered and cast Mara a resentful glance. "Ye'll be sorry ye brought him here, me girl." He walked back up the steps to the porch, his face livid with rage.

"Maybe and maybe not. But I don't think so. No one in need was ever turned away from this house while my father was alive."

Even at the school where fits of temper were common among the homesick girls Mara's temper was legendary. She held it in check now, even though a red rage burned deep within her.

"Trellis, go get someone to help get this man in the house." Mara issued the order and looked Aubrey directly in the eye. Something was going on that she didn't understand, but she had rights here. This was *her* home, *her* land; and from the looks of it, she should have come back long ago.

Aubrey McCall felt as if he had been kicked in the stomach by a horse. Why had Shannon McCall's daughter returned home? An educated miss such as she would have no reason to come to this place after all this time unless she intended to sell it. He suspected that Shannon McCall had left money in a bank in Denver to pay for her schooling, but had been unable to find out for sure until he had stopped sending money to the school after the first year and not a word had been said.

The girl had written she had a good-paying position at the school. What had caused her to give it up? Why hadn't she let him know that she was coming? He would have put a stop to her if he had known. She was going to be every bit as stubborn and self-righteous as her father, he could see that. Aubrey turned on his heel and went into the house. Damn her for bringing that bastard here! He ignored his wife's calls from the bedroom and went directly to the cupboard in the kitchen and poured himself a stiff drink.

Trellis returned with two men. Mara had no idea of the picture she made standing at the end of the wagon. Her straw hat was askew. Sun glinted on the copper in her hair that hung loose from its knot. Her dress was soiled, her cheeks were red and sparks of temper flashed from her emerald green eyes. Determination to have her way was evident in every line of her body.

She had a chance to observe the men as they approached. One was thin with a narrow face and eyes set close to his beaklike nose. His arms were long, hanging almost to the knees of his bowed legs. The other was strongly built and wore a high-crowned Texas hat designed to keep the sun off his skull. He was tall and had a long, lean, hard face burned brown from his forehead to a square chin. His clothes were those of a man who spent long hours in the saddle. A gun belt was strapped about his waist; the other man had a weapon tucked into his belt. Mara was used to seeing men wearing weapons as if they were part of the clothing, but it crossed her mind that these two didn't appear to be the type of men to work on a farm.

"Sam Sparks, ma'am." The tall man put his fingers to the brim of his hat and nodded politely to Mara before peering down at the man who lay in the back of the wagon. He whistled through his teeth. "Godamighty!"

"I found him about halfway between here and Sheffield Station. He's been shot in the side and in the leg, I think."

"He's in bad shape," the tall man said slowly in an accent of the deep south.

"Do you know who he is?" Mara asked.

"I've seen him around."

"Ma wants you to bring him into her room, Sam," Trellis said in a low tone, his eyes going from Mara to the tall man. "There's a bunk in there," he added.

Aubrey came out onto the veranda carrying the whiskey bottle in his hand and watched the injured man being lifted out of the wagon. The two men and Trellis staggered under his weight, but they made it up the steps and into the house.

Mara followed them, passing Aubrey without a glance. She kept her mind firmly on the injured man so that she wouldn't look at the destruction done to her mother's house. The layout of the rooms was familiar, four rooms downstairs, two rooms upstairs. They passed from the parlor into the kitchen and from the kitchen into the back bedroom, the room that had been Mara's parents' room.

Brita McCall was sitting up in bed with pillows behind her. Mara saw the fear and pain on her face. Her dark hair was streaked with gray, her face showed the lines of age, but it was still as sweet as Mara remembered. Blue eyes clouded with pain sought hers, and Brita lifted a crippled hand toward her.

"Hello, Cousin Brita."

"Hello, Mara Shannon. Ach, 'n what have they been doin' to me boy?" Tears came to Brita's eyes and rolled slowly down her cheeks.

"I don't know. I found him along the road."

"Pack, me darlin'," Brita murmured. "If only I could get up ter see ter yer hurts."

"Didn't you know it was Pack?" Trellis asked when he saw the surprised look on Mara's face.

"No." She shook her head. "Who would have done such a terrible thing to him?"

Trellis glanced first at his mother and then at his father who had followed them into the house, then shook his head.

" 'Tis not enough he be here in this house. 'Tis my bed he be takin'." Aubrey stood at the end of Brita's bed, the bottle still in his hand.

Mara saw Brita cringe. A tremendous dislike for her father's cousin was building rapidly within her. She threw Aubrey a disgusted glance, took off her hat and placed it on the bureau. The short man left, but Sam Sparks lingered beside the bunk.

"Will you be needing help here, miss?" he asked.

"Why, yes, if you would be so kind." Mara looked pointedly at Aubrey.

"Cullen'll not be likin' ye to be stickin' yer nose in, Sparks. Ye best be gettin' on back to the bunkhouse."

"This isn't a job for the young lady, McCall."

"She bit it off, let 'er chew it." Aubrey took a long swig from the bottle.

"Please stay, Mr. Sparks. Cousin Brita and I would appreciate your help." Mara saw that Brita was either too frightened to go against her husband's wishes or too worried about her son to speak.

"We'll need hot water and vinegar to start. He's out cold, and it will be easier on him if we do what we've got to do before he wakes up."

"I'll get it." Trellis moved around his father and left the room.

Sam took off his hat, hung it on the bed post, and knelt down to unwind the wool scarf from Pack's leg. Sam's thick hair was a dark russet brown. The upper part of his forehead was white where it had been protected from the sun. To Mara he looked much younger without the hat.

Mara gazed down at the unconscious man. She tried to compare this big man with the boy who had come to the school with her father so many years ago. Only the dark hair was the same. He was tanned almost mahogany to the waist, his great shoulders and arms narrowing to a sinewy middle. Mara had never seen a man as near naked as this one.

"I'm sorry your son is hurt, Cousin Brita. I'm just glad I came along when I did. I've no experience in tending to injuries, but I'm not squeamish and I'll do what I can if you and Mr. Sparks will tell me what to do."

Sam Sparks stood and looked down into Mara's emerald eyes. She saw that his eyes were clear and knowing, and a faint smile pulled at his lips.

"Looks like you've done all right so far, miss," he murmured.

"Mara." Brita spoke her name and Mara turned to her. "I can sit in a chair. Trellis will lift me."

"Oh, Ma!" Trellis came to the doorway. "It's hurts ya so much to move."

"I can stand the pain, Trell. Bring the chair. He be a sweet child," she said to Mara. "I don't be knowin' what I'd do without him."

"Is there something I can do, Brita?"

"Nothin', but I do be thankin' ye. 'Tis the misery in my joints that's made me as helpless as a babe."

The chair was placed close to the bed, and Brita's legs swung over the side. Trellis put his hands beneath his mother's arms, lifted her up, swung her around, and gently lowered her to the chair. Moans of pain came from Brita's lips in spite of her attempts to hold them back. Her feet and ankles were terribly deformed by her affliction, and her spine was curved in a permanent arc. Trellis settled her in the chair and placed a blanket across her lap. For the first time Brita got a good look at her son's face. She moaned and clenched her teeth as if in agony.

"Pack, me sweet boy. I told ye ter go, I told ye. . . ."

"Ma'am, he's got a bullet that's got to come out. It might not be something you want to see."

"I be seein' cruel things aplenty, Mr. Sparks. I got to be knowin' the worse. Will me boy die?"

"I don't know, Mrs. McCall. He's been shot, and it looks like they dragged him behind a horse and beat him."

"Sweet Holy Mother of God! How can they be so cruel?" Brita took a deep breath and closed her eyes for an instant. When she opened them, she began to give orders. "Ye've got to get the bullets out. Can ye sew him up, Mr. Sparks?"

"Yes, ma'am."

"Bring the hot water, Trell. Mr. Sparks will have ter wash his hands. They'll not like ye ter be helpin' him, Mr. Sparks."

Mara stood by and pondered their use of the word they. It was almost as if Brita, Trellis and even Sam Sparks knew who had tortured the man.

"Let me worry about that. I've got to strip him, ma'am."

" 'Tis not a sight for yer eyes, Mara Shannon." Brita's gentle face was creased with lines of worry. "Trell will help Mr. Sparks."

Mara picked up the bloody petticoat she had used to wrap about Pack Gallagher's torso and the wool scarf she had tied about his leg. She stepped out of the way when Trellis came with a teakettle of hot water and a handful of clean cloths. Her face reddened when she realized that Sam had opened Pack's trousers and was waiting for her to leave before he pulled them off.

"Call if there's something I can do."

Mara went into the kitchen and gazed in despair at the disorder. The iron cookstove that had been her mother's pride was still there. A fire behind it had charred the wall. The trestle table had a familiar look, but instead of ladder-backed chairs, two wooden benches now sat at each side of it. The range and the work counter were covered with piles of plates, cups, pots, and an assortment of cutlery. The floor was covered with grease and scraps of food embellished with chunks of dried mud. Cobwebs and soot hung like Spanish moss behind the cookstove.

A flicker of anger swept through Mara and threatened to burst into full flame.

The parlor had suffered as much damage as the rest of the house. A broken-legged table leaned against the wall where the window was boarded up. The loveseat was gone, as was the clock that sat on the mantel above the fireplace. Several heavy chairs stood in the room, and a barn lantern hung from a nail on the wall. Had Mara not been such a strong-willed woman she would have collapsed in despair. Instead she seethed with fury against those who had devastated her home. Her rage fed her determination to stay, take over the property her father had left her, and get a full accounting from Aubrey McCall.

Mara went to the door of the front bedroom and looked around. The bed in the corner was unmade, men's clothing was scattered about, a bridle and a set of reins had been flung into the corner, and an empty whiskey bottle lay on its side on the bureau. Fortunately the doors leading to the living room and the one going into Cousin Brita's were both still solidly hung and would afford her some privacy if she stayed here.

"Trellis," she called. "Who uses this room?"

"Cullen. He don't sleep there much. But he'll be sore if ya mess with his things." Trellis came to the bedroom door.

"Then he'll just have to be sore." Mara's voice was no-nonsense hard. She closed the connecting door and began ridding the room of Cullen McCall's belongings. Under different circumstances she would not have dreamed of touching another person's personal property, but anger, humiliation and disappointment spurred her on to clear the room as quickly as possible and make it her own again.

As she worked, a murmur of voices came from the other room. Trellis made trips to the kitchen, and once she heard him going upstairs. A cry tore from the wounded man. Mara stopped and put her hands over her ears for a long moment. The breath went out of her, and she felt her stomach suck in. Brita's low soothing voice could be heard over the grunts of pain.

Mara's mind kept pace with her hands as she worked. Someone had tried to kill Pack Gallagher. It was evident that Aubrey McCall hated him. There was something evil here, some reason why Brita wanted her son brought into her room. Did she think that whoever had done this terrible thing to him would come back to finish the job?

Mara felt a sudden homesickness for her neat, comfortable room at the school. The cooks would be getting dinner now, and the maids would be setting the tables with white linen and bone china. After dinner the girls would gather in the parlor to take turns at the piano or pair off to play cribbage or whist. On a night like this, Mara would take a couple of books to her room, undress in the soft light of the glass lamp with the hand-painted shade, and crawl into her warm, sweet-smelling bed to read.

No dinner was being prepared here, she thought, coming back to reality. And in order to have a decent place to sleep, she had to clean out this room and make up a bed with the linen from her trunk. There was no going back. Her bridges had been burned behind her. The unpleasant scene with Miss Fillamore when Mara told her she was leaving had opened her eyes to the fact that the affection the woman pretended to have for her was merely a facade. Miss Fillamore had called her a featherhead and said she was foolish to give up a secure position to travel to an uncivilized part of Wyoming; and if she went, she could not return. The schoolmistress had urged Mara to hire a broker, sell the property, and stay at the school. When she refused, Miss Fillamore had taken the attitude that she was somehow disloyal and had immediately hired a woman to take her place.

The sun had set when Mara went to the porch to drag in her trunk. She saw four men on horseback coming across an open field toward the house. She suspected one of them would be Cullen McCall, and Cousin Aubrey would be waiting to tell him the news. The look in Trellis' eyes when he came to help her with the trunk told Mara that the boy had also seen the riders and was uneasy.

"How is Mr. Gallagher?"

"Sam says he'll live if the fever don't take him."

Mara removed linens from her trunk and hurriedly made up the bed. She heard Sam Sparks leave the house and looked out the window to see him walking toward the bunkhouse where a group of men stood talking to Aubrey. She tidied her hair and opened the connecting door between her room and Brita's.

The room smelled of vinegar, whiskey, and burned alum. Pack lay on his back. A blanket covered him from his knees to his hipbones. Above that was a flat belly, a thick chest shadowed with dark curly hair, muscled shoulders, and arms as big as Mara's legs. Mara could see where Sam Sparks had stitched the flesh on his thumb. Brita's chair had been moved close to the bunk. She reached a crippled hand to turn the wet compress that lay across her son's forehead.

"He seems to be sleeping."

"Aye. He be dosed with laudanum."

"Do you want to get back into bed, Brita? I'll sit beside him for awhile."

"No, child. I be all right."

"I want to help you. My father was very fond of Pack. He brought him to the school one time."

"Pack was fond of Shannon. Child, why did ye come to this place?"

"I was homesick. I wrote that I was coming."

"Sure 'n ye did," Brita sighed deeply.

"Things are going on that I don't understand. Why are there no crops planted? If Mr. Sparks works here, what does he do? He doesn't look like a farming type of man."

"Mara Shannon, ye shouldna be here. Trell will be takin' ye back come mornin'. Ye can tell that to Cullen when he comes."

Mara searched the eyes of the woman who looked older than her years and found genuine concern there. She went to kneel down beside the chair because it was an effort for Brita to hold her head up to look into her face.

"I'm not going back. I own this property. My father worked hard to get the money to pay for it. Cousin Aubrey sent money to pay for my schooling, and I appreciate that; but I'm of age and I want to control my own inheritance. I plan to talk with Cousin Aubrey tonight.''

"Child, child." Brita shook her head sadly. "Let it be. Go back to yer school. This be no place for a gentle lass.''

"I can't go back. I've already been replaced. This is my home," Mara said gently. "Can't you understand that?''

"Home. Aye, would that we ne'er left the green land o' Ireland.''

Mara stood. "Don't worry. I'm not the type to fold up under the first hard blow." Heavens, she told herself, if that were true, she would have crumbled when she first saw the destruction done to her home. "Now, I'll fix us something for supper.''

"Mara Shannon, there be naught to fix. Trell brings me a plate from the cookshack.''

"A cookshack? How many men are here?''

"Why don't you ask someone who knows?'' The voice came from behind her and Mara turned.

A man lounged in the doorway. Her first impression was that he was a short man, young, and with a handsome, sullen face. This was Cullen. He resembled the father who stood beside him. Mara had steeled herself for the meeting with Aubrey and his son, and despite the uneasiness she felt, she was determined to face them boldly.

"Who are you?'' Mara knew who he was. She asked the question as an opening to what she felt was going to be an unpleasant encounter.

"I'm the one who runs things around here. Who are you?''

Bluntly Mara answered him. "I'm the one who *owns* things around here.'' She said the words curtly, snapped her mouth shut and waited for an explosion.

The surprised look on the man's face turned to smoldering anger. His eyes narrowed and he glared at her. "I advise you to get your prissy tail back to Denver.''

Mara forced herself to appear calmly contemptuous of his rudeness. "And I advise you to keep a civil tongue in your head if you plan to spend another night on this property.''

"Ha!'' He came into the room and looked down at the man

who lay on the bunk. "Do you think he'll help you throw me out?"

"No. But this will." Mara drew the pistol from her pocket and pointed it at him. She heard Brita draw in her breath.

Cullen turned cold, blue-gray eyes on the girl, aware of her defiant stance, her eyes that met his unafraid.

"You'd better put that peashooter away or you'll hurt yourself."

Mara looked into eyes that were level with her own. They were hard and cruel. She drew in a shallow breath but never allowed her eyes to waver from his.

"You should be worrying about yourself. It's pointed at the third button on your shirt."

"Cullen?"

"Shut up, Pa."

"Your things are on the porch. If you can't be civil, take them and leave." The anger that had started down in the pit of Mara's stomach had surged up, causing her to throw caution aside. She stood motionless, waiting for Cullen Mc-Call to make the next move.

"You'd best draw in your horns, *Cousin* Mara. You're in my territory. Out here it's the strong who survive."

"Are you threatening me? If so, you should know that before I left Denver, I made out a will leaving this property to the school. They have a battery of lawyers who will cover this place like a swarm of ants if they don't hear from me. Schools are hungry for money, *Cousin* Cullen."

Surprised at being able to lie so easily, Mara felt faintly giddy. She had no idea how much time went by while she stared at Cullen. She watched his face twist with bitterness and smoldering anger. Then he strode from the room. She could hear the beat of his boot heels on the parlor floor and then on the porch. Aubrey lingered.

"Ye had to go 'n get him riled—"

"Is he always so rude?" Mara put the pistol back.

Brita answered, "Cullen can charm the skin off a snake when he wants to."

"Evidently he didn't want to. Keep your son away from me, Cousin Aubrey. I won't tolerate his abuse."

"He'll cool off."

"I don't care if he does or not. Right now I'm more interested in something to eat. Brita tells me she get her meals from the cookshack."

"Trell will be bringin' it."

"After tonight I'll cook for myself and Cousin Brita. I want a list of supplies you have on hand, and you and I will go over the account books." Anger was still in her voice.

"Account books? There ain't no such."

Mara looked at him in stunned silence, and for a moment she almost felt sorry for him. He stood looking down at the floor.

"Do you mean to tell me that you don't keep records of what comes in and what goes out?" Aubrey didn't answer. "When did you cease farming?"

"This ain't farm country. Yer pa knowed it at the last."

"He's right, Mara," Brita said. "Shannon's dream of fields and fields of potatoes was naught but a dream. The land, the weather be not suitable."

Mara had to believe what they said when she looked down into Brita's pleading eyes. So many things crowded into her head that she found it incredibly hard not to keep asking questions.

"If you don't farm, what do you do? It takes money to live. Where does it come from?"

Aubrey shrugged. "Cullen runs some cattle."

"And the men in the bunkhouse are drovers who work with the cattle?"

"What else would they be doin'?"

Aubrey's face closed and he looked away. "Now 'n where else could it be comin' from?"

Mara tried to steel herself against softening, but it wasn't her nature to stay angry for very long. When she spoke again, her tone was softer.

"Now I see why you didn't want me to come here. But I'm here, and I'm staying. I want you to know, Cousin Aubrey, I can not abide disorder. This house, my home, will be put in order so that I can live here decently. You and Brita are welcome to stay as long as you want. I owe you that out of consideration for what you have done for me in the past.''

"Kind of ye," Aubrey muttered. Mara chose to ignore the sarcasm in his voice.

"I insist on having an accounting of how many cattle I own, because I assume it was my money that bought them."

Aubrey's shoulders slumped. Age and inactivity had thickened his waist, and his soiled shirt barely came together over his protruding stomach. His eyes, however, glittered angrily and his lips set defensively.

"Ye ain't goin' to let up, are ye?"

"No. Why should I?"

Aubrey was still. Only his eyes moved. They examined her from head to toe.

"What about Gallagher? Be ye set on keepin' him sniffin' 'bout ye?"

Mara turned her eyes from his and looked down at the unconscious man before she answered.

"Mr. Gallagher is your wife's son and my father's friend. Regardless of the disagreement you and your son have with him, it seems to me that you could be civil to him for Brita's sake. Pack is welcome in this house for as long as it takes him to recover from his injuries. Which, by the way, I feel you and your son know more about than you have let on."

Anger tightened the muscles in Aubrey's face. "Be ye accusin' me 'n Cullen?"

Mara let her silence speak for her. They stared at each other, and suddenly Mara felt good. Cousin Aubrey knew that she was no spineless creature who would scurry back to Denver and leave her property to be managed by him and his son.

"Do we understand each other, Cousin Aubrey?"

"What I be understandin' is that ye're a stubborn, foolish lass with naught but air for brains!" He wheeled and walked away.

Chapter
THREE

Mara slept uneasily in the strange bed with the pistol under her pillow. She had undressed in the dark because there were no coverings for the two windows. Physically and mentally she was exhausted. After the meeting with Aubrey and Cullen, her mind was plagued by even greater turmoil than that she had experienced when she arrived with Pack Gallagher.

Several times during the night she was awakened by voices in the next room, and once in that deep blackness she had awakened to a strange sense of unease that brought her to full awareness. She looked out the window to see four horsemen ride in and turn their horses into the enclosure beside the bunkhouse. She lay down again and closed her eyes wearily. She dozed fitfully and eventually fell into an uneasy sleep.

Morning came. As soon as she opened her eyes, she noticed the door that opened into the parlor was ajar. It made her realize how vulnerable she was. A poignant loneliness possessed her. She was alone, really alone in this hostile house except for poor, crippled Brita and the boy, Trellis.

Thoughts raced around and around in her head. Why had Cullen McCall been so antagonistic toward her? Why had Aubrey acted as if she had no right to be here? She knew she couldn't live here alone. She had to share her home with Brita and Aubrey. That thought held, and she resigned herself to it. But she would not allow these two overbearing men to intimidate her.

Mara lay thinking that it had been foolish of her to insist that she have her old room. What had been suitable for her as a child was not suitable for a young woman alone. She would take the upstairs rooms for herself where there was only one door to lock, the one leading to the stairway. There she would be able to dress or undress without the fear of someone seeing her through the windows. Where was her imagination taking her? She was planning to fortify herself in her own home! Well, if that's the way it had to be—so be it!

She got out of bed and used the granite chamber pot she had slipped under the bed the night before. Later, in a brown work dress, an apron tied snugly around her waist, her auburn hair secured in a topknot, Mara went out to the kitchen. A wave of hopeless despair swept over her when she viewed the clutter. Where to begin? She had just poured water into the basin to wash when she heard hard steps on the porch at the side of the house. Apprehension held her motionless. It had to be Cullen. Aubrey didn't move that fast. Mara wished she didn't have to face him so early in the morning. She needed time to adjust to the drab, unfriendly atmosphere of the house.

A boy looking amazingly like Trellis came tramping through the parlor to the kitchen. Carrying a pot of coffee with a rag wrapped around the handle, he walked past her, then set the pot down on the range with such force that the liquid came out the spout and splashed onto the hot iron, creating a hissing sound.

"There's your goddamn coffee!"

Mara was taken aback by the words and the vicious way the boy spat them out. She concentrated on soaping her hands and rinsing them.

"I can see that." Mara dried her hands on her apron

because there was no towel on the rack. "You must be Travor. I'm Mara McCall."

"I know who the hell you are. Everyone on this ranch knows who the hell you are."

Arrogantly he returned her stare. With feet apart, balancing on the high heels of his boots, the boy defied her. His face was so like the face of his twin, yet so different one would never mistake one for the other. This boy's face was hard, arrogant, and a sneer twisted his lips. He wore range clothes, and about his slender hips was strapped a wide gun belt.

"Good. I'm glad that they know the owner has arrived."

"Cullen said you threw that up to him. What does a prissy ass like you know about running a ranch?"

"Get out and leave her alone, Trav." Trellis came from his mother's room.

"Are you going to make me, sissy boy?" Travor put his hands on his hips and spit out the words spitefully.

"If I have to," Trellis said quietly.

Mara looked at the gentle boy with new respect. He was ready to do what he had to do to back his words.

"You don't have to, Trellis. I will." Mara thought it time she began to exert her authority, or there could be a fight. "Leave, Travor. Get out and don't come back until you can behave yourself.".

"Where do you get off ordering me to get out?"

"Because this is my house, and I don't have to put up with bad-mannered children."

A flush reddened his cheeks. Sparks of anger danced in his eyes. There was no doubt that by calling him a child she had hit upon a sore spot.

"I could show you a thing or two, *lady!*"

"No doubt you could, but I'm not interested in hearing anything from a spoiled little boy." She turned her back on him, went to the work counter and began to fill a pan with soiled dishes.

"You think you're so all-fired smart just 'cause you went to a fancy school. Well, you ain't nothin' but dirty Irish mick just like the rest of us!"

Mara heard his boot heels pounding on the bare floor, and

the sound of the door slamming behind him echoed throughout the house.

"He acts like that sometimes," Trellis said.

Mara turned. "Only sometimes? That's a relief."

"He was trying to impress you."

"He did that, all right."

"He wanted you to think he was a grown-up like Cullen."

"If he's trying to pattern himself after Cullen, he's made a poor choice to my way of thinking."

"Trav just wants to be somebody."

"You mean he wants to be a man who people look up to? He's sure going about it in the wrong way."

"Ma says he's goin' over fool's hill. He'll settle down."

"Why are you defending him? He's an ill-mannered, undisciplined, strutting little rooster who needs his tail feathers pulled." Mara poured water from the teakettle into a pan and dropped in a bar of lye soap. She would have to wash dishes before she could even drink a cup of coffee. "How is Pack this morning?"

"He's still sleeping. So is Ma. She had me give him another dose of the laudanum in the night, but she says that's all he can have. His stomach is growling. It's probably been a day or two since he ate anything."

"What does your mother suggest?"

"She'll say he needs meat to make blood. I'll get it from the cookhouse—that is, if you'll cook it."

"Of course I will. But I've got to clean this place first. How is it that you're willing to help Pack? Cullen and your father seem to hate him."

"Pack's all right. He's my half brother the same as Cullen. Besides, he's good to Ma."

"So are you, Trellis." Mara smiled so sweetly and sincerely at the boy that his face reddened. "Now that I'm here, I'll help you with your mother. We should be able to make things more pleasant for her." She found a cloth and dried two cups. "Let's have some of that coffee, shall we? Then I'll scrub out that iron pot and we'll cook some meat for Pack."

"I didn't know that you could cook. I thought you just

knew, uh . . . things like how to serve tea and that sort of thing.''

Mara laughed. "Every girl at Miss Fillamore's school takes a course in cooking. She learns how to cook a few things so that she will be able to supervise the cook when she marries a rich man and moves to a mansion.''

"Do they all marry rich men?''

"No." Mara laughed again. "Their parents send them to school thinking it will help them get a rich husband. Sometimes it does.''

"What about you?''

"I did have a proposal." Mara's eyes began to sparkle. "He was very rich, but he also was bald, had rotting teeth and was old enough to be my grandfather. Miss Fillamore thought I should consider it. She said he was on the verge of drinking himself to death and I'd be a rich widow.''

"Why didn't you marry him?''

"The cook at the school beat my time with him.''

Trellis grinned. "You're kidding.''

"No, I'm not. He and Mable were perfect for each other. I was at the school for seven years, and I hung around the kitchen a lot. Mable had worked hard; she deserved a rich husband more than I. Someday I'll make you a butter cake.''

"I eat down at the cookshack after the men have finished. Then I bring something to Ma. I'll get something for you this morning if you want me to.''

Mara brought the pot from the stove and poured coffee into two clean cups. The plate of food Trellis had brought her the previous night had been so greasy that she could hardly eat it, but the bread and butter had been good.

"I'll have some bread and butter. Who milks the cow and churns?''

"Steamboat. He hates cows. He named our cow Miss Fu—ah, well it's not for your ears, Mara.''

"Who is Steamboat?''

"The cook. I've not heard his real name. He came up the Missouri on a steamboat about five years back. It hit a snag and sank. He's told the tale so often that folks just call him

Steamboat. He came wandering in, down on his luck, and he's been here cooking ever since."

"If he works here, why not ask him to cook the meat for Pack?"

"I guess he could if you don't want to."

"I'll do it. I want to get this place cleaned today so I can cook supper in here tonight."

"It's not Ma's fault things are in such a mess. She kept it nice for as long as she could."

"I understand that. Who does the washing? I see there's a boiling pot in the yard."

"Miss Rivers comes every week or two. She can't see much, but she can do a lot. She helps me change Ma's bed and wash her things. Ma likes to have a woman to talk to. Miss Rivers likes it too. She doesn't get out much."

"Where does she live?"

"A couple of miles from here. She lives with her brother, Charlie Rivers. Their place is over along Lodgepole Creek. He's ornery as a steer with a crooked horn. He won't let a man get within a mile of her."

"Do they squat on our land?"

"Heavens no! Cullen would have shot him."

"Hmmm." Mara looked directly at the young boy sitting across from her. "Is that the usual way Cullen handles a problem?"

"He didn't shoot Pack, if that's what you mean. He might of roughed him up a bit—"

"Roughed him up? Do you call what was done to him roughing him up?"

"Well . . . they got carried away, I guess." Trellis looked away from Mara's suddenly cold stare.

"Who did it, Trellis? Who did that terrible thing to him?"

Trellis stood. "If Pack wants you to know, he'll tell you. It's best not to pry into things, Mara. There's bad blood between Pack and Pa and Cullen. Ma says they didn't get along right from the start."

"I can understand why if the welcome I received from your father and Cullen is an example."

"You surprised them, and—"

"And what?"

The boy shrugged. "They're afraid you'll sell the place out from under them, I guess."

"It would be my right," she said gently. "But I won't do that because my father loved the land, and because of Cousin Brita."

"Well, Pa and Cullen won't cool off until Pack leaves, you can bet your boots on that."

Mara watched Trellis walk toward the bunkhouse and the small cookshack that was attached to the end of it wondering how two boys, twins, could be so different.

A shaggy dog came out from under the porch of the cookhouse to meet Trellis. The dog was old and walked slowly.

"Hello, Maggie." He bent and patted the dog's head. "You've been out in the burrs again," he said and pulled a burr from the shaggy hair that hung over the dog's eyes. "I'll cut this hair off when I get time."

Maggie walked beside him to the cookshack and went back under the porch when Trellis stepped into it.

Sam Sparks, Cullen and two other men sat at the long plank table that stretched from one end of the small building to the other. Trellis nodded to them and went to the counter where Steamboat kept the tray they used for Brita.

"How's Pack this morning?" Sam asked.

"He ain't dead yet," Trellis answered and then gave Cullen a searing look.

"Too bad," Cullen answered.

"There'll be hell to pay if Miss McCall finds out who did that to him." Trellis set two granite plates on the tray.

"It ain't my style to drag a man to death. I'd just shoot the bastard." Cullen laughed harshly.

"He *was* shot. Did you do it before or after he was dragged?"

"You're getting pretty big for yore britches, boy."

"Pack came here to see Ma. Someday he'll kill you, Cullen."

"That would set fine with you, wouldn't it, sissy boy? It

just happens that I didn't even know he was around. If I had, I'd probably a done worse. Me 'n Pa both told him to stay away from here.''

"He's got a right to come see Ma.''

Cullen shrugged and banged his cup on the table for Steamboat to refill it. The thin, slump-shouldered man with a wrinkle-etched face, iron gray hair and a drooping mustache brought the heavy pot to the table and thumped it down. Cullen reached for the handle, then withdrew his hand quickly.

"Goddamn it, Steamboat! Leave the damn rag! That handle's hot as hell.'' The cook tossed the cloth on the table and hurried back to turn the meat cooking in the big spider skillet.

"There's men beside me that would take pleasure out of beating the hell out of Pack,'' Cullen said after he had filled his cup. "He was told not to win that last fight. He should a hightailed it out of the country. It's his own damn fault he got jumped.''

"Are you saying you had nothing to do with it?'' Trellis looked his brother straight in the eye.

"Yes, sissy ass. I'm sayin' I had nothing to do with it only because somebody else got to him first.''

Trellis ignored the slur and said calmly, "Mara thinks you did.''

"Shitfire! I don't care what she thinks.''

"She's not the mousy thing you thought she was, Cull. She'll stand up to you.''

"She'd better hie her prissy tail back to Denver, is what she'd better do.''

"You'd best be civil to her. She'll not take your sass. She put you out of the house, didn't she?''

"I didn't sleep there half the time anyhow. 'Bout the time somebody comes in on her she'll wish I was there.''

"I'm thinkin' she'd blow a man's head off with that little gun she carries in her pocket, eh Cullen?''

"Are you bein' *her* serving wench too, Trell?'' Cullen asked when the boy placed two plates on the tray for Steamboat to fill. He was stung by the mention of the pistol the girl had pulled on him. "You're turnin' into a real housemaid."

"Someday I'm going to bust your mouth, Cullen," Trell said calmly.

"Ya can dream about it. It'll be a cold day in hell, boy. 'Pears to me like you're suckin' up to Miss High-'n-Mighty. Are you thinkin' you'll be man enough to run this place someday?"

Sam Sparks watched and listened. The boy was showing much more maturity than his older brother. In a few years the boy's body would catch up, and Sam would like to be around to see what happened.

If Cullen and his bunch hadn't beaten Pack, who had? Sam mulled the question over in his mind, then dismissed it. Pack Gallagher wasn't his business. The fact that Cullen allowed outlaws to hide out here for a price wasn't his business. He was looking for bigger fish than a few two-bit outlaws. Sooner or later his break would come if he just remained patient.

Sam pondered Miss McCall's sudden appearance and how it would affect the situation here. Plenty of bangtails hung out in all the railroad towns—worn-out women who supplied a man with what he needed for the moment. But decent women were scarce out here in the Wyoming Territory, and pretty young single women rarer still. . . . Cullen had swallowed his story about needing a place to hide out. He'd paid for a month's lodging. The inactivity was about to kill him, but he'd stick it out for that length of time, and if nothing turned up, he'd mosey on over to Laramie.

"I've got to exercise my horse. I think I'll ride out to the lower basin." Sam got to his feet and reached for his hat.

"Stay away from the squatters' place. Rivers is liable to fill your tail full of lead if ya get too close." The bowlegged man who had helped him carry Pack into the house looked up with a grin that showed tobacco-stained teeth.

"What's he hiding out there?" Sam asked casually.

"His sister. She's pretty as a speckled pup 'n blind as a bat. I heard a woman singin' as I was ridin' along Lodgepole Creek. It come up over the hill sweet 'n clear as a bell. I rode on up close so's to hear. Bang! The next thing I knowed my horse got a load of rock salt in his rump 'n I went tail over teakettle. Rivers said next time it'd be lead. I ain't never heared of a man keepin' such a close eye on a *sister*. Haw! Haw! Haw!''

Cullen and the two men at the table all shouted with laughter.

"She's sightly. Ain't no two ways 'bout it." Cullen spoke as if he were privileged to something they knew nothing about. "If you want to get a look at her, hang around when Rivers brings her over to visit Brita. She comes every week or so 'n helps sissy pants with his ma."

Sam was getting more than a little tired of Cullen constantly belittling the boy because he took care of his crippled mother and bit back what he really wanted to say.

"He doesn't keep *too* close a watch on her if he lets her come here," he said almost absently.

"Charlie Rivers'll sit here on the porch 'n watch to see that no one gets close to her."

"What's he scared of?" Sam moved out of the way so Trellis could pass with the tray.

"Hell! I guess he's scared somebody'll get under her skirt 'n atween her legs. Hell! It ain't a bad idea." Cullen grinned. "Bet she ain't had no man . . . less'n it was Charley. She's so damn blind she'd not even know who it was anyhow!"

Sam looked down at the shorter man. "Cut out that kind of talk, McCall." His voice was more deadly because he spoke quietly. "Any man who forces himself on a woman, decent or not, will answer to me."

Cullen was taken aback by the quiet authority in the Texan's voice and was embarrassed to be chastised in front of the men.

"You Texans are sure touchy 'bout women." His need to redeem himself forced him to speak with a sneer in his voice. "Hell, they all got a slit. If'n they ain't goin' to let a man enjoy it, they ort a sew it up."

The laugh Cullen expected didn't come. The men got up and filed out the door, leaving him sitting at the table alone. Sam followed them out. He stood on the porch and looked off toward the mountains. Where in all this vast land was the man he hunted? Each time he thought he was close, the trail faded away. When he followed a trail on the ground, he also trailed with his mind. It was what made him good at his job. He had to think as the man he hunted would think. If he had someone on his tail, Sam reasoned, he'd want a far-off place where he could keep out of sight for a good long while. This was such a place. But hell, a hundred places such as this existed between here and Denver.

The dishes were washed and dried and stacked on the clean end of the trestle table. Her mother's service for ten had dwindled to a service for no more than four. Mara wondered what had happened to the pots and the iron spider that had hung on the nails behind the stove. She remembered the large wooden bread bowl, the churn, the caster set, none of which she had found. She would have cried had she not been so angry.

"Ma! What the hell am I doing here?"

As Mara dried her hands on her apron and hurried across to the door, she could hear Brita's soothing tones. Mara rapped on the door and then opened it. To her dismay the man on the bunk had swung his feet off and pushed himself to a sitting position. The end of the blanket lay across his lap, but otherwise he was completely nude. She quickly averted her eyes.

He looked up when she opened the door. His bruised face was still swollen and his dark hair looked as if he had been in a violent windstorm. He squinted at her, and a string of swear words dropped into the silence.

"Hell and damnation! Sweet Jesus! Good God Almighty, Holy Sainted Mother of God! What the hell are *you* doing here?"

The hostile greeting stunned her into silence and splintered her thoughts. Wildly she sought a reason for his fury. Finally she was able to speak.

"Mr. Gallagher, I must insist that as long as you remain in this house you refrain from taking the Lord's name in vain.

Hell and damnation are permissible; the rest of what you said is not!''

He gaped at her as she lifted her chin and looked down her nose at him and then away. "I'm Mara Shannon McCall. We met once, a long time ago."

"I know who the hell you are—"

"Oh, dear! I've heard that already once this morning. Should you be sitting up?"

"You were the woman who found me . . . helped me in the wagon! Jesus!"

"Mr. Gallagher." She made a restless movement with her hand. He continued to look at her. "Being hungry must account for your vile mood. Trellis is bringing some meat. I'll make a strong broth—"

"Broth! Hell and damnation, woman. I need something that will stick to my ribs and give me some strength so I can get the hell out of this vipers' nest before someone slits my throat. Where are my clothes?"

"I didn't take them off you," she snapped, her face going beet red. "Mr. Sparks did. They were nothing but rags anyhow." Mara deliberately turned her back on him and smiled at Brita. "I'll bring some water so you can wash. Trellis went down to the cookhouse to get your breakfast. I'll be able to cook our meals here after today."

"You're not staying."

Mara heard the shocking words and turned back to stare at the man before she remembered that he was naked except for the corner of the blanket. She found herself fascinated by his broad shoulders and wide chest marked by cuts and bruises. A triangle of soft dark hair covered his chest down to where the white bandage was wrapped about his middle. His thighs were rock hard and covered with soft black down. His legs looked to be as sturdy as tree trunks. She had seen a picture of a naked man in a medical book and knew what he covered with the end of the blanket. Her face flamed at the thought.

"What did you say?"

"You heard me the first time. I said you're not staying here. This is no place for you. I tried to head you off at Sheffield Station."

"You have no say in the matter, Mr. Gallagher, and I'll thank you to tend to your own business. I'm of age. I own this place, and I have a perfect right to be here."

"I said nothing about the *right*, you addle-headed woman. I said this is not the place for you. You belong back in Denver among your own kind."

"And what kind is that?"

"Society . . . where you can get a rich husband to take care of you properly."

"I'm not in the market for a husband, rich or otherwise. I'd think you would be pleased that I'm here. Your mother needs care that Trellis can't give her."

"I've got a Mexican woman lined up to come here and look after Ma. I'd have taken her away from this place long ago, but she wouldn't go. Something about honoring her marriage vows," he added sarcastically.

"Now, now," Brita said soothingly. "Ye be in no shape to be carryin' on, son. Yer head must be fair bustin'."

"Aye, 'tis. Damn women don't know when they're well off."

"Damn men don't, either," Mara said calmly. "Lie down before you bleed all over the place and I have another mess to clean up. And cover your nakedness!"

"Jesus, my God! Deliver me from a bossy woman."

"If one more word of blasphemy comes from your mouth, Pack Gallagher, you will lie there and starve to death before I cook for you."

Mara's level stare, daring him to defy her, effectively silenced his lips, but his eyes, as dark as midnight, gleamed with resentment. He eased himself down on the bunk and pulled the blanket up to his chest.

"I've got to have my clothes . . . ma'am."

Mara picked up the shirt that lay on the floor and held it up. "This is beyond repair."

"Jes—" He cut off the word. "That buckskin shirt saved me some skin. Where's Trell? Where are my britches? Hell, I'm as defenseless as a babe lying here."

"Trell's gone to get your mother's breakfast. You don't need your britches because you're not going anywhere, and you needn't worry about lying there defenseless. I'll guard you until you can take care of yourself.''

"My God, Ma! Did you hear that? She'll guard me!"

"Yes, I'll guard you with this." Mara took the pistol from her pocket. "I know how to load it and how to shoot it."

"Put that damn thing away before you blow my head off!"

"That's not a bad idea. Blowing your head off, I mean. I'm tempted to do it, but I almost broke my back getting you into that wagon. I'll not waste that effort by shooting you now."

"You are most kind and generous, ma'am."

"What did you mean when you said you tried to head me off at Sheffield Station? Did you intercept the letter I sent to Cousin Aubrey?"

"No, I did."

"You . . . Cousin Brita?" Mara was almost too stunned to speak.

"Trell went to town 'n brought the mail. Don't be blamin' Pack, darlin'," Brita pleaded.

Mara felt a wave of bitter disappointment and turned eyes dark with hurt on Brita. For the first time since she came home she felt like crying.

"Why? Why don't you want me here?"

"Child, it not be a matter of wantin' ye here." Brita rolled her head on the pillow, her eyes filled with tears. "There be no nice thin's here yer used to havin'. 'Tis rough 'n wild country, with rough 'n wild men. There be no one to stand 'tween ye 'n them."

"Do you mean to say Cousin Aubrey and Cullen wouldn't protect me if . . . if I needed protection?"

Mara heard a snort of disgust come from Pack.

"I don't be knowin' if they . . . could."

"Or would," Pack added.

Mara turned on him in a temper, feeling hot, uncomfortable, a little lost and unsure. He stared back at her, his eyes telling her that he knew of her uncertainty. When she spoke, there was nothing but cold determination in her voice.

"You keep out of this. I'm talking to your mother," she said frigidly. She was surprised and pleased that her voice came calmly from her tight throat because she was burning with uncertainty. She braced herself for a mocking jibe, but none came, and she turned back to Brita. "If you were worried that I would ask you and Aubrey to leave, you can rest assured that I will not. I owe you, as my mother's friend, and I owe Aubrey for working this place and keeping me in school."

"But, darlin'—"

Brita was interrupted by Pack. " 'Tis good of you not to throw my mother out."

His voice plucked at Mara's already taut nerves, and only a momentary burst of common sense prevented her from yelling at him. She turned a cool, superior gaze on him.

"Your mother will always be welcome in my home. However, that does not necessarily apply to her son, Mr. Gallagher. I have no such obligation to you," she said calmly, then turned quickly and left the room.

"Ye shouldn't rile her, son," Brita murmured. "She be a fine lass, 'n the spittin' image of Colleen McCall, but with more spirit. Ye should have seen her pull that little gun on Cullen."

"On Cullen? What did he do?"

"He be mouthin' off, like he does. She says be civil or be leavin'. Cullen come to yer bed, 'n cool as ye please the lass moved in 'n pulled the gun from her pocket. Cullen backed off. She ain't a lass to be pushed, son."

"What'll I do, Ma?" Pack said wearily.

"There be one thing—"

"No! That I'll not do unless all else fails."

"Ye got to be gettin' on yer feet. Do ye be feelin' a fever comin' on? Yer side ain't bad, just a cut as the shot went by ye."

"My damn leg burns like hellfire, I ache in a hundred places and I'm about to starve to death. Aside from all that I'm in pretty good shape."

"Ye be lucky to be alive," Brita murmured. "I be thinkin' ye'd not make it when ye was brung in."

"I wasn't sure myself, Ma."

"The Holy Mother was watchin' o'er ye, son. She sent Mara Shannon to see to ye."

"Holy Mother had nothing to do with it. More than likely it was old Jim at the station. He didn't want to be the one to help me. He sent Mara Shannon to do it."

"Was Cullen in on it?"

"I didn't see him."

"Who done it, son?"

"It's best you don't know, Ma. It'll not happen again."

"Ye can't be havin' more laudanum."

"I don't want any. I've got to keep my head clear."

Chapter
FOUR

Pack ate several soft biscuits for breakfast but was unable to chew the fried meat because of his sore jaws. Mara thought he hadn't missed anything. The meat was so salty that she could hardly eat it herself. She longed for a bowl of cold mush, honey, and cream and coffee that didn't taste as if it were made from boiled acorns.

After the meal Brita asked Mara if she would help Trellis change the bandage on Pack's side. She could feel his eyes on her face as she bent over the bunk and carefully pulled away the bandage. Sam had done a good job closing the wound. The bullet had apparently passed through the fleshy part of his side. Although Mara kept her eyes averted from Pack's face, she knew he was breathing faster than normal by the way his stomach moved beneath her touch.

When she finished, she found a reason to be out of the room and left Trellis to change the bandage on Pack's thigh which was the more serious of the two bullet wounds. The boy bathed it with vinegar water and placed a cloth sprinkled with burned alum against it when Mara brought it from the kitchen.

After they had finished, Brita motioned for her to come close and whispered in her ear. Trellis stood awkwardly at the end of the bunk with his face averted. Her own face flamed. She felt the complete fool for not realizing the man would have to, at times, relieve himself. Mara left the room and closed the door, vowing to have as little as possible to do with the tending of Pack Gallagher.

She worked in the kitchen, using what meager supplies she could find to make it clean. She tied a rag around the straw broom and wiped down the walls before she swept the floor. Making suds in the warm water with strong lye soap as she had seen the kitchen help do at the school, she washed all the utensils and scrubbed the workbench, trestle table, and wash bench before using the water to scrub the floor.

It wasn't work she was used to doing, but she welcomed it because she did her best thinking while her hands were busy. First things first, she told herself. Make the house at least livable, then make Aubrey give an accounting of the money so she would know how much they had to live on. Thank goodness she had saved a major portion of the allowance he had put in the bank in Denver. She was not entirely without funds.

Trellis brought a hunk of deer meat from the smokehouse. Mara cut it in cubes, browned it in the iron kettle, then covered it with water and set it on the cookstove to simmer. When the meat was tender enough for Pack to chew, she would make dumplings in the broth if she could get Trellis to bring her flour and lard from the cookshack.

Mara mopped the floor, poured several buckets of clear water over it, and swept it out the door with her broom. She smiled at the thought of what Miss Fillamore would say if she could see her now. No doubt it would have something to do with common labor being a disgraceful waste of an education!

Exhausted when she was finished, Mara viewed the room with satisfaction. It was clean and smelled of soap and damp wood. She arranged the few dishes in the cupboard and brought a cloth from her trunk to put on the table. The room was a poor imitation of what it once had been, but it was a start.

While carrying out a pail of dirty water to throw in the yard, she saw a group of horsemen coming up the road toward the house. She paused on the porch, wiped her hair back from her face with the back of her hand, and watched Aubrey and Cullen hurry from the bunkhouse to meet the riders. They stopped in the road, but one man came on up to the house.

"Howdy." The man tipped his hat to Mara and she nodded.

"Howdy, Marshal," Cullen said. "Looks like you've been ridin' for awhile. Bring your men on down to the bunkhouse, eat a bite 'n have a cup of coffee."

"This isn't a social visit, McCall. We're trailin' four men. The tracks led right here."

"Four men came in early this morning 'n wanted to do some horse tradin'. Said they were part of a posse trailin' a gang that killed a nester 'n his woman. They had badges—"

"You gave them fresh horses?"

"Why, 'course, Ace. They were part of your posse."

"You know goddamn well they were not part of my posse!" The marshal beckoned to his men. "Go on down to the corral and take a look at those horses. Who ya got here now, McCall?"

"Same as always. Me and Pa, the twins, Steamboat 'n old Riley."

"And that's all?" he asked. His disbelief was obvious.

"That's all." Cullen looked the man in the eyes and lied.

The marshal walked his horse toward the porch. "How do, ma'am?"

Mara came down the steps.

"I must apologize for my cousin's rudeness in not introducing us. I'm Mara Shannon McCall." She held out her hand when the man dismounted. He removed his hat before his calloused hand clasped hers. He was thin as a whiplash, had a strong, weathered face and sandy hair that contrasted with the dark mustache that swooped down on each side of his mouth.

"Ace January, marshal out of Laramie."

"I'm pleased to know you. Perhaps you knew my father, Shannon McCall, who built this place?"

"No, I've only been here for about five years. I came out after the war."

"I've been in Denver for the past seven years, but I'm home now to stay," she said smiling, and pulled her hand from his.

"That's mighty good news, Miss McCall."

"I'm glad to know there's a lawman in the area. You're welcome anytime, Mr. January." Mara glanced past the marshal and saw the look of agitation on Cullen's face. Let the little weasel squirm, she thought, and smiled sweetly at Ace January. "I'd invite you in, but I've just finished mopping and my floor is wet. The next time you come this way, stop by and I'll bake you a layer cake."

"I'll not let you forget that, ma'am." The lawman's eyes crinkled at the corners when he smiled. They seemed reluctant to leave her face. She was the softest, most wholesome-looking woman he'd seen in a long time. How in the hell could she be related to two no-good bastards like Cullen and Aubrey McCall? No matter, he thought. Her presence would not deter him one bit if he got proof the man he was looking for was here. He'd swoop down on this place and burn it out regardless of the girl and that poor crippled wife of Aubrey's just as he'd had to burn out other outlaw nests.

Mara stood on the porch and watched the posse leave the homestead. She had the feeling the lawman didn't like her cousins and that they didn't like him. Well, no matter. He seemed to be a nice man doing his job. The next time he came this way, the house would be put to order and she wouldn't be ashamed to invite a guest into her home.

"Cousin Aubrey," Mara called. "Will you please ask someone to move this pile of wood from the porch and carry it to the back of the house where it belongs?"

Aubrey glared at her but didn't answer.

A half hour later, Travor and Cullen, sullen and silent, moved the wood and piled it around a stump at the back of the house.

By the time the day ended Mara wasn't sure she was equipped to handle so much as one more abusive word or pull one more pail of water from the well behind the house. She had had a run-in with Travor when she asked him not to walk on her clean floor until it was dry. Cullen had demanded to know how long Pack Gallagher intended to hide behind her skirts, and Aubrey had refused to talk to her about the financial state of the property. Her pride and her body had taken a beating. She was exhausted, too exhausted to move her things up-stairs, too exhausted to do more than wash in the washpan when she longed with all her heart to sink down into a nice warm bath and let the tension flow out of her. In Denver all she had to do was request that the tub in the small room at the end of the upper hall be filled with warm water. Being here was like being in another world.

Mara pulled her nightgown over her head, loosened her hair from the coil, and crawled into bed. Tomorrow, she told herself, tomorrow she would work on the upstairs rooms, and then Trellis or Aubrey could have this one. She fell into a deep sleep almost immediately.

Something aroused her from that black, peaceful void. She stared into the darkness, shivered, and lifted her head from the pillow. After a long moment, she threw back the covers and went to the window to look out. The shimmering glow of the moon illuminated the landscape. Nothing stirred on the slope in front of the house. She went to the other window and looked toward the bunkhouse. All was quiet there. She was returning to her bed when she heard a hoarse whisper coming from Brita's room and tiptoed to the door to listen.

"Ma! Ma . . . wake up."

Mara lit the lamp, checked to see if the buttons on her nightdress were closed, then opened the door between her room and Brita's.

"Ma . . ." Pack's voice rasped out weakly.

In the soft glow of the lamp, Mara could see that he had thrown back the cover until it barely covered his privates. She placed the lamp on the bureau and went to the bunk.

"I'm burning up." He moved his hand down to pull the quilt up to cover himself. "Can I trouble you for a drink of water?"

Mara felt his forehead with her palm. "Oh, my. You *are* hot! You've got an awful fever!"

Brita roused. "Mara? What's the matter with Pack?" she asked anxiously.

"He's taken a fever. I'll get cold water and wash him down." Forgetting about being barefoot and in her night-gown, Mara hurried to the kitchen and the water bucket that sat on the shelf.

"Bring vinegar, child," Brita called. "Put the kettle on for sage tea." Brita could hear the stove lids clang and knew Mara had stuffed the firebox with wood and was putting the teakettle on.

Mara came back into the room carrying the water bucket and a pan. She placed them on the floor beside the bunk.

"Towels? Oh, I've got some in my trunk."

Pack's feverish eyes followed her. She floated out of the room and then back in like an angel out of a dream. She came to him, bent over him, and lifted his head to help him drink from the cup she held to his lips. He drank gratefully and sank back. She wet a large towel and laid it across his bare chest, wet a smaller cloth for his forehead.

"You've got to drink more water, Pack." Mara refilled the cup, slid her arm beneath his neck, and lifted his head. "Drink as much as you can." There was a concerned tone in her voice that he had not heard before. Her hair fell forward onto his chest. He could feel the softness of her body against his upper arm. He closed his eyes. Ah, her face, her sweet face. He had not thought he would ever be this close to her. As he drained the cup, she pulled her arm from beneath him.

On her knees beside the bunk Mara began to sponge his shoulders, then his upper and lower arms. She flipped the hair back over her shoulder and bent over the big oak of a man, and he suddenly stopped his restless movements and lay still. She touched the wet cloth to his bruised face, his torso with its hundreds of cuts and scratches, and shuddered at the pain he must have endured. His shoulders and arms bulged with muscles, yet the fever made him so helpless that he lay placidly still beneath her hands. When his eyes looked directly into hers, she was startled to see that they were blue, midnight blue, and the expression in them was soft, questioning.

"Mara Shannon," he whispered weakly, "you shouldn't be doin' for the likes of Pack Gallagher."

"Be quiet, Pack Gallagher," she said with gentle tyranny. "You're walking on these splintery floors with naught on your feet."

"My feet be no business of yours, Mr. Gallagher." Her whispered words were soft, without censure, and her eyes were shadowed with worry.

"Ye can call Trell—"

"Mara Shannon is not a squeamish woman. Ye just lie still. I be doing what has to be done to get the fever down. Then you'll be drinking the sage tea I'll be brewing." Unconsciously both of them had lapsed into Irish brogues.

Mara turned to dip the towel in the basin again. Her hair spilled over onto Pack's hand where it lay on the bed. His spread fingers combed through the silken strands when she turned back to lay the cloth once again on his forehead. The lamplight shone on the rich darkness of her hair, turning the strands to flame. The eyes that looked into his were soft emerald green, shadowed with concern. He liked what he saw in her eyes and longed to have it last forever.

Pack had never been so close to heaven, and never had he been more painfully aware of the difference between them. He could smell the feminine, sensual aroma of her woman's body, see the mysterious movements of her breasts beneath the cloth of her high-necked, modest gown. Mara Shannon was beautiful, proud, well-acquainted with all the social graces. He, Pack Gallagher, was a freighter, wild and rough, earning money with his fists, and could scarcely write more than his name. Pack closed his eyes, and the low moan that came softly from his swollen lips had nothing to do with his aching body and his pounding headache. It came from deep within his soul.

Stubbornly Mara stayed beside Pack and sponged his hot body, first with vinegar and then water. She held his head and forced him to drink cup after cup of the lukewarm sage tea. When the lamp began to flicker, she hurried to the kitchen for another lamp before the fuel ran out, leaving them in total darkness.

Brita watched helplessly, thanking God for Mara. The girl worked tirelessly through the long night hours as Pack dozed and became quiet, then roused and moved restlessly. Finally he slipped into a deep sleep.

"He seems cooler, Brita." Mara stood and looked down at his bruised face and the nose that leaned slightly to one side. She wondered what Pack Gallagher would look like when his face healed. He would not be handsome—his features were too craggy for that—but he would not be ugly.

"Dry him, lass. Dry 'n cover him."

Mara removed the wet towels and gently dried Pack's face and chest. She pulled the blanket up over his shoulders and tucked it in. She had never known anyone like him, had never before touched a man so intimately. Her palms had moved over the hard flesh of his shoulders and arms and her fingers had slipped beneath his thick wrist to lift his injured hand. Mara had sponged his chest, surprised to see the pink nipples nestled in the soft hair that ended where the bandage was wrapped about his middle.

Thank God the one time her forearm brushed against the soft bulge covered by the quilt he was asleep. She had jumped as if she had touched fire. After that she tried to avoid looking at the area below his hard, flat belly, but she knew that what was there was in proportion to the rest of him.

Pack was a rough man, yet he had been concerned about her, and more than one time during the last few hours he had urged her to rest before she wore herself out, to put on her shoes, to stop lifting the bucket of water.

Mara studied his face, his dark rumpled hair, and listened to his even breathing. It was a miracle that his ribs were not broken considering the bruises along his sides. It had taken more than one man to do this to him. She wondered if he would seek vengeance when he was well again.

"Come lie down, Mara Shannon. Like Pack says, ye must be wore out. Lie beside me. I'll wake ye if ye're needed."

"I think I will, if you're sure I won't bother you." Mara lay down on the far edge of the bed. "I don't know how you can be so kind and so patient, Brita. Don't you just want to scream sometimes?"

"Aye. Arthritis is what the doctor be callin' what 'tis cripplin' me. At first I be feelin' sorry fer meself. I be angry fer bein' locked in a crippled body. Now I got to be sayin' 'tis God's will. *He* don't be puttin' more burdens on a body than they be able to bear."

"Who did this terrible thing to Pack?" Mara asked, tilting her head on the pillow so that she could see Brita's face.

"I don't be knowin'. Pack says 'twas not Cullen, so we can't be blamin' him fer *that*."

"Where does Pack live? How does he make his living?" Questions she would not have asked in the daylight seemed perfectly reasonable to ask now.

"Sometimes he goes to Cheyenne, sometimes to Laramie or Denver."

"To Denver? What does he do there?"

"Pack's got a freight line, lass. 'Tis business what takes him there. My Pack, he be not afraid to work or take a risk. 'Twas haulin' cats to the mines what paid for his wagons 'n mules." Laughter shone in the blue eyes of the gentle-faced woman.

"Barn cats? Why in the world would he haul cats to the mines?"

"Mice 'n rats were eatin' up the grub he be takin' to the mining camps. There not be a cat in sight fer them to fear. Pack built cages atop his wagons 'n put the word out he'd pay twenty-five cents fer any cat what was brought to him. 'Twas not long till he had two loads a cats. He took them to the camps 'n they sold fer ten dollars each."

"That's robbery!"

"Not a'tall, lass. The next load went for more. 'Tis what

was needed. The cats ate the mice 'n rats. 'Twas a tidy savin' on the grub.'' There was a proud smile on Brita's face. "My Pack, he be knowin' how to make money."

"Then how is it that he doesn't have a proper home? What does he do with his money?''

"Pack be a grown man. I wouldna ask him, child.''

There was a long silence, then Mara asked, "Does he come here often?''

"Once, twice a month. Pack be wantin' me to go to Denver to see the doctor. But 'twould be fer naught." Brita turned her head so she could look at the girl lying beside her. "Mara Shannon, I asked Pack to head ye off at Sheffield Station. Ye can be seein' why. 'Tis a hard life out here. Things be goin' on that I don't be knowin' about. Trell 'n Pack know, but they . . . not be wantin' me to . . . worry." Brita moved her arm until her crippled hand lay on her chest, and she sucked in great gulps of air into her lungs.

Mara raised up. "What's the matter, Brita?''

" 'Tis nothin'. I get a pain at times. 'Tis from layin' abed." She closed her eyes and pressed her lips tightly together. As the pain eased her face relaxed. "Don't be tellin' it to Trell 'n Pack.''

"I won't. Does it come often?''

" 'Tis naught to worry 'bout, darlin'. It comes with the sickness.''

Mara lay back down. A question nagged at her. Was Brita's heart about to give out? Her mother had complained of pains in her chest before she died. Mara reached out her hand and touched Brita's arm. Please, God, she prayed, don't take Brita.

"I'm glad I came home, Brita," she whispered. "I wish I had come sooner. I'll take care of you now."

"Ye're a sweet child like yer mother."

"I've been lonely. It's good to talk to someone who knew my parents. Being Irish, I wasn't really accepted by the other girls at the school." Mara paused, remembering her loneliness when parents came to visit the students. Graduation had been held on the lawn in front of the school. A crowd of people were there, but not one of them had come to see her get her diploma. "I was considered a good teacher for a shanty Irish lass. Miss Fillamore thought I had risen far above my station in life. She couldn't understand why I wanted to leave the school. But Brita, I could see myself growing old and narrow-minded just as she was," Mara whispered. "Old, without ever knowing the love of a husband and children."

"Aye, 'tis why God made a woman. 'Tis lucky a woman be to have the love of a good man. I be one of the lucky ones. Me Gallagher was a big man, like Pack. He loved with all his heart . . . and hated the same. He was dear to me heart."

Brita fell silent. Mara waited for her to say more about her beloved Gallagher, but slowly sleep overcame Mara's determination to stay awake. She slept dreamlessly until she awakened with a dull headache and to the smell of coffee. She opened her eyes and found herself staring at Trell's young face bent over his mother.

"Pack?" Mara slid off the bed and hurried around the end of it to the bunk.

"He's sweatin'. Ma says the fever broke."

Pack was awake. His eyes were clear. He looked different this morning. His face was leaner, his lips thinner. Much of the swelling had gone from his face. Small beads of sweat stood on his forehead.

"Are you feeling better?" Mara placed the palm of her hand against his cheek.

"Much better."

"You're not at all feverish."

"You took care of that last night. Thank you."

"Why, Pack Gallagher!" she teased. "If you don't watch out you might be civil to me." Her smile was radiant. "Are you hungry?"

"Starved."

"I'll fix you something."

"You best be making yourself decent first unless you're wanting every man on this place to see you in your night-clothes." He swung his gaze down the full length of her body.

Mara backed away from him as if he had struck her. A rosy

redness rushed up her neck to flood her cheeks, and anger kept pace.

"I had no such thought in mind, Pack Gallagher! You're an evil man to even think it!"

"Evil or not, I am a man, Mara Shannon. A man who knows you're naked under that gown!"

"Oh! Why . . . damn your rotten soul! I needn't have wondered about you ever being civil. You don't know what the word means! You're a crude, rude, asinine man with cow dung for brains. And you can go straight to hell for all I care!"

"Swearing too! Your Pa didn't send you to school to have you come out talking like a mule skinner!" Pack's face was rigid with lines of disapproval.

There was silence, a bitter aching silence.

Mara seethed with anger. His criticism grated on her nerves like chalk screeching against a slate, filling her with a red rage. Not trusting herself to speak lest she bring forth more swear words that came to mind, Mara lifted her chin and walked from the room. Her legs were unsteady, but her shoulders were square and her back straight. Not until she reached her room did she give way to her anger. Then she slammed the door so hard the house shook.

The day had started off badly, and it didn't get any better as it progressed. By the middle of the afternoon Mara was tired and angry. She had sent Trellis to find Aubrey only to discover that her cousin had gone to town. Now she stood at the window of one of the upstairs rooms and looked down at the three men sitting on the porch of the cookshack. They had been sitting there for hours while she had been carrying trash down the stairs and piling it on the back porch. The two upstairs rooms had been filthy. Mouse droppings were everywhere. Mara vowed to buy a cat if she couldn't get one any other way. Finally the rooms were clean, the mop and pail were carried down to the back porch, and the windows were open to let a cool breeze pass through. She had done all she could do without help. She needed someone to carry the old musty mattress out into the yard to air, and needed help to carry her things up the stairs.

The bureau in the room was usable, as was the washstand. The bed and mattress in the room downstairs would have to be brought up as well as her trunk. Before winter she would purchase a rug for the floor. Up here she would at least have a measure of privacy.

Before Mara had quite realized that she had made a decision, she was down the stairs, out of the house, and heading for the bunkhouse. The breeze felt good on her hot face; the pistol in her pocket slapped reassuringly against her leg as she walked.

The men on the porch stopped talking and watched her approach. She recognized the man who had helped Sam Sparks carry Pack into the house. An old man without teeth sat on a bench, one leg crossed over the other, and a young man, hard looking with bold black eyes, sat on the edge of the porch. He wore down-at-the-heels boots and cruel-looking spurs.

"Do you men work here?" Mara asked curtly, addressing all three.

They looked at her silently, sullenly. Then the young bold-eyed man grinned at her, folded the knife he had been using to pare his nails, and put it in his pocket. He moved his eyes slowly over her body, then brought them back to linger on her breast.

"What ya wantin', sweetheart?"

Mara gave him a scornful glance that had sent schoolgirls scurrying to their rooms in tears. He didn't seem to notice her displeasure. His grin broadened, showing a missing tooth. He looked at her with his head cocked to one side.

"Do you understand English? I asked if you *worked* here."

"Work here?" he echoed. His eyes moved over her again before they came back to her face. "Sweetheart, I ain't likely to ever be that hard up!"

"Then what are you doing here?"

"Why, I'm just passin' the time." His eyes darted to the other two men.

"Then I suggest you pass the time someplace else."

"They work here." Cullen spoke belligerently as he came out the door. "What are you doing out here?" he demanded.

"If they work here, why aren't they working? It seems to me there's plenty to be done." Mara had to tilt her head to glare at Cullen who stood on the porch.

"Get on back to the house. What goes on down here is no concern of yours."

"Everything on this place concerns me. I want to know why these men have loafed out here all afternoon. Look at that corral. Look at that shed. A good wind would blow them away. They need repair as well as—" She caught herself just before she mentioned the outhouse that leaned perilously to one side. "Just about everything around here needs repair."

"I'm tellin' ya to mind your own business 'n get back to the house. I thought takin' care of that son of a bitchin' Gallagher would keep you busy."

"Don't you dare cast a reflection on Cousin Brita's character!"

"Don't be tellin' me what to do or *say!* I'm running things here, and if you don't like it, you can hightail it back to your fancy school!"

"You worthless, mouthy, slimy little piece of horse dung!" Mara sputtered. "You'll not be running things here for long. I can assure you of that."

"Whoopee! She's got some mouth on her, Cullen." The bold-eyed man slapped his thigh and shouted with laughter. Mara ignored him and spoke to Cullen again.

"When your father gets back, tell him that I want to talk to him . . . tonight!"

"Tell him yoreself."

Sam Sparks came out the door and stood behind Cullen.

"Afternoon, Miss McCall."

"Hello, Mr. Sparks." Mara's color was high. She didn't think she had ever been so angry in her life, but she would not give this group the pleasure of laughing at her. "Could I trouble you to help me for a short while, Mr. Sparks?" she asked calmly. "These *gentlemen* are too busy."

"Certainly, ma'am." He moved around Cullen and stepped off the porch.

"If'n you'd a asked me that nice, I'd a helped you do most anythin' you'd want done, little sweet thin'." The bold-eyed man stood. He was as rangy as a wolf and reminded Mara of one.

"Mister, I don't like your looks, and I don't like your manners." Mara spoke icily. She looked from the bold-eyed man to Cullen. "If this is an example of the men you have working here, it's no wonder the place is run-down. Get rid of him."

The man whooped with laughter. "Well, foofaraw! Ain't she uppity? You'd better set Miss Lacy Drawers straight about a few things, Cullen."

"Go on back to the house, Mara." Cullen's eyes were blazing with anger and his voice choked.

"Come on, ma'am." Sam took Mara's elbow in his hand and urged her toward the house. "It'd be best if you didn't come down here, Miss McCall," he said after they had walked a distance from the bunkhouse.

"Do you mean to say that it isn't safe for me to move about on my own property?"

"The property may be yours, Miss McCall, but it's not in your possession. Yes, I'd say it's not safe for a genteel young woman to wander away from the house."

"I have a pistol in my pocket, and I wouldn't hesitate to use it."

"Have you ever shot a man?"

"No, but I could . . . if I had to."

"I wouldn't count on gettin' the drop on a man like Sporty Howard. Stay away from him."

"Well . . . for goodness sake!"

"How is Pack?" Sam dropped his hand from her arm as they neared the house.

"Grouchy as a bear."

"He must be feeling better."

"Mr. Sparks, something is going on here that I don't like. I can't get Aubrey or Cullen to tell me a thing."

"It's not my place, ma'am, so don't ask me. It might be best, as they say, if you went back to Denver."

"No! If one more person tells me to leave my home in the hands of these incompetent fools and go back to Denver I'm going to throw a screaming fit!"

Sam Sparks grinned down at her. "I'm not sure I'd want to be around when that happens."

They had come into the kitchen. Mara flashed him a saucy smile, unaware that Pack could see them from where he lay on the bunk in the adjoining room.

"I'll tell you a secret if you'll not tell anyone." She moved close and spoke in a confidential tone. "I've never thrown a screaming fit in my life. But threatening to do it gets pretty good results . . . sometimes." She laughed softly.

"Someday someone will call your bluff; then what are you going to do?" Sam placed his hat on the table.

"I hadn't thought of that."

Mara's laughter floated into the next room, and the man on the bunk felt his muscles tighten.

"What was it you wanted done?" Sam asked.

"There's a mattress upstairs that needs airing, and I'd like help getting my bed and the rest of my things upstairs. I'm going to use the upstairs rooms because," she paused, then continued, "because I can bar the door!" She looked at Sam closely to gauge his reaction.

"Not a bad idea."

"Sam," Pack called. "Come in here."

Sam looked away from Mara and into the bedroom. "I'll be in shortly, Pack, after I help Miss McCall."

Mara walked past the doorway on the way to the stairs without looking into the room where Pack lay. Each time she passed, she tilted her nose a little higher. She would never forgive Pack Gallagher for the way he had talked to her that morning and vowed to do as little as possible for him. Trellis had brought his breakfast from the cookshack. She had carried a tray to Brita at noon, returned to set a bowl of beef and dumplings down on the stool beside Pack with a loud thump, and walked away. Since that time she had ignored him.

Sam carried Mara's trunk and carpetbags up the stairs and put the straw mattress on the back porch to air. The bed and mattress from Mara's old room was brought up and reassembled. After that Sam examined the door.

"This slip lock won't hold, ma'am. Ya need a stout bar to wedge under the knob. I'll cut one 'n leave it on the back porch tonight."

"Do you think I'll be needing it?"

"Ya can't tell, ma'am. A man gets to drinkin' at times 'n don't use no judgment."

"Thank you for helping me. Are you going to be here for a while, Mr. Sparks?"

"I'm not sure. I don't usually stay in one place long enough to get a growth a beard." He rubbed the stubble on his chin and grinned at her.

"Why are you here?" Mara asked.

"To rest my horse 'n eat grub I didn't cook over a campfire." He shrugged his shoulders. "I pay for bed 'n board."

"Do the other men pay to stay here too? Is that why they thought it so funny when I asked why they were loafing?"

"I only speak for myself, ma'am."

"I appreciate your honesty. I would have been disappointed if you had said you worked here."

After Sam went down the stairs. Mara stood in the center of the room, her arms folded across her chest, her mind crowded with questions. Sam was right when he said that although she might own the land, it wasn't in her possession. How in the world was she going to get control? And what would she do with it if she got it? She knew nothing about making a living off the land.

A feeling of utter despair came over her. Whom could she turn to for advice? Certainly not Cousin Aubrey or his son, Cullen. Her father had liked Pack Gallagher, but he had already told her to go back to Denver. He had troubles of his own and would not be around long enough to help her with hers even if he were willing. She suddenly thought of Ace January, the marshal. She filed it in the back of her mind to ask Trellis if he would take her to town to talk to him.

Sam sat down on the low stool beside Pack's bed. "How're ya doin', Pack?"

"I'll make it. I'm obliged to you for getting me in the house and sewing me up."

"Ya got yoreself worked over real good. I'd a swore ya was out cold when Miss McCall brought ya in."

"I was. Trell told me what you did. I'm surprised to see you out here, Sam."

"Why?"

"You know *why*. I never thought you'd have the need to hide out."

"It just goes to show that ya don't know everythin', Pack."

"Do you know the Rivers place over west of here?"

"I've not been there, but I heard a fellow by the name of Charlie Rivers has a place over along Lodgepole Creek."

"I'd be obliged if you'd ride over and tell him I need clothes and boots. Ma says he'll be bringing his sister over sometime during the next week or so, but I can't lay abed until then."

"I've been warned to stay clear of the Rivers place."

"Charlie's all right if you ride in and tell him your business. It's the ones that sneak around trying to get a look at Miss Emily that gets him riled up."

"How long's he been out there?"

"Three or four years. He's doing all right. He's got a little herd, does some trapping, and he gets along with the Sioux that come through there."

"Where's he from?"

"Ask him. I figure he'll tell you if he wants you to know."

Sam shrugged. "Guess he would. I'll ride over in the mornin'."

"I was riding a big, spotted gray, Sam. Have you seen anything of him?"

"I know the horse. There's not another like him in the territory. No, I've not seen him. Whoever jumped ya'd not take him to town. Ya can get hung for horse stealin' as quick as rapin' a woman."

"About Mara Shannon," Pack said in a low voice, his dark eyes holding Sam's, "she's not for the likes of anyone around here."

"Are ya warnin' me off, Pack?"

"You can call it that."

"If I set my mind on havin' her, yore warnin' wouldn't make a whit of difference. I'd fight ya for her with bullets, not fists."

"I know that."

"I'm not the one ya've got ta worry 'bout. Ya'd better look a bit closer ta home."

"Cullen? I'll kill that bastard someday. I know you're decent with women, Sam, and you'll not force yourself on her." His low voice had a warning in it.

"Ya don't want me courtin' her either, is that it?"

"That's it. What do you have to offer a woman like her? You're not a settlin' man."

"Yo're not the settlin' down kind either, Pack."

There was cold-eyed hostility in the look Pack gave Sam Sparks. "I know I'm not good enough for her, and I want you to know that you're not good enough either."

"I plan to be movin' on soon."

"What about the others? Who's down there?"

"Shorty Howard for one."

"Godamighty!"

"Ya'd best be gettin' her away from here, unless ya plan to stay around 'n ride shotgun."

"Godamighty!" Pack said again. "I'd be obliged if you stayed on till I'm on my feet."

"I plan to." Sam stood and looked down. "Galls ya to ask a favor, don't it? Can't say I'd not feel the same. Watch yoreself, Pack. Next time that bunch from Laramie will kill ya."

Chapter
FIVE

Sam left the McCall ranch, heading in a westerly direction toward the mountains. He rode cautiously along the two-wheel track, the mid-morning sun hot on his back. It was lonely, rugged country. These were the foothills of the Laramie Mountain Range, and there were more trees on the ridges, cutting down the visibility. In the valley the grass was truly green, but higher up where it was drier, the vegetation was stiff, harsh, more gray than green. He came to Lodgepole Creek and turned, following an animal path alongside it to find a place to cross.

Where the creek narrowed, he reined in, studied the land and listened. Far off to the south he heard the short blast of a train whistle, and then another and another. The whistling went on and on. Sam decided the engineer was trying to clear the track of buffalo. The crack of a rifle reached him, then another. Soon the sound of continuous shooting echoed from hill to hill.

"Goddamn stupid bastards!" Sam had seen the frenzy of killing displayed by Easterners when they saw their first herd of the slow-plodding animals. The waste made his stomach turn. All along the tracks were piles of bones, mangy hides and rotting carcasses. What the Easterners didn't kill for sport, the buffalo hunters killed for hides. The buffalo herds were small now. If the slaughter continued, in a few years there would be no buffalo at all. Who could blame the Indian for his hatred of the white man?

Sam touched his heels to the gelding, urging him down the embankment and into the fast-moving water of the creek. The horse cautiously tested the rocky bottom to find footing, then confidently moved on across to climb the bank on the opposite side.

Thoughts of Pack Gallagher sifted into Sam's mind. He had met Pack in '68, a couple of months after Laramie sprang up. Before the iron rails had reached the site, only a few tents had been pitched to house the tie cutters and grading crews working west of Cheyenne. Almost overnight a town of several hundred shacks and cabins of logs, sod, canvas and wagon boxes had appeared. Now, two years later, Laramie was a sprawling, brawling town of rutted, dusty streets, gamblers, dance-hall women, saloon keepers, and hangers-on.

Sam had known the big Irishman by reputation and, guided by intuition, liked him. He was honest, intelligent, and intensely loyal to his friends. The previous month Sam had seen the fight between Pack and the Pittsburgh fighter whom he had challenged. The sign nailed to the wall beside the saloon door by the cigar-smoking promoter had read: A HUNDRED DOLLARS TO ANY MAN WHO CAN STAY IN THE RING FOR THREE ROUNDS WITH BLACK BOB MASON. It created a flurry of excitement, and every betting man within a hundred miles had converged on the booming town.

The fight had been the main topic of conversation in every saloon in Laramie for days. The populace would bet on anything; horserace, footrace, shooting, knife throwing— even how long a chicken could survive in the rutted road in front of the saloon before it was carried off by one of the hungry dogs that roamed the town. A prizefight in a ring was a major event.

Pack's friends had urged him to fight.

"Ye can pick up a quick hundred, Pack. Ye ain't been beat yet."

"Yo're the only man we got to go agin that blowhard."

"I seen 'em fight in Cheyenne. He ain't no bruiser, like you, Pack."

"We be needin' a grub stake, Pack. We'll be bettin' on ya to brin' home the bacon."

Big money was bet on the Pittsburgh brawler. Amid the cheers of his supporters, Pack had knocked the man out in the third round. His friends had collected their money and headed for the gold fields. Later, Sam had discovered, gamblers from the Kosy Kitty Saloon had ordered Pack to lose the fight or suffer the consequences. The reason they had not killed Pack, Sam thought now, was so he could fight another day and they could recoup their losses.

Sam moved on down the trail. He had learned to sort out sounds. The shooting had stopped. Far off he heard the screech of a rabbit that had fallen prey to a soaring hawk. The horse's long tail flicking at the pesky flies made a swishing sound; the roan's hooves crunched the dry grass. As Sam shifted his weight, the saddle leather creaked.

Suddenly above these sounds he heard a woman singing. He pulled up on the reins, stopping the roan. He didn't want to make the same mistake the outlaw back at McCall's had made and have his horse get a load of rock salt in the rump.

The woman's voice was incredibly sweet and clear.

"Beautiful dreamer, waken to me,
    Starlight and dewdrops are waiting for thee.
Sounds of the rude world, heard in the day,
    lulled by the moonlight have all passed away."

Sam sat as still as a stone long after the woman stopped singing. The beautiful tones echoed in his head.

He shook his head to rid it of thoughts of another girl who had loved that song—his sister. Painful memories that he had shoved to the back of his mind came forward to torment him anew.

He had survived the war, but his family had not survived an attack by deserters who killed them for food and horses, then burned the house down so there was nothing left of his family to bury. Sam had gone back to his home on the Red River to find everything gone. Even the river had changed its course and flowed over the site of the homestead. Neighbors had told him of the vicious attack. His family was gone. Everything was gone except his childhood memories.

Just as Sam was about to ride on, the woman began to sing again. He waited and listened.

"Will you come with me, my Phyllis dear, to
      yon blue mountain free?
Where blossoms smell the sweetest, come rove
      along with me.
It's every Sunday morning when I am by your side,
We'll jump into the wagon and all take a ride."

The song was one sung by northern soldiers during the war. It gave Sam new food for thought. Had Charlie Rivers fought for the Blue or the Gray? Sam rode down the worn trail and through a stand of aspen, expecting any moment to be challenged by the homesteader. The scent he smelled was familiar although he hadn't smelled it for a long while. Soap was being made in a kettle over an open fire.

Sam moved out of the trees. He saw the homestead set in the clearing. A woman in a brown dress and a white apron was stirring the soap in an iron kettle with a large wooden paddle. He rode toward her cautiously. His eyes took in everything from the neat log house to the outbuildings and the long cords of evenly cut firewood stacked between the trees beside the house. He could tell a lot about a man by the way he kept up his place. Charlie Rivers planned well. He was methodical, hard-working and, from the looks of this place, there to stay.

The woman had heard the sound of his horse's hooves. She stopped stirring the soap and stood still, gripping the large paddle with both hands. She was as alert as a deer sensing danger. Sam pulled the horse to a halt a dozen yards from where she stood.

"Howdy, ma'am," he called. "I'm Sam Sparks and I'm bringin' a word from Pack Gallagher."

Long minutes passed. The woman stood so silent and so still, Sam wondered if she could speak.

"This's the Rivers' place, ain't it?"

"Yes. What do you want?"

"A word with Charlie Rivers. Is he here?"

"Oh, yes. He's in the house." She spoke so quickly that Sam knew she was alone. The quiver in her voice betrayed her fear.

"Will you ask him to come out?"

"Stay where you are. He'll be out in a minute." She pulled the paddle partially out of the kettle, holding it as if ready to swing.

"You needn't be afraid of me, ma'am. I'll keep my distance till your brother comes . . . out."

She didn't answer or move. Sam had a chance to study her. Somehow he had thought she would be a very young girl. She had the mature body of a woman past twenty. Her skin was golden from being in the sun, her hair light brown, and she wore it braided, Indian fashion. The eyes in her still face were enormous. He was surprised. Didn't Cullen say she was blind? He was not close enough to see the color of her eyes, but they were light, very light. She had turned her head slightly and was listening for him to make the slightest move.

A wave of anger swept over him when he recalled Cullen saying that she wouldn't know *who* it was under her skirts. She needed protection from the low-life that hung around McCalls even more than Mara McCall needed it. Sam searched his brain for something to say that would put the woman at ease, but nothing came to mind.

His eyes roved the homestead. It was a homey looking

place with the mountains for a background. A rope swing with a plank seat hung from the branch of a tree. The garden had neat weedless rows, and beside it a line was stretched for drying the wash. Hollyhocks grew around the privy that sat back from the house. Sam noted the line fastened from the privy to the house and realized it was for Miss Rivers' convenience. It was clear to Sam that Charlie Rivers thought a lot of his sister.

Sam's horse moved restlessly and nickered, peaking his ears and looking toward the stockade corral. A big gray horse trotted up to the fence and answered the roan's greeting with a trumpet of his own.

"Pack'll be glad to know ya found his horse, Miss Rivers. He was worried about him."

"Charlie found him. There was blood on the saddle. Is Pack all right?"

"He'll be all right in a day or two. He was worked over pretty good."

"Charlie thinks someone put Pack in a wagon. He found markings on the road. The tracks headed north toward the McCalls."

"Mara McCall found him on the road to Sheffield Station."

"He was going there to meet her. How is Pack's mother taking it?"

" 'Twas hard on her, seein' him so beat up."

"Poor Brita. Have you seen Miss McCall?"

"Yes, ma'am."

Sam saw a flicker of movement inside the house. Charlie Rivers must have come in through the back. Sam crossed his arms and leaned them on the saddlehorn, not wanting the short-tempered man to think he was reaching for a gun. Suddenly the man charged out the door with a sawed-off shotgun in his hands.

"Go to the left, Emily," he shouted. The woman dropped the paddle back into the kettle, turned to the left and disappeared behind the house. "State your business."

Sam's first thought was to wonder why someone hadn't told him Charlie Rivers was a one-legged man. The knee of his left leg rested in the cradle of a peg held by straps that wrapped about his thigh, the stump sticking out behind.

"I've a message from Pack Gallagher."

"What is it?"

"Pack needs clothes, boots . . . and his horse."

"What shape is he in?"

"Bad, at first. They dragged him 'n shot him twice. He's at McCall's."

"Hell of a place for him to be flat on his back."

"He's in the big house. His ma 'n Mara McCall are takin' care of him 'n doin' a fair job of it. Are you goin' to keep me sittin' out here all day?"

"You're not here by my invitation."

"Not by my own choice either. Pack said ya was a friend a his, 'n asked me to come."

Charlie Rivers took his time looking Sam over. Sam looked back at him steadily. Finally Charlie lowered the gun.

"Come on in."

"Thanks," Sam said dryly when he moved closer. "I'm about to wear out my throat yellin'."

Sam stepped down from the saddle and looped the reins over a rail. Charlie Rivers stepped down off the porch. He was a squarely built man, not as big as either Sam or Pack, but well-muscled and agile. He spun around easily on the peg leg.

"Sit," he said, indicating the edge of the porch.

"Hot for June," Sam commented as he sat down. He took off his hat and wiped his forehead on his sleeve.

"Guess it is." Rivers sat also, still holding the shotgun. The man seemed to wait deliberately for Sam to speak. Sam thought he might as well oblige him.

"I saw the fight in Laramie. Mason was no match for Pack a'tall. I figure Pack was told to lose the fight. When he didn't, he was jumped by the crowd that lost."

"Pack wouldn't throw a prizefight. He was fighting to get his friends a grub stake. Black Bob Mason was paid the same, win or lose. The gamblers were the ones set to make the money, not Mason." Charlie snorted with disgust.

"Have ya known Pack long?" Sam took a sack of tobacco

and papers from his pocket and offered them to Charlie. The man shook his head and Sam began to build a cigarette.

"Awhile."

Sam scratched a match against the porch post, cupped his hands about the flame and touched it to the end of the cigarette. He looked at Charlie Rivers over his cupped hands and tried to decide what part of the country he was from. His manner of speaking was not distinctly southern, and yet. . . . His beard was neatly clipped, his hair cut, his clothes of good quality and clean. He wore some type of signet ring on his right hand. Charlie Rivers, Sam decided, was an educated man who had adapted to the pioneer life rather well. Why would such a man come to the wild, untamed land of Wyoming Territory?

"Are ya from Ohio?" Sam asked after a long pause.

"No."

"I'm from Texas."

"I thought so."

"What made ya think I'm a Texan?"

"Tied-down gun, high-crowned hat, boots with a star on the side."

"You don't miss much."

"It didn't take many brains to figure that out."

They both turned to watch Miss Rivers come from the side of the house and go to the kettle. She carefully reached for the paddle. Charlie got up, went to the fire, and with his peg kicked the burning sticks beneath the pot. He came back and stood in front of Sam.

"Did they strip Pack?"

"They left him his shirt and pants, but they didn't amount to much after they dragged him."

"The bastards!" Charlie swore.

"It took a bunch of them. Gallagher wouldn't be easy to take down."

"Cowards travel in packs." Charlie's tone was bitter.

"So they do."

"I'll get the clothes." Charlie swung onto the porch by holding the post and went into the house.

Sam sat quietly, finished his smoke, and ground the butt beneath his boot heel. He could hear the thump, thump of the peg on the wooden floor inside the house as Charlie moved about. He watched the woman stirring the soap. She was not completely blind, he decided, when he saw her lift the end of the paddle and bring it up to within a few inches of her eyes and peer at it. And she had found her way to the house and back again to the pot.

He would like to hear the woman sing again, but he instinctively knew that she wouldn't as long as he was there. He turned his head slightly to look beyond her to the edge of the thick stand of trees where he had come out of the woods. His eyes moved back to her and at that instant a puff of wind blew her dress over the fire. A small ribbon of flame danced along the hem of her skirt and then spiraled upward.

Sam leaped to his feet, his long legs carrying him across the yard. The woman suddenly realized what had happened and screamed. In a state of panic, she began to run.

"Don't run," Sam shouted.

He sprinted after her, grabbed her about the waist and threw her to the ground. They both hit hard. The woman screamed again. Sam grabbed at the burning cloth, trying to smother it, trying to beat it out with his bare hands. They rolled. The woman continued to scream. Sam had to contend with her flailing arms and legs as he fought to put out the fire.

The sound of a shot echoed in Sam's head. Smoke from the burning cloth went up his nostrils. Suddenly the flames were gone. He found himself lying on top the woman, his head even with her knees, hands enfolded in what remained of her skirt.

"Get up you son of a bitch, I'm going to kill you! Goddamn your rotten soul!"

Sam rolled off the thrashing woman and onto his back. He looked up into the barrel of the shotgun and saw Charlie Rivers bending over him. The man jabbed at his chest with the barrel and Sam realized Rivers thought he had attacked his sister!

"Look at her, goddamn you!"

Charlie pushed the barrel harder against Sam's chest, then glanced at the woman on the ground. He withdrew the gun, dropped it, and squatted down beside her.

"Sister! Oh, my God!" He pulled his sister up into his arms. "Are you all right?"

Emily Rivers clung to her brother. "Yes . . . yes, Charlie. Don't worry." She was breathless and spoke between gasps.

Charlie ran his hand down over the burned cloth of her skirt. Charred pieces of cloth came off in his hand. Her legs were only slightly red from the burns.

"Oh God, Emily!" He hugged her to him. "That's the last time you'll be around that damn boil pot!"

"Don't be silly. I've got to wash clothes—"

"You'll wear a pair of my britches, by damn!"

Sam sat up and looked at the palms of his hands. At first he had not felt pain, but now it was making itself known. He was conscious that Charlie Rivers had turned to look at him and he turned his palms down.

"Are you burned?"

"Not much." Keeping his fingers curled over his throbbing palms, Sam put his forearm on the ground to help himself get to his feet.

Charlie stood and extended a hand to his sister. "I owe you a hell of a lot, mister."

"Ya don't owe me a goddamn thin'!" The pain in Sam's hands caused him to speak sharply.

"You burned your hands!" Charlie grabbed Sam's wrist with a surprisingly strong grip and turned his palm up. "Good God, man! Blisters are already coming up."

Sam watched the woman's head turn toward him. "Oh, my!" Emily gasped. "Are the burns bad, Charlie?" Then she looked at him with her great, light blue eyes for so long that Sam began to think she could see him.

"His palms are blistering."

"My aloe plant! The juice will take out the sting."

"What about yoreself, ma'am? Are ya burned?" His eyes roamed her face, and the strange feeling he had felt when he heard her sing stirred in him again.

"My legs are stinging, but it's not bad. I don't know how

to thank you. I shouldn't have run. Charlie has always told me that in case of a fire, I should lie down and roll. I was so scared that I didn't think.''

"I'm glad I was handy."

"Thank God Mr. Sparks was here. I couldn't have caught you, Emily, even if I had been here."

"I know, Brother." She placed her hand against his face. "Don't worry. It's over. I'll be more careful from now on. Now we've got to tend to Mr. Sparks' hands. Will you lift the kettle away from the fire, please, Charlie? The soap is ready to be poured into the trough and salt added to harden it.'' She appeared calm, as if nothing had happened. "I was going to put in some of that honey we didn't use up last winter. Oh, well, I'll make another smaller batch of bath soap later on.''

In spite of the pain in his hands, Sam's eyes couldn't leave Emily's face. She was not completely blind, but terribly nearsighted. Her eyes were large and light blue, surrounded by long, curly brown lashes. She was not a tall woman. Her head came to just above his shoulder, but she gave the impression of being tall because she stood so straight, her shoulders back, head up. Sam had seen many women who were more beautiful than this one. But Emily Rivers was beautiful in a completely unaffected way: natural, sweet and caring. When she spoke to her brother who was at least ten years her senior, there was love and respect in her voice.

"I'm terribly sorry, Mr. Sparks, that I misunderstood what was happening," Charlie said on the way to the house.

"No offense taken."

"If not for being afraid I would hit Emily, I would have killed you,'' he admitted with a tremor in his voice.

"Well now, I'm sure glad ya was afraid of hittin' your sister. I'm not wantin' to die for somethin' I didn't do.''

The house was one large room with a door opening into a lean-to attached to the side. As they passed, Sam saw a neatly made bed and clothes hanging from pegs in the wall. An open stairway with a hand rail went to the loft. Comfortable chairs sat on either side of the fireplace with an oval braided rug between. The house was homey and well-furnished.

Emily indicated that Sam was to sit down at a round table.

She immediately lifted a lid on the black iron cookstove and set the kettle directly over the blaze. The bottom of her skirt had burned and a good six inches of her leg showed above her laced, black leather shoes. Charlie caught Sam's glance.

"Go change your dress, Emily. I'll get a pan of cold water and Mr. Sparks can soak his hands. Then you can apply that sticky stuff from the plant."

The cold water felt soothing to Sam's palms. He flexed his right hand, looking closely at the blister rising on his forefinger, and hoped he'd not be forced to draw his gun any time soon. Charlie watched him from across the table with eyes a shade darker than his sister's.

"Are you a gunman, Mr. Sparks?"

For an endless moment Sam stared at the flint-eyed man, then he shrugged his broad shoulders.

"I don't call myself that. And call me Sam."

"This little episode doesn't make us bosom friends, Mr. Sparks." Charlie's eyes were as cold as steel.

"If that's the way ya want it, it's all right with me, *Mr. Rivers.*"

"Charlie." Emily had come down from the loft and her chiding voice came from behind the men. "Mr. Sparks is a friend of Pack's, and now our friend as well. Pack wouldn't have sent a man here if he didn't think he was worthy of our friendship." Sam could tell by the sound of her steps that she had changed into soft moccasins.

"Friendship? We know nothing about him, Sister. How are your burns?"

"Not bad, thanks to our new friend who burned his hands saving me when I was foolish enough to panic and run. I do thank you, Sam."

"You're welcome, Miss Rivers. I should've noticed when the wind started blowin' the flame your way."

"Charlie is used to my blindness; you are not," she said gently. "Now I must see about your burns." She placed a stack of white strips of cloth on the table, handed Sam a clean towel to blot his hands and took the pan of water to the work counter.

Emily held his hand up to within a few inches of her face

so she could see it clearly and clicked her tongue sorrowfully. Gently she applied the sticky substance from inside the spears of the aloe plant. Aloe grew in Texas, but the Rivers were not Texans. The puzzle of who they were became more complicated. Sam looked above the head bent over his hands. A bookcase on an inner wall held at least a hundred volumes. These were more books than he had ever seen at one time except when he was in the home of General Robert E. Lee shortly before the war ended.

The intense way that Charlie watched while his sister tended to his hands nipped at Sam's temper. Occasionally, when, with a flick of his lashes, his eyes skimmed over Emily's suntanned face and slender body, he was aware that Charlie had caught the look. Hell! What did the man expect him to do, shut his eyes?

Emily insisted that Sam stay for the noon meal. Charlie invited him to sit on the porch while she prepared it. Sam smoked and watched Charlie strain the soap in the kettle into a flat wooden box. When Emily called them to dinner, Sam left his hat on the porch and tried to smooth his unruly hair down with his bandaged palms.

They ate freshly baked bread, spring greens and venison steaks on a cloth-covered table set with good china and silver. Charlie bowed his head and prayed aloud before the food was passed. The table manners and the polite way the food was served confirmed Sam's previous belief that the Rivers were not the usual type of people who pulled up and moved west to settle on new land. Sam ate clumsily with his bandaged hand and prayed he'd not spill anything on the tablecloth.

Both of the Rivers were hungry for conversation once the tension was broken. Emily's acceptance of Sam seemed to rub off on her brother after awhile. They spoke of their friendship with Pack Gallagher and said that he sometimes left some of his belongings with them when he was going to visit his mother. They seemed to be fond of him, and Sam wondered if there was something more than friendship between Pack and Emily. They talked of Brita McCall and the kindly care given to her by one of her twins. Emily spoke of the winters when they were snowed in and laughed when she said that by spring Charlie was so sick of her company he was ready to pull his hair out. The Rivers wanted news from Laramie and Cheyenne, but they gave out no information about themselves.

When Sam was ready to leave, Charlie hung a bag containing Pack's clothes and boots over the saddlehorn.

"Tell Pack that gray devil was on his way back here when I run into him. I'll bring him over in a day or so. He's a frisky son of a gun, Sparks. I'm not sure you'd be able to hold him with those hands." Charlie stood beside the horse while Sam mounted. "I want you to know that I'm in your debt for what you did for Emily. It was fast thinking, and I do thank you for it."

"As I said, ya don't owe me a thin'," Sam said gruffly to cover his embarrassment. "I wasn't there when my sister needed help. I was off fightin' somebody's damn war. I'm glad I was around to help yours."

"I thank you anyway, Sam," Charlie said. "I'd like to shake hands . . . someday."

"Consider it done."

Emily walked up to the horse and held up a spear she had cut from the aloe plant. Sam placed it cut end up in his shirt pocket.

"Split it and rub the sticky juice on the burns," she instructed.

"Thank ya, Miss Rivers." Sam didn't mention that for as long as he could remember his family had used the plant for burns, insect bites, and rashes.

"When you're this way again, stop by for a meal." She voiced the invitation with a soft smile on her face.

Sam looked into her eyes and felt as if he were in another world. "I'll do that, ma'am." He spoke gruffly in an effort to bring himself back to reality.

Sam tipped his hat and turned the horse toward the trees. For some unknown reason he didn't want to leave. He wanted to turn and look at the woman standing in the yard beside the man with the peg leg. He couldn't resist, even knowing her brother might make something of it. He pulled the horse to a stop, spun him around and looked back. She clung to the porch post, the skirt of her blue dress pushed back against her legs by the wind. Sam raised his hand in farewell. Only Charlie lifted his hand in response. Emily wouldn't know that he had waved unless Charlie told her. Sam rode on, disgusted with himself for being disappointed.

During the ride back to McCall's, Sam's mind was troubled. He had spent several pleasant hours with the Rivers. He liked them, liked both of them, and he hoped to hell Charlie Rivers was not the man he was looking for.

As Sam approached the McCall ranch, he slowly unwrapped the white strips from about his palms and put them in his pocket. It hurt like hell to hold the reins with his burned fingers, but it wouldn't be wise, he decided, to let Sporty Howard, or any of the men that came to the hideout, know that there was anything wrong with his hand that would slow him down if he pulled his gun.

Sam Sparks and his horse were only a blur to Emily Rivers, but her ears were atuned to every sound.

"Why did he stop?"

"He waved." Charlie felt a strange uneasiness when he saw the look of sadness on his sister's face.

"I wish you'd told me. I would have waved to him."

For the first time in a long while Emily wished that she could see like other people. She had grown accustomed to the small world she lived in and only at times thought about what her life would have been like if she could see and if that . . . other thing had not happened. Most women were married and had several children by the time they reached her age. She thought she had reconciled herself to the fact that she would never know the love of a man or have his children.

Sam Sparks had been different from any man she had ever met. He had not once mentioned her poor eyesight. She liked his voice, the polite way he spoke. He was a clean man. The only smell about him was of saddle leather and tobacco. His hands were long, slender, twice the size of hers, and she had felt him trembling when the back of his hand lay in the palm of hers, almost as if he were not used to having a woman hold his hand. It had been a long time since she had been close to any man other than Pack and her brother.

Once she had lifted her head as Sam bent to look at his palm, and his face had come into the perimeter of her vision. His cheeks were smooth, as if he had shaved that morning. His mouth was wide and firm, his chin square. She remembered dark brows, white teeth, and hair that curled down on his forehead. But what she remembered most of all was his warm breath on her lips. It was almost as if he had kissed her.

"He was nice, wasn't he, Charlie?"

"I guess so . . . for a drifter. He didn't say much about himself."

"He said he was from Texas, and that he had a sister."

"Most men are from somewhere and most of them have a sister. Sam Sparks will take Pack's stuff to him and ride on, if I read him right."

Charlie Rivers looked at his sister standing against the porch post. He had detected a longing in her voice that tore at his heart. Had he been wrong to bring her to this lonely place? But dear God, what would she have done without him? He couldn't stay where he was. Alone, she would have been taken, used, degraded. There were very few men who would take a blind woman for a wife, love her, cherish her. For awhile Charlie had hoped that Emily and Pack would come to love one another; but after a friendship of four years, there was no sign that they were more than friends.

"We'll take Pack's horse over to the McCalls in a few days, and you can visit with Mrs. McCall and Mara McCall if she is still there," Charlie said in an attempt to lighten Emily's spirits.

"Pack seemed to be angry because she was coming. He was going to head her off at Sheffield Station and send her back to Denver. I wonder what happened?"

"That bunch of no-goods from Laramie who wanted him to throw the fight caught up with him before she got there. That's what happened. It was lucky for him the girl came along. I might not have found him before he bled to death."

"I wonder if Mara McCall is pretty," Emily murmured absently.

"Pack has never said anything about her other than that she was the daughter of an old friend and her father had put her in the school so she could learn how to be a lady." Charlie snorted with disgust. "People get a distorted idea of the word."

"Do you miss your old life?"

Charlie was surprised by his sister's question. They seldom talked about the old life.

"At times, but not enough to make me want to go back."

"Poor Charlie. You would have had a brilliant career if not for your blind sister."

"You're indulging yourself in a spell of self-pity, Sister." His voice was stern. "You'll get no sympathy from me. I've seen men with both arms and legs shot off and head wounds that made them look like animals. What if you had no mind, Sister? The insane asylums are full of people who have no more mind than a chicken. And you pity yourself because you can't see clearly beyond a few feet. You—"

"Should be ashamed of yourself!" Emily finished, and laughed. "Charlie, dear, I hear that same speech every time I get down in the dumps. Please think of a new one!"

"Really? I didn't think I'd said that over a time or two." Charlie chuckled.

"Well, you have. Would you like to hear my speech about how lucky you are that you have one good leg?"

"Heavens no! I've heard it a hundred times."

Emily laughed again. Charlie smiled with relief. Things were back to normal once more.

Chapter
SIX

Mara had been at the homestead a week before she met Steamboat. He came reluctantly when she sent for him. She invited him into the kitchen, seated him at the cloth-covered table, and served him coffee and slices of bread spread with butter and sprinkled with sugar and cinnamon. She had dreaded meeting him, thinking she might have been eating food prepared by a slovenly cook; but he was a quiet, clean, stoop-shouldered man, and she liked him. By the time he left the house, he and Mara had an understanding. Steamboat would milk the cow and bring the milk to the house. Mara would churn, and they would share the butter and milk. The hens were laying eight to ten eggs a day. Mara said she wanted four of them in order to make nourishing meals for Brita.

When she inquired about the garden, he told her that he had planted onions, potatoes, cabbage, turnips, kale and a small patch of corn.

''The next time you go to town for supplies, I'd like to go with you. I've not had experience managing a house, but I'll learn . . . if you'll help me." Mara smiled so sweetly she could have asked for ten years of his life and he would have given them to her.

"I'd be jist plumb tickled to escort ya to town 'n show ya around, ma'am. I'll see to it that nobody cheats ya."

Pack, lying on the bunk in his mother's room, rolled his eyes to the ceiling as he listened to Mara sweet-talk the cook. The old fool would roll over and play dead if she asked him. This was just going to make it all the harder for him to jar her away from this place.

During the next few days Pack spent most of his time on the porch. He walked to and from the privy and up and down in front of the house trying to work the stiffness out of his joints. Sam came to talk to him, and sometimes he played cards with Trellis or Travor to pass the time. Travor was still resentful of Mara.

One afternoon Mara came out onto the porch just as Travor sank his knife into one of the turned porch posts and cut off a sliver of wood.

"Don't do that, Travor," she said sharply. "I've asked you any number of times not to damage the post with your knife."

"Don't do that, Travor. Don't do that, Travor," he mimicked. "Is there anythin' 'round here I can do?"

Bluntly Mara answered him. "You can cut wood for the cookstove. The box is empty."

"Cut yore own damn wood, Miss Prissy Ass!"

Pack's hand lashed out, closed about the boy's arm and jerked him close to him. He gave him a vicious shake.

"If I hear you talk to your cousin like that again, boy, you'll think you've run into a hornets' nest." For an endless moment Travor stared, his senses shocked by the anger in his half brother's face and the savagery of his tone.

"I . . . I ain't—" He started to say something more, but Pack shook him again.

"That's right, you ain't! You'll not be giving Mara or Ma any more of your sass. Do you understand? If you don't, I can make it plainer."

Travor's face turned a fiery red. "She don't . . . let a man do nothin'."

"You call yourself a man? You're a smart-mouthed, wet-eared kid trying to act like some of the trash that hangs out at the bunkhouse. A *man* doesn't talk to his womenfolk the way you've done. Give your mouth the rest of the day off, boy, and fill that woodbox." Pack pushed the boy from him.

Mara watched Travor until he disappeared around the side of the house.

"He'll never like me now," she said almost wistfully. Then she turned to Pack. "Thanks to you!" With that she went back into the house.

Mara passed through the parlor, the kitchen, and out onto the back porch. She stood by the support post and shivered. "Please God," she prayed, "let me get accustomed to these people and their ways."

Her troubled eyes turned toward the bunkhouse where Cullen and Aubrey lolled on the porch. They had not been to the house since the day she arrived, not even to inquire about Brita. If Brita was hurt by her husband's neglect, she never voiced her feelings; in fact, she never mentioned him or Cullen at all.

In the span of a week, a remarkable change had come to the house. The days were long this time of the year, and Mara worked from dawn to dusk with what help Trellis would give her. Because Brita told her that it rankled the boy to have the men see him washing and cleaning, she asked him to do what repair work he could handle. Trellis took measurements so that the broken windowpanes could be replaced. He nailed a new board to the back step and put new hinges on the privy door. Mara scrubbed floors, washed walls, and polished wood.

One afternoon, several days after the incident with Travor, Mara saw Cullen and Aubrey ride away from the ranch. She asked Trellis to go to the bunkhouse and bring back everything that had been taken from the house. The boy brought back one chair and the mantel clock. Everything else was beyond repair. Disappointment was not exactly the word for what Mara felt: heartsick might have described her feeling better. She went upstairs to her room, shut the door, and allowed herself the luxury of tears.

Later, her small, round chin tilted, her dignity returned in the guise of a very stiff, proud posture, she went back down to the kitchen, more determined than ever to make a place for herself.

Pack was recovering from the ordeal faster than she thought possible, but he was weak, trembly, and in a foul mood most of the time. The problems now were the wounds in his thigh and side. They were healing, but not fast enough to suit him. Mara didn't know what condition they were in because he no longer needed help in changing the bandage. Since the morning after his fever, when he had railed at her for being in her nightclothes, Mara had avoided him when possible. His insults had shaken her to her very roots, and she vowed that she would never forgive him. She had spoken to him only when he asked a direct question and was civil to him only for Brita's sake.

When the evening meal was ready, Mara carried a tray to Brita and called Pack to the table. She sat across from him, eating without appetite. No words passed between them, but she could feel his eyes on her often. She avoided looking at him, finished eating, and got up from the table to take her plate to the dishpan.

"Mara Shannon! Sit down!"

Pack's commanding voice was like a lash on Mara's back. It caught her by surprise and startled her so much that she almost dropped the dish she was carrying from the table. She hesitated a minute to fight down the anger that rose up to redden her face, then turned.

"Yes? You want something more?" she asked formally, determined not to allow him to know how his harsh voice grated on her already taut nerves.

She couldn't help noticing that the swelling had left his face and the bruises were fading. With the dirt and blood washed from his hair, it was as dark and shiny as a crow's wing. He had made an attempt to control the mop of unruly curls without much success. They flopped over his ears and tumbled down over his forehead.

"I don't want anything more. Sit down." His dark eyes met her emerald green ones and refused to look away.

As his eyes held hers for several seconds, some of the hardness left. The silence between them seemed to crackle. Neither of them moved nor spoke for what seemed an endless space of time. Pack stared at her, holding her eyes like a magnet with his. For an instant there was a flicker of recognition in some small part of Mara's brain. It was as if she suddenly knew this man well, was bound to him with invisible ties. His face was not strange to her, nor was his body or his feelings. The reflection lasted for only an instant.

"Is that an invitation or a command?"

"Call it what you want. We've got to talk."

"We? I have nothing to say to you."

"But I have something to say to you."

Pack watched her move from the table to the workbench, her color intensified by the heat from the stove. He let his eyes travel the room, taking in every change she had made. The kitchen was pleasant; the shining chimneys on the lamps helped give the room a rosy glow. Her woman's touch had made this house a home again. She was a nesting type woman who could make a home anywhere.

"Say it," she said more calmly than she felt and turned her back on him. It irritated her that his presence made her nervous. Each time he looked at her the bold masculine magnetism he emitted aroused a sense of excitement in her.

"I'll be leaving as soon as I get my horse." The words were softly spoken to Mara's back.

"What has that got to do with me?"

She calmly wrapped the freshly baked loaf of bread in a clean cloth and placed it in a tin. She thought briefly of asking him if he knew where she could get a cat. Each morning she found mouse droppings in the kitchen, and it offended her sense of cleanliness.

"Goddamn it, woman, you can't stay here!" he snarled, low-voiced.

She turned, leaned her back against the workbench, and folded her arms across her chest. This past week, from dawn to dusk, she had worked harder than she had ever worked in her entire life. At the end of the long day she was so exhausted she could only wash herself in the water she carried to her upstairs room and fall into bed. Now this . . . this big, stupid Irishman was sitting at her well-scrubbed table, after he had eaten the meal she had cooked, and was telling her that she couldn't stay here—in her own house!

"Maybe I didn't understand you, Mr. Gallagher. Surely you didn't say that I couldn't live in my own home."

"That is exactly what I said, Miss Mara Shannon McCall." His dark brows were drawn together and his big hands lay palms down on the table as if he were going to stand. But he didn't.

"My father would be terribly disappointed in you. He was fond of you and considered you a friend."

"Aye, he did. It's because of my love for Shannon McCall that I'm telling you that this is no place for you." Shannon McCall had taken the place of the father he had barely known, and they had loved each other like father and son.

"And why is that?"

"I told you before. Ma told you. What's the matter with you that you can't see it? This is a hard, lonely land full of hard, impatient men without women. Who will stand between you and the ones who'll have you when I'm gone? Sam's a decent man. He'll see that no harm comes to you while he's here, but he's a drifting man. Go back to town and get a teaching job. It's what you were schooled—"

"Why don't you like me?" Mara interrupted.

"Jesus! Godamighty! Holy sh— You didn't hear a word I said!" Pack pushed himself to his feet. He was so tall Mara had to tilt her head to look into his furious eyes.

"I warned you about taking the Lord's name in vain."

"You're enough to make a preacher swear! Do you know that?" He was angry and his voice was loud.

"Don't shout!" Her words came out in a throaty rush. "You know it upsets Brita. You'd best be paying attention to her. She's not well."

Pack swore under his breath. "Do you think I'm blind, girl? I know she's not well. If I could get her away from here, I'd set the two of you up in a place in town. I'm not so poor I can't take care of my own ma, for God's sake!"

"She won't go and neither will I. Brita feels her place is with her husband and the twins. She took Aubrey for better or worse. Vows are sacred to her." Mara stared at his angry face, transfixed, literally shaking inside.

Pack stood in troubled silence. Mara remained stiff and proud, her fine-boned profile set, her clearly etched features perfectly composed and cold. The thought of leaving her here brought a dull ache that spread through Pack until it occupied every part of his body.

Small bits of things had been coming back to him. *Help me, you damned stupid dolt!* She had shouted the words while he lay in the dirt, and they had seeped into his dull senses. *What kind of man are you to sit there like a stubborn jackass and not help yourself?*

If he were a different type of man, Mara Shannon would be the woman for him. She was soft and feminine, yet she had a will of iron. She had gotten him moving and saved his life when he would have just as soon lain there and bled to death.

With anguish he realized that he was what he was, and she was what she was; there was no way on God's earth he could have her. She had dominated his thoughts while he lay flat on his back, his chest tight, his face hot, and his manhood tenting the covers. Now that he was on his feet and could watch her moving about the house, he was aware of her every move, every glance in his direction.

Pack knew little about women, but he knew men and their ways. There wasn't a man here except for Sam who wouldn't have his way with her if given half a chance. The little fool had the face of an angel but the brains of Paddy's pig! She hadn't known when she was well off. Bedamned! How was he going to convince her that he knew what was best for her?

"Think about it," he said gruffly. "Think about what can happen to you. There are men here who would use your body to satisfy their lust. You would be no more to them than a hunk of meat.'' The talk was plain and he saw the color rise up her neck to her cheeks.

"I have thought about it.'' She spoke in a kinder, more reasonable tone after she had swallowed several times. She was crying to herself inside that it was so hard to be a woman alone and to stand up for her rights.

"Then think about it some more,'' he said harshly.

"I have to live somewhere, for heaven's sake! My money wouldn't last long in town, but it will see me through here for awhile.'' She wanted to unload the heavy burden of fear that ate at her every night as she lay in her upstairs bed with the post wedged against the door, but it would just make him more determined to make her leave.

"You can't live here alone! No!'' He raised his voice when she would interrupt. "You'd be about as safe as a snowball in hell.''

"What do you mean alone? Your mother is here, for crying out loud! I've convinced Cullen and Aubrey that I've left everything to the school if something should happen to me. That should keep me safe for awhile.'' Her cheeks, suffused with color, were the only indication that she was nervous. "I thank you for your concern; but I'm not your responsibility and you needn't worry about me.''

He stared at her for a long moment, then let his hard-held breath out in a long sigh.

"You may be the prettiest woman in all Wyoming Territory and maybe the smartest when it comes to school learning, but you're also the most mule-headed, unreasonable female I've ever known. You don't know anything about life in this country. A pretty woman without a man beside her is considered fair game by every horny drifter that sees her. Men from miles around will be camping on your doorstep with two things on their minds: getting your land and getting under your skirts!''

Her face flamed. "You needn't be so crude! You think I'm mule-headed because I don't do what you want me to do— pull out and leave my inheritance to Aubrey and Cullen to manage. Surely you're not so blind that you can't see what they're doing here.''

"And what is that?"

"They're not living off the land. It's just sitting here. Where do they get money? Why were they nervous when the marshal was here? Now you get this straight, Pack Gallagher, I'm not a complete idiot, and I'll not let you ramrod my life!"

"I'm trying to help you, Mara *Stubborn* Shannon!" His eyes battled with hers. He wanted to shake her. "Ah hellfire! You're naught but a scrap of empty-headed *baggage!*" He headed for the porch.

Mara followed him through the parlor. Somehow she wanted to cry but fought back angry tears. She had tried to be civil and what had it gotten her? She saw that he was still standing at the edge of the porch. Empty-headed baggage was an insult she couldn't ignore. It goaded her to throw angry words at him.

"I'm not empty-headed, Mr. *Loose-mouth* Gallagher. I want you to know that my high marks in school set a record. And I deeply resent being called a baggage which, according to Noah Webster, means an unchaste woman, a trollop, hussy, or slut. In other words a bad, loose, easy woman lacking moral goodness. Don't you dare refer to me in those terms again."

He turned and looked at her outline in the doorway, unable to see the stricken look in her eyes.

"Is this Webster fellow your beau?"

"Damnation! Holy Saints preserve me!" The unguarded words burst from her mouth. "He's a dictionary! Oh! You make me so angry that I don't even know what I'm saying!" She darted back into the darkness of the parlor.

Wearily Pack sat down on the edge of the porch and watched the moon come up over the treetops. One dismal truth stood out above the others; his hands were tied because of his mother. She would not abandon her husband and the twins. He rested his elbows on his thighs and cupped his chin in his hand. What to do? He had his freighting business in Laramie to see to. He had no doubt that old Willy was taking care of things, but there was just so much the old man could do. The paid thugs who jumped him were long gone by now, but the gamblers who worked the Kosy Kitty Saloon were still there; and he would not rest until they paid for what they had done to him.

Pack sat with his puzzled thoughts long after the light disappeared from Mara's upstairs room. He felt like the restless lobo who howled his frustration into the night and was answered by his own kind. One unwelcome fact stuck in his mind: Mara Shannon should be in town, living in a fine house with all the conveniences, with someone like that Webster fellow who knew the meaning of words. It was what her father had wanted for her.

Recognition of how hard Mara Shannon had worked to clean up the house came to Pack's mind. She had toiled from morning until night and seemed to be content while doing so. He had even heard her singing while she worked. But she would soon get tired of scrubbing, washing, doing without, and fending off women-hungry men. After one long, cruel, lonely winter she would be sorry she ever came to this place, and then it might be too late.

It seemed to Pack that every time he opened his mouth he made her angry. He had not meant to insult her when he called her baggage. Hellfire and brimstone! He hadn't known it meant all the things she'd said. He had thought it meant a package . . . an empty package. He had heard women called baggage, and they hadn't made such a to-do over it.

Pack ran his fingers through his dark hair and massaged the back of his neck. Life was not simple when it involved a woman. At times, when he looked into Mara Shannon's emerald green eyes that so clearly reflected her feelings, he felt as if he had been run through one of those fancy clothes wringers that fastened to a washtub. He was a man with urges like any other, he thought now, and sometimes he ached to have a woman, not just any woman, but his own woman who wanted him and only him. He'd had a strong yearning for a permanent home for a long time—had dreamed about it at night when he lay alongside his wagons in some remote mountain pass and wondered how it would feel to be lying in his own bed with his own woman beside him, coming eagerly into his arms when he reached for her. It wasn't that he just wanted a woman to satisfy his lust; there were whores for that. He yearned for something more, a commitment to a good woman who would be the heart and core of a family. He wanted *this* woman, he told himself harshly, but she wasn't for the likes of Pack Gallagher, teamster, prizefighter, brawler.

Pack cursed himself softly. One thing was certain: he had to think of something. Cullen and Aubrey were just waiting for him to leave before they made their move. Perhaps they were going to let her stay and try to force her to marry Cullen, thinking to get control of the ranch that way. She would resist, but Cullen would go to any length to get what he wanted. He might decide to get into her room some night, rape her, and shame her into marrying him. Pack's jaws tightened and he ground his teeth in frustration.

At length Pack stretched wearily, feeling an ache in each and every muscle, a stiffness in his bones, and a heaviness in his heart as he wrestled with the problem. He was unaware of it, but within a very short time the decision would be made for him.

Morning came and with it Ace January. Brita was sleeping and Pack and Trellis were hunting in the hills behind the house. Mara Shannon saw the marshal ride up to the hitching rail, dismount, and tie his horse. She went to the door, stepped out onto the porch and called a greeting.

"Morning, Mr. January."

"Mornin'." The marshal stepped up to the porch. He removed his hat. "I'm surprised you're still here, Miss McCall. I thought you'd be back in town by now."

Her smile turned into a puzzled frown. "Why would you think that?"

"Town girls don't usually like livin' away from town."

"I'm not a 'town girl.' This is my home and I'm here to stay." Irritation stirred within her, making her welcome a trifle cool.

"I'm right glad to hear it."

"Come in and have a cool drink, or coffee if you prefer."

"I'd be pleased to have the coffee, ma'am."

Ace followed Mara Shannon through the parlor and into the kitchen. She was even prettier than he remembered. She was all woman. He liked the way she looked and the way she smelled—like freshly baked bread. Her dark auburn hair curled about her face and stuck to her cheeks that were flushed with heat. He especially liked her full mouth that tilted at the corners when she smiled. The wide band of the apron tied about her small waist showed the curve of soft, full breasts. He pulled his gaze away from them and mopped his forehead with the sleeve of his shirt.

"It's goin' to be a hot one."

"Would you like a drink of water first?"

"Thank you, ma'am. I'd be obliged for a drink of water."

Mara Shannon took the ladle from the pail, dipped it into the water bucket and handed it to him. He drank the water with his eyes on her face.

His eyes were such a light gray they appeared almost colorless. The look in them was frank admiration and something more that implied . . . intimacy. Mara Shannon knew instinctively that it had been a mistake to look directly into them. She moved to the other side of the room, took a cup from the shelf, and filled it with coffee from the pot on the stove. Her mind would have frozen had she known what he was thinking.

Ace was wondering how she would look naked, stretched out on a soft bed, her legs and her mouth open beneath him, his hands full of her breasts, hers on his bare buttocks. He pictured her naked in the kitchen cooking a meal for him, naked in front of a fire, naked running through tall grass with her hair streaming behind her like a banner.

He wanted her. Her wonderful woman's body was made to cushion a man, to ease his impatient body. The feeling was ten times stronger than when he'd first felt it that day he rode in with the posse. He pulled his mind back when he felt desire so potent that it threatened to embarrass him. He lowered his hat to cover the sudden bulge in his britches. It would not do to scare the hell out of her now. He'd have to go slowly, be patient. His facial features reflected none of his thoughts after he returned the dipper to the pail.

"Sit down, Mr. January." Mara Shannon indicated the place where she had set the cup of coffee. "Pack and the boys will be back soon."

"Is Gallagher still here?"

"Yes. His mother is very ill."

"I'm sorry about Mrs. McCall."

Mara Shannon sat down at the far end of the table. "Are you on official business, Marshal?"

"Business and pleasure. Seein' you again is the pleasure part."

"Thank you," she said. "And the business part?"

"How many men do you have here now, Miss McCall?"

"What do you mean?"

"Just what I said. How many men work here?"

"I wouldn't know. You'll have to talk to my cousin."

"Cullen or his pa?"

"Cullen. You'll find him at the bunkhouse if he's not out seeing about the cattle."

"Where is that? The south slope?"

Mara Shannon felt her face grow hot beneath his intense stare and was relieved when she heard Pack call out to Trellis, then heard his steps on the back porch. She stood, grateful for his return. Something about the marshal's inquiries made her nervous. She was sure that he was thinking one thing while saying another.

Pack came in. He looked first at Ace January and then at Mara Shannon. A look in her eyes told him that she was glad to see him.

"Howdy, January. I thought I recognized that horse."

"Howdy, Pack. Looks like you're gettin' over the roughin' up the boys gave you."

"You knew about that?"

Ace laughed. "It's all the talk. Everybody in the territory knows about it."

"You knew before it happened and you did nothing." Pack pulled out the bench, straddled it and placed his forearms on the table.

"You made the choice, Pack. You knew what you were in

for when you went against the crowd.'' Ace looked Pack straight in the eyes, then drained his cup.

"So I did.'' Pack stood and pushed the bench back with his foot. "Let's talk outside.''

The marshal rose and held out his hand to Mara Shannon. She could think of no way to avoid placing her hand in his. He squeezed it tightly, let up, and squeezed again.

"Thanks for the coffee, ma'am. I'll be back one of these days soon for that cake you promised me.''

"Good-bye, Mr. January.'' Mara Shannon pulled her hand from his.

Pack had gone to the door. Mara, looking past the marshal, saw a look of impatience on his face. An imp inside her tempted her to ask the marshal to come back real soon, but her common sense told her to keep quiet and she did.

At the door Ace looked back at Mara. Her thighs were against the table as she reached for his coffee cup. She looked up into his eyes and he slowly lowered one eyelid. When it occurred to her what he had done, her face flamed. The girls at the school had told her about the flirtatious wink of an eye when a man wanted a woman to know he desired her. Somehow, instead of angering her, it made her want to laugh.

Pack walked around the house until he reached the front hitching rail where the marshal had tied his horse.

"Are you here on business, Ace?''

"Mara asked me that. I told her business and pleasure.'' He saw the tightening of Pack's facial muscles on hearing him say the woman's name with familiarity. It amused Ace that he could make the big man angry. If Pack wanted the woman, it would make the taking of her all the more enjoyable.

"I take it you've had the pleasure. What's the business?'' Pack asked bluntly.

"You should know that. This place is a hangout for any outlaw with the price for room 'n board.'' Ace mounted his horse. Although he was tall, Pack Gallagher topped him, and he despised looking up at a man.

"If you know that for a fact, why don't you clean it out? You're the marshal."

" 'Cause I'm not ready. That's why."

"There are half a dozen petty crooks down at the bunk-house. You could take them in and collect a couple of hundred dollars in reward money."

"I'm lookin' for a really big fish to come floatin' in. I'd be a fool to dam up the stream afore he gets here."

"Little fish turn into big fish if they're not caught," Pack said dryly.

"Old Willy is wonderin' when you'll be back. He said if I saw you, to tell you to come on back and tend to the business."

"I doubt if Willy said that. He can run that freight line as well as I can."

Ace shrugged away the contradiction. He glanced toward the house, rolled and lit a cigarette before he spoke.

"Are you hidin' out here, Pack?"

"What do you think?"

"I think you're afraid you'll get your clock cleaned again if you go back to town."

"Yeah, Ace. That just plumb scares me to death."

"It'll not be a scare that's the death of you." Ace paused and looked steadily at Pack. "It'll be a bullet," he said softly, then wheeled his horse and rode back down the lane toward the road.

Pack watched him go, glad he was leaving. Ace January seemed to be a good marshal. He had not heard anything to the contrary, but something about the man made him uneasy, and he didn't know why.

"Why in the hell did you let that man into the house?"

Mara Shannon would have forgotten Ace January's visit if not for those angry words Pack spat at her. He had stomped back into the house and told her in no uncertain terms that she was not to invite the man into the house again. When she demanded the reason, he sputtered and told her it wasn't *decent* for her to be in the house alone with a strange man. At that she laughed, making him even more angry. She wondered what Pack would say if she told him Ace January had winked at her.

Several days passed, and Pack's words still made her angry when she recalled them. She pushed thoughts of him and the marshal from her mind, broke the shell of an egg and carefully spilled the contents into a bowl. She added another and beat the eggs until they were a light yellow.

"What next, Brita?" she called.

"A teacup of sweet milk." Mara and Trellis had moved Brita's bed so that she could look into the kitchen. "Then ye be addin' a lump a butter the size of an egg."

Mara hummed while she worked. She liked to cook, and Brita was teaching her to make what she called everyday cake. The tired look on Brita's face worried Mara. Brita hadn't wanted to get out of bed since the day Pack was brought home. For most of the day she lay and stared out the window after Mara had washed and straightened her bed.

"It looks like a wet mess, Brita."

"Put in a teacup a sugar 'n grate up part of a nutmeg."

"These nutmegs look as old as I am."

"They be all right, darlin'."

"Brita, I wish we had a cat. Do you think Trell could get us one when he goes to town?"

"Emily Rivers promised one to me. Charlie took her big tabby to town . . . at just the right time. Be ye ready . . . fer the flour?"

Brita was getting breathless again. Each time it brought back memories of her own mother's breathless whispers and caused a hard lump of dread to settle around Mara's heart. She called out to Brita cheerfully in spite of her fear.

"I've sifted it twice. Did you say two teacups?"

"Aye. 'Fore ye put it in, fill the hollow a yer hand with bakin' powder. Not too much, now."

When Mara scooped the powder, she went to the door so that Brita could see how much she had in her hand. "How's this?"

" 'Tis only half enough, darlin'. Ye don't be wantin' yer cake flat as a pancake."

Mara finished mixing the cake, poured it in a flat pan, and put it in the oven. In about half an hour she would stick a straw from the broom in the middle. If it came out clean, it was time to take the cake out of the oven.

When Trellis came into the kitchen half an hour later she was sifting sugar over the top of the cake. Mara's mind flashed back to the time Pack had come to the school with her father. Trellis was not as big or as quiet as his half brother, but he had the same black curls and dark blue eyes. He was going to be a handsome man.

"Is that for the company?" Trellis wet his finger in his mouth and swiped it through the sugar.

"What company?"

"Charlie Rivers and Miss Emily." He spoke as if company were an everyday occurrence, but his eyes shone with mischief. "Trav come down off the big hill and said he saw them comin'. I'll go tell Ma."

Mara followed him to the bedroom and smoothed the bed-clothes over Brita's slight body.

"Would you like to get up and sit in a chair to meet Miss Rivers? Trell will help us."

"No, darlin'. This be fine. Ye'll like Emily."

Coming through the parlor and into the kitchen, Pack stood in the doorway of his mother's room.

"Did I hear you say the Rivers were coming, Trell?"

"Yup. They've got your gray tied on behind the wagon. They ought to be comin' 'round the hill 'bout now."

As Mara turned to go back to the kitchen, Pack's big body filled the doorway. Their eyes met. A sincere yearning shone in the depths of his dark blue eyes. Did the thought of seeing Emily Rivers put that look there? Sam said his horse was headed toward the Rivers place when Charlie Rivers found him. Pack had been there many times if the trail was so familiar to the animal. An unexplainable uneasiness began to confuse Mara's thoughts.

"Excuse me," she said when Pack didn't move from the doorway. He stood for a few seconds longer, then moved. Mara brushed past him, her head down, embarrassed because she had been staring at him.

She looked around to make sure things were tidy, then raced up the stairs to her room. Her heart began to thump. She felt as if new life had been suddenly pumped into her body. It's the company, she thought. This was the first time she'd had guests for dinner in her home. She would use the tablecloth with the scalloped edge, make tea for herself and Miss Rivers, coffee for the men. While her mind was busy with plans for dinner, she took off her brown work dress and slipped a blue sprigged cotton dress over her head. With sure swift fingers she fastened the front buttons, whipped a clean white apron from the drawer, and tied it about her waist.

She looked at her face in her ivory-backed hand mirror, one of her most prized possessions, and grimaced. Freckles she had kept at bay with lemon juice had popped out on her nose. She loosened the ribbon that held her hair at the nape of her neck, bent over and brushed it to the top of her head, and coiled it. After fastening it with her silver hair pins, she set a comb in the back to hold the loose hair off her nape.

Each Christmas for the last five years a package had been beneath the tree for her. The year she was sixteen it had been the comb and brush, the next year the mirror and the curved comb for her hair, and the next year the hair-saver and a beautiful Mexican shawl. The fox cape was the gift at Christmas the year she graduated, and at graduation she had received a beautiful cameo brooch. These things were Mara's dearest possessions. She had fantasized that they were from a secret admirer, and that someday he would present himself at the door of the school. He would be handsome and charming and madly in love with her. He would sweep her up into his arms, carry her away to his castle, and love her to distraction.

When she questioned Miss Fillamore, the woman told her that she had bought the gifts with the funds she collected from the parents of girls Mara had tutored privately.

Mara carefully placed the mirror glass down on the dresser scarf. She remembered how desolate she had felt when she discovered that Miss Fillamore had not given her the presents because she was fond of her. Oh, well, it did not matter now that the gifts were payments for services rendered. That part of her life was over. She had no time to spend on schoolgirl sentimentalities. She was a grown woman, responsible for a house.

And company was coming.

Chapter
SEVEN

Mara went out onto the porch and stood beside Pack. The large green eyes she lifted to his were as full of pleasure as a child's with a new toy. Their gazes met, warmed and played within the depths of each other's eyes. The harsh lines that usually furrowed his brow were gone. There was no hostility between them now. Pack felt his heart jump out of rhythm, felt his blood pound and drain away. He chuckled to hide his confusion.

"What did you get all dressed up for?"

"I didn't. This isn't a *good* dress."

"It looks good to me."

Her breath was insufficient. She drew in a deep, long one. Her eyes lingered on his smiling mouth and the creases on each side of it.

"Thank you," she murmured breathlessly.

"You'll like Emily."

"Brita said that."

"She's almost blind—"

"Trell told me. Are they our nearest neighbors?"

"There are a couple more homesteaders east of here."

He wanted to keep talking to her, but he couldn't think of anything safe to say. An almost domestic tranquility existed between them. Sharing this sweet intimacy with her made Pack almost light-headed with pleasure.

The wagon stopped in front of the house. A man with a neat beard and a wide-brimmed hat pulled low over his eyes wound the reins around the brake handle and climbed down. Mara was surprised that no one had mentioned Charlie Rivers had only one leg. Pack went down the steps to the wagon just as Charlie reached up to help his sister down.

"You don't look too beat up to me," Charlie said to Pack. "I bet you've been playing possum, letting a pretty woman take care of you."

"Something like that." Pack laughed and held his uninjured hand out to Charlie.

"I expected to find you flat on your back, being waited on hand and foot."

"I'll not be running any footraces for awhile, but I'm out of the woods."

"Glad to hear it."

"Are you sure you're all right, Pack?" Emily placed her hand on his arm and lifted her face toward him. "Let me see your face. Is your nose still there?"

"I think so, but it might not be in the right place." Pack laughed, bent down and put his face near hers. "One nose, two eyes, and all my teeth." He snapped them at her.

"Your poor nose. I expected to see it smeared all over your face . . . again." Emily reached up to grasp his nose with her thumb and forefinger and wiggle it. "Pack Gallagher, I swan to goodness you can get into more trouble than a drunk hoot owl."

Watching from the porch, Mara saw a new side to Pack. The brother and sister were genuinely fond of him and he evidently returned their affection. He handled Emily as gently as if she were a prized possession, taking her arm and leading her toward the porch. The thought came back to her that Pack might be in love with the blind girl and she with him.

"Come meet Mara Shannon, Emily. She dashed upstairs,

changed into her Sunday go-to-meeting dress and gussied up
her hair when she heard you were coming." Pack's face was
relaxed, and his usually grim mouth was slightly parted and
tilted at the corners. His teasing eyes caused a bubble of
happiness to burst from Mara in the form of trilling laughter.

"Pack Gallagher! I did no such thing! My dress and apron
were dirty. Pay him no mind, Miss Rivers. He's got a loose
mouth."

"I know what a tease Pack can be. I'm glad to meet you
at last, and please call me Emily."

Emily stumbled on the step, but Pack's hand beneath her
elbow steadied her as if he had done it many times before.

"I'm glad to meet you, and call me Mara, or Mara Shannon if you wish." As Mara held out her hand, Pack lifted
Emily's forearm. Mara grasped the girl's hand and smiled
into her face. Her eyes were large and smiling, and it was
hard for Mara to believe that her eyesight was so poor she
could scarcely see her hand in front of her.

"I'll call you Mara Shannon. That's what Pack calls you."

Mara's eyes went quickly to Pack's. He was looking down
at her with a broad smile and something like pride in his eyes.
A dull red started up from her neck and she turned quickly to
the man beside him. Charlie Rivers was not nearly as tall or
as heavy as Pack. Silver strands shone at his temples; his eyes
were clear gray with wrinkles at the corners, and they moved
over Mara with interest. When Mara extended her hand to
Charlie, he clasped it firmly.

"How do you do?"

"It's a pleasure to meet you, Miss McCall."

"Charlie and I will see to the horses. Take care of Emily,
Mara," Pack said.

"Of course I will. Did you think I'd leave her standing out
here on the porch?" Mara said in a tone of mock exasperation. Then as an aside to Emily she said, "Some men don't
think women know anything, and Pack Gallagher is one of
them. Let's go visit with Brita. She speaks of you often, and
I'm sure she is eager to see you."

"Set the basket on the porch, Charlie, before you take the
wagon away," Emily called.

"Some women don't think men know anything, eh Charlie?"

Mara struggled to bring some order to her thoughts in view of Pack's behavior as she led Emily through the parlor to Brita's room and placed a chair beside the bed. He was completely different from the cantankerous man she had faced several nights before. He smiled, teased, and his voice was gentle. Seeing him with the Rivers opened up new avenues of conjecture as to his real nature.

Emily held out both hands to Brita. "It's been awhile since I've been here, Brita, but I knew you had Mara Shannon with you."

" 'Tis glad I am to see ye, Emily. Ye look well."

"I can smell cake. Have you been telling Mara Shannon how to make your everyday cake?"

"That I have. The lass takes to cookin'."

Emily removed her bonnet, groped for the chair behind her, and sat down.

"We were worried about Pack until Mr. Sparks came over and told us he was here with you and Mara Shannon, and that he was going to be all right."

"Aye," Brita said heavily. "Until next time."

"I'll see about starting the noon meal," Mara said.

"I'll help." Emily started to rise, but Mara placed a hand on her shoulder.

"No. Visit with Brita. I'm sure she's tired of hearing the sound of my voice."

"Charlie will bring in the basket if he doesn't get to talking with Pack and forget about it. I brought along a baked chicken, a loaf of wheat bread and some pickled beets that Brita is fond of. The raisin cookies are for Trellis."

"Cookies!" Mara exclaimed. "You'll have to tell me how to make them."

"Did I hear my name?"

"Trellis! You scamp! You heard *cookies!*" Emily's face creased with a beautiful smile. She reached for the boy's hand. "How dare you sneak up on me. Just for that, if I catch you, I'll give you a hug."

"Now that wouldn't hurt me none a'tall, Miss Emily."

Mara saw the pleasure on the boy's face.

"We'll be having dinner in a little while, Trell. Stay and eat with us."

"Can't, Miss Mara. Me 'n Trav are goin' to town."

"What are ye goin' fer, son?" Brita's eyes were anxious. "Is yer Pa in town?"

"Yes, ma'am. Me 'n Trav thought we'd go in 'n ride home with him."

"Aye. Ye be good lads. Ye're to be careful, hear?"

"Yes, ma'am. Don't worry."

"Take the cookies with you, Trellis." Emily, sensing the tension, spoke lightly. "You and Travor enjoy them. There'll be none left once Pack gets his hand in the pan."

After Pack brought a fresh bucket of water to the kitchen, he and Charlie sat on the porch while Mara prepared the noon meal. She fried meat, made cream gravy, boiled potatoes and eggs. While the food was cooking, she changed the tablecloth and set the table, placing the everyday cake in the center. After taking Brita a tray, she removed her apron and called the men and Emily to the table.

Pack's eyes met Mara's as soon as he came into the warm kitchen. A pleased look lit up his rugged features. Flushing, Mara shifted her gaze to the guests and told them to be seated. Emily and Mara sat across from Pack and Charlie. It was Emily who brought up the subject of Sam Sparks.

"Did Mr. Sparks' hands heal all right? Oh, I hope he didn't get any infection."

"I didn't know there was anything wrong with them." Pack turned to Charlie. "What happened to his hands?"

"He didn't tell you?" Charlie spoke up after seeing that his sister was going to leave the telling to him.

"Tell me what?"

"That he saved Emily from serious burns, if not worse."

"Godamighty!" Pack glanced quickly at Mara because of his slip of the tongue, and then anxiously from Emily to Charlie. "What happened?"

Emily answered. "I was foolish enough to get too close to

the fire when I knew the wind was behind me blowing my skirt toward the flame. I panicked and ran. Mr. Sparks caught me and put the flames out with his hands.''

"He never said a word about it." Pack sat with his fork and his knife in his hand and looked searchingly at Emily. "Were you burned?"

"A little bit on my legs, but it was nothing compared to Mr. Sparks' hands. Blisters were all over his fingers and his palms. Is he . . . still here, Pack?" The slight hesitancy in her voice was only noted by her brother.

·"He's down at the bunkhouse as far as I know. I haven't seen him ride out today."

"Charlie, you must go see about him."

"I'm not sure Charlie should go looking for him down at the bunkhouse," Pack said slowly.

"Why not? His burns could have gotten infected."

"He'd know how to take care of them."

Although Pack's face was clear of all expression, Mara had the impression that he was not pleased about Emily's interest in Sam. A feeling knifed through her that could only be jealousy. Emily had two men who cared for her, guarding her from both emotional and physical hurt. Lucky, lucky Emily. Charlie's voice broke into Mara's thoughts.

"I'll see about Mr. Sparks before we leave, Emily."

"Are you ready for cake?" Mara had caught the look that passed between Pack and Charlie. Mara had a dozen questions to ask Pack about Sam and the men in the bunkhouse, questions that he would soon answer—or she would know the reason why.

Sam knew that Charlie and Emily Rivers were at the house without ever seeing the wagon or Pack's big gray horse in the corral. It was what the men talked about during the noon meal and what they talked about while they loafed in the bunkhouse.

"I'd shore like to get me a bite a that blind gal's titties." Sporty Howard let his knife fly through the air toward a paper he had pinned to the bunkhouse wall. "She's purtier than that Irish baggage that come struttin' down here switchin' her tail like a bitch in heat."

"Ya best be careful, Sporty. Our Texas friend ain't likin' to hear no nasty talk 'bout the 'ladies.' " The voice came from the table where four men sat playing cards.

Sporty ignored the warning.

"Ever'time she goes ta the privy she looks fer me, pokes out her tits and wiggles her ass. She's jist beggin' fer it."

"Sheeit, Sporty! Ya must think yer ahidin' a fence post in yore britches."

"I'll tell ya right now, it ain't nothin' to be 'shamed of, by God! I ain't had me no complaints."

"Well then, jist wave it at Miss McCall and jist maybe she'll give ya a invite to the privy." Loud laughter followed the card dealer's remark.

Sporty threw the knife, speaking as he jerked it from the wall.

"If I had my druthers, I'd take the blind gal. Her legs is long enough to wrap a man 'n give him a good long ride."

"She'd not give ya the sport Mara would." Cullen sprawled on an unmade bunk and rolled a smoke. "That redheaded heifer would be hotter'n a brushfire if a man could get close enough to light her up."

Sam saw Cullen's eyes flick to him. They were deliberately trying to rile him. Sporty Howard retrieved his knife and stepped back to make another throw.

"Hell! I ain't wantin' to get my pecker burned off, Cull. I like to do my plowin' slow 'n deep 'n make it last. I can have me a high ole time goin' up 'n down like I was bouncin' on a featherbed. That blind gal'd do me jist fine." *Plunk*. The knife sank into the wood again.

"I wonder how ole Charlie gets his rocks knocked off. He don't go to town much." The man who spoke was watery eyed and had a mustache soiled with tobacco juice.

Sporty laughed lustily. "What'd ya suppose, ya goddamn, stupid asshole!"

The man grinned as if he had just been given a compliment.

"I'd shore not be wearin' out my hand if'n I was him! Haw! Haw! Haw!"

Sam's chest was tight. He took a deep breath. They were trying to bait him into a fight. Why? Was the man he was looking for here in the bunkhouse, and had he somehow got wind he was being hunted? Sam decided that he wouldn't play into the hands of a gun-happy, knife-throwing piece of horseshit like Sporty Howard. He'd not be forced to show his hand to this wolf pack. The time would come, he vowed silently, when Sporty and Cullen would eat their words. He got to his feet, keeping his eyes on the shifty-eyed Howard. The man grinned at him impudently.

"Ya goin' up to the house ta pay your respects to the *ladies*, Sparks?"

Cullen sat up on the bunk. "Ya ain't got no chance at all with the redhead, Sam. Ole Pack'll be all over yore ass like sorghum on a hotcake if ya blink a eye at her."

"And ole Charlie ain't lettin' nobody sniff up to his woman, neither," Sporty added.

The desire to kill a man knifed through Sam like a hot blade. All that kept him from going for the man's throat was years of self-discipline. There was a sudden quiet that lasted for a few tense seconds. When Sam's words fell into the silence, they were clipped, but soft, and carried a weighted message to each man in the room.

"A man that talks bad 'bout good women is lower than a snake's belly. If any of you gents want to make somethin' of it, speak up." There was silence as Sam turned eyes, hard as steel, on the knife thrower. "All of yore brains is in that stick 'tween yore legs, Howard. One day I'm goin' to break it off and shove it up yore ass."

"Now that jist plumb scares me, Sparks." Sporty tried to speak with bravado, but his voice failed to carry its former confident tone.

Seething with anger, Sam stood with his hands on his hips. His eyes circled the room and moved back to Sporty. The men were watching quietly. Finally Sporty grinned at him and palmed the knife. Sam waited until the knife left the hand

and struck the wall before he turned, walked out the door, and headed for the corral.

"And one a these days I'm goin' to blast that bastard clear to hell!" Sporty yanked the knife from the wall.

"Ya had yore chance," one of the card players said dryly. "What stopped ya?"

"Best do it when he ain't lookin'." Cullen stood and glanced out the window. "He's steady 'n quick. Quicker 'n a goose shittin' appleseeds."

"So he's steady 'n quick. Ya think I ain't?" Sporty sneered. "What's he runnin' from?"

"I didn't ask him, no more'n I asked you. But I'm leery of him."

"Ya think he's the law?"

"No. I think he's lookin' for somebody, 'n when he finds him he'll kill him."

"Glad it ain't me." The man dealing the cards slapped the deck down on the table. "The bastard'll not give up till he finds him. Them Texans ain't got no quit a'tall. I fit in the war with 'em. I'd ruther have me one steady 'n quick Texan on my side than six a anybody else."

"Yo're right as rain 'bout that." The man with the soiled mustache spit in the can beside his chair. "I come up the Cimarron with one a 'em. He'd have a smile on his face like the wave on a slop bucket while he was gunnin' a man down. It beat all I ever saw."

"Sheeit! If they were so good, why'd they let a bunch a pepper eaters whip their asses at the Alamo?" Sporty wiped his knife on his pants and shoved it in the scabbard. "What ya goin' to do with that redhead, Cull?"

"What do you mean?"

"Goddamn it! Ya know what I mean. Is she goin' to mess up what's goin' on here? Hell! We'd best start lookin' fer another place to spend some time."

"Don't get yore ass over the line. I done got it figured out what to do. All I got to do is wait till Pack leaves. I wish to hell them roughhousers had finished him off when they had the chance."

"You scared a him, Cull?"

"Scared? Hell! I'd a killed the son of a bitch long ago, but the ole man was set against it. But it'll happen. I ain't havin' my plans ruint by no prissy ass woman 'n a dumb muleskinner."

"I ain't likin' that marshal nosin' 'round either."

"He didn't even come down here," Cullen said with a nonchalance he didn't feel. "Might be he's got a hard-on for Miss Prissy Ass."

"Yeah? Well, I'm gettin' antsy. I ain't feelin' easy here no more." Sporty pulled his gun out of the holster and spun the cylinder like a kid playing with a toy. He waited for someone to say something, but no one did.

"Sam! Hey, Sam!"

Pack was calling from the back porch of the ranch house and waving his arm. Sam glanced back toward the bunkhouse. The porch was empty. The building was set a good three hundred feet back and to the north of the house, and Sam had plenty of time to wonder what Pack wanted to speak to him about as he walked up the path. He had not intended to go near the Rivers, although he wanted to see Miss Emily again and had even thought up several excuses to ride over to their place. He wanted to see her and yet he didn't want to see her. What the hell was the matter with him? This was not the time for him to be lollygagging over a woman.

Pack stood waiting on the porch. "Come in for coffee, Sam."

"Ya got company, Pack. I'm not wantin' to be no bother."

"Charlie and Miss Emily want to see you."

Sam stepped up onto the porch. "I'm not much for visitin', Pack." He took off his hat and followed Pack into the kitchen.

Charlie stood and held out his hand. "Howdy, Sparks."

"Howdy."

"I said I was going to shake that hand. How is it?"

"Fine, thanks to Miss Rivers."

"Hello, Mr. Sparks." Emily's large clear eyes were turned

in Sam's direction and there was a smile on her face, also a blush, noted by everyone except Sam. She held her hand out to him.

"Howdy, Miss Rivers." Sam took her hand gently and would have dropped it quickly, but she refused to let it go.

"Not so fast! I've got to see if it's healed."

"It has, ma'am. It's fine."

Emily brought his palm up close to her face and ran her fingertips over the rough places where the blisters had broken. Dear God, she was pretty! Sam thought. Prettier and sweeter than he remembered. He could feel her warm breath on his palm, and he feasted his eyes on the top of her head where her hair was piled and pinned. When he had seen her before, it had been braided Indian fashion, hanging in two long ropes down over her breasts.

"I brought a tin of salve. It's not as good as aloe, but not as messy either."

"I thank ya, ma'am, but I'm not wantin' ya to feel beholden fer what I done." Sam gently pulled his hand from Emily's.

"Whether you want it or not, Sparks, we are beholden," Charlie said firmly. "We'll be forever in your debt. Emily would feel better if you took the salve."

"Why shore, if that's how ya want it. And I'm obliged."

"Sit down, Sam. Mara Shannon made cake. I'm not saying it would take any prizes, but it's eatable." Pack gave Mara a wicked, teasing smile.

"Then you'll only want a tiny little slice," she retorted.

"No, I'll manage to choke down a *big* slice."

"Pack Gallagher, today you're nothing but a . . . a big *bosthoon!*"

"Bosthoon? What's that?" Charlie asked.

"It means big, lovable darlin'." Pack gazed unabashed at Mara's suddenly scarlet face.

"You—you liar!"

"Ach, ach, Mara Shannon. Behave yourself. We got company." His face was wreathed in smiles and his eyes seemed to burn with a blue light.

Pack's teasing words and smiling face left Mara speechless

and sent a tingling all the way to her toes. This camaraderie was so new to her that she didn't know how to handle it. Shaking her head as if to clear it, she turned to serve the cake.

When the meal was over and the men went to the front porch, Mara put the dishes in the pan and covered them with water. Her intentions were to wash them after the company had gone, but Emily insisted on helping.

"It will take no time at all. Brita is napping and we can visit. I talk better when my hands are busy."

"All right." Mara handed her a clean dishtowel. She was fascinated as she watched the near-blind girl rinse a glass in the clear hot water and dry it with the towel. "Emily, you're amazing. I don't know how you manage to do what you do."

"You don't miss what you've never had, Mara Shannon. It's as simple as that."

"Have you ever had eyeglasses?"

"None that helped. Charlie says that someday we'll go back east and see what can be done. But I don't really care if we do or not. I'm used to my blindness. I've lived all my life in a blurred world. I'm a coward too. I'm afraid of getting my hopes up and being disappointed."

They worked silently for a few minutes, then Mara asked, "Have you known Pack long?"

"Four or five years. When we came up the Missouri on the steamer, Charlie hired Pack to meet us and take our things out to the homestead. We think the world of Pack." Emily placed the plate on the table and reached into the pan for another.

"I've only known him a short while."

"I thought he and your father were very close."

"They were. Papa brought him to the school once. But it was so long ago that I didn't even know who he was when I found him lying in the road."

"Pack knew that those men were waiting for him, but he was determined to meet you at Sheffield Station. He often leaves things at our place. This time he emptied his pockets and left his saddlebags. After his horse came back, Charlie went looking for him. He saw where you had put him in the wagon and brought him here."

"Sam was the one who took care of him. I was at a complete loss as to what to do."

"Mr. Sparks is nice . . . and, I think, kind of shy."

"Shy? I hadn't thought of him as shy. He's terribly polite. Maybe he just seems shy to you because Pack is so . . . so bold." Mara carried the dishwater to the back porch and threw it out into the yard. She came back in, wiped the pan with the dishrag and hung it on a nail at the end of the work counter.

"I never thought of Pack as being bold," Emily said quietly, draping the wet cloth on the handle of the oven door and spreading it out carefully.

"Maybe not bold. I should have said bossy."

"I've not noticed him being bossy. He's one of the sweetest, kindest men I ever knew."

There was a tremor in Emily's voice. She was standing quietly with her hand on the back of the chair. Mara looked at her with a faint trace of confusion. She was suddenly aware that the subject of Pack Gallagher was not one she could discuss with Emily if she wanted the blind girl's friendship.

"Brita is still asleep," Mara said, hoping to get the conversation on a more friendly basis. "Would you like to sit in the parlor or go to the porch where we can catch the breeze?"

"Why don't you like Pack?"

Mara was startled to hear the softly spoken words so like the ones she had said to Pack a few nights before. *Why don't you like me?*

"I don't dislike Pack. He sees things one way; I see them another. We constantly . . . butt heads." Mara turned when she heard a small noise come from Brita's room. She was grateful for the distraction and hurried to her cousin's bedside.

"Are the boys back from town?"

"Not yet. Would you like a cool drink?"

"That I would, darlin'. Did ye have a good visit with Emily? She be such a fine . . . lass." Brita's voice was weak and there was a momentary catch in her breath, followed by a faint moan. Fear bloomed in Mara's heart as it did each time she became aware that Brita's condition was worsening.

"We've had a grand time. The next time she comes over we're going to make a big batch of cookies, and she's going to show me how to make doughnuts. We made a list of the things we'll need."

Emily had moved quietly into the room and stood at the end of the bed. She was smiling.

"I forgot to tell you about the kittens, Brita. Cinderella had four girls and two boys. As soon as they're weaned, you can have your choice."

"That'll be grand! Mara Shannon be wantin' a cat."

"Cinderella. What an unusual name for a cat," Mara said, but her mind was on the blue tinge around Brita's mouth.

"Pack brought me the cat from Laramie, so he got to name her. A few years ago he was snowed in at our place and Charlie read us the *Tales of Mother Goose* by Charles Perrault. My favorite was 'Beauty and the Beast,' but Pack liked 'Cinderella,' and that's what he named my tabby."

"Then we'll name our kitten Beauty. Is that all right with you, Brita?"

"Aye, lassie. 'Tis a fine name."

Mara straightened the pillow and smoothed Brita's hair with a loving hand. "I'll get you a cool drink."

Moisture had come to Mara's eyes. She quickly left the room, went to the kitchen, and stood beside the almost empty waterbucket, gripping it with both hands. *Brita was going to die!* She clenched her jaws as fear ripped into her. The memory of her mother's death and the terrible loss she had felt afterward came back to haunt her. She just barely choked back a sob as she tugged the heavy oak bucket off the shelf. Mara turned to see that Emily had come into the room and was standing beside the back door.

"You're worried about Brita." The words came out on a mere breath. She reached for Mara's hand when she approached her. The blind girl's face was creased with worry.

"She's so much worse than when I first came here." Mara whispered the words close to Emily's ear. "She's getting weaker all the time, and now there's a blue tinge to her skin."

"I thought as much. Her voice is so much weaker and it's harder for her to breathe."

"I wish she would let us take her to town."

"She won't go. I think she knows that nothing can be done. She wants to be here with her boys." Emily's hand squeezed Mara's. "If ever you need me, send one of the twins."

"Thank you."

On her way to the well, Mara saw three riders coming up the road. They rode single file. One twin was leading Aubrey's horse, the other rode behind. Aubrey lay against the horse's neck, his arms dangling. Mara wondered with disgust how he could stay in the saddle. A fine example he was setting for his boys.

She unhooked the rope and the weight of the well bucket carried it to the bottom where it landed with a plunk. She waited for it to fill, then pulled the rope through the pulley to bring the full bucket to the top. Pack's large hands reached over her and the weight was taken from her hands.

"It's too heavy for you, Mara Shannon."

"I'll have to get a lighter bucket." She moved out from between Pack's outstretched arms. "I can't depend on someone being here every time I need water. Pack. . . ." She waited until he had drawn the well bucket to the top and poured the water into the one they would carry to the house. "Pack, I'm worried about your mother."

"So am I," he replied with regret.

"She's sinking fast. Isn't there anything we can do?" Mara asked while he lowered the bucket and secured the rope.

"I had the doctor out from Laramie a couple of months ago. He said her heart was missing a beat every once in a while and there wasn't anything he could do to fix it. It was just wearing out. Rest would help more than anything. Lord knows she gets enough of that."

"Her mind doesn't rest, Pack. She worries about you, about the twins, and about Aubrey."

"And you, Mara Shannon." He stopped walking and

looked down at her. "I'm obliged to you for the care you give her. I'm glad you're here. She loves you." His voice was raspy as if his throat hurt; his dark eyes were shadowed with worry.

"I love her. She's so much like my . . . mother." Tears threatened and Mara blinked rapidly.

He looked at her face searchingly. "You've got to prepare yourself."

"I know." The words came out on a sob. Pack's hand closed about hers, and she let it stay there.

"Let's get on back to the house. Charlie'll be wanting to leave soon."

"Pack." She looked up at him with a sparkle of tears on her lashes. "How did you know I was at the well?"

"I heard the pulley squeak."

The riders were approaching. Mara wiggled her hand from Pack's. His eyes followed hers and an expression of intense dislike came over his face. An expletive dropped from his lips.

"Son of a bitch!" he said in a voice as brittle as ice. He watched the twins and their father until they reached the bunkhouse. Then, almost rebelliously, he recaptured her hand and held it until they reached the house.

Charlie and Sam were in a deep conversation about longhorn cattle when Pack returned to the porch.

"They're usually yeller in color," Sam said. "They got a bony form, long legs, light hindquarters 'n a backbone that sticks up like a ridge. Tough animal. All meat 'n bone, no fat. Looks somethin' like a deer, only bigger. Most weigh 650 to 950 pounds."

"Do you think they'd do well in this country?"

"No doubt in my mind. They'll live on a handful of grass 'n take care a themselves. I ain't so sure a cougar could take one down. They're a mean breed 'n got horns to back it up. They'll kill ya if they get a chance. Longhorns can't be handled on foot 'n they're bitches to drive."

"I heard that some ranchers up north were putting their money in Texas longhorns, and a herd of a hundred thousand was on the way."

"Whew." Pack whistled through his teeth. "Do you want to get into the cattle business, Charlie?"

"Do you?"

"Hell! I can't take care of my freight business right now. I'd be in a hell of a mess without old Willy. Are you givin' it thought, Sam?"

"I got to settle down sometime. I'm gettin' partial to this country. Plenty a water 'n open range left. I've thought of drivin' up a herd next spring."

Charlie stood and knocked the ashes from his pipe on the heel of his boot. "Country is filling up. Before the railroad came it was a right peaceful place."

"Squirrely still around, Charlie?" Pack asked.

"Yeah. He's squirrely as ever, but a good old coot. He watches the place while we're away."

Sam, rolling a smoke, looked up at Pack. "That's his name? Squirrely?"

"I've not heard another. He's a genuine old-time mountain man." Pack grinned. "Claims to have been here before the Indians. Hellfire! He's so damned old he could have been here before the mountains."

Charlie chuckled. "I'd better hitch up and make tracks for home."

Emily, coming through the parlor, heard the exchange and went to the door leading to the porch. She could see the dim image of her brother and the taller form beside him that was either Pack or Sam Sparks.

"Mr. Sparks," she called.

"Yes, ma'am?"

"I want to give you the salve before we go."

Charlie Rivers looked from his sister to Sam, hesitated, then walked away. Pack followed. Sam saw the look of concern on Charlie's face before he turned away. He glanced at their retreating backs and wondered if he should excuse himself and catch up with them. He looked at Miss Rivers waiting beside the door.

What the hell? He didn't have to have the man's permission to spend a few minutes with his sister.

"Mr. Sparks?"

"I'm right here, Miss Rivers." He went up the steps and stood a few feet from her.

"I can see your outline. You're very tall."

"I guess so. I've not given it much thought."

"Charlie says I'm about average."

"I'd say Charlie's right."

"It would be nice to be taller. Especially when I want to reach something." She chided herself for making such inane conversation, but she was afraid he would leave.

"My sister was about your size."

"What was her name?"

"Rose."

"My name is Emily Rose. I wish you would call me Emily."

"I'd be right proud to, Miss Emily."

"Here's the tin of salve. Put it on your palms at night. It will soften the skin that was burned."

He took the tin from her fingers. It was warm from being held in her hand. He slipped it into his breast pocket, trying to think of something else to say. His eyes moved over her. The dress molded her high breasts and slender waist. Little gestures revealed her nervousness; the movement of her hands, her darting tongue as it moistened her lips. Sam had had his share of women, but what he felt now had nothing to do with lust. He feasted his eyes on her face, her pink cheeks, her soft lips and shiny hair. It was her eyes that fascinated him. Large and unblinking, they seemed to be looking straight into his. Emily Rose, sweet Emily Rose. He could only say her name like that in his thoughts.

A small nervous laugh suddenly burst from her lips. "I'm trying so hard to think of something to say."

The honest confession surprised and pleased him. His chuckle came from deep in his chest.

"So am I. I can't think of anythin' either. I feel like a fool jist standin' here."

"I'm not usually so tongue-tied." She laughed again softly, happily this time. Her mouth remained smiling and Sam had an aching desire to kiss it.

"Don't—" they both said at the same time, then laughed together.

His eyes were on her face, hers were on his, but he didn't know how clearly she could see him.

"Don't what?" she asked.

"Don't go in. What were you going to say?"

"Don't leave," she whispered with her lips barely moving.

"I don't want to, Emily Rose," he said softly.

"I like you calling me that. Will you be here long?"

"I'm not sure."

"If you're over our way, will you stop by?"

"Wild horses couldn't keep me away." The words came out so easily that he was hardly aware he had said them.

Emily's pounding heart released a flood of happiness that was reflected in a brilliant smile which ended in soft laughter. It was the sweetest sound Sam had ever heard. God! What a wonderful, sweet woman! Just being with her caused years of frustration and pain to drop from his shoulders. For an instant he thought about running away with her to some faraway place so that he would have her all to himself. She was still smiling and was such a pleasure to look at—warm, sparkling and pretty.

Sounds of the horses' hooves and the creaking wagon reached them.

Emily held out her hand. Sam took it and held it tightly between his two rough palms.

"Good-bye, Sam."

"Bye, Emily Rose."

The smile on her face was genuine, unguarded, natural and beautiful. Once Sam had been thrown from his horse, and when he made solid contact with the ground, he had lain there, hearing nothing but a pounding in his head. That was how he felt now. Only this time he had another discomfort: his guts were wrenched with a spasm of longing.

Chapter
EIGHT

"She can go anytime. Her heart is worn out. I told you that when I was here before. I didn't think she would live this long." The doctor turned from Pack and spoke directly to Mara. "All you can do for her is make her as comfortable as possible."

The day before Mara had written out a detailed description of Brita's condition, and Trellis had taken it to town. The doctor had arrived in a handsome black buggy with a man riding guard. He was very professional and also very blunt. After spending some time with Brita, he spoke with Mara and Pack on the porch.

Pack held out some bills.

"I'm sorry I can't do anything for her." The doctor took the money and put it in his pocket. "I heard you got roughed up a bit, Gallagher. Is there anything I can do for you?"

"Not a thing."

The doctor shrugged. He put his bag in the back of the buggy and climbed up on the seat.

"You know where to find me . . . next time."

Mara was so upset that the doctor's words failed to register in her mind. She cried when he left. He had only confirmed what she believed to be true.

In the days that followed, Mara devoted herself entirely to Brita. She hurried through her housework while Brita slept. During Brita's waking hours she sat beside her bed, telling her about her life at the school or reading to her from the small collection of books she had managed to accumulate. She finished *Moll Flanders* and started *Robinson Crusoe*. Pack and the twins seemed to enjoy the stories as much as their mother. In the evening they would come quietly into the room, sit on the bunk and listen. Mara could tell that it gave Brita great pleasure to see her boys together. Her eyes would rest lovingly on each of their faces.

Pack spent time alone with his mother each day. He sat beside her, held her crippled hand, and talked to her in low reassuring tones. Mara never intruded on these private talks. It seemed to her that Brita was worrying about something, and he was trying to put her mind to rest. He shared in every phase of his mother's care, even to emptying the chamber pot and boiling the soiled bed clothes in the big pot in the yard.

Mara found herself watching him more and more, marveling that he was such a big, rough man and yet so gentle with his mother. She admired his constant attention to her needs, his attitude toward his young brothers; but it was more than that. It was something in the man himself, an integrity, an inner strength, and it was also a sexual attraction that was entirely new to her.

Pack's strength was almost back to normal. With the help of the twins he had snaked logs down out of the hills, and they were sawing them into lengths to be split for firewood. It was something to do that kept him close to the house. He pulled on the saw and tried not to think about the pain in his leg.

On the other end of the two-man saw, Travor's arms felt as if they were about to fall off. He gritted his teeth and pulled doggedly. He'd be damned if he'd cry quit before they had sawed through the log. The chunk fell, Travor let his end of the saw drop, and straightened his back.

"You done real good, boy!" Pack grinned at his young brother. "I was about to holler uncle."

"I bet!" Travor returned the grin and painfully flexed his shoulders.

"Keep the blade out of the dirt. It'll be a hell of a lot harder to saw the next one if it's dull."

Travor picked up his end of the saw and they placed it lengthwise on the log. Pack drew an oily rag over the jagged teeth. "We sure as hell don't want that bastard to rust up on us."

"You goin' to stop now?"

"For awhile. I need a rest and a cold drink. How about you?" Pack tried not to limp on the way to the well. He had tied a tight cloth about his leg to keep the skin from stretching and breaking over the wound. He had to work. The inactivity, the *waiting* was even more painful.

Travor drew the water, and they drank from the dipper that hung on the nail beside the well. A change had come over the sullen twin during the past few days. He spent more time at the house and less time with the men at the bunkhouse, although he still slept there. He willingly shared work with Trellis and had been civil to Mara, but it was Pack whose company he wanted. If they were not working together, he sat near him on the porch. During meals or when evening came, he quietly disappeared.

"Ma's goin' to die, ain't she, Pack?" Travor looked off toward the mountains as he spoke.

"Yes, Trav."

"I see a light at night. You 'n Trell sit up with her."

"Yeah. Mara Shannon takes a turn too. But either me or

Trell have to move her in the bed. Mara Shannon isn't strong enough for that.''

"I could . . . do that. I'm as strong as Trell."

Pack made a to-do of wiping the sweat from his face and neck while he blinked away the moistness from his eyes. He wanted to throw his arm about his young brother, but he didn't dare, fearing that the line holding together this fragile friendship they had forged would snap.

"Ma would like that."

"What's goin' to happen . . . when she's gone? Mara Shannon won't let us stay here."

"I don't know what will happen," Pack said honestly. "But you and Trell will have a place with me if you want it."

"We couldn't leave Pa. He don't have anybody but Cullen, and Cullen don't care nothin' for him."

"How old are you and Trell?"

"Fourteen. Fifteen in the fall."

"I didn't realize you were that old. Time goes by fast."

"Do you know how to read, Pack?" They were on the way back to the woodpile.

"Some."

"Do you read as good as Mara Shannon?"

"No, but I can make out most of the words, given time."

"When she reads about the man on the island, I feel like I'm right there." Travor picked up the oily cloth and moved it along the saw blade. "Did the man who wrote the story just make it up in his head and write it down?"

"I guess so. I never heard that he was left on an island." Pack retied the cloth about his thigh. "Charlie Rivers has a lot of books. If Mara Shannon reads all of hers, maybe we can borrow some from Charlie."

"I wish I could read like Mara Shannon. I'd read those stories to myself."

"Well," Pack said, blowing out a long breath, "I bet Mara Shannon would teach you if you asked her."

Travor lifted his head to look up at his brother. Unashamed tears blurred his eyes.

"There ain't no time," he said hoarsely and picked up his end of the saw.

It was nearly midnight. On the hill behind the house a man sat on his haunches and waited for a light to appear in the upstairs window. He began to feel the same excitement he had felt the night before when he saw Mara move about the room preparing for bed. It had been late. He had waited for several hours just as he had tonight. He lifted the small telescope to his eyes and saw movement in the room downstairs where the light burned all night. Minutes later a light shone from the upstairs window.

The man sat as still as a stone and watched as Mara passed the window and back again. On the next trip her arms were lifted. She was taking down her hair! It fell over her shoulders and down her back. She massaged her scalp with her fingers and then moved into the center of the room. The man almost groaned with fear that she would move out of his sight. She unbuttoned the top of her dress, wiggled her shoulders and arms out of it and let it slide down over her hips. A white chemise with a drawstring covered her breasts. As she reached for the string, she stepped out of his sight.

He drew in a ragged breath and cursed. All too quickly the light was gone. He lowered the glass and stared at the darkened window, waiting for the desire that made him hard and uncomfortable to lessen.

Ace January moved quietly to his horse and led him to another area where he had a view of the bunkhouse, settled himself against a tree, and raised the spyglass. Nothing stirred, yet he waited. He would like nothing more than to lie down and sleep, but the stakes were too high for him to indulge himself. If his hunch was right, he would be sleeping in a featherbed for the rest of his life. It was very possible Mara Shannon McCall would be beside him. As desirable as she was, she was like any other woman. He had no doubt that he could have her once she realized what he could give her.

*   *   *

Mara awakened the instant Pack called her name. It seemed
to her that she had just closed her eyes. She had stayed with
Brita until midnight while he napped on the bunk. Wide
awake, she sat up in bed, clutching the cover up over her
breasts, a lump of dread in her throat. Pack stood, a vague
shadow, filling the doorway of her room.

"Pack? What is it?"

"Come," he said simply and backed away.

Mara Shannon pulled her dress on over her nightdress,
took a ribbon from her pocket and tied her hair at the nape of
her neck. She groped in the dark for her shoes, couldn't find
them, then left the room in her bare feet. At the bottom of the
stairs she followed the ribbon of light to Brita's room.

Pack had moved the lamp to the bureau behind his mother's bed. He sat on the stool beside her, the light shining
down on his dark head, his face haggard. Trellis stood beside
him and Travor sat on the bunk, his shoulders hunched, his
hands clasped between his knees. Mara moved to the bedside, her eyes anxiously scanning Brita's face. Her head
moved restlessly on the pillow and a froth of bubbles flew in
and out of her mouth as the slow, gasping breaths came and
went. The only sound in the room was the sobbing, dragging
sound of her breathing.

No words were necessary between the four people grouped
around the bed, only a silent waiting—a period of suspense
that had no relation to reality. Mara drew close to Pack and
placed her hand on his shoulder.

"Shouldn't we call Aubrey?"

"No." The word came from Travor who moved up beside
her. "No," he said again. "He's drunk."

Mara's other hand inched over and clasped the boy's cold
one. His fingers accepted hers gratefully and tightened. He
was holding his grief tight inside him, not even allowing
himself the comfort of tears. Trellis, standing at the foot of
the bed, was crying silently. Pack sat hunched, his eyes on

his mother's face. He was still except for his large fist which rested on the bed beside her milk-white hand. His fingers opened and closed, opened and closed.

The minutes spun into an hour or more. They waited, each wishing, hoping, but knowing the inevitable. The three sons knew they were spending the last few minutes with the mother who had given them life.

A rooster crowed, announcing a new day. Shortly after that the clock on the mantel in the parlor struck five times.

Then, sudden silence.

Mara looked down at Pack's hand. It had closed into a tight, hard fist and did not open again. The silence went on and on with all four pair of eyes on Brita's face, peaceful now that she no longer had the agonizing task of drawing breath into her lungs. As they watched, color faded from her face.

"She's gone." Pack spoke the words that penetrated each of them and sank into their senses with cold finality. No one else spoke. He reached over and gently cupped his mother's chin in his large hand to close her mouth.

Travor turned and sought the darkness of the kitchen. His twin went with him. Mara stayed beside Pack, her hand gripping his shoulder, her face wet with tears. He reached for her hand and held onto it tightly. He was holding his grief inside, hurting hard with a kind of knotted pain that wouldn't loosen. Finally tears rolled from the corners of his eyes and down his cheeks to his set jaws.

A sound like none Mara had heard when he had been so badly hurt came from his throat. He turned, leaning his head toward her. Her fingers forked through his hair around to his cheek and pressed his head to his breast like a mother comforting a child. His arm wrapped around her thighs, pulling her close, his shoulders shaking with soundless sobs. She had no thought but to give him comfort. Pack's tears wet the front of her dress, but she was unaware of it until later. She held him, stroked the crisp blue-black curls at his temple, moved her hand down his nape to his shoulders and back.

"Shhh . . . shhh . . . she's at peace now," she crooned.

"But—she suffered—and had so—little."

"She's not suffering now, and she had all that she wanted.

She had a great and enduring love for your father. She had you, and she had the boys. It gave her pleasure to see the three of you together.''

Mara was conscious of nothing but great sorrow and the need to comfort. She held Pack's head to her breasts, smoothed his hair back from his brow and cupped his cheek with her palm. When the twins came back into the room, she drew back with no feeling of guilt for having been caught holding and comforting him.

"I'll take care of her now." Mara reached over and smoothed the hair back from the still warm face of the woman on the bed.

Pack stood looking down at his mother, feeling deserted and terribly alone.

"Tell us what to do."

"We wash and dress her. My mother . . . died in the night and that is what my father did."

"I'll heat water." Travor left the room as if grateful to be doing something.

"Ma don't have many clothes." This came from Trellis. His lips were still trembling and he was trying desperately not to cry.

Mara knew that only two worn dresses were in the bureau drawer. Brita had spent the last years of her life in loose gowns.

"I have a dress that would be pretty on her. Do either of you mind if I furnish the burial garments?" Mara's voice thickened as she spoke the final words. Tear-filled eyes went from Pack to Trellis and back again.

"I think Ma would be pleased to wear something of yours. Don't you, Trell?"

The boy nodded wordlessly.

With Pack's help, Mara washed and dressed his mother in a rose pink dress with a white lace collar and cuffs. It was one of Mara's favorite dresses. They made a fold in the back of the dress because it was too big for Brita's slight body. Mara put a pair of white stockings on her legs and brushed her hair. When she had finished arranging and pinning the soft gray hair to the top of Brita's head, she went up to her room and brought down her curved ivory comb. With infinite care she placed it in Brita's hair, lifted her hands, and folded them across her breasts. When she straightened, her eyes, glistening like wet emeralds, met Pack's.

"The comb was given to me at Christmas a long time ago when I was lonely and homesick. It means a lot to me, and I want her to have it."

The sun was up by the time they finished laying Brita out on the bed and cleaning the room. While Pack hung blankets over the windows to darken it, Mara carried the teakettle of hot water to her room, washed herself, put on a clean dress and apron, and pinned up her hair.

Pack was shaving at the washstand when Mara returned to the kitchen. She made a pan of biscuits and put them in the oven. When they were done, she set them on the table with butter and syrup. No one ate much, but they all made a show of swallowing a few bites.

"Trav, we'd better go tell Pa." Trellis spoke as if he were going to choke on the words.

"He might still be drunk."

"In that case we'll have to sober him up."

Pack followed his brothers to the porch. "If you see Sam, ask him to come up." He watched the two boys go down the path to the bunkhouse, then came back to the kitchen. Mara was massaging her temples with her fingertips. "You're worn out. Why don't you sleep awhile?"

"No. There's too much to be done. Brita would want us to make things as nice as we can. How many will come when they get the word?"

Pack regarded her for a long while, his eyes filled with grief. When he spoke there was deep regret in his voice.

"Not many. Aubrey and Cullen never made neighbors feel very welcome. No one came to see Ma but Charlie and Emily. She hasn't been to town but a time or two since they came here."

"It won't matter. Brita will have her sons," Mara said firmly. "There will be a good meal for them and anyone who does come."

Later, Mara saw the twins walking with Aubrey toward the

horse tank. As she watched, she saw Travor give him a shove. Aubrey toppled in backward, and it was Trellis who helped him out. Mara shook her head sadly. The boys were trying to sober up their father so he could attend their mother's wake.

When Sam came up the path to the house, Pack went out onto the porch to meet him.

"I'm shore sorry, Pack," he said with his hat in his hand. "I'm just plumb sorry. Is there anythin' a'tall I can do?"

"Yes there is, Sam. I'd be obliged if you'd ride over and tell Charlie and Emily."

"I'll be glad to."

"And Sam, if it isn't too much to ask, I'd sure thank you to ride on into Laramie. Go to the preacher's house, the one next to the church with the stained glass window in front. I don't remember if he's Methodist or what. Tell him to come out in the morning. Tell him to come and bring the best box he can get, and I'll cancel the bill he owes me for hauling in that window and his church pews."

"Did ya think he wouldn't come?" Sam asked and screwed his hat down tight on his head.

"I'm not exactly a friend of his," Pack said dryly. "I'm just making sure."

"I'm thinkin' yo're right. Them righteous fellers can be plumb aggravatin' at times if a man strays from their way a thinkin'."

"When he wanted the pews for his church hauled in for damn near nothing, he came to me, but when I stepped in the ring to fight Black Bob Mason, I was nothing but pure dee old Irish trash leading his flock to hell." Pack's voice was laced with dry amusement. "A hell of a lot of his flock were there too, and more than a few of them won some money."

"Knuckle fightin' would raise a lot more money fer the church than box-suppers." Sam grinned one of his rare grins and stepped off the porch. "I'll get on over to Rivers' place 'n tell them the buryin' will be in the mornin'."

"Sam, when this is over, I'd like a word with you about another matter."

"Sure, Pack."

"You'll be welcome to come up for the meal . . . after the burying. We can talk then."

"I'd be proud to come. There's a thin' ya'd best be knowin' 'n it ort a be knowed now. Somebody's hangin' round here nights spyin' on the house. I found his tracks more 'n once up there on the ridge." Sam jerked his head toward the west. "Keep a sharp eye out, hear?"

Sam went back down the path to the corral, saddled his horse and rode out. Pack watched from the porch, his mind busy with the information Sam had just given him.

The twins came back to say that Aubrey would be up in a little while. He was in the cookshack where Steamboat was forcing him to drink a mixture of raw eggs and buttermilk.

"Phew!" Mara Shannon shuddered. "That sounds terrible."

"It ain't no worse than some of that other rotgut he drinks." Travor's young face was set rebelliously and not an ounce of sympathy was in his voice.

"Will you boys be here for awhile?" Pack came through the parlor and into the kitchen. "I'd like to go down to the creek and wash, but I don't want to go off and leave Mara Shannon here by herself."

"Go ahead. We'll be here." Trellis poured coffee for himself and his brother.

"Sam's gone to tell Charlie and Emily. Emily will be here by this afternoon." Pack looked at Mara as he spoke. "She'll be a help to you. She was fond of Ma." His expression became as bleak as his voice.

"I'll be glad for her company."

"Sam will go on into town and tell the preacher to come out in the morning."

"Pack . . . what'll we do about a . . . a box?" Trellis could just barely get the words out.

"The preacher will bring one from town." Pack placed his hand on his young brother's shoulder. "We're going to make it just as nice for Ma as we can." He cleared his throat. "Later this evening the three of us will go up to the place where Mara Shannon's parents are buried and pick out a spot."

"Ma liked that place. She used to put flowers up there when she could walk." Trellis turned his face away. "Is there room inside that fence you built?"

Mara's eyes went to Pack's. "You built a fence?"

"I didn't exactly build it. I dug a few holes for corner posts and fastened some sections of iron fence around the plot to keep it from being overrun."

"It was thoughtful of you, Pack."

Pack shrugged, a gesture he used when he was embarrassed and didn't know what to say. When he did speak, it was to change the subject.

"Trav, why don't you talk to Steamboat and see if he'll cook up a hindquarter of beef? We'll want to put on a spread and Mara Shannon is worn out from being up all night."

"I don't know if he'll do it, Pack. Cullen's bein' a asshole." Travor looked quickly at Mara to see if she was offended by the word, but her face was turned away. "Cullen says Steamboat works for him."

"Steamboat works for the owner of this property," Pack said quietly. "Ask him to cook the meat. I'll take care of Cullen if he makes trouble."

Mara and the twins were in the kitchen when Aubrey came up the path to the house. Trellis had filled the firebox of the cookstove, and Mara was stirring up the everyday cake that had been Brita's favorite. Aubrey had tried to clean himself up. He had shaved with shaking hands as indicated by the small nicks on his face made by the razor. His shirt was wrinkled but clean, and he had combed his hair.

He stood silently in the doorway as if expecting to be turned away. His watery eyes were swimming in tears. Finally he pushed himself away from the doorjamb and went into Brita's room and closed the door. Mara went about her work. The twins sat in stoney, uncomfortable silence, hunched over their coffee cups. When Travor could stand it no longer, he picked up the water bucket and went outside. Trellis followed.

Mara was pulling the cake from the oven when Pack returned. Her face was flushed from the heat; her auburn hair was damp from sweat and stuck to her cheeks and forehead.

Pack's hair was wet and glistening from being in the creek. His shirt clung to his broad, wet shoulders and deep chest like a second skin. He had a fistful of wildflowers in his hand.

"Oh, Pack! The flowers are beautiful. Where did you find them?"

"Down by the creek. There's more. We'll gather them in the morning."

"Ouch!" The cloth Mara was using to hold the pan slipped and her fingers came in contact with the hot pan. Pack tossed the flowers to the table and was at her side in an instant.

"Here, let me take that." He grabbed the towel from the wash bench, took the hot pan from her hand and set it on the table.

"That towel's dirty, Pack," she chided gently because she couldn't think of anything else to say.

"Where did you burn yourself?" He grasped her wrist and pulled her up close to him.

"My fingers."

His big hand held hers in a gentle grip. He turned it and looked closely at the pad of her forefinger, rubbed his thumb across it, then lifted her hand quickly and stuck her finger into his mouth. Shock waves washed over Mara from the top of her head all the way to her toes. Pack's lips formed a firm cocoon around her second knuckle. His tongue, rough and wet, bathed the pad with gentle strokes. She drew in a gulp of air that came out with a sigh from between unconsciously parted lips. She started to speak but forgot what she was going to say.

He seemed to be completely absorbed in what he was doing. He towered over her, filling her world with his masculine presence. Mara looked up at him. Her green eyes, darkened by confusion, sought his. What she saw in the blue eyes looking into hers was bittersweet and oddly haunting. Then her dark lashes came down, shutting him out lest he see the debilitating weakness that his touch elicited.

"What . . . are you doing?" Her voice was gritty, thick. Her brain was fogged with bewilderment. All that registered was the exotic feeling of her finger in his mouth, his tongue stroking her flesh.

"I'm making it better," he said calmly when he pulled her wet and glistening finger from between his lips.

They were standing so close that she had to tilt her head to look up at him. His clean, damp scent filled her nose, her head. His brows were drawn together as he examined first the finger and then her thumb. She watched him through a haze of sensuality as he lifted her hand to his mouth again. His eyes, dark and clouded with concern, looked down into hers as his firm lips closed around her thumb. His tongue lathed the pad with a circular motion. Her eyes were eloquent with unspoken questions. Why did his touch leave her defenseless and cause her breath to come out in fragments?

"Feel better?" he asked.

She nodded. "It isn't a bad burn."

"Water takes out the fire."

"I'll remember."

"Your fingers taste like spices."

"It's from . . . the cake." She wet her lips and pulled her hand from his. "I should get the flowers in water. I've got just the thing to put them in."

She went to the shelf that stretched along the wall above the wash bench where she had placed the small crocks and reached up for a gray one with a blue stripe around the top. Her fingers could only touch the bottom.

"Is this the one you want?" Pack's chest was against her back, his chin stirred the top of her hair. Thick, muscular forearms with a shadowing of dark hair enclosed her as he reached above her head for the crock.

Mara nodded, then waited until he moved from behind her before she turned. She could not understand what was the matter with her and tried to swallow the excitement that bubbled up each time this body came in contact with hers. The sight of him with his sleeves pushed up to his elbows intrigued her. The buttons near the neck of his shirt were open, showing more dark hair. His powerful masculinity caused her heart to carom crazily, and even more shocking to her was the thought that floated into her mind. She wondered if God had made her from the rib of such a man as Pack Gallagher.

"This will be perfect." Mara said the words, knowing instinctively that they were the right words to say. She filled the crock with water and placed the flowers in it, pulling at the stems to spread the blooms. She lifted her head to see Pack frowning at the closed door going into his mother's room.

"Who's in there?"

"Cousin Aubrey."

"What the hell is he doing here *now?* He didn't bother to came yesterday or for days before that." His lips clamped down hard, his head came up, and he shot a furious sidelong glance at the door. When he started for it, Mara quickly stepped around the table and placed her hand on his arm.

"Pack—don't. Don't make a scene. For the twins' sake. Travor is just now beginning to see his father for what he is. We don't want to put that boy into the position of having to defend him."

"But . . . goddamn it, Mara Shannon, he put Ma through hell with his drinking and slipshod ways." The bitterness of his words drew the corners of his mouth down and caused his eyes to become rock hard.

"I know, but it's over. The twins will be the ones to suffer now if there's unpleasantness. Their mother was all that was good, stable, and secure in their lives. They need you more than ever now that she's gone."

She stood still. Her large emerald eyes pleaded with his as her fingertips lightly touched his arm. Their gazes met and locked. Pack slowly brushed the hair off her cheek with the back of his hand; his knuckles nudged her chin when he lowered his hand to cover the fingers on his arm. He took such a deep breath that his chest heaved.

"You're a sweet little thing, and you've got a good head on your shoulders." He dragged his eyes from hers and glanced at the door. "How long has he been in there?"

"Quite awhile. We can go in and put the flowers on the table beside Brita's bed. She loved flowers."

Mara moved ahead of Pack and opened the door. Aubrey was sitting on the bunk in the darkened room with his elbows on his knees, his face in his hands. He looked up when the door opened, then got to his feet.

"There's coffee in the pot on the stove, Cousin Aubrey, if you care to have some." Mara set the flowers on the table beside the bed. "Pack found these down by the creek. Aren't they lovely?"

Aubrey nodded and slipped out the door as if he expected Pack to attack him. Pack followed and Mara hurried after them. Aubrey slumped down on the bench, leaning his elbows on the trestle table. While Mara poured the coffee and placed it in front of him, Pack stood on the other side of the table. Aubrey's hands were shaking so badly that he could scarcely lift the cup. Pack put a foot up on the bench, rested his forearm on his knee, and leaned across the table.

"If you as much as smell the cork on a whiskey bottle between now and the burial, I'm going to break every bone in your miserable body." His face and his voice were so impersonal that Mara found it hard to believe he had spoken the threatening words.

Aubrey was under no such illusion. Pack's words sank into his mind like a stone dropped into a deep well. He nodded without looking up.

Chapter
NINE

Sporty Howard tilted his chair back against the wall and looked out the door toward the house. It was quiet in the rough log building. The men talked in muted tones out of respect for the dead. None of them had ever seen old drunken Aubrey's crippled wife; but she was a mother, and mothers were to be respected and cherished regardless of who they were. The majority of men in the bunkhouse had known only the love of their mothers and it was sacred to them.

"The useless old bitch finally give up the ghost," Cullen remarked. Two men rose up out of their seats and stared at him menacingly. After that he too had been quiet.

"Do ya think Sam's gone for good?" Sporty asked Cullen in low tones, not out of respect for the dead, but because he didn't want the men at the card table to hear.

"Naw. He'll be back."

"He took his bedroll."

"He always takes his stuff when he leaves. I'm thinkin' he don't want ya prowlin' through it, Sporty."

Sporty took no offense at the remark. He didn't even seem to hear it. His face was turned toward the door, and he was watching Pack draw water from the well.

"Pack'll be leavin' now. There ain't no reason fer him to be hangin' round. Do ya reckon he'll take the prissy ass redhead with him?"

"I suspect he'll try. The ole man thinks he will. He thinks Pack's got his nose to the ground 'n is smelling out a place for himself here. I think Miss Mara Shannon McCall will stay. She's as stubborn as her old man was. But there's ways round that. Pack's got to leave sometime 'n see bout his business in Laramie." A hint of a threat was in Cullen's voice.

"Ya plannin' on courtin' her?"

"Sheeit! I'm plannin' on gettin' her on her back 'n gettin' in her drawers. That's the only way I'll get this place. If it takes sweet talkin', I'll sweet-talk her. Hell! She's so proper she'd wed me like a shot if I plowed her. She'll figure she's been ruint 'n won't ever get another man." Cullen chuckled nastily. "I'd sure enough like to get me a blanket colt outta Miss Mara McCall. Whee! I'd be set."

"That ain't decent," Sporty said coolly.

Cullen looked at him with amazement. "What the hell ya taking about? Ain't decent? Hell! Ya wouldn't know *decent* if it jumped up 'n hit ya!"

"Don't ya be makin' no fun a me, Cullen. My folks was church-goin' folk. She's yore kin, yore cousin, ain't she? Ya wantin' to get ya a bunch a idiots?"

Cullen's expression turned to disgust.

"There ain't nothin' to that ole tale. 'Sides, her pa was my pa's cousin. Our blood ain't close enough to make idiots."

"What about that fat gal in Cheyenne ya was tellin' me bout?"

"I'd jist as soon hump a young heifer." Cullen snorted. "I'd a not messed with her a'tall if her pa didn't own the livery."

Sporty watched Aubrey cross the porch and go into the cookshack.

"Yore ole man's goin' to be pissin' coffee fer a week. He ain't touched his bottle today a'tall."

"He's scared shitless of Pack."

" 'N you ain't?"

"Hell, yes! I'd be a fool not to. He'd kill a man in a brawl. He's bigger 'n me, but I got more brains."

"If'n I was you, I'd get myself all slicked up 'n pay my respects to Mrs. McCall. It'll make gettin' yore foot in the door a lot easier later on."

"I been thinkin' on doin' jist that. Do ya have a clean shirt I could borrow?"

Mara stood beside the black wool scarf she had tied in a bow and fastened to the wall beside the front door, a symbol that there was a death in the house, and watched as Pack helped Emily from the wagon. As soon as Emily's feet were on the ground, her arms went about his waist and she hugged him.

As Mara watched this open display of affection, she was struck once again by the thought that Pack was in love with the near-blind girl and that her brother approved. For a reason unknown to her, chills chased over her skin. Charlie gripped Pack's hand warmly with one hand while squeezing his shoulder with the other. With a firm hand beneath Emily's elbow, Pack guided her up the steps to where Mara stood waiting. She greeted Mara with a hug.

"I thought about coming over yesterday, but Charlie was putting new traces on his harnesses and I hated to bother him. I had Brita on my mind. Oh, I wish I had come."

"Thank you for coming now. Come in and let me get you a cool drink of water. It turned out to be a warm day."

"Charlie, be careful with the basket when you bring it in." Emily spoke to her brother and then turned back to Mara. "I was baking a berry pie when Sam came by to tell us the news. I brought it and a few other things along. I came prepared to spend the night, if you need me."

"That's kind of you, Emily. You're most welcome."

Brita's body lay in the parlor beneath the clock that had been stopped at the time of her death. Pack and the twins had removed a door and placed it on two barrels. After Mara covered it with a quilt, Pack carried his mother's body from the bedroom. In the darkened parlor she appeared to be sleeping peacefully. Her lower limbs were covered with a sheet and the flowers Pack had picked were beside her pillow.

Mara waited beside the door while Pack and his friends stood beside the bier. When Emily reached out, Pack guided her hand to where his mother's hands lay folded. Emily placed her warm palm on Brita's cold hands for a moment, her head bowed. When she lifted her head, her eyes were filled with tears.

"She fulfilled her destiny," Emily whispered tearfully. "She came to this earth and left something behind to mark the time she spent here. She left you, Pack, and the twins."

The misery was so clearly etched in Pack's face that Mara was overwhelmed by the tenderness and concern she felt for him. Pack's arm moved across Emily's shoulder. Emily leaned against him, Pack's dark head tilted toward her light one, and he placed his cheek against her hair.

Feeling as if she were intruding, Mara slipped out of the room and went to the kitchen. A surge of emotion unlike any she had experienced touched her to the core. Pack was not alone. His friends were there to give him comfort. But she had never felt more alone in her life.

Mara was distracted from her dark thoughts when Travor and Trellis came to the kitchen on their way to the creek. She supplied them with soap and clean towels and volunteered to iron the shirts they would wear to the funeral service. Mara had developed a genuine fondness for the boys.

"Supper will be ready at sundown," Mara said. "Ask your father to come up to the house and eat with us."

"He won't," Travor said and opened the screen door.

"But you'll be here, won't you?"

Trellis answered. "We'll be here."

The boys and Charlie ate heartily of the supper Mara and Emily prepared. Pack ate little while he and Charlie talked in muted voices, as befitted a house of mourning. When Charlie was ready to leave, he and Pack went to hitch up the team.

Sam returned from Laramie shortly after Charlie left for home. When he rode his tired horse up the path toward the corrals, Pack went to the back door and hailed him.

"Hey, Sam!"

Sam turned his horse and rode up to the porch.

"The preacher'll be here before noon. He'll be bringin' his missus 'n a nice box from the furniture store."

"Much obliged, Sam. Did you have to do any arm-twisting on the reverend?"

Sam grinned. "Not much. He's mighty proud a that colored glass window, 'n he ain't wantin' no rock bustin' it up."

"Son of a bitch," Pack muttered under his breath because Mara had come out to hang up the wet dish towels. Emily stood in the doorway.

Sam's eyes rested on Emily's quiet face. He put his fingers to the brim of his hat and nodded his head in greeting, then cursed himself for forgetting that he was probably only a blur to her.

"Howdy, ladies."

"Come in and let us fix you some supper, Sam. There's plenty left over."

"Thank ya, ma'am, fer the invite, but I'll get on down to the cookshack 'n see what ole Steamboat has hashed up. I got pounds a road dust on my back that's got to come off before I'm fit fer a lady's company."

"Come up this evening for coffee."

"Yes, ma'am. Thank ya."

Sam turned his horse toward the corral. Glancing over his shoulder, he saw Emily's face turned toward him. As he watched, she brushed her feathery hair from her forehead with the back of her hand, a gesture that was becoming familiar to him. *She didn't even let on that she knew he was there.* Now why in the hell was that so damned important to him? He knew why even as he asked himself the question.

The image of her face and the fantasy of holding her in his arms had lurked in the back of his mind during the long ride. He had ridden his tired horse harder than he should in order to get back, knowing that she would be there and that he would have a chance to see her. The truth suddenly struck him like an unavoidable shot from ambush. It was there instantly, big as life and twice as powerful. He was not going to be able to ride away from this woman and forget her when his work was finished.

As darkness approached, candles were lit in the parlor and the family gathered for the death vigil. Mara was surprised to see Cullen, bathed and shaved, quiet and respectful, arrive with Aubrey. They swung around the house, came in the front door, and took the chairs at the end of the bier. When the twins came, she asked them to carry in a bench from the porch to sit on. She and Emily sat on the straight wooden kitchen chairs, and Pack, ignoring Cullen and his father, sat down on a box with his forearms resting on his thighs, his huge hands clasped between his knees.

Minutes turned into an hour. Mara's mind went over the events that would take place the next day. The preacher and his wife would be out in the morning with the burial box. The scarcity of furnishings in the house would be embarrassing to her, but there was nothing she could do about that now. Working with what she had, she had made the house as presentable as possible.

The stars came out. The moon came up, its light making a shadow of the house across the yard. A breeze moved through the treetops over the homestead, bringing with it the sound of an owl hooting.

Inside the parlor Mara began to squirm. Not only was the chair hard on her bottom, but each time she looked up, Cullen's bold, admiring eyes were on her. Being so nearsighted, Emily was unaware of the stare, and Pack was unable to see from where he sat on the box. Trellis had noticed Mara's discomfort, shuffled his feet to get his half brother's attention, then scowled at him. Cullen merely gave him an insolent glare. One time the corners of Cullen's mouth had lifted in a half smile when Mara's eyes met his. After that she refused to turn her face in his direction.

"I'll go make fresh coffee," Mara whispered to Emily

when she felt she could sit still no longer. She tiptoed from the room without a sound.

In the kitchen she leaned against the trestle table and massaged her temples with her fingers. She couldn't remember ever having been so tired. Her hands felt as if each weighed a hundred pounds when she lifted the chimney to light the lamp. For a long excruciating moment she stared around her.

The kitchen was the largest room in the house, and here she had worked the hardest. The oak slab top of the table had been scrubbed and polished to a glowing finish. On the work counters, food for tomorrow's dinner was covered with clean dish towels. The cloth curtain that was strung on a rod to hide the utensils stored below was starched and ironed. The cookstove was cleaned, the woodbox was filled, the lamp chimneys were polished, and the plank floor scrubbed. She had even mended the rips in the screen door with a heavy wool thread. The work had kept her mind so busy that she'd had no time to think of how she was going to stay now that Brita was gone.

Working quietly, Mara shook down the ashes in the firebox and filled it with kindling, prodding it until it blazed. She filled the coffeepot from the water bucket, removed a round cap from the top of the range with the lid-lifter, and set the black-bottomed pot down in the hole.

The bud of the thought that had been in the back of her mind since morning came forward in full bloom. *Pack would leave after the burial.* No longer would there be a reason for him to stay. What would she do then? She was sure that because of his friendship with her father he felt responsible for her. He would insist that she go to Laramie, Cheyenne, or Denver and get a teaching job. That she would never do!

The thought of not having her own home and having to live in a boarding house, teaching children who didn't want to learn, working without adequate supplies and kowtowing to the school board members and their wives was so repulsive to her that she felt a hard, heavy knot begin to form in her stomach just thinking about it.

She would not do it! She had the right to make her own

decisions. Women in Wyoming Territory had been given the right to vote. Earlier that year six women had served on a jury in Laramie. If a woman was capable of meting out justice, she was capable of deciding her own future. Mara considered herself as smart as any woman on that jury. She'd not be pushed into leaving her home.

Mara's mind was so distracted with miserable thoughts that she failed to hear Cullen come into the room. She turned to see him standing a few paces behind her and gasped with fright.

"Don't you dare sneak up on me like that! You scared me!" she snapped.

"I just wanted to know if there was anythin' ya needed."

Cullen was only slightly taller than Mara's five and a half feet. His face was charmingly handsome when he smiled, but the smile never quite reached his eyes. There was something cold and unfeeling about him. Her eyes flashed contemptuously over him before she swung around, opened the curtains below the workbench and took out the cups.

"There's nothing I need now. But the day after tomorrow you and I will have a talk. You will tell me about the men who spend their days playing cards in the bunkhouse, and you will tell me where the cash money has been coming from to run this place. Something underhanded is going on here, and I intend to find out what it is."

"I agree, Mara Shannon. As the owner it's your right to know everythin' that goes on."

Mara was so startled that she gaped at him for a moment. She had fully expected him to be as sullen and obnoxious as he had been the other two times she had spoken to him.

"I want an accounting of the cattle—"

"Sure," he broke in, nodding in agreement. "I know every steer and heifer on this place."

"You've kept accounts?"

"I ain't had much book learnin', Mara Shannon. I got the figures up here." He tapped his head with his forefinger.

"That's a risky way of doing business."

"You've got the book learnin' to keep accounts. I got the know-how to do the rest. If we work together, we can make this place pay. We'll sell off some of the cattle and fix up the house. We'd have enough to buy a buggy so ya can go to town when ya want.'' He rolled his hat around in his hands and looked down at the floor. When he lifted his eyes to look at her, they were filled with remorse. ''I'm sorry about what happened when ya first come, Mara. I ain't got no excuse but to say it was a jolt havin' ya drop in on us like ya did.''

He seemed so sincere that Mara could almost believe him.

''There's no point in looking back, Cullen. I never—'' Mara broke off when Pack came striding into the room.

''Get the hell out of here, Cullen. Stay away from Mara Shannon.'' Pack's tone and his expression reflected his anger. He loomed over the shorter man, his clenched fists at his sides. All pretense of civility was gone.

''Sure, Pack. If that's what ya want. I've too much respect for your ma to cause a fuss when she ain't even in the ground yet.'' Cullen's eyes went to Mara with a look of apology.

Pack snorted. ''Respect! You've never respected anything in your miserable life. You don't even respect yourself. But I'll not argue with you. Heed my words and stay away from Mara Shannon or else I'll tear your head off.''

''I said all right.'' Cullen spoke soothingly. ''Let's not start anythin' with your dear, dead mother lyin' in there.'' At the end there was a trace of mockery in his voice.

A blanket of silence covered the room.

Pack went very taut, a muscle twitched at the corner of his mouth. His face turned a dull red and his eyes, dark and fiery, compelled Mara's to meet them. She knew he was near the breaking point.

The sudden hissing sound of water dancing on the top of the hot range as the coffeepot boiled over broke the silence.

''Tend to the coffee, Mara Shannon,'' Pack said quietly.

A prickle of uneasiness went up Mara's spine. Pack's muscles were as tight as a coiled spring. Instinctively she knew that he was on the verge of slamming into Cullen. The smaller man stood his ground, seemingly unperturbed. Finally he edged toward the back door.

''I'll go, Mara Shannon. I ain't goin' to be the cause a any trouble." He cast Pack a glance of disgust. "It ain't decent at a time like this."

Cullen can charm the skin off a snake when he sets his mind to it. The words Brita spoke the day she arrived came to Mara's mind. Too many things had happened between that day and this for her to believe Cullen was sincere. She was glad when he went out the back door instead of returning to the parlor. Unpleasantness had been avoided for the time being, but she dreaded what the next day would bring.

Mara wrapped the end of her apron around the handle of the coffeepot and lifted it out of the hole. She replaced the lid by sliding it across the iron top with the lifter. It made a grating, familiar sound that eased the tension. The aroma of freshly ground coffee filled the air as Pack turned the crank on the grinder fastened to the wall beside the stove. When the jar beneath it was half full, Mara removed the lid on the pot, and he dumped the grounds into the boiling water.

"What did he say to you?"

"He said he would tell me about the men in the bunkhouse and give me an accounting of the cattle."

"That's all?"

"That's all, except he expects me to stay here."

"The bastard!" Pack snorted. "He'd like nothing better than to have you here all by yourself."

A silence fell while Mara dipped the granite ladle into the water bucket and drank. Pack leaned his shoulder against the wall and watched her. She had worn a pink dress during the day while she was working. It was faded from many washings, but it had added color to her cheeks and emphasized her breasts and small waist. She had looked young and pretty in the pink. Now in the black dress, she still looked young and pretty, but dark shadings beneath her green eyes told of sleepless nights and a day of unceasing labor. He studied her face, unable to pull his eyes from her delicate features and huge emerald green eyes. A sprinkling of freckles dotted her nose that he hadn't noticed before.

Something tightened in Pack's throat. He wanted to pull her to him and tell her that his grief had been easier to bear

because she had been with him. And yet he wanted to shake
her for coming in the first place and for not realizing that
there was no way on God's green earth she could stay now
that his mother was gone.

"Mara Shannon?" Emily came into the kitchen, feeling
her way along with her hand on the wall. "Do you need any
help?"

"There's not much left to do. The coffee will be ready as
soon as I pour in a little cold water to settle the grounds."

"It's awfully hot in there. Phew! It's almost as hot here in
the kitchen, but the little breeze coming in the door helps."

"Do you want to go out onto the porch and cool off?"
Pack asked when she pulled her handkerchief from her pocket
to wipe her brow and fluttered it in front of her face to create
a slight breeze.

"I'll step out there for a minute. I should have worn
something cooler, but this is my only black dress." As she
moved around the table, Pack took her arm. "I can find the
way, Pack. I'll stand just outside the door."

Pack went ahead of her and opened the screen door just as
Sam stepped up onto the porch.

"Evenin', Sam. Miss Rivers was coming out to get a
breath of air."

"Evenin', folks." Sam reached for Emily's elbow as she
stepped over the threshold. "Will ya allow me to stay with ya
for awhile, ma'am?"

"I'd like that, Sam. Oh, my! The breeze feels good."

"We'll stay here on the porch, Pack. I'll see that she don't
fall off the edge."

Pack shut the screen door. When he swung around, his
hard gaze sought Mara's. The muscle stood out in the hard
plane of his cheek and his mouth was grim. She waited for
him to voice his disapproval, but he remained silent. From
the harsh expression on his face, it was clear to Mara that he
was not pleased about Emily being alone in the dark with
Sam.

*   *   *

On the porch Emily reached out for Sam's arm. "Do we have to stay on the porch, Sam?"

"I told Pack we would."

She laughed softly. "He's as bad as Charlie about not letting me out of his sight. We could walk a few steps out into the yard. He could still see us."

"All right. I reckon it's worth gettin' a beatin' from Pack just ta hear ya laugh, ma'am."

She laughed again. "He wouldn't do that. He's as gentle as a lamb."

"Bull-foot! There ain't nothin' gentle about Pack when he's riled up. I'd say he's more like a tornado. One thin' about him, he's touchy where womenfolk is concerned. Stop here 'n let me lift ya down."

Sam stepped off the porch, placed her hands on his shoulders and his at her waist, then swung her easily off the porch and to the ground. He didn't know why he got so loose-lipped all of a sudden.

"You're awfully strong."

"Yore just not very heavy, ma'am."

"The other time you called me Emily Rose."

"I've been thinkin' of ya as Emily Rose."

"What did you think?" It was a mere whisper as she placed her hand in the crook of his arm.

Sam looked down at the white blur that was her face. Without thinking his hand came up and covered the one on his arm. He couldn't tell her that sometimes thinking about her made him feel all mixed up and shaky inside, and at other times he was surprised by the burst of happiness that washed over him.

"What did you think, Sam?" she asked again. She could feel the trembling in the hand that covered hers.

"Well . . . I was wonderin' what ya was doin'. If ya was well."

"I thought about you too."

"Did ya? What was ya thinkin'?"

"I was wondering what you were doing. If you were well."

They both laughed, unaware that they had stopped and were facing each other.

"Sam . . . I say stupid things when I'm with you. And for the life of me, I don't know why."

"I do it too, 'n cuss myself after."

"I'm twenty-four years old." Her eyes seemed to be looking right into his.

"I'm twenty-eight."

'I'm a . . . spinster."

"It means ya ain't married, don't it?"

"It means that I'm what's known as an old maid. A woman who lives with her family. A woman without a husband. A woman whom men consider too old to court."

"Ah . . . that's bull. Pack seems to be right fond of ya."

She laughed again, her face not far from his. Sam could see her soft lips part, smell her fresh woman's body. He liked the feel of her hands on his arms, clinging to him, trusting him, depending on him to keep her safe.

"I'm fond of Pack. I love him the way I love Charlie. He's the only male friend I've had besides old Squirrely who lives up in the hills behind us."

"Why is that?" Questions filled Sam's mind, questions he didn't want to think about now and spoil this magical moment, but things he'd have to think about later.

"Charlie is afraid someone . . . will take advantage of me because I'm almost blind."

"Charlie's right to keep the riffraff away from ya. It's what I'd a done for Rose."

"Charlie feels guilty because he was off fighting the war when . . . when. . . ."

"Someone took liberties?" A sudden, desperate anger made his words come harshly before he could stop them.

"Yes," she whispered. "During the war. Does it make a . . . difference?"

"A difference?" he asked, not understanding. Then, as the meaning of her words soaked into his brain, "Good God! 'Course not!" He would have started walking again, but she refused to let go of his arms.

"Are you sure?"

"Emily Rose." The husky syllables had the sound of a plea.

"It was bad, Sam. There were three of them. I'm telling you this because I don't want you to think that I'm . . . pure—" She stopped talking suddenly. Her stricken face turned up to his. After an instant of frozen stillness, he spoke in a grating whisper.

"Where are they?"

"Charlie came home, found them, and killed them."

"It's what I'd a done!" The breath he was holding came out in a rush of air. "Oh, you sweet, sweet woman!" His voice was low and raspy. "The goddamn, dirty low-down bastards!"

Her hands dropped and his arms closed around her, holding her warm, safe, strong. It was a mutual coming together. Neither of them was conscious of making the first move. Her soft, slender form came against his tall hard one. Her cheek found a place on his shoulder, her nose and mouth against the firm, warm flesh of his neck. She took a deep, shuddering breath and was still.

The breeze came up and wrapped her long skirt about his legs.

A great tenderness welled up in him. She had been so honest, wanting him to know this terrible thing that had happened to her. Now she was so trusting in his arms. He swallowed, fighting the constriction in his throat. He wanted to kill again the ones who had violated her, but never had he wanted to do anything so much as he wanted to protect and cherish this wonderful creature in his arms.

"Sam?" she said softly against his neck. "I'm twenty-four years old and I've not known a lover's kiss."

"Then I think it's time ya did." He lowered his head and pressed a gentle kiss to her lips.

It was over all too quickly for Emily. The first gentle touch of his lips awakened a bittersweet ache of passion. She lifted her arms and wound them around his neck. His arms held her so closely against him that she could feel the hard bones and muscles of his body thrusting against the softness of hers. It was so strange being this close to him, her breasts flattened against his chest, his knees touching her thighs. A curiously warm, exciting feeling fluttered in her stomach. Sam's hoarse, ragged breathing accompanied the thunder of his heartbeat against her breast.

Her hands moved around and framed his face. The soft bubble of laughter that broke from her lips was a mere whisper in the night.

"What are you thinking about me now, Mr. Sam Sparks?" Her voice was a soft happy sound. "I bet you're thinking this is a brazen woman if I ever saw one."

"I'm thinkin' it's yore turn to kiss me now."

He waited, trembling with the desire to crush her to him, to move his hands down her back to her buttocks, to press her against his aching arousal, to caress the softness of her breasts, and to kiss her until she wanted him as much as he wanted her.

Dear God! What was he thinking? She had endured so much pain and humiliation at the hands of the scum that attacked her! How could she ever accept a lover? His arms loosened and he moved back until her breasts were no longer pressed to his chest.

"Emily Rose, ya needn't if ya don't want to."

Her hands remained on his shoulders. "I want to, Sam. Have you changed your mind about wanting me to?"

"Yo're the purtiest 'n sweetest woman I ever did know. I've got no right to even be touchin' ya, much less kissin' ya. Ya best mind yore brother. He knows what a man gets to thinkin' 'n feelin' when he's holdin' a sweet, purty woman. I ain't wantin' to hurt ya or scare ya with my rough ways."

"I was afraid it was . . . the other thing. Back home I was considered ruined, no longer fit for marriage. My friends stopped calling. They pitied me but didn't want to associate with me. That's why I wanted you to know. Pack knows, but I'm not sure Mara Shannon will want me for a friend after I tell her, which I will."

"They weren't yore friends if they turned their backs on ya. They were a bunch a goddamn fools!"

Hungrily his eyes slid over her upturned face as she rose on tiptoe, nuzzling his hard lips with her soft ones. Their breaths mingled for an instant before he covered her mouth with his. He held her with gentle strength. There was no haste in the kiss. This time it was slow and deliberate. He took his time with closed eyes and pounding heart. She offered herself willingly, their bodies meshed, close and warm and hard. Her mouth opened under the force of his, yielding, molding itself to the shape of his. There was a soft union of lips and tongues as their mouths parted and clung with wild sweetness that held still the moments of time. A lovely feeling unfolded in Emily's midsection as she allowed herself the pure joy of kissing and being kissed by him.

Abruptly he seized her arms and held her away from him.

"Sam . . ." she said weakly.

"I'm sorry, Emily Rose. I never meant for it to go that far." His voice was husky with regret.

"I'm not one bit sorry." She reached for his face with her palms. "Please don't regret kissing me."

"Regret it? God knows I don't!"

"I've thought about being with you like this since that first day when I bandaged your hands. Remember? I wanted to see your face, and I finally got up the courage to put my face close to yours so I could see you. You're handsome, Sam!"

"Emily Rose," he whispered huskily. "I've got nothin' to . . . to offer a woman."

She drew back from him and her body stiffened. "I don't expect anything. You're not to feel obligated because you kissed me, for heaven's sake."

"What are ya talkin' about?"

"I know what I am, Sam. I'm a spinster whose innocence was taken by morally corrupt men. I wanted to know how it felt to have a good man hold me and kiss me. I'm a blind woman who would be like a millstone about a man's neck. Charlie has extracted a promise from Pack to look after me if something should happen to him. Poor Pack. See what our friendship has done to him? I'll be his burden instead of Charlie's—"

"Hush up talkin' 'bout yoreself like that." Sam's hands on her arms gripped and pulled her to him. "Ya'd not be a burden to any man."

"What I said was true, Sam. All true." She pressed her face against his shirt, not wanting him to see the spurt of tears that filled her eyes. She was aware of the heavy beat of his heart and placed her hand over it.

"Emily Rose, look at me. Oh, hell, what am I sayin'? I keep forgettin' ya can't see." Sam held her away from him and looked down into her face. "Ya know nothin' 'bout me. Fer all ya know, I could be low caliber like the ones who did ya harm."

"I can see you, Sam. Not plain, but I can see you. You'll never make me believe you're anything but an honorable man."

"Pack's lookin' out the door." His whispered voice was husky with emotion. He lifted her hand and pressed his lips to her palm. "We don't want him comin' out here with blood in his eye."

Emily would have been content to stay there forever. The last few minutes had been the most wonderful moments of her life. She had a hundred sweet memories to store away and bring out during the long nights when she lay in her lonely bed. She drew away from him and lifted her hands to tuck the stray hair into the knot at the nape of her neck.

"No. We don't want that. Do you mind walking for a few minutes before we go in?" Her voice was strangely quiet. He guided her hand into the crook of his arm. "Tell me about your sister, Sam. Tell me about Rose."

Chapter
TEN

———

Had someone called her name?

Mara awakened from a sound sleep and lay staring into the darkness; her muscles tense, heart thumping. The wind rippling the tin roof, so close to the bed tucked beneath the sloped ceiling, moaned like a woman in pain. A feeling of relief washed over her when she realized what had awakened her. Pitch darkness stretched out beyond the window. She lay still for a long while, afraid to move, to risk waking Emily.

When she could stand it no longer, she eased out of the bed and groped in the darkness for her dress. She slipped it on over her nightgown and crept down the stairs. A faint light led her to the parlor door. Pack sat on the bench, his head against the wall, his long legs stretched out in front of him. She thought she had not made any noise, but his head rolled toward her the instant she appeared in the doorway.

"What are you doing up, Mara Shannon?"

"I came to relieve you. Go lie down and get some rest."

He reached a hand out to her. "Come sit with me."

Mindless, she put her hand in his. How tired he looked. His cheekbones stood above hollowed cheeks shadowed with a day's growth of dark beard. The deep blue eyes that squinted up at her were ringed with dark smudges. His hair was a tangled mass of dark curls.

He pulled her down onto the bench beside him.

"Have you had any sleep at all?"

"Some." His hand curled around hers, pressing their two palms together.

"You didn't get much sleep last night," she chided gently. She was so close to him that her shoulder fit snugly against his arm and her thigh and hip nestled against his.

"I couldn't leave her here alone, Mara Shannon. She's going to be alone for a such a long time."

The pain in his voice almost broke her heart. She gripped his hand tightly, wishing desperately for words that would ease his grief.

"Ah, Pack . . . don't grieve so. It isn't your mother you'll be putting in the ground tomorrow." Her voice was a trembly whisper. "It's the shell she lived in while she was here. She's happy now and free from that tired, crippled body. She's walking beside your father, her hand in his." Pack let out a long shuddering sigh, and Mara blinked rapidly so that she could see him through her tears. "She spoke of him only one time, but when she did, her face glowed with pure happiness."

"It almost killed her when he died." The voice didn't sound like Pack's voice.

"She's with him now, and she wouldn't want you to take on so." Mara spoke with trembling lips, but with a firmness in her voice despite the constriction in her throat. "How long have you been here alone?"

"When the old man left, I sent the boys to bed." He tilted his head back against the wall again and closed his eyes. "I'm glad you're here." Her arm was held firmly against his body, his fingers finding the spaces between hers.

She glanced at their clasped hands resting on his thigh, then up at his face. Her insides quivered. To her he looked almost as young and defenseless as his young brothers. Six weeks ago she had not known who he was. Now he was very . . . dear to her. She snuggled contentedly against him, lifted her bare feet to the bench and covered them with her skirt.

Pack had replaced the candles with the kerosene lamp from the kitchen. It was turned low, and occasionally it flickered, causing the shadows to dance on the floor. It was peaceful here in the room with Brita and Pack. She was comfortable leaning against his warm strength. Mara glanced up at his profile. His mouth was slightly open and he was breathing steadily.

He had gone to sleep.

Mara closed her eyes, and in spite of herself, yawned. Soon her head drooped against his shoulder. When she awakened, the light of dawn was coming in through the window. It took a short while for her to realize where she was. It was deliciously warm against him. She had turned during her sleep and his arm was between her breasts. She kept perfectly still for a long moment, then gradually tilted her head and looked up. His eyes were open and he was looking at her.

"Mornin'."

"Is it morning already?" Her voice was slurred with sleep.

"The rooster thinks so. He crowed a long time ago."

"I'm sorry," she breathed. "I should have stayed awake and been company for you."

He continued to look at her, lifting her hand and bumping it gently against his thigh. The light of dawn had softened the tired lines in his face, yet his eyes were such a deep blue they were almost black.

"Sweet little Mara—" His hand slipped up beneath her hair and stroked the nape of her neck. "I'm going to kiss you. I was thinking about it while I watched you sleep. Don't say anything, don't make a fuss. I need it."

She felt herself succumb to the gentle pressure of his hand at her nape. Slowly he bent his head until his lips touched hers. She was surprised that his lips were so soft, so gentle, surprised at the pleasant drag of his whiskers on her cheek.

He held her head in his large hand, working his fingers through her hair while his lips made little caressing movements against hers. His hand was firm, his lips soft.

With a swift motion he wrapped her in his arms and his kiss deepened. He gave her no chance to withdraw. Nor did she want to. Her stomach knotted. The touch of his tongue on her lower lip caused surging motions deep inside her and drove her to press closer. She wanted it to go on and on but knew it had to stop.

Together they drew away. It was over quickly and she let her breath out slowly. She hadn't wanted the kiss to end. She wanted more! What had started out to be a chaste, sweet, comforting kiss ended in a kiss of an entirely different nature! She looked into his eyes. He had wanted more too. She could see it reflected in the tense lines of his face. Then why had he stopped?

In the flickering illumination of the mantel lamp, his eyes were as dark as midnight and, like the lamp, they glowed. Mara became conscious of his hand stroking the length of her hair and his low voice speaking to her again.

"Is that the way that Webster fellow kissed you?"

"No! I told you—"

He wasn't listening. He held up her hand, looked closely at each broken nail, and stroked her palm with his thumb.

"You've worked too hard here. When you came here this little hand was as soft as silk and each little nail rounded and smooth."

"Pack—"

Shivers of awareness went through her. She tugged on her hand, but his fingers tightened and refused to let it go. Instead, he lifted it and gently pressed his lips to her knuckles. A long moment passed while his eyes held hers. She held her breath. Her heart almost stopped beating when he turned her hand so that the ridges of her knuckles rubbed back and forth across his lips.

"It will be soft again, Mara Shannon. I promise." His soft words echoed through the storm that shook her, but she couldn't comprehend them.

She unfolded her cramped legs and placed her feet on the

floor. As soon as the tingling stopped, she tugged her hand from his and got to her feet.

"I'll start breakfast."

"You'll get splinters in your feet. Go put on your shoes; I'll start the fire." He stood and gave her a gentle push toward the door.

The bewildering moment was over, but it was not gone from her mind. It stayed with her as she dressed and caused her to converse absently with Emily who had already washed, dressed, and tidied the room. Finally the other girl, sensing her preoccupation, lapsed into silence and waited until they could go down to the kitchen together.

While she was preparing breakfast, irrational anger at herself for what she had allowed to happen surged through Mara. She had sat there like a lump of lard and allowed Pack to kiss her, knowing perfectly well that he didn't even *like* her! What had gotten into her? She didn't care much for him either! Anger and humiliation caused her to set the iron skillet down on the top of the range with a bang. Immediately she was sorry and glanced around to see if Emily had noticed. Thankfully she had stepped out onto the porch to hand Pack the empty water bucket.

Mara's thoughts continued to churn. She had merely been decent to Pack for Brita's sake. He had said all manner of vile things to her after she had almost ruptured herself getting the big ox into the wagon and bringing him here! She hadn't forgotten the morning he accused her of parading around in her nightclothes to attract attention. And she hadn't forgotten that he called her baggage! How could she have been so stupid as to allow him to kiss her?

Pack came in and spoke quietly to Emily. Mara kept her back to him until he sat down at the table. He and the twins ate hurriedly and, to Mara's relief, left immediately for the burial site to prepare the grave.

"They're taking the wagon and Sam's going with them," Mara said to Emily when she came in from hanging the wet towels on the porch line. It was becoming a habit with Mara to relate things to Emily that the near-blind girl couldn't see. "Sam and Pack seem to get on well together."

"Pack never mentioned anything to me or Charlie about knowing him."

"I like Sam. He's different from the others who hang around the bunkhouse. I don't know why he's here or what he does every day when he rides out, but he has something on his mind." Mara was aware of the interest on Emily's face. "Did Sam tell you where he's from?"

"He said he was from Texas and that he had a sister named Rose who was killed while he was away fighting in the war."

Emily turned to place a stack of plates on the table, but not before Mara saw the blush that covered her cheeks. Questions began to form in Mara's mind. If there was something between Pack and Emily, why did she blush at the mere mention of Sam Sparks? And was Pack so low-down that he would kiss Mara when he was in love with another woman? Mara desperately wanted a quiet time so that she could be alone to think about the triangle, but too much depended upon her today. Nevertheless, it lurked like a dark shadow in the back of her mind.

Because all had to be in readiness for the burial by the time the preacher arrived, Pack and the twins went to the creek to wash as soon as they returned to the house, taking with them soap and towels Mara had laid out and the clean shirts she had ironed the day before.

Steamboat sent word up to Mara that the hindquarter of beef he had started to cook at midnight would be ready by noon. Now, with the preparations for dinner complete, the women were free to carry the teakettles of warm water up to Mara's room so that they could wash and dress for the service. Mara was in a better frame of mind. She had decided to cope with each event of the day as it happened in the best way she knew how. Tomorrow would be time enough to think about other things.

In somber black dresses, their hair pinned back so severely that not a single frivolous curl was allowed to escape, Mara and Emily went to the parlor. The twins, Pack and Charlie were there. Charlie wore a black serge suit and Mara found herself wishing that Pack had a coat to wear. The shirt she had ironed was tucked neatly into his breeches and he was wearing a black string tie. She didn't know where the tie came from unless Charlie had brought it.

The twins didn't even look up when their father came to stand in the doorway. Aubrey looked worse than Mara had ever seen him. His face showed the ravages of dissipation even though he had gone to great pains to make himself presentable. Mara went to him.

"Come sit over here, Cousin Aubrey." She took his arm and led him to a chair at the head of the bier.

"The preacher's comin'." It was Cullen who called the words from the porch.

Pack got to his feet. "Mara Shannon? Will you come with me to greet the preacher's missus?"

"Of course." She went ahead of him out the door, stood beside him at the top of the steps, and watched the approach of the black buggy pulled by a handsome black horse. A lone rider rode behind, and behind him was a wagon carrying the burial box.

Mara heard a low hissing sound that came from Pack. At the same instant she recognized the rider as Ace January. She looked up quickly and saw a flicker of anger on Pack's face. Why, for heaven's sake, was he angry because the marshal had come to his mother's burial? She had no time to think about it because the buggy pulled up in front of the house, and Sam came off the end of the porch to stand at the horse's head while the preacher climbed down from the buggy. He removed his duster, folded it, and placed it on the floor, then helped his wife to alight. She also wore a duster, a cape that her husband lifted from her shoulders.

Pack ignored the man and woman and went to the wagon that had pulled up behind the buggy. He jumped into the wagon bed to inspect the box, picked up a rag, and wiped the dust from the top. When he jumped down again, he saw that the marshal was still sitting on his horse watching Mara. A muscle jumped in Pack's jaw as he ground his teeth together. Later, he told himself, later he would have a word with Ace January.

"Let me do this, Pack." Sam came to take the end of the box and the driver took the other end. They carried it past

Cullen who stood on the porch, his thumbs hooked in his belt. Pack elbowed him out of the way and held open the door for the men to take the burial box into the house.

Ace January continued to lean on his saddle horn, watching Mara, making no move to step down from the horse.

Mara went down the steps to meet the preacher and his wife. "Mrs. Piedmont, I'm Mara Shannon McCall."

The woman looked at her with her head tilted to one side, her small mouth pursed. She was not as tall as Mara, but her bosom was enormous, making her look top-heavy. Her stiff, black taffeta dress was buttoned up to her chin. Black hair threaded with gray was coiled and pinned over each ear, and she wore a small straw hat trimmed with a black feather plume. She was sweating profusely.

Mara held out her hand. The woman held her breath as if the air was filled with an offensive odor. Her face reflected her reluctance to take Mara's hand.

"How do you do?"

Mara was puzzled by the hostility. The woman spoke briskly and touched her hand as if it were not clean. The minister's face was red, his flabby jaws shaking. He looked like a puffed-up toad about to explode. From the looks of the pair, Mara thought, they had not missed a meal in their entire lives.

"Reverend Piedmont, it's unfortunate we have to meet under these sad circumstances. Welcome to my home."

"Thank you, Mrs. McCall."

"Miss McCall. I'm not married."

"Ah . . . I assumed you were married to the younger McCall."

Mara didn't answer. She would not satisfy the morbid curiosity of this pompous pair. They had not wanted to come. It was written on their fat faces and in their pious, stiff-necked attitudes. Mara wanted to tell them to get back in the buggy and leave, but good manners had been ingrained in her by her mother and later by Miss Fillamore's teachings.

"Would you like a cool drink?" Mara lifted her brows and spoke in a tone of quiet reserve that Miss Fillamore used when she was forced to be polite.

"Yes, I would. It's more than six miles out to this . . . place. It's a miserable ride and I've not been well." Mrs. Piedmont waved her handkerchief before her face.

"I'm sorry to hear it. Come in. It's a bit cooler in the house."

Mara led them through the parlor where Pack and Sam were lifting Brita's body and placing it in the coffin. When they reached the kitchen, she dipped into the water bucket with the dipper she took from the nail on the wall and handed it, brimming full, to the woman. Mrs. Piedmont hesitated, gave her husband a withering glare, then carefully inspected the dipper. An Irish imp inside Mara prompted her to speak.

"You needn't be afraid to drink from it. The dipper is clean." The tilt of her lips was more a sneer than a smile. Her chin was high and her eyes as cold as ice. She prayed she'd be able to endure this woman at least until after the services.

"A body can't be sure." Mrs. Piedmont sniffed and took a few sips from the dipper before handing it to her husband.

"Hrumph!" He cleared his throat noisily before he drank. The auburn-haired woman before him looked as cool as a cucumber in spite of the hot day. She wasn't at all what he had expected to find in a place like this, but he knew well that a ladylike appearance could be deceiving. Didn't the whore at the Diamond Saloon look like a lady during the light of day? But at night her true identity was revealed. She turned into a painted, naked siren, drawing unsuspecting men into her den of iniquity, corrupting their souls with lust.

"I have written a eulogy I wish you to read at the gravesite." The woman's voice broke into the minister's thoughts. He took the paper from her hand, glanced at it, and nodded.

Reverend Piedmont wanted nothing more than to get the service over with and head back to town. Since the marshal had volunteered to ride out with him he felt safe enough. It was his congregation he feared. He didn't know what their reaction would be if they found out he had come running at the request of the infamous pugilist of Laramie.

Mara rode on the seat beside Emily and Charlie on the way to the burial ground, and Aubrey sat on the tailgate. They followed Pack and the twins who walked behind the wagon carrying the coffin. The preacher's buggy, the marshal, and Cullen on horseback completed the procession.

The place where Shannon and Colleen LaMont McCall were buried was a quiet, beautiful spot shaded by tall pines. The knoll was fresh and green. Wild violet and buttercup blossoms nodded in the late morning sun. A slight breeze ruffled the rich green grass, and from far away came the melodious sound of a mourning dove. In the branches overhead a robin sang a merry song.

The procession stopped alongside the fenced enclosure. Pack, the twins and Sam carried the coffin and lowered it gently to the ground beside the gaping hole. The mourners gathered around. Pack reached back, grasped Mara's hand and pulled her up beside him and the twins. Reverend Piedmont took his place and opened his Bible.

Mara, determined not to allow the minister to rush the services so that he could leave, began to sing. Her voice rose sweet and clear. After the first few words, Emily and Charlie joined her. Pack bowed his head and squeezed her hand.

> "Shall we gather at the river?
> Where God's angel's feet have trod.
> With it's crystal tide forever,
> Flowing by the throne of God.
> Yes, we'll gather at the river,
> the beautiful, the beautiful river,
> Gather with the saints at the river,
> that flows by the throne of God."

When the song ended, a hush fell over the group. The minister looked at Mara. She nodded to him and he began the service by reading the eulogy she had written. When he finished, he read a short verse from the Bible, then began to recite the Lord's Prayer. Sam stood beside Charlie and Emily. His voice and theirs joined with the minister's and Mara's.

The ceremony ended and the coffin was lowered into the grave. Sam and Charlie each took a spade and began to fill the grave. Pack stood as still as a stone, holding tightly to Mara's hand while spadeful after spadeful of dirt was dropped on the box. The twins, tears streaming down their faces, stood beside him. With his head bowed, his hat in his hand, Aubrey stood apart as if he were not a member of the family.

During the service Mara had managed to keep the tears from her eyes, but after the grave was filled, Travor and Trellis came forward with a waterbucket full of wildflowers and carefully placed it at the head of their mother's grave. Mara's control gave way, and tears ran down her cheeks in a steady stream. She moved up between the twins and put an arm around each boy. They clung to her, and the three stood silently together until Pack moved up close behind them, his chest against Mara's back, a hand on the shoulder of each of the boys.

Charlie led the others away, leaving Brita's sons and Mara alone beside the grave.

Reverend Piedmont and his wife walked past Sam as he was putting the shovels in the wagon.

"The ladies fixed up a good meal, Reverend. We'll all go back to the house to eat."

"We . . . ah, got to be getting on back to town."

"Ya're not in no hurry," Sam said flatly.

"Yes, we are," Mrs. Piedmont blustered.

"I'm sayin' ya've got time to be sociable." Sam's face was like a stone carving.

"But . . . we don't have time, do we, Arnold?"

Sam's sharp eyes pierced the wavering eyes of the other man. "You have time, don't you, *Arnold?*"

"We'll take time."

"That's better. Wait up 'n follow us back."

Sam walked away as Mrs. Piedmont began to sputter. "What's the matter with you? Where's your backbone? I'm not eating a bite in that house! The idea! You know what the ladies in the circle will do if they find out we were consorting with that—that McCall trash? They'll not help fix up the parsonage. We're going back to town.''

''Shut your mouth for once!'' Reverend Piedmont snarled and grabbed his wife's elbow. He propelled her toward the buggy and boosted her up onto the seat.

''Don't you dare talk to me like that!'' she hissed.

''I'll talk to you any way I can to shut you up! We're going back there; you're going to eat and be decent. Understand?''

''Heavens! I'll not be able to hold up my head if they find out—''

The marshal edged his horse up to the buggy and leaned from his saddle. ''Sparks giving ya any trouble, Preacher?''

''None at all.''

''Yes, he did,'' Mrs. Piedmont snapped.

''He did not!'' The minister dug his elbow into his wife's side. ''He invited us for dinner.''

''Invited? It ain't his place to do no invitin'.''

''He was extending the invitation from Miss McCall.''

Ace rubbed his chin thoughtfully and moved his horse up beside the wagon where Charlie and Emily waited. He had met the one-legged rancher and his near-blind sister in Laramie and had stopped by their place one time. As Mara approached, Ace quickly stepped down from his horse and waited to help her up onto the wagon seat.

''It was nice of you to come, Marshal.'' Mara smiled. ''You must stay and have dinner.''

''Thank ya kindly, Mara. Let me help you.'' He placed his hand beneath her elbow when she placed her foot on the spoke of the wheel. Charlie reached for her hand and pulled her up to sit beside Emily.

Ace stood beside the wagon, unaware that he was staring. Mara was not the most beautiful woman he had ever seen, but there was something about her that made him unable to drag his eyes away. Her hair was curly and shining like the coat of a young roan in the spring after it had shed its winter coat. Emerald eyes flashed at him when she became aware of his stare, and color flooded her face. He imagined that her eyes could turn as fierce as those of a treed wildcat when she was loving a man. By God, he would have her!

The wagon began to move. Ace chuckled and twisted the ends of his mustache with shaking fingers. Goddamn! Even at a funeral he only had to look at her to visualize having her naked in his bed. He mounted his horse and pulled his coat together to cover the throbbing length of his swollen manhood. She was everything he thought she would be. Sensible when it was called for, fiery when mad. Since the first time he had seen her he had wanted to throw her to the ground and satisfy himself right then and there. Mara Shannon was a woman worth waiting for. His time with her would come.

Tables were set up in the shade of the oak tree beside the house when the mourners returned to the homestead. Steamboat worked over the joint of beef, placing slices on a huge platter. Riley, the stooped old man who worked the garden and helped the bunkhouse cook, had built a fire in the yard and was boiling water for coffee.

After the preacher and his wife were seated in the shade, Mara led Emily into the house. They took off their hats, tied aprons about their waists, and began setting out the food they had prepared. Each time Mara carried a dish from the house to the tables she could feel the marshal's eyes on her. She looked for Pack and saw that he was deep in conversation with Charlie and Sam.

"I'm surprised the marshal is here," she whispered as Emily handed her a bowl of boiled eggs to take to the table in the yard.

"So am I. Charlie doesn't like him. I don't think Pack does either."

"Then why did he come?"

"Maybe the preacher asked him."

"He has a habit of staring that makes me uncomfortable," Mara confessed.

"He stares at you? Oh, I hope Pack holds his temper."

"What do you mean?"

"Only that Pack . . . will feel responsible for you now."

"I'll not need protection from the *marshal*, for heaven's sake!" Carrying the bowl of eggs and a pan of bread, Mara left the kitchen.

Mrs. Piedmont sat at the table beside her husband, and both ate a hearty meal. After several attempts to draw the preacher into a conversation, Charlie gave up and talked with the man who had driven the dray wagon. Aubrey and Cullen sat at the far end of the table. Aubrey ate with his head down, but Cullen watched the preacher and his wife as if having them there was a huge joke.

Mara cut the pie and filled the plates when they were passed to her. Each time she looked up, she caught Ace January watching her. After the meal when she carried the butter crock to the house, he followed. She set the crock on the counter and went quickly through the parlor and out onto the porch before he could catch up with her. After that she stayed beside Emily until the Piedmonts were ready to leave and then walked out to where the overweight preacher was helping his overweight wife into the buggy. Ace brought his horse from the hitching rail and stood waiting.

"I trust you'll have a pleasant trip back to town." It was all Mara could think of to say. She certainly wasn't going to thank them for coming or say she was pleased to have met them, because she wasn't. It would please her, however, never to see the pious pair again.

"The bill's paid." Pack's voice came from behind Mara, and she turned to see him looking at the minister with hard cold eyes.

The minister's grunt was noncommittal. He slapped the reins against the mare's back and the buggy moved away, leaving Ace January standing beside his horse.

"Good-bye, Ace." There was no mistaking the firm tone of dismissal in Pack's voice.

Smoldering anger was reflected in the marshal's face. His squinting eyes went from Pack to Mara. They were as cold as Pack's, but there was a strange little sneer at the corners of his mouth.

"I want to speak to Mara—"

"Some other time," Pack broke in.

Mara had to force herself to appear calm as the marshal took a second look at Pack. She was aware of Pack's defiant stance, his possessive hand on her shoulder. She had to act quickly if an unpleasant encounter was to be avoided.

"Good-bye, Mr. January."

"Some other time," he echoed Pack's words.

Ace glared into Pack's face, his jaw muscles pulsing as he fought to contain his anger. He mounted, and as soon as he was settled into the saddle, he gigged his horse cruelly. The powerful hind legs bent, the front legs stretched out and he was off down the road in a cloud of dust. He passed the buggy and was soon out of sight.

"I want to speak to you." Pack's hand slid from Mara's shoulder to her elbow. He swung her around and propelled her toward the porch.

"You too?" It was all she could think of to say.

Pack didn't speak until they were in the darkened parlor. He turned her to face him and held her in place with his hands on her shoulders.

"Get your things together," he commanded. "You're going home with Emily and Charlie."

Chapter
ELEVEN

Mara's mouth opened in astonishment. She had known that Pack would try to convince her to leave the homestead, but it had come so unexpectedly. He had not *asked*, he had *demanded* that she pack her things and leave . . . today! She was shaken, hurt, but now was not the time to dwell on it.

"Who are you to be telling me what to do?" Her voice shook with resentment and fury. "I like Emily very much, but I'm not going to be thrust upon her and her brother like a penniless orphan. I'm staying in the house my father built and left to me."

"No, you're not. Get up there and get enough together to last a day or two. I'll bring the rest of your things over later. I've already told Charlie you're going home with them. He has chores to do. He can't be waiting all day while you lollygag around."

"Then you can just untell Charlie, Mr. Know-It-All Gallagher, because I'm not going. I have a home and I'm staying in it."

"Mara Shannon, I've told you that you can't stay here, I've told you why, and that's all there is to it."

"And I've told you to tend to your own damn business. I'm of age and no longer need a guardian."

Pack ran his hand through his dark hair. His face was tense with anger and frustration as he struggled to hold onto his temper.

"I can force you to leave, Mara Shannon. Don't make me do it!"

"That's nonsense! You can't make me do anything I don't want to do." Mara rubbed her hand over lips that had gone chalky with anger. "Why are you doing this to me, Pack? How are you going to benefit if I abandon everything my father worked for?"

"How am I going to *benefit?*" Huge hands grasped her shoulders and he shook her. "Damn you for a stubborn, stupid little fool! I'm not asking you to abandon it. You'll be *paid* for every acre, every blade of grass, if I have to work my fingers to the bone."

Mara took a couple of deep, steadying breaths. "I want to be here!"

"You don't want to face the fact there are things a woman can't do alone. You saw the way Ace January looked at you. He was thinking about getting you in bed! And he's only one of your problems. Cullen will crawl on you the minute my back is turned!"

"You're being crude and hateful."

"Crude and hateful won't hurt you, Mara Shannon. *Rape* will! Do you understand what it means to be raped? A man will force entry into your body and you will feel pain such as you've never felt before. Pain and . . . shame. Once I saw a woman, a pretty young woman, after several men had been on her. She begged me to shoot her. Sometimes women are used so cruelly that they bleed inside until they die!"

"Stop it!" Mara squeezed her eyes shut and tried not to hear the words.

"An unattached woman in this country attracts men like flies on a honey pot," Pack continued doggedly. "A *pretty* unattached woman living out here by herself is enough to cause a shooting war among the men who want her, especially if they think she's got money or land.''

She glared up at him, dry-eyed and furious. "If you don't get your hands off me I'm going to—to kick you," she said between her teeth.

"I mean what I say. I'm responsible for you."

"You're not! You're not even blood kin!"

"You haven't got the brains of a buttercup if you think old Aubrey would stand between you and Cullen. Trellis and Travor will try. One or both of them will get killed. Be sensible and go home with Emily until I can find a place for you in town. You can teach school and make friends among your own kind."

"No! No! No!" Her voice rose to an almost hysterical pitch. Her color was vivid, her eyes as sharp as polished emeralds. "I'll not live in a rooming house, sleeping on someone else's bed, eating at a community table with a bunch of dullards. I won't do it, Pack. My roots are here. I'm staying here on McCall land. It's my right, by damn, and you're not taking it from me."

"Damn you for a stubborn *baggage*." He said the word deliberately. "You can't stay here without a man—a husband to protect you!" His voice rose with every word. "Are you so wrapped up in the possession of this land that you can't understand that?"

His hands, rough and calloused, were like vises on her arms. He held her so close she could feel the heat of his anger.

"If I've got to have a husband in order to live in my own home on my own land, I'll get one."

"Who do you think will come courting you out here?" he demanded. "Cullen will shoot the first man that comes calling. Or did you have the marshal in mind?"

"I had *you* in mind, Pack! Are you man enough to marry me, stand up to Cullen and protect what is mine?"

The words were out before she realized what she was saying. Her breath was coming fast, her upper lip glistened with sweat. She would have snatched back the words if she could, but when she saw the look of horrified surprise on his face, she was glad she had said them, and it goaded her to say more.

"You're like a stray dog that's all bark and no bite, Pack Gallagher. You're great at telling me what to do, but you've not got the guts to make a decent life for yourself. Most men would be glad to settle down on a piece of land as fine as this and build something to leave to their children as my father did. You're satisfied to float over the surface of the land, living in a freight wagon going from one mining camp to another."

"Damn you for an educated fool with more temper than is good for you. You don't know a damn thing about me or what I do. It's true that I'm a teamster, but it's honest, hard work. I'll not always *float* over the land. I've got dreams of my own."

"I just bet you have. Dreams of whores and barroom brawls?" she jeered. "Let's see what you're made of, big, bad, teamster Gallagher. My father was fond of you, but for the life of me I don't know why. Half of this land will belong to the man who marries me. Have you ever had a better offer?"

Pack's eyes narrowed to blue-black slits. An inarticulate sound came from his throat, breaking into the charged silence that held them after her words.

"You'd marry a man, any man, to stay here?" His voice was controlled yet savage. It curled around her like a whip, hungry to bite into her flesh.

"Not *any* man. You're not choice husband material, but better than Cullen. And being Brita's son, along with the fact that my father saw something good in you, is in your favor. You may be rough around the edges, but you can't be *all* bad." Her smile was like a slash across his throat. The emerald blaze in her eyes told him that she was sure she had backed him into a corner and he would retreat.

"Think twice, my girl," he snarled. "Marriage is forever."

"Not necessarily. Only until one of us dies," she responded casually, shrugging his hands from her shoulders.

"All right!" His voice roared in her ears as his patience

snapped. He shoved her down in a chair and stood over her. His hands balled into hard fists and he swore. "Don't ever forget, Mara Stubborn McCall, that this was your idea! *You* asked *me!* And don't forget another thing: I'll not be lashed by that sharp tongue of yours and slink away like a whipped dog. You need a strong hand, by God, and you'll get it." He turned to leave, then turned back. "Don't move out of that chair."

Quick steps took Pack to the door and out onto the porch. "Sam!" he bellowed.

Sam, sqatting on his heels, was talking to Charlie. Emily sat on a stump nearby. Sam turned at the sound of urgency in Pack's voice and hurried to the porch.

"I've got one more favor to ask, Sam. Ride after that preacher and bring him back, will you? Get him back here if you have to bring him at gunpoint."

"Well, shore, Pack. But—"

"He's got a marriage service to read, but don't tell him that. Just bring him back. I don't think you'll have any trouble with the marshal. He rode on ahead."

After Sam left, Pack beckoned to Charlie. The brother and sister came up onto the porch.

"Is Mara Shannon getting ready?" Emily asked.

Pack stepped aside to let her enter the house. "She's not going. She's in the parlor."

The thump, thump of Charlie's peg leg on the floor echoed loudly as they entered the room.

"Mara Shannon?"

"I'm here, Emily."

"I'd love for you to visit for awhile. Please say you'll come."

"Thank you, but if I leave my house, there'll not be a stick of anything left when I return."

"But . . . you can't stay alone out here. Pack can tell you that."

"He has. I'll not be alone."

"Mara Shannon asked me to marry her." Pack's voice had a sneer in it. "Sam's gone to fetch the preacher back. Funerals and weddings are much the same. A man dies and is put in the ground; a man weds and he's got a millstone around his neck for the rest of his life.''

''A thousand acres of land is some millstone,'' Mara said dryly.

''You'd wed the devil himself to stay here.''

''That's most likely what I'm doing, but I'll survive. My father's dream was to build a home for his family on land to call their own. He worked from dawn till dark to get it. I'll not leave my land, and I'll not leave my house sitting idle to be ravaged even if I have to wed you to keep it.''

Pack swore. ''You'd be the one to be ravaged by that bunch in the bunkhouse!''

Mara sat on the chair, as prim and proper as if she were sitting on a church pew. Her hands were clasped in her lap and her ankles were crossed neatly. Emily moved toward her. Mara took her hand to guide her to the chair beside her. It suddenly occurred to Mara that she may have broken her friend's heart, and she felt a wave of regret that eased when her friend spoke.

''You and Pack were made for each other. I knew that as soon as I met you,'' Emily said softly.

Mara bent forward to look into her face. ''Emily? Are you sure you don't mind? I was afraid that—''

''Mind? Oh, you thought that I was in love with Pack?'' Emily laughed. ''I do love him . . . in a way. But Pack and I are friends, nothing more.''

Mara glanced at Pack. He was rubbing his hand through his hair in a gesture of frustration that was becoming familiar. He was still angry and no doubt regretting his hasty decision. Emily might not be in love with him, but what about Pack? Did he love her? Did he think that as long as he couldn't have Emily, he'd take her?

''Well,'' Mara said flippantly, in spite of the unease that made her stomach flutter. ''I didn't want to buy him away from you. He agreed to marry me for half of my land.''

Mara knew that she was being unnecessarily blunt. She hated herself for saying it, but it was best that Charlie and

Emily knew that this was not a love match, but strictly a business deal. If Emily didn't want her friendship knowing that, it was better to know it now.

Pack's mouth flattened into an unyielding line. He wanted to lift the stubborn little redhead out of the chair and shake her until her teeth rattled. God almighty! Was he letting himself in for a lifetime of misery? She would never see him as anything except a rough, uneducated teamster who married her for her land. Hell! What was he to do? Ride out and leave her alone? He couldn't do that even if he hated her. She was Shannon's daughter, for Christ's sake. He would do his best to protect her from the scum who would have her, but who would protect her from . . . him?

"There must be a way around this if neither of you want this marriage." Charlie finally spoke. "People are coming in on the train every week looking for a place to settle. You'd not have any trouble finding a family that wants a little land."

"I'm thinking Mara Shannon isn't willing to give up any of *her* land to homesteaders. What good would that do anyway? She'd still be here alone and Cullen would run off the homesteaders." Pack's mouth snapped shut with a soft click of his teeth.

"You could find someone to come stay with her," Charlie persisted.

"Another woman? Ha!" The snort accompanied a venomous glance at Mara. "That would only give the bunkhouse crowd two women to sport with."

"A man and his wife—"

"I'll not have strangers living in my house," Mara said firmly. "If Pack wants to crawfish out of the deal, he only has to say so."

"There are times when I'd like to beat your butt!"

Pack stood over her with his thumbs hooked in his belt. His voice carried a real threat, but she was determined not to be humbled by him. If she was sure about one thing it was the certainty that he would not hurt her—for her father's sake, of course. So she looked up at him defiantly.

"You've a habit of repeating yourself, Pack. You've said

that before. And," she added with a lift of her brows, "a few other things that I've not forgotten."

A low rumble of laughter escaped Charlie. It was one of the few times Mara had heard his laugh. The insufferable man! How dare he laugh at her!

"I fail to see any humor in the situation," she said coolly.

"I'm sorry, Mara. I was just thinking that there'll not be a dull moment at the McCall ranch from here on out."

"The *Gallagher* ranch," Pack corrected firmly, his dark eyes boring into Mara's, daring her to contradict him.

The Gallagher ranch? Dear God, what had she gotten herself into?

The sound of boots on the porch and words of protest from the preacher told her it was too late now to consider another alternative.

The preacher was inside the house for a total of ten minutes. During that short time, Mara's life was changed forever. She was no longer Mara Shannon McCall. She was Mara Shannon Gallagher. She stood beside Pack, his hand holding tightly to hers as if he thought them she would flee, while the sputtering preacher pronounced them man and wife. Sam had returned to the buggy where Mrs. Piedmont waited impatiently and brought the folded leather envelope with the blank marriage and death documents. The marriage paper was filled out and signed. Emily and Charlie signed as witnesses.

Pack shoved a few bills at the preacher.

"Register this in town. I'll be in next week to check to see if you've done it. And keep your mouth shut about it. Understand?"

The preacher fled the house and the men followed to see him on his way.

"I can't believe I've done this, Emily." Mara stood in the parlor shaking her head as if she were in a daze and spoke huskily, not quite sure her voice would work. "It's not at all like the wedding I dreamed of having. I . . . I didn't even change my dress. I'm still wearing funeral clothes."

"Ah, Mara Shannon. I know how you feel, but sometimes

things are taken out of our hands. It's said that some of the best decisions we make in our lifetime are spur-of-the-moment decisions. Pack is terribly fond of you and wants what's best for you.''

"Fond of my land, you mean.'' The sound that came from Mara was something between a snarl and a jeering laugh. She lifted her hands to her hair and slid her fingers along her scalp to loosen it from the pins. "Better Pack Gallagher than Cullen McCall,'' she said, then added tiredly, "What's done is done. I'll make the best of it.''

"Pack will be . . . gentle with you. He is such a kind man for all his rough ways.''

"What do you mean, gentle with *me?* Oh, you think that we'll— No! Absolutely not! He understands that this is not *that* kind of marriage.'' Mara's face had turned brick red, and her mouth clamped shut so hard that her teeth clicked. "He'll keep his distance or I'll shoot him.''

"You wouldn't do *that.*"

"Oh yes I would.'' Mara had to fight to make her voice sound convincing. She knew as well as she'd ever known anything that she'd not shoot Pack Gallagher, regardless of what he did or did not do. "I want you to take a pie and some of the meat home, Emily. It'll just take a minute for me to put them in a basket for you.''

Mara had a great need to be alone. Within the last few minutes she had taken a step that would change her life forever, and the enormity of it was making itself known to her as her mind swam back to reality. She escaped to the kitchen, leaned against the wall, and covered her face with her hands.

When Pack went with Charlie to bring up the wagon, Sam stepped back into the house. He had not had a private word with Emily all day. He stood hesitantly inside the room with his hat in his hand, feeling like a bashful schoolboy.

"Miss Emily?''

"Sam? Is Charlie ready to go?''

"Not yet. I just thought I'd . . . tell ya he'll be along soon."

Emily drew in a long breath and stood perfectly still. When she heard him coming toward her, a smile lighted her face. She held out her hand and felt a fierce pleasure when he grasped it and placed her palm against his chest. She filled her lungs with the scent that was typical of him, pine, leather, tobacco. She loved the size of him, the strength of his hand, the heavy beat of his heart.

"I was afraid I'd not get to talk to you again. Oh, Sam, I never wanted to be able to see as badly as I do right this minute."

Sam raised her hand to his lips. "Ah, Emily Rose, I'm not much to look at."

"Oh, but you are!"

"I may be leavin' here soon. There's not been a place I wanted to come back to since I went home that first time after the war till now. I want to come back to you, Emily Rose. I'll have somethin' to offer when I come."

"You don't have to have anything but yourself," she whispered with tears in her voice.

"I've got to be able to give ya at least as good as ya got now."

"I don't need much, but you—"

"Yore brother's right to be lookin' out fer ya like he does. When I come back, I'll tell him I want to take over the lookin' after ya."

"Oh, Sam! Do you mean it? Are you sure?"

"I was never more sure a anythin' in my life."

"Will you come to see me before you go?"

"If you want me to."

"I do! Oh, I do!"

"I hear the wagon comin'. Can I kiss you?"

"I was hoping you would."

"Sweet, sweet Emily Rose." His voice was husky and intimate.

Slowly he bent to brush her lips with his. Then his arms slipped around her, pressing her body to the length of his. His lips were warm, sweet and moved over hers with gentle strength. The tip of his tongue teased her lips until she sighed, giving herself up to his kiss with sensual abandon, wanting, needing to increase the pressure. She felt his breath against her ear and a shiver of delight raced down her spine. This was Sam, her Sam, her love. His touch was more wonderful than any dream she had ever had of a lover's touch. Her arms tightened around him and his around her until she could hardly breathe.

He drew in a shaky breath when he raised his head. "Ya taste as sweet as a cool mountain spring."

She reached up and kissed him with trembling lips. The freedom to do so went to her head like heady wine. "You taste good too," she whispered before kissing him again.

"Emily, sweet Emily Rose, I like saying your name." His voice was a caress as sweet as his kiss.

Sam felt as if his heart would leap out of his breast. But over its pounding he heard the jingle of harnesses.

"Charlie's out front with the wagon."

He placed a warm kiss on her parted lips, then, holding tightly to her hand, he led her out onto the porch and down the steps. Still holding her hand, he drew it up into the crook of his arm and covered it with his. This was his woman, and her brother might as well know it now. Come hell or high water, he intended to have her. He watched for Charlie and Pack's reactions to the possessive way he held her close to him. Neither man appeared to notice.

Sam helped Emily up onto the wagon seat.

"Bye, Emily Rose. I'll be over soon." His words were for Emily, but he made sure that they reached Charlie too.

"Emily!" Mara came out of the house and ran lightly down the steps to the wagon. "Are you leaving already?"

"Charlie has chores to do before dark."

"Thank you for coming. I couldn't have managed without you."

"I was glad to come, Mara Shannon. Now it's your turn to come see me."

Sam stuck out his hand to Charlie. "I'll be over soon," he repeated and looked the man in the eye.

Charlie took his hand, his sharp eyes narrowing as they held Sam's steady gaze. Finally he nodded his head.

"You'll be welcome, Sam."

Pack saw the relief that slumped Emily's shoulders, then the brilliant smile that lighted her face. Realization came to him slowly, but definitely. Sam and Emily had feelings for each other. *Lucky Sam.*

"Bye, everybody," Emily called, suddenly happier than she had been in her entire life. "Pack, as soon as you and Mara Shannon are settled, bring her over."

"Take care of yourselves," Pack said, without responding to the invitation. He drew back as the wagon began to roll.

Mara stood between the two tall men and watched the sister and brother ride away from the homestead. Now she was alone with this man, this stranger who was her husband. Never had she imagined it would come to this; never had she thought she'd be forced to give over the control of her life to a man like Pack Gallagher. She turned and went back to the house, her back straight, her head up, but the confident pose was completely superficial. Inside she was tied in knots.

She paused to look about the kitchen before she went up the stairs to the room above. Today she had married a man, joined her life to his until one of them died. There had not been a tender word, a kiss, nor a ring during the ceremony that had made them man and wife.

"Sam," Pack said and walked a few paces across the circular drive to lean against the large oak tree with branches spreading almost to the edge of the porch. "I owe you, Sam. I'm obliged to you for standing by through this."

"I figured ya'd do the same." Sam squatted down on his heels, picked up a twig and absently began to skin back the bark. "Ya've bit off a big chaw, Pack. Mara jist might be a widow afore she's a wife."

Pack snorted. "I'm not counting on her being a *real* wife. She hates my guts."

"That bad, huh?"

"That bad. She's not suited for this life, but she's got feelings about this place. Hell! She could have gone to town, taught school, married one of them lawyer fellers."

"She might be more suited than ya think. She ain't afraid a work."

"I've got to make it safe for her here. That means I'll have to clear out Cullen and his bunch."

"Cullen'll back down. He'll not face ya. He's the back-shootin' kind."

"How about Sporty Howard?"

"In a crowd he'll make a show to save his face. By hisself he's got a yellow streak a yard wide."

"How many are down there?"

"Five, countin' Cullen. I plan on backin' ya."

Pack's blue-black eyes narrowed. "Why?"

"I want to stay round for a while."

"You can do that anyway, Sam. You know that."

"Yeah. Ya ort a know I'm lookin' fer a feller. I trailed him here, then he disappeared. I figure he up 'n got hisself killed 'n is buried here abouts."

"You a law man?"

Sam studied Pack before he answered, surprised at the hint of anxiety in his voice. If he didn't know better, he'd think Pack had something to hide.

"Not exactly. The man I'm lookin' fer made off with some gold bars he stole from the Confederacy durin' the war."

"Then you're a government man."

"I guess ya could call me that. I got asked to do the job cause one a the fellers in on it was my lieutenant."

"A lot of men on the other side of the law have come through here the last couple of years. Cullen put the word out they were welcome."

"I figure the feller roamin' round here nights watchin' the place might a trailed the lieutenant here same as I did. Funny thin' about it though. The same feller rides a different horse each time, tryin' to cover his tracks."

"How do you know it's the same man?"

"He sits in the grass the same, always puts his hat down on the left side, gets up by diggin' in his left foot. Horse veers to the left cause the feller holds the reins in his left hand. I figure he watches with a spyglass."

"Do you think he's after the gold?"

"What else?"

"If the man's dead, whoever killed him took off with the gold."

"Maybe not. I'd a buried it, waited till thin's cooled off."

"Do you think Cullen knows about it?"

"I'm not thinkin' that. He'd a already tried to sell the bars, dumb as he is. The bars ain't surfaced yet. They ain't no good till they're turned into money."

"Dust or nuggets wouldn't be talked about. But gold bars—"

"Yeah. I'm not lookin' to do anythin' outside the law, Pack. I'm aimin' to get the reward money. It'll be enough to buy me that herd a longhorns 'n give me a start."

"Well, luck to you, Sam."

"This is damn good cattle country, Pack."

"Aye. I'd like to run longhorns if I could raise the money to buy 'em."

"Charlie'd like a slice a the pie if we could swing it to drive up a herd."

"He told me."

Sam stood. "Ya ain't plannin' on doin' nothin' till mornin', are ya?"

"That's time enough."

"I'll keep an ear out."

"I'm obliged."

Pack's brow furrowed. He watched Sam head for the bunkhouse. Just for a moment he had thought it was Charlie that Sam was after. He would have hated to go against Sam, but he would have. Charlie Rivers was the best friend he'd had after he lost Shannon McCall. But, hell! That business in Evansville was over and done with long ago. Sam was a steady, deep-thinking man. He'd be a good man to stand by Charlie, especially if he had feelings for Emily, and it sure as hell looked as if he did. By damn. Sam had been as bold as brass about letting Charlie know it. And Emily looked as happy as a dog with two tails.

Despite the worry on Pack's mind, the corners of his lips tilted in a grin.

Chapter
TWELVE

Trellis and Travor came into the kitchen from the back porch at the same time Pack came in from the parlor. The boys stood beside the door with their hats in their hands. They looked more alike than ever now that Travor had stopped his swaggering and attempts to act tough. Pack could tell them apart when he saw them together, but he doubted he would know which was which if he met them one at a time in a crowd.

"Want some coffee?"

"We want to talk to you."

"Can you talk and drink at the same time?" Pack poured coffee into granite cups.

"Guess so." They hung their hats on the pegs beside the door and came to the table.

"What's on your minds?" Pack straddled the bench and sat down.

The twins sat also, avoided looking directly at Pack, and fiddled with the cups. Finally Trellis spoke.

"Me and Trav've been talkin'. We ain't thinkin' Mara

Shannon ort a be left here by herself. Cullen wouldn't a done anythin' while Ma was here, but now that she's gone, there ain't no tellin' what he'll do."

"What do you think I should do about it?" Pack took a sip from his cup.

"I, ah, we think you ort a take her with you, or stay here and see *they* don't bother her."

"They, meaning Cullen and his bunch."

"You know what they are, Pack." Travor gave his older brother a disgusted look. "Cullen thinks to marry up with Mara Shannon and get this place."

"You don't think that's a good idea?"

"Hell!" Travor rose off the bench, then sat back down. "Cullen ain't fit to wipe her feet."

"Why the interest in Mara Shannon? You said she was prissy and bossy."

"She was good to Ma, and she's been square to me and Trell." Travor faced Pack, his gaze daring him to scoff because he had changed his mind.

"What do you boys want to do now?"

"We been talkin' about that too." Trellis lowered his lashes over his blue eyes and stared into his coffee cup. "We'd go with you, but we ain't leavin' Mara Shannon here by herself."

"What about your pa? What's he going to do?"

"We'll find out when he sobers up. He took to the bottle right after the buryin'."

"Cullen won't give up without a fight. He's got too much to lose."

"We figured that. We ain't runnin' out on Mara Shannon, like you're doin'." Travor spoke resentfully, clipping each word.

Mara stood at the top of the stairs listening to the conversation below. She had changed into a work dress, taken down her hair and tied it at the nape of her neck. When she had first gone to her room, she had stood just inside the door, shivering with the knowledge that she was now the wife of a big, battle-scarred man who had the devil of an Irish temper. Now that she'd had time to think, her senses had come back full force, and she realized that to marry Pack had been the only option available to her.

It was Travor, the twin who had been so resentful, who was now taking up for her. She recognized his voice. It was a little louder than his brother's, and he talked a little faster. She had worked hard to reach the lonely boy who hid his real feelings behind his scowl and his swagger. Now, listening to him, Mara could feel her own heartbeat shaking her, and at the same time tears of gratitude brightened her eyes.

"Can't you stay here, Pack?" Trellis asked.

"He ain't goin' to stay, Trell," his brother sneered. "He's got to get back to that blond whore at the Diamond."

"You seem pretty sure, Trav." There was a mocking tone in Pack's voice.

"Ever'body knows that you 'n that woman they call Candy are thicker'n eight in a bed."

"Is that right?"

"Bedurned and bedamned! You know it is. Why'd you rather have her than a woman like Mara Shannon? Mara Shannon can read and she knows things about history and cipherin'. 'Sides, she's sweet and pretty. She's Irish, too, like us. That other woman ain't nothin' but a bangtail."

"Watch your mouth when you talk about Miss Camp. You're pretty quick to judge someone you don't know anything about."

"I ain't deaf and dumb, for God's sake. I know she works at the Diamond Saloon, and I know that's where men go to get their rocks knocked off." Travor's young, squeaky voice quivered with temper.

"You know a lot for a wet-eared kid."

"I might have wet ears, but I ain't got sawdust atween 'em!"

"And I have?"

"You ain't got no brains, if you don't look out for your own kin."

"I'm not blood kin to Mara Shannon. You are."

Mara's brow knitted in a puzzled frown. She wondered why Pack didn't stop arguing with the boys and ease their minds by telling them that he was staying. He was probably sorry he had married her, and was thinking about the woman who worked at a saloon where men went to "get their rocks knocked off." She wasn't sure what that meant, but she certainly knew what a whore was.

So *that* was the kind of man she had married! A man who consorted with whores. Defended them! Well! It was no wonder he was reluctant to marry Mara when he had a skilled lover waiting for him in town. For some reason unknown to her she felt both insulted and hurt. Mara placed her hand over her heart and vowed that she would never forgive him. Never, if she lived a million years!

Mara reached behind her, slammed the door smartly, then walked down the stairs into a silent kitchen. Be casual, she ordered herself, while the pulses thudded angrily in her wrists. He had a lot of nerve to sit at her table, eyeing her the way he was after he had just defended a fallen woman, a woman so tarnished that even a boy like Travor knew her reputation.

She stopped behind the twins and placed a hand on each of their shoulders. "Are you hungry?"

"No, ma'am," they answered in unison.

Mara looked over their heads and into Pack's midnight blue eyes. "Has Pack told you the news?"

Twin heads swiveled to look at her. "What news?"

"I'll leave the telling to him. After all, he's the one who will have to balance his *loss* against his gain."

Mara's chin angled up as she turned away. Pack couldn't suppress a twitch of his firm lips. So she had been listening and heard what was said about Candy. Mara Shannon McCall Gallagher would never understand about a woman like Candace Camp, better known as Candy to the miners and railroaders who spent their money at the Diamond Saloon. The uppity little snob didn't know what it was to scrounge to keep body and soul together. She'd had a soft life at the school. She looked at him now as if he had just crawled out of a pig sty. Damn her! Charlie had been right. He might not have any peace from now on, but life with her wouldn't be dull. They'd start off right. He'd teach Miss Priss not to bait the bear.

"Come around here and we'll tell the boys our news."

"You're the one with the Irish gift of gab. You don't need me." Mara went around the end of the table on her way to the wash bench to wash her hands. Pack's arm shot out and circled her waist. She didn't have a chance against his great strength. She lost her balance and he pulled her back and down onto his lap before she could take a deep breath. "What in the world do you think you're doing? Let go of me . . . damn you—"

"Hush, wife. I'll not have you cussing. Boys, meet your new sister. Mara Shannon and I are married. Sam rode after the preacher. He came back and tied the knot—good and tight and legal. We're man and wife. What do you think of that?"

Mara could feel Pack's hard thighs beneath her buttocks and the arm that locked her to him was unrelenting. She squirmed, trying to break free. At least he hadn't told them that she had asked him.

"Let me up—"

"Sit still, sweetheart. And don't look so embarrassed. The boys will have to get used to me holding you on my lap. We're all going to be living here together. We want them here with us, don't we, darlin'? Tell them that they have a home with us for as long as they want it."

"You're married?"

Mara didn't know which twin had spoken. It didn't matter. Pack pulled her back against him so tightly her rib cage rested on his forearm. She considered butting him in the face with the back of her head. Considered it and rejected it. He would be just mean enough to retaliate.

"Tell them, honey," he whispered. His lips nuzzled her ear before he caught the lobe gently between his teeth. "You taste just as sweet as ever, darlin'."

"I . . . we want you to stay. You can have the room at the front of the house." The words burst from Mara's mouth, then she snarled between clenched teeth, "Let go of me, you dolt!"

"You're married? Well, doggie! Well, confound me for a two-headed hoot owl!" Trellis jumped up and slapped his brother on the back. "I tole ya. Didn't I tell ya, Trav?"

"Trell said you'd not go and leave her here. He said you'd think a somethin'. I just never thought a you *marryin'* her. I never thought Mara Shannon'd have you. Why, she could have any town man she wanted. She could've even got a railroad conductor if she'd a wanted." Travor had a pleased grin on his young face. Neither of the boys seemed to notice Mara's struggles to free herself from Pack's tight hold.

"I guess I must be more important than I thought if Mara Shannon would take me over *all* them other fellers—even a railroad conductor. My, that's aiming pretty high."

Because her head was whirling, Mara sputtered when she tried to explain. "Some . . . times circumstances—"

"Bring lovers together." Pack interrupted her with such a quick tightening of the arm locked about her waist that it forced a puff of air from her mouth. "Isn't that what you were going to say, sweetheart?"

Trellis' admiring eyes stayed on Pack. "Ma would be real tickled about it."

"I take it you boys approve of your new sister?"

"You bet!"

"It'll put a end to Cullen's plans. He's goin' to have a shit-fit! Oh . . . sorry, Mara." Travor didn't look as if he were sorry. He was still grinning, but his twin's smile faded to a frown.

"Yeah. Cullen ain't going to like this none a'tall. You're goin' to have your hands full, Pack. But me 'n Trav will stand with you."

"Thanks, but no," Pack said firmly. "Cullen's as much your brother as I am. I'll not ask you to go against him. I'll take care of Cullen, but I'll need you to stay here in the house and take care of my . . . sweet wife."

Much to Mara's embarrassment, he had moved her hair aside and his lips were making little forays down the side of her neck. She all but bared her teeth and snarled. "Stop that!"

Pack laughed softly. "Don't be skittish, honey. The boys don't mind if I give my woman a little lovin'. You're just so pretty and soft and sweet-tempered, it's hard for me to keep my hands off you."

"I'll get even with you," she murmured between clenched teeth.

"What'd you say, darlin'?"

"You heard me, you—you—jackass!"

Pack laughed with his lips against her neck.

"She's a hell of a lot prettier than that Candy woman at the Diamond Saloon." Travor chortled happily, and Mara suddenly hated him, hated Trellis, and most of all hated Pack Gallagher.

"I don't know about her being prettier, Trav." The fingers on her rib cage spread and Pack's thumb rubbed back and forth across the underside of her breast. "For sure, she's plumper, but she's not as loving as Candy," he murmured. "I liked blondes best till just lately. Now I *think* I like redheads better. But then, blond women don't have freckles on their bottoms like redheaded women."

Pack's lips were fastened to the skin of her neck below her ear and Mara could feel little sucking movements. She was shamed to the bone, to the heart. What he was doing could be a beautiful thing between a man and a woman, but he was doing it now to mock her. She would scream if she stayed on his lap a second longer.

Her arms were locked against her sides, but her hands were free. She wanted to hurt him and hurt him! She lowered her hand down to his thigh, slipped it behind her, and viciously pinched him where he had received the bullet wound.

"Yeow! Goddamn it, you little devil."

His arms loosened. She sprang to her feet and backed away. Just for an instant she regretted the vicious pinch. Then she looked into a face flushed with anger and knew that she would do it again if she had to.

"What's the matter . . . dear?" she asked in a breathless voice filled with exaggerated concern.

"You know damn good and well what's the matter, you little imp of satan! If you broke open that wound I'm going to whip your hind end."

"Oh, dear. I'm sorry if I accidentally hurt you."

"Accidentally, my—"

The last word was mouthed, but Mara was pretty sure she

knew what it was. She lifted her reddish brown brows, opened her emerald eyes wide with playacting horror, and stared into his fiery dark ones. Her manner was light, but her thoughts were heavy. It was best to set the rules right now. If he tried to manhandle her again, he'd get a poke in the eye with a stiffened forefinger for his trouble. If that didn't work, he'd get a fist in the gut. She was fully prepared to do what was necessary to see that he kept his distance.

"Gosh, I just can't believe you and Mara Shannon are married." Totally unconcerned, Trellis propped his elbows on the table and rested his chin in his hands.

"That makes two of us," Pack growled, and threw Mara a dark look.

"Three," Mara said with a bright smile. "Are you boys hungry now?"

"Sure." They both spoke at the same time.

While Mara was setting the food left over from the noon meal on the table, Travor hesitantly asked about his father.

"What about Pa, Mara Shannon?"

"Cousin Aubrey has a home here for as long as he wants it. Heavens! Did you think I'd turn my father's cousin out after he worked this place and paid for my schooling?"

"God save us from a stupid woman!" Pack snorted and rolled his eyes to the ceiling.

The words didn't even rate a glance from Mara.

"I'm glad you're not going to run him off," Travor said.

"He's worried about it," Trellis echoed.

"Tell him not to worry. I haven't fully decided what I'm going to do yet, but there will be room here for him."

"So you haven't fully decided what you'll do?" Pack snarled. "I know what you'll do. You'll tell Aubrey McCall that he can have a bed in the bunkhouse if he works for it. There'll be no dead wood on this place from here on out."

Mara dismissed him with a haughty stare, then spoke to the twins.

"We have almost two thousand acres here and it's all paid for. Of course, half of it is Pack's. We've got to think of a way to make a living on the other thousand. It's not suitable for vast fields of potatoes as my father dreamed, but there are other things we can do with land besides growing potatoes.''

It was killing Pack to hold back the cutting words that sprang to his lips. The fiesty little baggage was showing her sharp edges. She was trying to provoke him into a shouting match so he'd come off looking bad to the twins.

''I heard fellers sayin' this would be good sheep country. You could start a sheep ranch.'' Trellis was getting warmed up to the conversation and the fact that Mara was including him and Travor in the planning.

''Oh, no, Trell. I can't stand sheep. They stink to high heaven. Or is it goats that stink? Oh, well, I'm thinking very strongly about raising turkeys. They don't stink at all.''

Three pairs of eyes turned to look at her, three mouths opened in awed silence, then three voices joined in a chorus. ''Turkeys?''

''Jesus, my God! Are you daft?'' Pack's voice exploded in the hushed silence of disbelief.

''I've warned you about taking the Lord's name in vain. Don't do it again.'' She spoke in her schoolmarm voice and set a pan of bread down on the table with unnecessary force to emphasize her demand.

''But, Mara Shannon, I don't think turkeys are . . .'' Trellis' voice faded. His young face was a mask of disappointment and confusion.

''People in Denver are wild for a taste of tame meat. We could sell every turkey we raise.''

''How do you plan to get them there, *Mrs.* Gallagher?'' There was an insulting tone in Pack's voice that raised Mara's hackles and made her more determined to speak calmly and rationally.

''Drive them,'' she said as if he were an idiot for not knowing that was the logical way to move turkeys from one place to the other. ''A few years ago a man and two boys, not as old as the twins, drove a flock of five hundred turkeys from Nebraska to Denver with the loss of only a few birds. The man said the birds ate grasshoppers along the way and roosted on and around the wagon loaded with corn at night. People lined up for blocks to buy the turkeys.'' She looked down her nose at Pack, then took her place at the table. ''Supply and demand. You should understand that. Didn't you get your start selling cats to miners?''

"There's a mite of difference between a twenty-five dollar cat and a two-bit turkey."

"Who said my turkeys will go for two-bits?"

Pack slammed his fork beside his plate. "You'll not be raising feed on this land for wolves, fox, wildcats—''

Mara held up her hand, palm out. "We will not discuss it now," she said, her calmness in direct contrast to his agitated state.

Pack looked every bit the black Irishman as he glared at her. Finally he made a show of eating a few bites, then got up and refilled his coffee cup. He listened to Mara's chatter as she told the boys that they could sleep in the front room that had been hers when she was a child. And that, if they were interested, in the evenings she would read to them or teach them to read and to write. The choice was theirs.

Travor sat in openmouthed admiration. Pack supposed he should be glad that his brothers had such a warm feeling for his new wife. But at that moment he was unable to be glad about anything. His leg hurt, Mara Shannon was acting as if he had the plague, he had the problem of what to do with his business in Laramie, and in the morning he faced the task of getting rid of Cullen and the petty thieves who had paid him to stay there.

Mara was telling the boys that she planned to wash the following day and that they were to leave their dirty clothes in a pile at the foot of the bed. Her voice was calm as if she had not a care in the world, but Pack knew she was as nervous as a cat on a tin roof. She pushed her loose, curly hair over her ear with shaking fingers. Five times in the next few minutes she made the same gesture, only there was no loose hair to brush away.

Pack didn't speak until the boys were ready to leave the table.

"One of you will be responsible for keeping the woodbox filled and one the water bucket. In the morning both of you will help Mara Shannon fill the washtubs and the boiling pot.

Later, after we're settled in, we'll sort out the rest of the chores. But first there's fixing up to do.''

"We figured to help her." Trellis picked up a fried pie and followed his brother to the door.

"Another thing," Pack's voice stopped them. "Not a word about me and Mara Shannon to anyone, hear?"

"Oh, shoot!" Travor said, coming back to pluck the last pie off the platter. "I was hopin' to throw it at Cullen and see him have a fit."

"Sorry to spoil your fun, but that's the way it'll be. The morning is time enough for them to be knowing. Bed down in the bunkhouse tonight. I want to be alone with my . . . bride."

Mara's heels scraped on the floor as she shot to her feet. She opened her mouth to protest but closed it when she saw the black scowl on Pack's face and the way the twins had accepted the order. She turned to the workbench to hide her flaming face from Pack's direct stare.

As soon as the door slammed behind the twins, Pack got up and went into the room where his mother had spent her last days. Now that he was alone, he allowed his shoulders to slump wearily. He was tired, but there were things to do, plans to make. He lit a lamp, then pulled a small, very old, wooden chest from under the bed. It had been painstakingly made with grooved ends and held together with pegs. The forged hinges were long and reached across the top and down the back of the box. His father had made the chest in Ireland, and it had held all of their meager possessions when they made the perilous trip to the New World. Pack took an iron key from a hiding place behind the bureau, unlocked the box, and lifted the lid.

As the familiar scent of rose petals wafted up, his lips tightened and he blinked his eyes to hold back the tears. He would always associate the scent with his mother. For as long as he could remember she had kept the letters his father had written to her in this box amid the rose petals. He had never read the letters, nor would he now. He gently moved the bundle aside and took out a packet of letters addressed to him. He sat back on his heels, removed a letter, and scanned it. When he was finished, he returned it to the envelope. He picked up a tintype of himself that he'd had made for his mother years before when he was no older than the twins. He looked so young. Where had the time gone? Pack locked the box and shoved it far back under the bed.

He lifted his holster and gun from the peg on the wall, picked up the rifle that stood in the corner, and brought them to the bunk. For the next half hour he cleaned and oiled the weapons. His hands worked automatically, allowing his thoughts to stray to Mara Shannon. It had cost the haughty little colleen dearly to ask him to take her as his wife. He was sure that it ate at her guts to have to admit that she needed him. It was almost a relief to have her say something snide to him during the meal. It gave him a reason to stay angry with her. Rage lashed at him now as he recalled her words to Emily and Charlie. *I bought him for half of my land.* He understood that the words were a salve for her pride, but nevertheless, someday she would eat those rash words.

His face hardened and his hands became still on the gun. He didn't want to think about the cruel words they had thrown at each other because it hurt inside. Nor did he want to think about her sweetness or her response when he had held her and kissed her. When the preacher had pronounced them man and wife, he had felt for a brief moment that every sweet dream he had dreamed had come true. The elation was quickly dampened when she turned away from him and turned up her nose as if he were a necessary evil.

Pack's gaze lifted from the gun to the doorway leading into the kitchen. His midnight eyes examined every inch of her proud body as she moved back and forth, hurrying he was sure, to finish the cleanup so she could escape to the room upstairs. She was alone and scared. She was his wife by her own choice, and she wasn't sure whether or not he would insist on his marital rights. Her only defense against him was her sharp tongue. He still held the rifle in his hands, and his rough thumbs moved gently, caressingly over the polished stock. If only he could make her understand that he would never hurt her. If she only knew how gentle he would be.

She passed the doorway without a glance into the room. He heard her footsteps going up the stairs and the soft click as the door closed. Ah, sweet, scared little woman. If he wanted to go in, that closed door wouldn't stop him.

Mara undressed in the dark, slipped her gown over her head and crawled into the bed as if the covers were some protection. She wrapped her arms about her body hoping to stop her shivering. This had been her wedding day. The day that should have been her most joyous day had been a nightmare. She and the man downstairs had been circling each other from the moment she brought him here, sniffing and fighting like two tomcats. Now she was married to him for life, because divorce was unthinkable and was granted only on rare occasions and only to the ones who could afford it. No, the vows she'd made today would hold until one of them died.

There was no way that she could ever go back to the old life now. The feeling of vulnerability and isolation swept over her, making her feel sick, making her heart feel like a stone in her chest. Slow tears slid from the corners of her eyes and into the auburn curls on her temples. She cried silently, and then a thought so terrifying came to her that she sat up in bed holding her hands to her cheeks.

What if Cullen killed Pack?

Pack had been sitting on the bunk rubbing a cloth over the barrel of a rifle. Did he think he'd have to use it against Cullen? Had she, by asking Pack to marry her, put his life on the line?

Of course she had!

The knowledge ate at her. She fell back onto the pillow. In the past she had been able to deal with the nightmare of being alone and had refused to let herself be turned into a frightened shell. She wondered now if she would be able to live with the horror if Pack were killed because of her. Desolation such as she had never felt before washed over her like a giant tidal wave and she felt the walls closing in on her, stifling her.

Mara turned to look out the window. Through it she could see a million stars shining against the black void of the night sky. There were so many they made her feel small and as insignificant as one grain of sand on a beach.

The tree limb scraped on the tin roof, an owl hooted, both familiar sounds. Pack's face nudged itself into her mind's eye. Pack's words came back to her. *Sweet little Mara, you've worked too hard. These little hands will be soft again, I promise.*

The sound of footsteps coming up the stairs sent her heartbeat into a wild gallop. She lifted her head from the pillow and gazed wide-eyed at the door. She hadn't expected him to come to her! Surely he wouldn't—didn't mean to—to sleep in the bed with her! She held her breath. In the stillness she heard the doorknob turn against the prop wedged beneath it. Seconds of breathless silence followed. Then a rap on the door.

"Open the door, Mara Shannon."

He didn't sound angry, but his voice sent shivers of dread knifing through her. Dread so acute that she couldn't speak. She only had time for an indrawn breath before he rapped again.

"Open the door." This time he spoke with some agitation.

"I'm asleep." Her voice squeaked. How could she have said anything so stupid?

"Mara Shannon, open this goddamn door. I'm not going to ask you again." The loud thump that shook the wall could only be his heavy boot as he kicked the bottom of the door. "If I rip this door down it will not be replaced. Stop acting like a quaking virgin and open the door."

Mara was out of the bed before she realized his goading words had moved her. She pushed the hair back from her eyes and went to the door. It was difficult to dislodge the prop beneath the knob, but she yanked on it and it came loose. Holding it in her hands she backed into the corner of the room.

The door was thrown open. Pack's big form was a shadow that filled the doorway. He stood for a moment, then took two steps into the room, his head turned to Mara, who was like a white ghost against the wall.

"You've no reason to cringe from me, Mara Shannon. I'm not here to rut on your virginal body. If you thought to keep me out by barring the door, you needn't have gone to the trouble. I'll not have this door or any door in this house barred against me. In case of fire, I might not be able to break down the door in time to save you." His voice changed from calm reasoning to one filled with contempt. "Go back to bed and dream your silly, schoolgirl dreams. I'm not so desperate for a woman that I'd find pleasure in taking an unwilling one."

Mara stood in a kind of frozen agony, clutching the heavy timber. His contemptuous words hit her like stones. The shadow disappeared, and she heard Pack going down the stairs.

Chapter
THIRTEEN

Mara looked worried when Pack came out of the bedroom with the holster and gun strapped around his waist; worried and anxious and tired. He looked at her steadily, up and down, with no regard for politeness. She flushed beneath his look. Damn, she was pretty! She reminded him of a cameo he'd seen in a shop in Denver. But there was nothing hard and rigid about her fine-boned features, only anxiety, fatigue and dark smudges beneath her eyes. He had never seen a woman who was so soft and feminine, sensual and exciting. She was all warm tones from the top of her auburn hair and emerald eyes to the flushed skin of her face and neck. His gaze moved down over her soft, full breasts and narrow waist, and he found himself wondering how it would feel to hold her naked in his arms. Pack tore his eyes away from her to rid his mind of the thought.

The feeling in Mara's stomach was not pleasant. It churned with fear as her heart beat slowly and heavily.

"Do you think you'll need that?" She waved her hand at the gun on his hip.

"Better to have it and not need it than to need it and not have it," he said, retreating behind a wall of stony silence.

She searched his face for a hint of what he was thinking but saw only eyes as hard as steel, a firm thrusting jaw and an implacable mouth. Right now he was as unapproachable and as distantly remote as a stone statue on a high pedestal. He was the most self-assured person she had ever met—hard, clever, knowing exactly what he was doing at all times. She could think of nothing to say to him.

"Stay in the house." He issued the order coolly without looking at her and walked out the door.

Pack had waited until he was sure that the men were eating breakfast before he walked down the path toward the cook-shack. The only plan he had was to pick a time when all the men were together in one place. He didn't know who would stand with Cullen and who wouldn't. In the past when he had been in a tight spot he had played it by ear. That's what he would do now. If he had to fight Cullen, he would. He understood well that a fight meant a gunfight. Pack hated violence, hated the thought of killing a man. But years of struggling for survival among rough men, in rougher country, had taught him that a man did what he had to do to stay alive.

He looked back over his shoulder. One of his young broth-ers was at the well; the other was building a fire beneath the wash pot. He had told them to see to it that Mara Shannon stayed in the house. He was sure that they'd do just that.

A half a dozen men were seated at the long plank table when Pack walked into the cookshack. He sized up the layout in a single glance. Cullen sat at the far end, Sporty Howard two seats away on the left.

"Mornin'." Steamboat spoke before he even saw who had come in. When he did, his mouth opened in surprise. He set a platter of fried meat down on the table and scurried back to the cookstove.

The men at the table glanced at Pack, then at Cullen, but continued to chomp their food. A big-bellied, florid-faced man banged his cup on the table for more coffee, and Steam-boat hurried to fill it. Sporty Howard speared a biscuit with his knife and grinned at Cullen.

"Ya come to say good-bye, Pack?" Cullen's eyes flicked over the faces of the men at the table, seeking support, then back at the giant standing on spread legs, his hands on his hips.

"Aye."

For a moment Cullen's pale blue eyes flashed a victory sign to Sporty Howard. Then a crafty gleam came into them when a blanket of silence covered the tension-filled room. Cullen came out of the chair and rested his hands on the table.

"Well, ya've said it. What're ya waitin' for?"

"I'm not going. You are."

Pack heard the screen door open, but he didn't take his eyes off Cullen. Instinctively he knew that it was Sam who stood against the wall beside the door. Only Sam would have entered in such a way as to not distract him.

Cullen took a deep breath, and the words exploded from him. "I ain't goin' nowhere."

Still looking at Cullen, Pack spoke. "I've got no quarrel with the rest of you men. But as soon as you've finished eating, ride out and don't come back."

The florid-faced man started to object angrily. "I paid to stay here, by Gawd—"

"Cullen will give you your money back."

"Like hell I will." Cullen's stunned silence had passed and blind anger took over.

"I'll have my money back or I'll nail yore ass to the floor. Ya said ya was owner here." The man who spoke had sun-bleached hair and a narrow, sardonic face.

The words stung Cullen. His eyes flicked over the faces of the men and on to Pack.

"You ain't the owner here. You—you ain't nothin' but the ole woman's by-blow."

The gun was in Pack's hand before Cullen could blink an eye. He was a heartbeat away from death and he knew it. In the silence that followed no one moved. Cullen's face paled, and he cursed himself for letting his anger control his words.

"I could shoot you down like the dog you are, but I'll wait till you're armed and do it legal." Pack shoved his gun back into the holster. His eyes moved to Sporty Howard. "You got something to say?"

"Ain't my fight."

"It will be if you palm that knife." He looked back at Cullen. "Be off this land in an hour. Aubrey and the boys will stay."

"Ya backin' off, Cullen?" The question came from one of the men.

"What about your plans to wed that redheaded bitch that's been swinging her ass—"

With a move as powerful and sudden as a whirlwind, Pack swung an arm. His rocklike fist sent Sporty back over the bench, slamming him to the floor. He lay sprawled, his nose gushing blood. Pack reached him with one long stride, grabbed him by the nape of the neck and hauled him to his feet. The men moved quickly out of the way. Pack loomed over the smaller man like an angry giant and shook him viciously.

"You low life, egg sucking son of a bitch! The lady you're talking about is my wife. If you want to keep that tongue in your head you'll not mention her again. Understand?" Pack plucked the gun from Sporty's holster, the knife from his scabbard and tossed them on the table. "Pick them up on your way out." He shoved him toward the door.

His wife! Cullen's face was cold with suppressed fury and helplessness. He looked past Pack to where Sam Sparks leaned against the wall, seemingly relaxed, but his hand was hanging at his side.

"Mara Shannon wouldn't wed you. She . . . wouldn't."

"She did. I run things now."

"Ya ain't jist gonna run us off!"

"Are you going to stop me? I wish to hell you'd try. I'd like to put a bullet in each kneecap, hipjoint and elbow, and watch you squirm before I put one between your eyes and blow your stupid brains out."

"The men here'll help me." Cullen looked around at the men who were getting up from the table and heading for the door.

"They want no part of your fight. They've been using you like you've been using them. All they want from you is their money back. You'd better give it to them or you'll find yourself hanging from a tree."

"You're not gettin' away with this. I've been here five years—"

"Five years too long."

"I'll take Trav—"

"Go near him and I'll kill you."

"I've got horses and cattle. I built this bunkhouse and cookshack. I'm entitled to a share."

"You're entitled to nothing. You'll leave here with nothing but your worthless hide and one horse. You'd have been gone long ago but for old Aubrey. My mother honored her wedding vows."

"Pa'll tell you that Shannon McCall wanted us to have this place."

"You're lying. Shannon McCall knew you for the worthless scum that you are. Stop your whining and get the hell out."

Cullen stood his ground a moment longer, then turned to go. At the door he paused. "You're not gettin' away with this," he repeated.

Pack watched the men go into the bunkhouse. When he turned back, Steamboat was pulling a pan of biscuits from the oven. Old Riley hovered near the cookstove.

"Where do you two fit in?" Pack asked.

"I work here for bed and board," Steamboat answered.

"Me too."

"Are you hiding out here?"

"Ya might say that. I got a wife in Ohio I'd just as soon not run into."

"You can stay and cook for ten a month."

Steamboat shrugged. "It's more'n I was gettin'."

"Eight a month for you, Riley."

"I don't need that much."

"That's what you'll get and I'll expect you to earn it. Where's Aubrey?"

"In the bunkhouse—dead drunk."

"Leave him there until the men are gone, then throw him in the horse tank to sober him up."

"I ain't playin' nursemaid to no drunk," Steamboat said flatly and waited.

Pack looked sharply at the slight, thin-haired man. Finally he nodded. "You're right. It's not your job. I'll do it."

He went to the porch to watch as the men carried their bedrolls to the corral. He watched as they saddled up and rode away. Cullen was among them.

Pack waited a few minutes before going to the bunkhouse. The place smelled like a boar's nest. Spittoons were full, cigarette butts had been ground out on the floor, empty whiskey bottles were strewn about. Aubrey lay in a drunken stupor on one of the bunks. Pack went back to the cookshack.

"It'll be your job, Riley, to clean up that bunkhouse. Aubrey will help you. You can start as soon as I get him sobered up." He sat down at the table beside Sam. "Thanks for the backup, Sam."

"Didn't do nothin'." Sam poured sorghum syrup over his biscuits. "I got so caught up in what ya was doin', I let Cullen ride off with my board money."

"You're getting plumb careless, Sam. I'll take some of that coffee now, Steamboat."

Mara stood in the doorway and, with relief, watched Cullen and the other men ride away. She saw Pack go to the bunkhouse and then return to the cookshack. Her nerves and muscles were wound up tight and had been since the faint light of the new day appeared when she had heard the first boastful crow of the boss rooster in the yard. She had tried to reason that this was why she had married Pack. He was earning his half of her inheritance by getting rid of Cullen and his undesirable friends.

A half hour went by. She went to the stove and moved the coffeepot to a cooler part of the range. She had made fresh coffee thinking Pack would return soon. They would sit at the table and he would tell her what had taken place. She had been wrong again.

Mara tried to shove her thoughts to the back of her mind, but over and over again they rolled, like the turning of a wheel in her brain. She was mortified when she recalled his words. *Go back to bed and dream your silly schoolgirl dreams. I'd find no pleasure in taking an unwilling woman.* How was she going to live in this house with this stranger who was her husband?

For now, work was the answer. Today she would wash clothes. Tomorrow she would work in the vegetable garden. In a few days she would ask Pack to take her to town to buy glass for the parlor window and new screening to put on the doors. She would go to the bank and have her money sent up from the bank in Denver. Things to do and things not to do were listed in her orderly mind.

Mara roamed restlessly about the lonely house, touching the few familiar things left from her childhood, smoothing her fingertips over a table, the back of a chair her father had made one winter while they were snowed in. She went to the mantel and rubbed her palm over its smooth surface. The pendulum on the clock was lifeless. She had forgotten to wind the springs. She opened the glass-fronted case and inserted the key. The eyes in the painted face on the pendulum seemed to rebuke her for her neglect. Eight to ten turns for the chimes, eight to ten turns for the clock. Because she had no idea what time it was, she set the hands at six o'clock, replaced the key, and closed the door.

"It's half past eight."

Pack's voice came from the doorway, and she turned to see him returning a flat, gold watch to his pocket. Damn! Damn! How could a man so big move so silently? She leaned on the mantel for support, her brain whirling, as she moved the hand down to six. The peal as the clock struck the half hour was loud and seemed to be saying, Why are your knees so weak?

"Did you have any trouble?" she asked as she turned.

"None to speak of. Trell wants to know if you want the bench and the washtubs set up on the porch or in the yard."

"Under the shade tree."

Mara followed him through the kitchen and out onto the porch, hoping that he would share with her what had happened between him and Cullen. He walked out into the yard and spoke with the boys, then headed for the shed. Halfway there he turned and came back.

"Steamboat said to tell you that he had already started a big pot of beans and meat. You won't have to stop your washing to cook today."

Mara worked furiously throughout the day, trying to tire herself out so that she would sleep when night came. She washed, scrubbed, carried out ashes. Sheer willpower and determination forced her to smile occasionally, speak pleasantly when spoken to, and choke down a portion of the food she took on her plate when she went to the cookshack to eat. Not once did her expression reveal the panic that rose in her throat each time she thought of the long, lonely, loveless years ahead.

Toward evening, while she was taking the clean dry clothes off the bushes, Pack and Sam came from the corral leading their horses. They mounted and, without a word or a look in her direction, rode away, adding yet another doubt to the growing list of doubts regarding the man she had married. When Trellis brought her a plate of food from the cookshack, she asked him where Pack and Sam had gone.

"Scoutin' round, I guess. They'll be back. Pack said for me 'n Trav to stick close to the house."

"Good of him," Mara mumbled and watched the young boy go to the porch and seat himself on the back step. Disappointment slowed her steps. Even Trellis had aligned himself with Pack to keep her in the dark as to what was going on.

After she ate, Mara carried the teakettle of warm water up to her room, closed the door and washed herself from head to foot. She longed for a bath in a tub but didn't know how she could arrange it with so many men coming and going from the house. She slipped her gown over her head and crawled wearily into the bed. The ache in her muscles and bones was nothing compared to the ache in her heart.

It was a luxury to be alone. Tears came. Mara allowed them to roll down her cheeks. *What had she done?* The more she thought about it, the more miserable and confused she became. Finally weariness overcame her and she slept fitfully, dreaming that she was being chased through the woods by a big black horse. The animal reared over her when she fell and slashed at her with sharp hooves.

She awakened. A startled cry broke from her when she saw a dark form bending over her. She whimpered and tried to move, but her muscles refused to obey.

"Shhh . . . don't be scared. I heard you call out and wanted to make sure you were all right." Pack's familiar voice came out of the darkness. Her panic ebbed.

"I . . . was dreaming. I—"

Suddenly it was too much to hold inside her. A huge convulsive sob came from deep within her and disrupted the silence of the dark room. Mara could not have choked it back if her life had depended on it. She turned her face to the pillow and cried for herself because she was alone and frightened, for her father who had come to this country looking for a better life for his wife and daughter. She cried for her mother, gentle and refined, who had loved this house and lived for such a short time to enjoy it and for Brita, whose life had been short and painful.

Pack's weight on the side of the bed tilted her toward him. The hand on her shoulder was warm and soothing. She welcomed it. When she was lifted and held close in Pack's arms, she clasped her arms around him and clung. She didn't think of him as being the man she had married in desperation. He was a link with happier times. He was someone her father had known and trusted and loved. She burrowed her face into his shoulder and melted against his hard chest.

"Ah . . . don't cry. Hush now."

She stirred against his shoulder. "I . . . can't stop!"

"It'll be all right. You're here where you want to be, and Cullen is gone. You've nothing to be scared of."

Large, rough hands stroked her hair, then moved beneath the heavy mass to work gently at the nape of her neck. Her sobs continued until she was drained and empty. At the moment she wanted nothing but to cling to the warm, living man who held her. Gentle arms rocked her, a soothing voice crooned to her as if she were a small child.

"You worked too hard today. You're worn out." The words, a gentle rebuke, were murmured against her ear in such an inexpressibly moving, deep voice that she started crying again.

"No . . . I didn't," she sobbed. "I like to . . . work."

"You try to do too much at one time. You're tired. Don't cry." His hand stroked up and down her spine. He kneaded the muscles in her shoulders and back. "Does that feel good?" His voice, kind and comforting, was still close to her ear.

"Uh huh, but you don't have to."

"I want to." Silence stretched between them. He sat on the side of the bed holding her and rubbing her back. There were no more tears left within her. She took a shuddering breath and let it out slowly.

"I'm sorry. It's been a long time since I gave way like that."

"You earned it. You've been through a lot lately."

"I'm sorry, too, for being so hateful to you and hurting your leg."

She could feel the deep chuckle in his chest and the heavy pounding of his powerful heart against her breasts, but she felt safer than she had in weeks.

"I wanted to spank your bottom. That was a powerful pinch, but it didn't do any real damage." He continued to rub her back. "I'm not your enemy, honey," he said quietly. "You don't have to be afraid of me." He drew the words out on a long breath. "I'll not hurt you and I'll do my best to see that no one else hurts you."

"I know that. I've been unfair to you."

"No." His lips turned into her hair. "You've given me the world." He pulled her arms from around him and lowered her to the bed. "Go to sleep. Things will look better in the morning.'' His voice was strained. His hand moved to smooth her hair back from her cheek, then away.

Mara wondered for a moment about the words he had whispered in her hair. Her body's weariness overcame her churning thoughts. Her lids drooped and she slept. Once during the night she was vaguely aware that her back was against something warm and solid. It was such a pleasant, comfortable and safe feeling to know that she was not alone. She drifted back to sleep.

When morning came, she lay listening to the sounds of an awakening homestead. She heard a mourning dove's plaintive call, the creak of the pulley as the water bucket was lowered into the well, the plop as it hit the bottom. The rooster crowed, announcing a new day. The hens in the chicken house clucked contentedly. The clank of iron as the ashes were being shaken down in the firebox of the cookstove told her Pack was starting the morning fire.

Mara lay for awhile wondering if Pack had really come to her, held her while she cried, and murmured comforting words, or if she had dreamed it. No, it wasn't a dream. He had been real, solid and warm. She had felt his breath on her wet cheeks. She remembered now that when he pulled her arms from around him and she lay back on the pillow, she had missed his warm strength and had wanted him to stay with her. He *had* stayed! It had been his solid body she had felt against her back. Oh! How could she face him? She was mortified that she had allowed him to hold her last night, and even more distressed that she had liked being in his arms.

The days that followed were filled with work. Pack and the boys labored from dawn to dusk repairing first the barn and horse stalls, then the chicken house, sheds and the corral. The privy was straightened up and made more solid. The twins carried bucket after bucket of lye water and scrubbed out the inside, then dirt was poured into the cesspit so that they could no longer smell it from twenty feet away.

Mara worked in the house, at times so lonely she wanted

to cry. Although she had told Trellis and Travor they had a room in the house and would have welcomed them as a buffer between her and Pack, they had settled in the bunkhouse with Aubrey, Sam, Steamboat and Riley. They worked willingly and seemed to enjoy being with Pack. They trailed after him as if he were something wonderful.

Mara didn't know what had taken place between Aubrey and Pack. She knew that Aubrey and Riley had scrubbed the bunkhouse, had spread the manure from the barn on the vegetable garden and had taken a scythe to the weeds and brush that would threaten the buildings if they should catch on fire. Aubrey stayed clear of the house, and neither Pack or the twins mentioned him to her.

Each morning Pack managed to be up before Mara came down the stairs. He had coffee made and went after the milk while she made the breakfast. At noon he came to the house, and they ate a nearly silent meal together. At dusk he went to the creek to bathe, then came to the kitchen to eat. While she cleaned up after the meal, he sat on the porch and smoked or walked down to the bunkhouse and stayed until she had gone to bed.

They never mentioned the night he came to her room and demanded she open the door, or the night he held her while she cried and lay beside her while she slept. It was as if neither of those events had happened.

To Pack, however, the memory of holding her in his arms with only the cloth of her nightdress between them was both an agony and an ecstasy. He remembered the terror that had knifed through him when he heard her cry out. And he thought about how soft, how sweet smelling, how trusting she had been when she wrapped her arms about him. The scent of her warm woman's body had intoxicated him. He had wanted to pull her onto his lap, cuddle her and murmur foolish things in her ear. It was an odd and uneasy sensation to want only to comfort a woman without thinking of her as a way to satisfy his own bodily needs.

She was his now.

Mara Shannon had accepted his touch when in despair, and now he waited for her to become accustomed to his company before he could expect her to accept the most intimate touches between a man and a woman. Once she realized that he was going to take care of her, she'd settle down and accept their mating as natural. He didn't dare hope that she would come to love him, but she could become fond of him. That much would make life bearable. It was unthinkable to him that they live their lives together and sleep apart. He wanted a family. That was what made a home.

Her coolness hurt him in ways he had never thought he could be hurt. It was vital to him that he learn all he could about her before he would be able to close the distance between them. He wanted to know where her mind went when she sat across the table from him and looked out the window toward the distant mountains.

His hunger for her consumed his every thought. It was not just physical release he needed, but the need to go inside her, give her his child, and bind her to him for all eternity. At night he paced the floor, thinking about walking up the stairs to her bed, holding her as he had done the night she cried out in her sleep. The agony of being rebuffed or having her retreat from him completely kept him from taking the first steps. As much as he wanted her, longed to have her put her arms around him and hold him, he wanted something more than the union of their two bodies.

He wanted her love.

A couple of weeks after Pack and Mara were married, Pack decided it would be safe to leave Mara and go into Laramie. He and Sam had scouted the area, and there had been no sign of Cullen slinking around. Nor were there any fresh tracks of the mysterious night watcher.

He made his announcement at breakfast.

"I'm going into town today."

Mara set a pitcher of milk on the table and watched as he poured some of it on his mush.

"I'll go with you. I can be ready in just a few minutes."

"Not this time." He bent his head over the bowl and

refused to look at her. She stood at the end of the table looking down on his dark head.

"What do you mean, not this time? I want to go, Pack. I need some things."

"Give me a list and I'll get them for you."

"No! I want to get them myself."

He looked up, his eyes dark and velvety. "I don't want you to go this time, Mara Shannon. You'll be better off here where Steamboat and the boys can look after you."

"I'm not a baby to be looked after." Anger raced through her. She tried to keep it out of her voice and almost succeeded.

Pack stared at her. Her face was set in a blank mask and her lashes veiled her eyes, allowing only a thin glittering line of emerald green to show.

"No, you're not a baby, but you don't know this country. You'll have to trust me to do what's best for you." The coldness of his tone angered her all the more.

"Then go. I'll not force my company on you." She turned back to the stove. Her legs trembled and her voice wavered out of control. In a sudden fit of temper, she slammed the round iron lid back over the hole in the top of the range and threw the poker in the woodbox.

"Be reasonable, Mara Shannon. I can't take you this time." Pack got up from the table and went to stand behind her. He placed his hand on her shoulder. She jerked away from it.

"You've made that quite clear."

"There's a man in town who is interested in buying my freight line. I've got to see what he's willing to offer, and there's another matter I need to attend to. I can't leave you standing on the street while I do that."

"Of course not. You wouldn't want me to accompany you to the Diamond Saloon while you do 'business' with Miss Candy. You needn't worry. She can have *that* part of you. I certainly don't want it."

"And you've made that quite clear." He repeated her words.

He wanted to grab her and shake her. Instead he stood for

a moment longer looking on her auburn hair with its hidden
fire, her rigid back and her fists, clenched and pressed against
her thighs.

When she refused to turn and look at him, Pack slammed
his hat down on his head and, swearing under his breath, left
the house.

Damn her for a high-tempered *spalpeen!* He couldn't tell
her that he didn't know what awaited him in Laramie. He
couldn't tell her that he wanted a chance to tell Candy that he
was married. There were matters to settle with the gamblers
at the Kosy Kitty Saloon before he could take Mara to town.
Willy had sent word by Sam that he had a buyer for the
freight line. He intended to see about that first, just in case he
wasn't able to talk business after he cracked a few heads at
the saloon.

He wanted to tell her that it hadn't been his idea to wed!
And because he had married her, didn't mean that she owned
him or that she'd always call the shots. If she was so damned
stubborn she wouldn't even listen to reason, she could stay
here and stew in her own juice for all he cared.

Maybe by the time he got back she'd be cooled off.

Chapter
FOURTEEN

Pack and Sam rode into Laramie and down the rutted busy street that ran parallel with the shining tracks of the Union Pacific Railroad, the lifeblood of the town. Nothing had changed. Even at mid-morning the street was clogged with wagons, horses, and mule teams. They passed a saloon just as the bartender was throwing a drunk into the street. They walked their horses slowly, weaving in and out of the traffic. Both men scanned the town with careful eyes, alert to any attention they might be getting.

At the end of the first block was a two-storied building with a porch that extended out eight feet, offering shelter to a couple of wooden benches polished by the seats of many breeches. Over the door was the sign: DIAMOND SALOON. A sweet potato plant sat in a jar on one side of the shiny window, its long reaching vines tied to the top of the window frame. Voices and music coming from the Diamond Saloon were muted. Miss Candace Camp, the owner, allowed no toughs in her place of business.

They crossed the intersection and rode past Flannery's

Dining Hall on the corner. In the middle of the block was a building with a stairway going up the side. Across the front was a crudely lettered sign: BARBERSHOP, MISS NAN NEAL, PROPRIETOR. In Nan's shop a man could get a shave, haircut, bath, and twenty minutes in bed with the bawdy Nan, all for ten dollars. Of course, if he needed more than the twenty minutes, it would cost him another five unless he was one of Nan's favorite customers. In that case the time in bed could extend to an hour or two without extra charge while other customers waited. Nan Neal was a woman who clearly enjoyed her work.

A loafer leaning against the rail in front of the eating place glanced at the two tall riders out of the corners of his eyes, then jerked his head to see them better. "Holy shit!" He ducked under the hitching rail and headed for the Kosy Kitty, proud that he would be the one to spread the news that Pack Gallagher was back.

Pack and Sam turned the corner and rode into what was considered the "tough" part of town. They rode past the Kosy Kitty, a long, narrow building with a long bar and a good many tables. It had been the hangout for the town's rougher element as well as for an occasional outlaw drifter since the town's beginnings two years earlier. Next to this a one-room bunkhouse served as a place for casual sleeping with a dozen tiers of bunks and a few tables for playing cards. The usual rowdy sounds issued from the Kitty, but no one came out to see the riders pass.

Beyond that was the small headquarters building of Pack's freight business and the corrals where he kept his horses, mules and freight wagons.

The old man sitting on the stump in front of the building did not change his position as the riders approached him. He alternately stroked his drooping mustache to the right and then to the left, with a little twist at the end each time. His eyes, sad with a perpetual mist, watched the two men on horseback. As they neared, he raised a browned forefinger to the bush on his upper lip, lifted it, leaned back a little, and spat. The brown juice struck squarely on the stone he had been aiming at, and had rarely missed for the past four days.

"Howdy, Willy."

"Ya took yore sweet time 'bout gettin' here."

"Did you miss me?" Pack stepped down from his horse and tied the reins to the rail.

"Humph! Like I'd a missed a bellyache."

"You know Sam?"

"I know 'em. Sent word by 'em, didn't I? Howdy." With that he dismissed Sam. "I'll swear, Pack, yo're the bestin'est man I ever saw. I been sittin' here four days waitin' fer ya."

Pack looked at the juice-spattered rock. "Only four days?"

"I got a feller here what'll take the mules, wagons 'n the whole kit 'n caboodle off'n our hands. Ya know freightin's 'bout played out in these parts."

"I've been telling you that for the past year, Willy. Did you pay off the two drivers?"

"Ya don't see 'em, do ya? Ain't no sense in a man sittin' doin' nothin' 'n drawin' pay. Even I know that."

"Find the fellow that wants to buy and we'll get to dickering."

Sam listened to the exchange between the old man and Pack and grinned. The two were fond of each other but neither would admit it.

"I'll mosey round. See ya back 'bout noon." Whistling between his teeth, Sam turned his horse toward the main part of town.

It took the rest of the morning for Pack and the buyer to agree on a price for his wagons, mules and his contract with the army to haul supplies from the railroad to Fort Laramie. The man, a mule skinner from Nebraska, would finish out the contract, then move on south where the railroad was not expected to eat into the trade for years.

When Sam returned they ate a meal together at Flannery's Dining Hall, which was nothing more than a tent with a board floor and board siding. While they ate, they were forced to listen to the Nebraskan brag about the places he'd been and the sights he'd seen. Afterward, Sam went to tend to some business of his own and Pack walked with the man to the bank where he signed the bill of sale. He deposited the money, shook hands with the Nebraskan and wished him luck. As Pack started to leave, the banker invited him into his private office.

"Sit down, Pack. Have a cigar." The banker held out a box of Cuban-made cigars. He was a man of middle age with a large paunch and a shiny bald spot at the top of his head. He parted his side hair just an inch above his right ear and combed the long strands carefully over his bald pate.

Pack selected a cigar and lit it. It amused him that now that he had a substantial amount of money in the bank, Herman Flagg considered him worthy of being invited into his private office.

"What are you planning on doing, Pack?"

"I'm not sure."

"I was sorry to learn you'd been set upon by that bunch of poor losers after the fight with Bob Mason. I had hopes Marshal January would run that element out of Laramie, but he seems to spend most of his time out of town."

Pack shrugged his shoulders and drew deeply on the cigar. He looked the banker in the eye and remained silent.

"I've been asked to find a buyer for the Shamrock Hotel, Pack. Interested?"

"Lord, no."

"I didn't think so." Flagg templed his fingers and leaned back in his swivel chair. "But I've another proposition to put to you. We're planning a big shindig at the end of August to celebrate Union Pacific Day. It's sure to draw a crowd of thousands. A fight promoter from Kansas City came to town last week. He's looking for someone to fight his man."

"Who's his man?"

"Moose Kilkenny."

"He's tough. He's no whiskey-soaked drifter."

"I think you're tougher."

"Maybe, maybe not. Moose is a first-class fighting man." Pack dusted the ash from his cigar into the can of sand at the end of the rolltop desk.

"He's Irish; you're Irish. It would be a good fight."

"Let the stinking Irish micks kill each other, huh?"

"You said it, I didn't," Flagg said quickly. "A good fight is what I want. I'm a gambling man."

"Do your depositors know their money is in the hands of a gambling man?"

Flagg ignored the sarcasm. His eyes roved over Pack's broad shoulders, immense forearms and the hard fist that lay on his thigh. Flagg put his cigar on the edge of the desk where other cigars had left a row of burns and smoothed his already slicked-down hair.

"Have you seen Kilkenny fight?"

"I've seen him."

The banker picked up the cigar and puffed rapidly. "Do you think you can beat him?"

"I never climb into the ring expecting to lose."

Flagg looked into cold eyes and had no doubt that Pack was speaking the truth. He had not believed it when he had been told that Pack would throw the fight. He'd followed his instincts and won a substantial amount of money when Black Bob Mason had been unable to stand after Pack had knocked him down three times.

"It would be a fair and square fight using the London Prize Ring Rules."

"What's in it for me?"

"A fourth of the purse."

"A third."

"With a decent crowd a fourth of the gate could be a thousand dollars. If you think you've a chance to whip him, you can always make your own side bet. You could come out with quite a bit of money. I'll bet a couple thousand myself."

"The celebration should bring more than a decent crowd to town. I want a third if I win. If I lose, which I won't, I'll take an eighth to pay for my time . . . and my pain."

The banker stood. "Agreed." He offered his hand and Pack took it.

"Agreed. I don't welsh on my deals, you'd better not either."

"I didn't get to where I am by welshing on deals. Where can I get in touch with you?"

"Send word out to the McCall place."

Herman Flagg raised his brows. "The McCall place?"

"That's right."

"You'll get yourself killed or crippled out there. That place is a hideout for every petty outlaw who can find it."

"Not anymore. I'm running the place now. You can spread the word."

Pack walked out the door. If he had looked back he would have seen the banker holding the cigar between his teeth and smiling around it.

Willy was lounging against the building and moved up beside Pack when he stepped to the edge of the walk to throw the cigar butt in the gutter.

"What are you going to do now, Willy?"

"What ya do. I been lookin' out fer ya fer so long, I don't know how to do nothin' else."

"I thought you'd say that. What do you know about ranching?"

"Ever'thin'. I been a drover since I was ass-high to a duck."

"Good. You can teach me all you know about ranching some night after supper."

"I ain't funnin', goldurn it. I know ranchin'. My pappy ranched down on Purgatoire Creek near Raton Pass in the early forties. That country was so full a wildcats 'n bears my maw had ta kick 'em outta the way to get to the privy." Willy stepped off the walk and out into the street to let a lady with a parasol pass. "Howdy, ma'am."

Pack reached into his pocket, took out some bills and shoved them into Willy's hand.

"Go up to the livery, buy a good wagon and hitch it to that pair of blacks. We'll take it and that six head of horses out to the McCall place."

"What 'n hell do ya want to go out there fer?"

"Because my wife is out there, that's why."

"Wife!" Willy backed up a step as if he'd been dealt a blow. "Who in hell'd marry you?"

Pack grinned. "Why are you so surprised? There's plenty of women who'd jump at the chance to marry me."

"All bangtails," Willy snorted. "Only decent woman what ever looked at ya was old Mrs. Eliza Swain. That's cause she wanted help gettin' 'cross the mud puddles to the votin' place. Haw! Haw! Who'd a thought she'd be the first female in the whole world to vote in a election 'n ya helped her 'cross the puddle." His weathered face took on a serious expression. "It warn't decent what she done."

"Decent or not, it put Laramie on the map. The news went clear around the world. Mrs. Swain isn't my only admirer. There's Nan." Pack had started walking down the street, Willy taking two steps to his one to keep up.

"Yep, there's Nan. What was that ya said 'bout havin' a wife?"

"I said I had one. Her name is Mara Shannon. She's out at the McCall place."

"They ain't nothin' out thar but a nest a cutthroats. Ya went and married one a them? Why'd ya go 'n do that fer?"

"The cutthroats are cleaned out or I'd not have left my wife and two young brothers out there. From now on it'll be known as the Gallagher Ranch."

"Jesus, my Lord! I dunno what'll become of ya! How'd ya manage that? Where'd the woman come from anyhow?"

"You can ask her when you get there."

"Pack! Pack, darlin'. Where've ya been?"

Nan Neal came from the back room when Pack entered her barbershop, Willy crowding in behind him. Nan was a pencil-slim girl with black curly hair, a wide mouth and laughing brown eyes. Her calf-length dress exposed skinny legs. The bodice barely covered her small, bouncy breasts. She was a bundle of energy. Nan never walked when she could run, never spoke softly when she could shout. She took a few running steps and leaped into Pack's arms. He backstepped a few paces to keep his balance and grabbed her around the waist. Her arms encircled his neck and her legs his hips as she placed loud smacking kisses on his face.

"Darlin', darlin', darlin'," she screeched. "I missed ya!"

Pack chuckled. He put his hands beneath her arms and peeled her off him and lowered her until her feet were on the floor.

"One of these days you're going to get me shot." His

voice scolded, but he was grinning down at the pixie face snuggled against his arm. "One of your lovesick customers is going to do me in if you don't stop that."

"Oh, poot on them! Are ya all right, love? Did them dirty, low-down bastards hurt ya? Do ya need a shave today? Or a bath?"

Pack laughed. "Yes to the first, honey. No to everything else. I've got business to tend to."

"Business with Miss Candy?" She hugged his arm and her bottom lip came out in a pout.

Nan had come to Laramie two years before riding on one of Pack's freight wagons. He had found her in a mining camp, beaten almost to death by the gambler who claimed to be her husband. When Pack walked into the tent that served as the whorehouse, he had taken one look at her, and all his pent-up desire had faded in an instant. She was sick with a fever, and her face, arms and upper body were covered with big red and purple bruises. Lying there listlessly, she looked up at him with dull, disinterested eyes, waiting for him to use her slight body in any way his lust demanded.

When he left the camp, Nan had been with him. The gambler lay on the cot, his face swollen beyond recognition. He had been no match for Pack's fists. As soon as he was able, the gambler headed farther west toward San Francisco hoping never again to run into the Irish freighter with the terrible temper and rock-hard fists.

Pack was the moon and the stars as far as Nan was concerned. He was up there somewhere near to God in her eyes. He had set her up in the barbershop and left her to build the life she wanted. Pack sat in her barber chair and in her bathtub, but he had never been in her bed. She had become something like a younger sister to him; and although he knew what she was, he offered no advice or criticism.

"Are Ballard and Wilson still in town?"

"They're the ones that done it." Bright red spots appeared in her cheeks, the sign of anger rising. "They set them toughs on you."

"Are they still here?" He put his hands on her shoulders

and held her away from him when she would have wrapped her arms about his waist.

"Ballard is. Wilson hightailed it." Her pert nose, sprinkled with dark freckles, wrinkled when she giggled. "He come waltzin' in here for a bath just like he was the only rooster in the hen house. I waited till he was naked as a jaybird, then I tippytoed in aswingin' my razor. I says, 'There's a dozen men in this here town that want to stay on my good side. All I got to do is crook my little finger and they'll hold you down while I cut off that little bitty old peanut you call a pecker.' " Nan grinned and lifted her chin as if she had accomplished a great feat. "He didn't know that everybody in town knew what him and Ballard had been up to. Lordy! He was out of that tub like a shot. He threw on his clothes and took off like a turpentined cat!"

"Is Ballard down at the Kitty?"

"As far as I know. That's where he hangs out. He's not been in here yet. Must be gettin' his bath over at Jake's."

"You're a rapscallion, that's what you are." Pack put his forefinger on her nose and smiled down into her beaming face.

"I figured you'd want me to leave one a them for you."

"You figured right. I'd have been mad as hell if you hadn't."

"Well, are ya goin' to stand there lollygaggin' all day?" Willy snorted impatiently.

"You still here?" Pack asked over his shoulder.

"I'm waitin'."

"Waiting for what?"

"Fireworks."

Pack turned and gave Willy a cold stare. "You've got things to do, Willy."

"Don't ya want me to go with ya to the Kitty?"

"What the hell for? The last time you horned in on one of my fights you lost two teeth, busted a rib, and were crippled up for a month." Pack went to the door, paused and looked back. Nan had climbed up into the barber chair. "Take care of yourself, honey."

"You too. Will you stop by afterward?"

"I'm not sure."

"Why didn't ya tell her ya'd up 'n got yoreself married to a McCall?" Willy asked as they walked on down the street.

"Because it's none of her business. It's none of yours either."

"She'll think it is."

"No, she won't. I set her straight about that a long time ago. See ya at the corrals later."

Pack went through the double doors at the Diamond Saloon. The room was cool and the light was dim. The long bar down one side gleamed with polished wood and shining glasses. The tables against the opposite wall were spaced to permit a private conversation. There were no nude pictures behind the bar and no loud, bawdy music. The brass spittoons that sat on the floor behind the bar rail, where up to twenty men could stand and rest a booted foot, were cleaned and polished. Tall crocks of sand stood between the tables for cigarette butts. The Diamond Saloon was not a place where a man spit on the floor or threw his cigarette butt to the floor and ground it with his boot heel. The atmosphere prohibited loud talk, obscene language, and banging on the table to get service from the bar.

A few of the tables were occupied by men in dark suits, mostly merchants and traveling men. The Diamond was too quiet for the rowdy element in town. Pack walked up to the bar. The man behind it was polishing glasses. His beard was almost as white as the apron tied about his waist.

"Howdy, Boston. Is Miss Camp upstairs?"

"She hasn't been down this morning. Want a beer before you go up?"

"A small one."

"You don't look bad for what they say happened, Pack."

"I made out all right." Pack put a coin on the counter and took a long drink from the glass.

"Miss Candy was fit to be tied when she heard the news. There's nothing secret in this town."

"Did the men come back here?"

"One did. He was crowing about what they'd done when he got hit in the mouth. He went out like a light. When he woke up, he found himself in old Mrs. Swain's hog pen. It's a wonder the hogs didn't eat him. You got friends here, Pack."

"Where did he go?"

Boston lifted his shoulders. "Who knows? His coattail wasn't touching his backside when he left town."

Pack set the empty glass on the bar. "Thanks, Boston."

He went up the stairway at the end of the saloon. At the top he turned the corner and rapped softly on the door. It opened almost at once.

"Hello, Pack. I saw you leaving the bank."

The blond woman swung the door open wider. Pack took off his hat and came into the large, airy room. The windows were open and the lace curtains fluttered in the breeze.

"I sold out to a Nebraskan and put my money in Flagg's bank. I guess it's as safe there as anywhere."

"I suppose so. Sit down. I'll get you something to drink."

"I just had a beer downstairs."

"Well, sit down." She moved to the chairs that flanked a small table. "I was worried about you. It's been more than a month since I heard about you being hurt."

Pack sat down carefully. He was always uneasy in Candy's rooms. He didn't trust the chair to hold him, and he was afraid he'd knock over some knickknack she had sitting around.

"It wasn't too bad."

"But you were shot." Her large blue eyes took on a worried look.

"Flesh wounds. Almost all healed now."

"Were you at the Rivers' place?"

"No. I was out at the old McCall place. My mother and Mara Shannon McCall, her niece by marriage, bandaged me up. My mother passed on a couple of weeks later. I guess you could say those thugs did me a favor. If not for them, I wouldn't have been with her during her last days."

"I'm sorry about your mother."

Candace Camp was one of the few people in whom Pack had ever confided. She knew about his mother being married to Aubrey McCall, his dislike for Cullen McCall, and how he had tried to get his mother to leave Aubrey and come to town where he could find someone to take care of her.

Little lines at the corners of Candy's eyes and at the sides of her mouth were evidence that she was somewhere between five and ten years older than Pack. Yet she was still a beautiful woman with soft white skin, silky blond hair and curves in the right places. She was neat and perfectly dressed at all times. Pack had known her for several years and he had never knocked on her door and found her with a single strand of hair out of place or wearing a wrinkled or soiled dress.

A stranger seeing Candace Camp sitting in church on Sunday morning would never think that she ran a saloon, or that a few select men, of which Pack was one, were welcome in her bed. Pack had enjoyed the physical part of their relationship. Candy was a giving woman and at times a lusty one who enjoyed the physical union. More than that, she was the only woman with whom he had ever been able to converse on a variety of subjects. She didn't preach to him about his boxing or condemn him because men bet on his fights and lost money they couldn't afford to lose. She simply took him for what he was.

"Has Cullen been to town?"

"I've not heard that he's been here."

"He must have gone to Cheyenne. I don't care where the hell he goes as long as he stays away from . . . the twins."

Pack's dark eyes held her light blue ones. His eyes were so dark blue, so mirror dark, that she could see her own reflection in them. Candy felt a spurt of intense pleasure as she did each time she was with him. A tingling thrill traveled down the length of her spine, making her almost giddy.

"Do you want to go to bed, Pack?" she asked softly and reached for his hand. "It's been a long time."

Pack took her small, soft hand and held it between his calloused palms.

"No, Candy, not that the offer isn't tempting. I came up to

tell you that I was married a few weeks ago. When the preacher came out to read my mother's funeral service, he married me and Mara Shannon McCall.''

Candy's face paled. She pulled her hand from beneath his before he could feel the trembling that started with her heart and traveled the full length of her body.

"You're married?" The smile she gave him was the practiced one she gave the customers at the saloon. "Congratulations."

"It was sudden. I hadn't intended to wed."

"Do you love her?"

"I've known her since she was a little girl. She's been in a school in Denver. Her father was Shannon McCall, the best friend I ever had."

"I know. You told me about Shannon McCall, but you never mentioned that he had a daughter."

Candy put a happy smile on her face. Pack would never know that she was dying inside, that all she had wanted in the world was to have his love, to spend the rest of her life with him. She might as well have wished for the moon.

"Will you be going to Denver?"

"No. We're going to ranch on the old McCall place. There are two thousand acres of land out there and more lease land if we need it. I'm going to raise some money to buy longhorn cattle. A fellow I know is bringing a herd up from Texas next spring."

She could see the excitement in the eyes and hear it in his voice.

"And to raise the money you'll fight Moose Kilkenny."

"You've heard about that?"

"Kilkenny's promoter is in town. He's a very nice man. We've become . . . acquainted."

"Does that mean you'll bet against me?" he teased.

"I'll never, ever bet against you," she said emphatically and stood. "Now that you're married, you'll have no need of me, but I want a kiss for old times' sake."

Pack got to his feet and put his arms around her. Her hands moved up his chest and locked behind his neck.

"We can still be friends, Candy. I'd like you to know Mara Shannon. She's headstrong, like most of us Irish, but I think you'll like her after you get to know her."

"It would be best for both of us if we never met. It's foolish for you to think she'd like me."

Candy closed her eyes so he'd not see the sudden moistness there. He kissed her gently on the lips.

"You'd make a man a hell of a wife."

Candy laughed. "Believe it or not, several have asked me lately: a railroad woodchopper who wanted to take me back to camp, three track layers who have their own tent at the end of the line, and two gamblers who wanted to set up their tables downstairs."

"Do Judge Moore and Doc Billings still come to see you?" Pack asked on the way to the door.

Candy smiled with her lips, but not with her eyes. "Occasionally. And I've come to know the promoter from Kansas City quite well. He's handsome, gentle and refined. I won't be lonesome."

"Good-bye, Candy. You're a sweet woman." He kissed her on the lips again and went out the door.

When she was alone, Candy leaned her forehead against the thick slab. She could hear his footsteps going down the stairs. "But being sweet didn't do me any good, did it, Pack?"

On the way down the stairs Pack screwed his hat down tight on his head. He had one more chore to do before he could head for home. Suddenly he wanted it to be over. He wanted to get out of town and out into the open. A pair of emerald eyes had haunted him all day. Sooner or later he had to bring Mara Shannon to town. Lord! What would she think of Nan? She had already heard about Candy from the twins. Her opinion of him would take another nosedive when she found out he was going to fight Moose Kilkenny. One more fight would give him enough money to buy in with Sam and Charlie, and Sam could bring up that herd of longhorns.

He saw Sam coming toward him from the corrals as he neared the Kosy Kitty. He was walking beside a tall, well-dressed older man with a neat gray beard. Pack raised his hand in greeting, then turned into the saloon. Ballard was his trouble, and there was no need for Sam mixing into it.

The Kosy Kitty was noisy. A dozen card games were going on and the bar was crowded. Booted feet scraped on the plank floor. Pack stood inside the door, letting his eyes become accustomed to the light before he began scanning faces for Ballard, for any one of the four men who had waylaid him, and for Cullen. He had almost completed his search of the room when a sudden hush fell. Chair legs scraped on the floor as necks were craned to get a look at him. Pack finished his methodical search, then spoke to the man leaning against the back bar, beneath the picture of the naked woman reclining on purple robes.

"Ballard here?"

"Hell, no, Pack. As soon as he got word you were in town he left here like he was shot out of a cannon." The man roared with laughter. "He'd sooner meet up with the devil than you, Pack."

"When I catch up to him he'll wish to hell it was the devil that caught him."

"No doubt he knows that. Wilson left town a couple weeks ago. Nan up at the barbershop put the fear in him. She threatened to get some of the fellers to hold him while she cut off his whacker. Goddamn it was funny! He was so scared when he was telling it, he 'bout wet his drawers." The bartender laughed again. It was an unusually loud laugh for such a small man.

Pack didn't laugh. "How come you're still here, Anderson?"

"Wasn't no reason for me to be feared of you, Pack. I didn't have nothin' to do with any of that. Ask any of the men here. Hell, I won a hundred and ninety dollars. I knew you wouldn't throw the fight."

Anderson was a small man with a big head. His hair was parted in the middle and slicked down on both sides. He wore a walrus style mustache that he was very proud of.

Pack nodded, then turned his back and leaned on the bar. He believed him. Anderson would have never stayed and faced him if he'd had any part in having him waylaid and beaten.

"If any of you men've got a bone to pick with me, speak up. Wilson and Ballard tried to bribe me to throw the fight. I refused and told them so. If you believed them and lost money on me, it's your hard luck." Pack looked at each face in the room while he waited.

"Ballard said you'd agreed to throw it." The surly voice came from one of the card tables at the end of the room.

"He lied. Go settle your complaint with him. I told my friends I could win for them and I did."

"I lost a month's pay," the man grumbled.

"Why are you whining to me about it? Did it occur to you that Wilson and Ballard might have told you I was going to throw the fight to get you to bet on the other man? If I come on to either of them, or any one of the four who ambushed me, they'll be gumming their eats for the rest of their lives."

"We'd not blame ya none, Pack," Anderson said from behind him. "It was dirty what they did."

"No. We'd not blame ya none a'tall."

"I've never stepped in the ring and not given it my best, and I never will." Pack turned back to the bar. "Give me a beer, Anderson."

The men began to crowd around. "You goin' to fight Kilkenny, Pack?"

"By God, I'd bet on ya. Ya sure whupped Black Bob Mason."

"Hell, Kilkenny couldn't stay two rounds with ya, Pack. Take him on. I'd shore like to see it."

Pack lifted his beer and grinned. Today they were his friends. After he had beaten Mason and they had lost their bets, they had been ready to tear him apart. Pack gulped his beer to the bottom of the glass and elbowed his way out of the crowd. He was sick of the stench of sweat and stale ale. He wanted to go home to Mara Shannon.

Outside Sam was waiting for him. "That didn't take long."

"I was spoiling for a fight and nobody would give it to me." Pack grinned.

"This here's a friend of mine, Pack. Meet Zachary Quill."

"Howdy, Mr. Quill." Pack held out his hand.

"I'm pleased to meet you, Mr. Gallagher. Sam has been telling me you're the best bareknuckle boxer west of the Mississippi."

"I don't know about that." Pack eyed the older man sharply and wondered if he was the promoter Flagg had mentioned.

"I've seen a few matches back East." The man spoke with an accent that was not unlike that of Charlie Rivers. "They're beginning to adopt the Marquess of Queensberry Rules back there that call for opponents to wear gloves."

"It sounds plumb sissified. I can't see a country boy from Ireland fighting with gloves on."

"I heard there was to be a fight here in late August."

"I was thinkin' you were the one promoting it."

"No." The man waved a hand at Sam. "But Sam and I have been in a few fights of a different kind. Huh, Sam?"

"Me 'n Zack met up a time or two durin' the war. Once his company damn near wiped us out."

"Not without a hell of a fight. Texans don't know what it means to quit. Terrible war, terrible war." Zack shook his gray head, and a sad look came over his face. "I lost a lot of good friends."

Pack propped his foot up on a water trough and rested his forearm on his thigh. "Are you looking to settle out here, Mr. Quill?"

"No, but I'll be here for awhile. Sam, I hope your young lady will be able to see with the eyeglasses. I'd like to meet her and her brother."

"I'm obliged to ya for bringin' them, Zack. I'll be back in town in a day or two. We could take a day 'n ride out. I'd like ya to meet Emily."

"It seems my friend here is in love." Zack winked at Pack. "I'll be at the Shamrock Hotel, Sam. It was a pleasure to meet you, Mr. Gallagher."

Sam and Pack watched the tall dignified man walk down the boardwalk toward the hotel.

"Yo're curious as a cat. Ain't ya goin' to ask what that was all 'bout?" They stepped into the street and headed for the corrals.

"No." Pack glanced sideways at his friend. "You're just busting to tell me anyway."

"I knew Zack was comin'. I wired him several weeks back to bring magnifying eyeglasses. I've known people who couldn't see a lick without 'em. I'm thinkin' they'll help Emily."

"Charlie said she had a pair when she was little, but they weren't right. They made her dizzy. Then the war came and their folks were killed."

"Charlie's closemouthed. I don't even know what side he was on. Not that it matters none."

"It didn't sound like you and Quill was on the same side."

"We wasn't, but we are now. He's the man that sent me out here. But he's not here checkin' on me. The governor of the territory sent him to find a site for a penitentiary."

"Penitentiary?"

"Ain't no secret. Congress set aside the money ta build one in all the territories. Governor Campbell asked Zack to come out 'n find a place. Him 'n the committee has 'bout decided ta build it west of the Big Laramie River atween Haley 'n Hunter's Ranch. Zack says it's a good site, close to water 'n stone for the buildin's. But he wants to look around to be sure there ain't a better place."

Pack whistled. "He must be an important man."

"He's become a legend like his pa. His pa was Farrway Quill, Congressman from Illinois. There's a town on the Wabash named for him. It's called Quill's Station. It's where Zack grew up. He still lives there when he's not off doin' business for the government. Zack's a fair man 'n a hell of a scrapper. Too bad he was on the other side."

They walked the rest of the way in silence. Pack was thinking about getting home to Mara Shannon, and Sam was wondering what the eyeglasses would do for Emily's eyesight and if she had been looking for him.

" 'Bout time ya got here," Willy shouted as they came alongside the corral fence. "If'n I don't miss my guess, there's a real turd floater comin'."

"In that case you'll get a bath without having to pay for it."

Pack looked toward the south and saw the bank of dark clouds rolling their way. Rain or no rain, he wasn't staying in town a minute longer than it would take to put the horses on a string and head out. An explosion of sheet lightning lit up the darkened sky, followed by a low rumble of thunder. The lightning was not unlike the feeling of elation that raced through Pack, making him want to laugh aloud. His pulse accelerated and the skin on his face and neck tingled.

He was going home. Home to Mara Shannon.

Chapter
FIFTEEN

Anger kept Mara going until noon. After that it was the desire to finish what she had started regardless of her aching back and the blisters on her palms. With an old felt hat on her head and a hoe in her hands, she chopped at the weeds in front of the house, raked them into a pile to carry away later, and set to spading a flowerbed. The ground was soft, the spade sharp, and the bed grew to be larger than she had planned.

Trellis and Travor had offered to help with the spading when they saw her carrying the long-handled tool from the shed. With a strong hint of impatience in her voice she told them they had best be doing the chores Pack had assigned them, which was pulling deadfalls out of the woods and getting them ready to saw into lengths to split for firewood, or he'd be madder than a stepped-on skunk when he returned. She then added out of pure spite, "At that it would be an improvement over his usual pigheaded disposition."

At noon she ate a cold biscuit, drank milk, and tried not to think about Pack in town with the woman from the Diamond

Saloon. She would not ask him again to take her to town. A wagon was in the shed and horses were in the corrals. They belonged to her every bit as much as they did to him. She would have Riley or Steamboat hitch a horse to the wagon and she would drive herself to town. The foot of her crossed leg began to move back and forth in a rhythmic movement that reflected her frustration. She would come and go as she pleased, she fumed silently. She would not be dictated to by that mule-headed, arrogant, opinionated, jackass of an Irishman.

By late afternoon Mara was dead tired but viewed her day's work with satisfaction. Her flowerbeds were a myriad of blossoms. It had taken trip after trip to bring the plants from where they grew along the creek bank. Outlining the bed and along each side of the walk leading to where the white fence once stood she had planted creeping phlox in shades from dark to light purple. In the big bed, arranged according to color, were buttercups, black-eyed Susans, wild iris, lily-of-the-valley and delicate little violets. Among the plants known to her were others she could not name. One had small white flowers much the same as those on the bridal wreath bush; another had blue blossoms that looked like small fuzzy heads.

The bank of dark clouds in the south was a promise of rain. Overhead the sky was suddenly gray except for small white clouds that scuttered before the wind. A gentle rain would be just the thing for her flowerbeds, but she couldn't count on it. Rain clouds had a way of scattering and disappearing. One or two more trips to the well and her plants would be safe until morning.

Mara caught a glimpse of a rider coming up the road just as she was pouring the last of the water on the purple phlox. The wind had become stronger and gustier and had torn her hair loose from the ribbon holding it. The long strands of auburn hair blew across her face. She couldn't see. She tried to brush the hair away with the back of one hand while holding her skirt down with the other. At first she thought the rider was Pack, then she remembered that Pack had ridden away on his big gray horse. This horse was a roan and coming fast, the rider leaning forward in the saddle.

The mud on her hands was smeared on her hair as she captured the windblown tresses with her two hands and held them back from her face, squinting her eyes against the wind as she watched the rider approach. It was Ace January, the marshal. Behind him lightning flashed and from a distance came the muttering of thunder. Silhouetted against the dark sky, the horse and the rider with his duster flapping was an ominous sight.

Ace January pulled his horse to an abrupt stop beside the hitching rail. He slid from the saddle and twisted the reins around the top bar. The horse was blowing, his sides heaving, and white foam covered his flanks. What had happened to cause the marshal to run his horse almost into the ground? Had something happened to Pack?

Taking long determined strides, Ace came up the walk to where she was standing. His face was as dark and as angry as the thunderclouds he had been racing. He didn't take his eyes from her face, nor did he greet her.

"Get in the house."   •

"Has . . . has something happened?"

"It sure as hell has." He took her elbow in his hand and propelled her up the porch steps.

"Just a minute!" Mara tried to jerk her elbow from his grasp. "What is it? What's wrong?" Alarm caused her to raise her voice.

He didn't answer or look at her. His strides carried them across the porch and through the doorway. He shoved her inside and marched her through the parlor and into the kitchen. By this time her stomach was quaking, her legs seemed to have no bones in them, and she was dangerously close to crying. Pack! Had Pack been hurt or . . . killed? Oh, God, that couldn't be what he was going to tell her!

Ace pushed her down in a chair and loomed over her. Her heart sank to the pit of her stomach and lay there, thumping in a strange and alarming way.

"Why 'n the hell did you marry that son of a bitch?"

She looked at him stupidly. "Why . . . what?"

"You heard me, damn you!" he gritted out harshly. "I just found out today that you married that Irish bastard. Why?"

As soon as his words sank into her mind, relief swept over her like a warm, caressing hand, leaving her giddy and trembling. Pack was all right! Ace had not come to tell her something dreadful had happened to him. Dangerously on the edge of hysteria, she tried to swallow the laughter that bubbled up in her throat. Mara looked up into Ace January's angry face; her smile spread, her eyes sparkled. With her arms folded across her chest, she rocked back and forth. Shrill, uncontrollable gasps of giggles burst from her mouth, then bloomed into laughter.

With the swiftness of a striking snake, Ace lifted his hand and slapped her, hard. The blow cut off the laughter and sent her reeling sideways. He grabbed her shoulder to keep her from falling off the chair. She straightened and looked into his blazing eyes, her own filled with tears and disbelief. For the first time in her life she had been struck in the face. She was so shocked by the blow that she scarcely felt the pain on her cheek.

"I asked you why you married him? Answer me, goddamn it! If you laugh I'll slap you again."

"It's none of your business," she gasped. She came to full awareness. "It's none of your business," she repeated. "Get out of here! Get out of my house!"

"Have you slept with him?"

"Have I— Why, you unspeakable, crude—"

"Have you?" He grabbed her shoulders and hauled her to her feet.

"Have you lost your mind? Get out!" Mara began to panic, but her common sense exerted itself. "Your behavior is totally unacceptable. I want you to leave." She tried to speak calmly and with dignity, but her voice trembled.

"Unacceptable, huh? I'm one of the most respected men in the territory, yet you chose to marry up with a mule skinner, an ignoramus who knows nothing but whoring, brawling and bareknuckle fighting. You chose him over me! I'd of given you anything you wanted if you'd just waited awhile longer."

"I don't know what you're talking about." Her words were strong, not at all a reflection of her apprehension.

"I'm talking about you and me. You and me! The first time I saw you you looked me in my eyes, then down at my crotch. I got the message. You wanted me!" His hands moved to her upper arms and shook her to emphasize his words.

Mara's face flamed. "I did no such thing! I never even thought of you as a . . . as a suitor."

"The next time I was here, here in this kitchen, you switched your tail at me. Lady, I know when a woman wants me." His hard mouth made a thin line, his eyes blazed, and there was white-hot anger in his voice. His hands were hard and cruel on her arms. "I want to know if he's been between your legs. Answer me!"

"No!" The word exploded from her.

"If you're lying I'll kill you!"

Mara darted a look out the door and saw lightning flash. She desperately wished the twins would come, and then she hoped they wouldn't. The marshal was out of his mind, and there was no telling what he would do.

"You're crazy to talk to me like this!" She wanted to add that Pack would kill him for saying these things to her, but she didn't dare mention Pack's name for fear of infuriating him even more.

"Crazy? Mad? Insane? Maybe. I've done nothing but think about you since I met you. I had plans for us. Still have them. Why did you do it? The preacher said you didn't want to marry, so I figured you'd not let him in your bed. He said Pack threatened him if he told it. Did he force you to marry him so he could get his hands on this ranch? Is that what he did?"

"No! He . . . didn't force me to do anything I didn't want to do."

"I was going to take you to Denver or San Francisco. I was going to take you anywhere you wanted to go and buy you anything you wanted."

"I don't want to go anywhere. This is my home, this is where I want to be."

"You don't know what you want. All women want pretty dresses and furs and perfume—"

"I don't! Let go of me and get out!"

"Shut up!" He slammed her against him. "Whether you know it or not, this is what you want, and when I get you away from here you'll get plenty of it."

He put his mouth to hers, hard, hot and wet. The shock of it numbed her to her toes. She silently shrieked a bitter protest and resisted with all her strength. The harder she pushed against his chest the tighter he held her. He cupped the back of her head with his hand, holding it in a viselike grip. His mouth ground into hers, his rough and wet tongue laved her tightly pressed lips, his hard nose pressed into her cheek, his mustache brushed against her nostrils. Mara couldn't breathe. She felt as if she were being drawn down into a horrendous black pit. Wildly she struggled to break free, but her efforts were useless against his strength. Finally he released her mouth.

"Open your mouth . . . damn you!"

"No!"

He cupped her chin and pressed his thumb and forefinger into her cheeks. His mouth, open and hot, seemed to devour her. His tongue found the break in her lips and thrust against her tightly clenched teeth. His body pinned hers flat against the wall while his hand squeezed and cupped her breast. He spread his feet to lower the long hardness that had pressed her stomach and ground it against her mound. He thrust his hips against her with quick jerky movements. She fought against black panic as she fought him. She kicked and turned her head from side to side until his mouth was dislodged from hers.

Suddenly his body was no longer pressing hers to the wall, but he held her there with one hand on her upper arm, the other on her breast, cupped about its fullness. She choked back sobs and tears of humiliation.

"Dear God!" he murmured. "I've done it now. I'm sorry, Mara. I never meant to do that. But you have driven me half out of my mind."

Mara was relieved to hear the remorse in his voice, but his

hand was still on her breast, stroking and squeezing. He looked into her eyes as if he didn't know it was there, as if his hand belonged to someone else.

"I want you to . . . leave." Her heart was racing beneath the breast he was holding.

"I'm just so goddamn mad and hurt, Mara. I'm hurt that you would go behind my back—"

"I'll forget what you've just done . . . if you'll go."

"Something must have pushed you into marrying Pack, but that doesn't mean you have to stay married to him. I'll make Piedmont tear up the wedding paper. That son of a bitch hasn't got the guts to go against me."

"What are you saying?" She pushed on his chest. His hand dropped from her breast after a gentle squeeze, and he backed away from her.

"I'm saying I want you. Old Piedmont will do what I tell him. He'll get your marriage to Gallagher off the record. We'll leave here and no one will know."

Mara moved to put the table between them. It was almost dark in the room. She could hear the wind swooping down the chimney, and the low rumble of continuous thunder.

"You'd better leave. Pack will be back soon."

"He won't be back tonight."

"He will. He told me he'd be back."

Ace's mood changed almost instantly from remorse to anger and resentment.

"You're going to have to learn not to contradict me, Mara. I know what I'm talking about. I said Pack won't be back tonight. He's with his whores." The malice in his face and the venom in his voice were terrifying. "Pack's as horny as a rutting moose. He's got two whores in town that spread their legs every time he crooks a finger."

His words ravaged her. She could feel the blood leave her face. But not a sign of the pain showed when she met his eyes. He was insane. She had to get away from him. But where could she go? If she went to the bunkhouse he would follow, and someone might get killed.

"You'd better go. It's going to storm."

"Pack Gallagher is not fit to lick your feet. Don't you

know that?'' To her utter disappointment, he shrugged out of
his duster. He hung it and his hat on a peg beside the door just
as if he lived there.

''Please go, Mr. January.''

He rounded the table and backed her against the wash
bench. Mara cringed away from his caressing fingers on her
cheek.

''Don't be scared of me, little sweetheart. I just lost control
there for a minute. Didn't you like what I did? I liked it . . .
a lot.''

''No! Please, Mr. January—''

''Don't call me Mr. January again. Call me Ace, or darling, or lover. And don't act so scared.''

''Why should I be scared of you? You're the marshal.
Your job is to protect people.''

His hand went to her throat. Mara stood quietly, refusing
to humiliate herself by struggling. He looked down into her
face and gently brushed the strands of hair from her cheeks.
Then, to her relief, he stepped away from her.

''I've got to think about what I'm going to do. The easiest
way to solve the problem would be to kill the Irish bastard.''

The hatred on his face caused Mara to almost choke on the
lump of fear in her throat. ''You can't do that! That would be
murder.''

''Yeah? What do you think he's done to me? He murdered
my dreams.''

''But he didn't know—''

''Light the lamp and fix me some supper, pretty woman.
We've got plans to make.''

Mara felt as if the breath had been kicked out of her. Oh
sweet Jesus, she prayed, don't let him kill Pack. She had
been the one to throw out the challenge. Pack had married her
because she had goaded him into it. He couldn't die because
of her stubbornness.

Aloud she said, ''The lamp is in the parlor. I'll get it.''

Mara sighed as if in resignation and walked around the
table. Out of the corner of her eye she saw Ace go to
the window and look toward the bunkhouse. She went into
the darkened parlor, then through it. Without a plan in mind

she went swiftly to the door and out onto the porch. The wind
tore at her hair and whipped her skirts up and around her
thighs. She hurried to the end of the porch and jumped down,
then hesitated. If she ran to the bunkhouse he would be sure
to see her. Her eyes sought a hiding place. In the gloom she
could make out the outline of the privy. It was the only place
she could go and not be seen from the kitchen window.

A sharp crack of lightning sizzled across the sky overhead,
followed by a deafening blast of thunder that shook the rain
from the heavy dark clouds. It came down as if a cold river
poured from the sky. Fear set Mara's feet in motion, and she
ran through the rain, crying soundlessly. Running against the
wind and the rain was like a bad dream. It seemed to take
forever to get to the outhouse. The bursts of lightning out-
lined the privy. The ground beneath her feet became slippery.
She staggered and slid against the door when she reached it.
The board that swiveled on the nail to hold the door shut was
tight. Mara clawed at it frantically, turned it, and pulled open
the door.

Inside the small dark enclosure she fumbled for the latch
which was nothing more than the end of a razor strop nailed
to the door. A slit in the end of the strop looped over a nail
on the doorframe. A man, not even a strong man, pulling on
the door could break it loose. Knowing this, Mara leaned
against the wall, her heart beating like a hammer.

For long moments she was too frightened even to wonder
if she had done right by hiding. Then questions flooded her
mind. Would he go down to the bunkhouse and hurt the
boys? Would he wait for Pack? She hoped he was right about
Pack staying in town. Oh, it cut her to the quick to think he
was with that woman, but if it meant his life, she didn't care.
Maybe she should have stayed in the house. Ace wasn't
going to *kill* her.

The wind buffeted the small building. From between the
cracks in the walls, Mara could see flashes of lightning followed by ear-splitting cracks of thunder. Pack and the twins
had pounded stakes into the ground on each side of the
outhouse, but the boards in the building creaked and groaned
against the pressure of the wind.

Huddled in the corner, Mara began to tremble both from fear and the cold. She was wet to the skin. Her hair was plastered to her head, her wet skirts to her legs. Ace would have gone through the rooms looking for her when she didn't return to the kitchen. By now he knew she was not in the house. *Would he come out into the storm looking for her?* She strained her ears for any sound above the roar of the storm. Surely, she told herself, she would hear a gunshot.

A heavy gust of wind struck the outhouse and rocked it precariously before settling down. Mara cried out and held onto the heavy timbers. The stench from the cesspit which had been so repulsive to her earlier was unnoticed now. Her head whirled, her stomach churned. Into her dulled mind drifted the thought that Ace January, the marshal of Laramie, was utterly ruthless, insane, or both. He must be to be able to talk so calmly of murdering a man to get him out of the way.

The storm raged on. It seemed to Mara that hours had passed. Finally she got up the nerve to open the door a crack. It was as dark outside as it was inside except for the flashes of lightning. An exceptionally bright flash knifed the dark sky. The clap of thunder caused her to whimper with fear, close the door and fumble with the strop to hold it. Thunder rolled and the rain beat down on the tin roof. Mara hung onto the timbers, leaned her forehead against the rough wood and waited for Ace to pound on the outhouse door. She had never felt so alone, so abandoned. Dazed with fear, she was almost unaware of the cold that sank into her very bones and the ache on the side of her face where Ace had struck her.

Sometime later, between the claps of thunder and over the roar of the rain on the tin roof, she heard someone shout her name. Sobbing with terror, she slid down on the floor and covered her face with her hands.

It took Pack and Sam an hour to load the wagon, catch the horses, put on halters and attach lead ropes. Pack debated about going to the mercantile. He had wanted to take something home to Mara. Flashes of lightning convinced him that he didn't have the time. He tied two mares behind the wagon and told Willy to head out. Sam led three docile geldings and Pack the young, frisky stallion. They followed the wagon through the town. When they reached the outer edge Pack moved up close behind the wagon. The young stallion had rutting on his mind and followed along behind the mares, sniffing the air and occasionally releasing a trumpeting call.

Already the wind had picked up. In the darkened sky lightning flashed and thunder rumbled. Willy pressed his hat down on his head and whipped the team into a trot. He shouted mixed curses and warnings back over his shoulder at Pack, some of which were lost in the wind. Pack didn't even try to understand what the old man was saying. He had been with Willy long enough to know that he was going to grumble until the day he died and then would complain to Saint Peter, if and when he reached the Pearly Gates, that they weren't open wide enough.

Pack, Willy and Sam were only a few miles from home when the heavens opened and the rain poured down on them. The young stallion tried to rear. It took all of Pack's strength to hold him. The mares became frightened, and their fear was passed on to the other horses. Willy pulled the team to a halt and Pack came alongside, dragging the protesting young stallion.

Willy shouted that they should find shelter, but Pack waved him on. The old man cursed and sputtered and spit. But he snaked the whip out over the backs of the team and they moved on. The storm worsened. Overhead lightning cracked. Pack knew that it was dangerous for them to be on the road, but he had an overpowering urge to get home.

"What do you think?" he shouted to Sam.

"Might as well keep goin'. There ain't nowhere to hole up here nohow."

Pack nodded and moved out ahead of the wagon, setting a faster pace. He wondered if Mara Shannon had missed him, if she still had her back up because he hadn't taken her to town. He wondered if she was afraid of the storm, if she had a hot supper ready for him. Tonight he would tell her about his trouble with Ballard and Wilson. He'd tell her about Nan, and try to make her understand about his friendship with Candy. Just thinking about his wife warmed him. She *was* his wife, and soon he hoped she would be his wife in all the ways a woman belonged to a man.

Pack's arm felt as if it was about to be pulled from his shoulder, and his hand was raw from holding onto the wet rope. He was tempted to take his quirt to the stubborn young stallion but reasoned that the naturally frisky animal was scared, and the quirt would do nothing but make him more so.

When they reached the homestead, Pack took the trail to the corrals and the bunkhouse, bypassing the house. He peered through the rain but could see no light. To him it didn't mean that there wasn't one. He gave it no more thought. His mind was set on getting the horses into the corral, his mount and Sam's in the barn, and himself into the house.

The rain was still coming down in a steady stream, and the wind was still strong by the time they were ready to leave the barn. They stood for a moment before going out into the night.

"Willy, there's a good bed in the bunkhouse and the cook will fix you some vittles. Go along with Sam and get settled in. I'll see you in the morning."

"It'll be a pleasure to get dry. I'm wet as a drowned rat." Willy wiped his face with a wet sleeve.

"I'm obliged to you, Sam, for the help with the horses. I expect you wanted to ride straight to the Rivers' place."

Sam grinned. "It'll keep till morning. Get along 'n see 'bout your woman. I 'spect she's edgy 'bout the storm."

"Yeah. I expect so."

Pack held onto his hat and took off running toward the house. Once he slipped on the muddy path, cursed because he'd track mud on Mara Shannon's clean floor, then leaped up on the porch.

The screen door was open and banging against the side of the house. Pack took hold of it and realized the back door was also open, and the house was pitch dark. Long years of being cautious made him pause and listen before entering. He could hear nothing but the banging of the front door as the wind sucked through the house and the pounding of the rain on the roof. A cold circle of fear was forming around Pack's heart. Mara Shannon wouldn't have gone to bed and left the doors open.

Pack darted inside, paused, then felt his way to the table. His groping hands found the lamp. He struck a match, lifted the chimney and held the flame to the wick. Light flooded the room and he looked around. Rain had blown in through the open door. The floor was puddled with water. His feeling of apprehension growing, Pack hurried to the parlor. The door stood open, and there, too, rain had blown in.

"Mara Shannon," he bellowed while closing the door against the wind.

No answer.

He took the stairs two at a time. The door to her bedroom was open. He charged in and stopped. She wasn't there. He felt as if he had been kicked in the stomach by a mule. His first thought was that she had left him. His eyes swept the room. Her comb, brush and hand mirror lay on the embroidered scarf on the bureau. Her trunk was at the end of the bed, her clothes in the bureau drawers.

Suddenly he paused and chuckled. What a fool he was. When she had seen the storm coming, she had gone down to the bunkhouse. He shook his shaggy, wet head. He had tracked mud all over the house looking for her. She would scold him, but he didn't care; he was relieved.

Downstairs he set the lamp on the kitchen table, took a wad of cloth from beneath the wash bench, and mopped up the floor. He would go fetch Mara and carry her back, but first he had to clean up the mess he had made. When he finished, he took a slicker from his room to wrap her in and ran out into the rain again.

Sam and Willy were standing beside the potbellied stove in their underwear when Pack threw open the door. The twins, Aubrey and Steamboat sat at a table playing cards. They all looked up. Willy was the first to speak.

"Thought ya was goin' to yore woman. She throw ya out a'ready?"

Pack's dark eyes circled the room. "She's not here?"

"Ya think I'd a took off my pants—"

"Mara Shannon's not in the house. I thought she was here."

"Not in the house?" Trellis got up. "She's been there all day. She made a flowerbed."

"She's not there now! The front and back doors were open and rain was coming in. Who was here today?"

"Nobody," Trellis said. "Did you see anybody, Trav?"

"How could we've seen anybody? We been sittin' here playin' cards."

"She wouldn't have just pulled foot and gone without taking her things. When was the last time you saw her? Goddamn it, Trell, I told you and Trav to stay close." Anxiety made Pack's voice unnecessarily loud and harsh.

"We did stay close. She was in a grouchy mood today. She didn't want nothin' to do with anybody. The last time I saw her she was carrying water to put on her flowerbed, and it was cloudin' up to rain."

Sam had already pulled on his wet pants. He dug a dry shirt and a slicker out of the bundle on his bed.

"Yo're sure she's not in the house?"

"I'm sure," Pack snarled, but Sam didn't seem to notice.

"We know she ain't in the barn," he said calmly. "We'll fan out and search all the outbuildings. Steamboat, have you got any lanterns that'll stay lit in this downpour?"

"I'm goin'," Trellis said and pulled a poncho over his head.

"Me, too." Travor got up so fast his chair turned over. He grabbed a slicker from the peg on the wall.

"Do ya suppose she went to the cookshack?" Steamboat opened the small door going out of the bunkhouse and into the back part of the cookshack. He was back in a minute shaking his head. "She ain't there. I'll get ya a lantern that'll stay lit."

Pack stood on the edge of the porch and waited for Steamboat to bring him the lantern. Never in his life had he felt more like praying. Never had he felt such an overpowering feeling of dread. When he closed his eyes, horrifying scenes danced behind his closed lids. Sweet little Mara Shannon could be lying out there in the rain. A tree could have fallen on her, an Indian could have whisked her away. Cullen or one of the no-good bastards who hung around here could have carried her off.

Many men had tried to knock Pack off his feet and had failed. Now, fear and worry over one small missing woman had almost brought him to his knees. If he found her, when he found her, he vowed to tell her everything. Everything.

"Take one of the boys 'n go circle the house, Pack. I'll take the other 'n go through the shed and stock pens."

Pack stepped off the porch into the rain, one of the boys with him. He held the lantern waist high and sloshed through the water and mud. He squinted his eyes, trying to penetrate the darkness. In the driving rain, the light from the lantern didn't do much good.

"Mara!" he shouted. He circled the house and started off toward the well. "Mara!"

"Pack." Trellis shook his arm. "Do ya think she could a got caught in the privy when the rain come?"

"She wouldn't have stayed there. Mara!"

"I'm goin' to go look anyway." Trellis ran ahead. Soon he was back. "Pack! That board we nailed on the outhouse to keep the door closed is up! I pulled on the door and it's latched on the inside."

Pack's heart leaped with hope. "Mara!" he bellowed, and ran toward the privy. The board was turned up! "Mara! Mara, are you in there?"

No sound came from within.

"Somebody's got to be in there." Trellis pulled on the door.

"Here." Pack shoved the lantern at the boy. He yanked on the strap he had put there as a door handle. It came off in his hands. He cursed. "Mara, if you're in there, open the door." He ground his teeth in frustration when no answer came. Pack forced his fingers between the door and the frame, cursing himself for making it so tight. Using all of his great strength, he jerked on the door and felt it give. He jerked again and the nail holding the strop bent. The door opened.

The light from the lantern fell on Mara hunkered down in the corner, wet and shivering, her knees drawn up to her chest, her hands over her eyes. Pack's knees were weak with relief.

"Thank God!" he breathed. He was on his knees beside her in an instant.

"Godamighty," Trellis said. "What's she doin' down there?"

"Mara Shannon . . . sweetheart?"

Pack was unprepared for what happened next. She seemed to explode with hands and feet. They flew out in all directions. She kicked out at him with her feet and beat him in the face with her fists. She tried to scratch, then bite. Screams of outrage came from her and she fought him with an amazing strength. He held her away from him by putting his hands on her upper arms. The strange look on her face frightened him, as did her unfocused eyes.

"Get away from me! I'll not let you kill him! Bastard! Belly-crawling snake! Stinking polecat! I'll die before I go with you!"

"Mara! Mara Shannon, stop it!"

Pack was forced to step back out into the steady rain. He dragged her with him, holding her at arm's length. She still tried to kick him and twisted and reared until he was afraid he was going to hurt her.

"What's the matter with her?" Trellis' young voice was shrill with anxiety.

"She's out of her head. I don't think she knows me."

"You make me want to puke! Pack's ten times the man you are, even if he does have two whores. He'll kill you when he comes home!"

"Stop it, sweetheart." Pack's voice was desperate. "Mara Shannon, it's me, Pack."

"He'll be back . . . he said he'd be back and he will." Mara's face suddenly crumbled and she began to cry. "It's my fault. He didn't want to marry me. He did it because he loved Papa."

"Ah, sweetheart. Don't cry." Pack pulled her to him, wrapped his arms around her, and held her close.

"Has she gone looney, Pack?"

Suddenly it was as if the starch had been washed out of Mara's back and legs. She drooped and hung in Pack's arms. He lifted her up, cradled her against his chest, and started for the house.

"I've got to get her out of these wet clothes. Go tell the others we found her."

Trellis struggled to keep up with Pack's long strides. "What happened, Pack? What was she talkin' 'bout?"

"She's scared half to death. I'm thinking that goddamn Cullen's been back here. I swear I'll find him and kill him."

"I don't think he's been here. Steamboat thinks he went to Cheyenne. He's got a girl there."

Pack stepped up on the back porch. "Somebody's scared the daylights out of her. When I find out who it is, I'll strangle him!"

"Do you want me to come back after I tell the others that we found her?"

"No, I'll take care of her."

Pack passed through the kitchen, turned, and angled through the bedroom door. He lowered Mara to the bed, knelt down beside her, brushed the wet hair back from her face and kissed her gently on the lips.

"Darlin', darlin', I thought for sure I'd lost you."

Chapter
SIXTEEN

Pack stripped Mara of her wet clothes. He didn't know if she had swooned or fallen into an exhausted sleep. She had no injuries as far as he could tell. When he took off her shoes and stockings her feet were as cold as ice. She was as limp as a rag doll when he removed her dress. Under it she wore a chemise trimmed with white lace and tied with a pink ribbon. He wished fervently that he was undressing her under different circumstances, that she would open her eyes, hold out her arms and come to him with love in her eyes.

He dropped each piece of sodden clothing on the floor beside the bed. Her breasts were high, round and firm when he bared them to his gaze. Her pink nipples were puckered into hard buds. For a moment he gazed at them, feeling a tightness in his loins. The temptation to touch them was great but he couldn't bring himself to take advantage of her. Relief flooded over him when he saw that the buttons on her drawers showed no signs of a man's fumbling attempt to remove them. He pulled the knee-length garment down, exposing the growth of dark, soft hair that covered her mound. She would be furious with him for undressing her, but he couldn't let her sleep in her wet clothes.

Her body was whiter and slimmer than he had imagined. Then it occurred to him that she had lost weight. She looked so small and helpless with her mud-streaked face and wet straggling hair. He covered her with a soft blanket and went to the kitchen to stoke up the fire and bring warm water from the cookstove reservoir.

On his knees beside the bed, Pack toweled her hair, then wrapped a dry one around it. He washed first her face and then her hands with the warm water. What he had thought at first to be dirt was a bruise on her jaw and cheek. He wiped it gently with the warm cloth. How did she come to have a bruise? It worried and angered him.

Her face was a magnet, drawing his eyes to it time and again. He sat back on his heels and looked at her. Suddenly he wished that Shannon McCall could see her. His skinny little girl with the big wistful eyes had grown up to be a beautiful, proud, spunky woman. Lord but she was something to look at with that white skin, rich auburn hair, and breasts shaped to fit a man's hands. He lifted her limp hand and placed his lips on the blister on her palm. Something had happened to frighten her while he was gone. Thank God it wasn't attempted rape.

The poor little thing had been scared so bad that she hadn't even recognized him when he found her. His indrawn breath hissed roughly through his gritted teeth. Goddamn that Cullen! Who else would have told her that he had two whores in town? Pack swore aloud, his voice quiet and controlled. Explicit, obscene words fell from his lips. He would find the sneaky little weasel and choke the life out of him! He closed that avenue of thinking just before black rage consumed him.

Pack was still in his wet clothes although he'd had the presence of mind to leave his mud-covered boots beside the kitchen door. After a long look at Mara's sleeping face, he stripped. His legs and thighs were stiff and cold. He rubbed himself with a towel before he pulled on a pair of soft doeskin britches and a cloth shirt. Barefoot, he went to the kitchen stove where the teakettle was sending out a plume of steam. Behind the curtained cupboard he found a half empty bottle of whiskey. He poured a generous amount in a cup, filled it with hot water and added a bit of sugar. He carried the cup back to the bedroom and sat down on the edge of the bed.

His hands trembled as he raised the cup to his lips and drank deeply. His gaze moved over the perfection of Mara's face. Lord! He had to find a way to make her want him. Did she love someone else? Had she given her heart to that Webster fellow? The thought tormented him because he knew that there was such a great difference between the life he had lived and her life at the school. He had scrounged, fought, even stolen in order to eat and had had to kill to stay alive. She had known nothing but kindness and plenty. He had known many women, but none of them had satisfied the yearning in him or moved him the way this one had, even when she was a skinny twelve-year-old schoolgirl.

What would she think if she knew how many nights he had lain beneath his freight wagons during the dead of winter or the blistering heat of summer thinking of her? While he was driving the lumbering wagons over the mountains, he had never even dreamed that someday he would be her husband, that she would legally carry his name. Somehow he had to make this marriage work. He would use any means necessary to make her see him as a man who needed love and who had love to give.

Pack had never felt so uncertain before. He had lived his life among rough men. His mother and, later, Candy were the only soft, feminine things in his life. He was rough, impatient and at times brutal. Life had made him that way. He felt a stirring of hope that someday she might accept him not only in her bed, but in her heart. His chest warmed with the quickening of his own heart and he questioned himself silently. Could he live up to her expectations?

His hand slid beneath the blanket. His fingers closed around her foot. It was still cold, as was her calf when he touched it. He set the cup down on the floor and placed his palm against her cheek. Her face was cool. Her nightdress would give her extra warmth. She would be mortified if she awakened and found herself naked. Why hadn't he thought of that? Pack picked up the lamp and hurried up the stairs. He took her nightdress from the peg on the wall, turned down the covers on her bed, and left the lamp on the bureau. The decision to bring her up to her own bed had been sudden.

Pack lifted Mara carefully and slipped the nightdress over her head. Goose bumps covered her arms. Her cold body reminded him of the coldness of his mother's body when he and Mara had washed her and dressed her for burial. He felt a moment of terrible fear that Mara Shannon would sicken and die.

He went to the front and then to the back door and dropped the heavy bars across them, not that he expected Cullen to return, but he wanted no surprises.

He returned to the bedroom and lifted Mara up in his arms. He carried her up the stairs as easily as if she were a child. It felt so right to hold her; her head lay on his shoulder, her hair hung down over his arm. His heart thumped heavily in response to her nearness.

Before he lowered her to the bed, he lifted her so that his face fit into the curve of her neck. He nuzzled it gently, breathing in the sweet smell of her woman's body. Reluctantly he eased her down onto the bed, covered her, and pulled her damp hair up over the pillow. He stood for a long while looking down at her. And then, without thinking about the right or the wrong of it, whether or not she would hate him when she awakened, he blew out the lamp and stripped off his clothes.

Pack wrapped her in his arms and pulled the covers up over them. Her cheek lay against his shoulder, her arm across his chest. His large hand moved down her back to her firmly rounded buttocks and long, sleek thighs. He pressed them between his, offering her every bit of the warmth of his body. She fit so perfectly against him. He could feel every bone and every soft curve in her body.

Pack thought he had been in heaven when, with the covers between them, he had lain with her back to his chest, giving her the comfort of his presence the night she had awakened from a bad dream. It was nothing compared to having her in his arms with only her thin nightdress between them, her soft breasts pushing against him, her thighs between his, her warm breath on his neck. Her fragrance filled his nostrils. He closed his eyes tightly as tides of desire rippled over him. The male part of him reared up, hard and painful, and before he could stop himself he flexed his hips to press it against her thigh. Delicious thrills rippled through him. Every instinct in him screamed to bury himself in her soft body, but an even stronger need overrode the physical one—the need to have her love and trust. He groaned aloud. It was torture to move his extended sex away from her, to lie still and listen to the sound of the rain on the tin roof and the thunder of his heartbeat.

Mara stirred and straightened her legs. She was in that state halfway between sleep and reality. She was warm and comfortable, secure in the instinctive knowledge that she was safe.

"Pack," she murmured. "Pack."

"Yes, honey, I'm here." Pack's voice came reassuringly out of the darkness. "Don't be scared," he added quickly when she tried to draw away.

"Pack!" she cried out in alarm as she awakened to full awareness. Her hand moved up to his face. A sob rose in her throat. "You came back!"

"Yes, I came back. It's all right now. You're in your bed—"

"I knew you'd come back." She was unable to stop the tears that flooded her eyes or to choke back the sob in her throat. She clung to him. "Is *he* gone?"

"There's no one here but you and me. I'll not leave you alone again," he whispered hoarsely and pressed his lips to her forehead.

"He said you'd not come back. He said you had two whores—"

"I hurried back to my sweet wife. I'd have been here sooner but for the storm."

"He said if he killed you, it would solve the problem." Her arm tightened around him and he snuggled her tear-streaked face into the warm flesh of his neck.

"That's just talk."

"I ran out into the storm."

"I found you in the privy."

"I couldn't go to the bunkhouse. He'd have seen me and might've hurt the boys."

"It's over. Don't cry."

The warm safety of his arms was heaven. Mara wanted to forget everything that had happened and that would happen tomorrow. She had never been held so lovingly or comforted so tenderly. This strong, hard man was holding her as gently as if she were a baby. She moved closer in his arms and ran the palm of her hand over his back.

He was naked!

Pack felt her reaction the instant of her discovery and loosened his arms. "Don't be scared. I was trying to get you warm."

"I'm not scared. It's just that . . . I've not been this close to anyone without clothes on."

"I don't have a nightshirt," he mumbled apologetically.

"You could have put on one of mine," she whispered. Then a series of gasping giggles came from her.

Pack lay perfectly still. Was she still out of her mind with fright? The sweet intimacy of holding her and the soft whispers in the dark had erased all else from his mind. He felt a moment of panic. He wanted her to have a clear mind and to know who was in her bed, who was holding her.

"Mara Shannon?" He leaned away and put his fingers beneath her chin. "Are you all right?"

"I think so."

"You've had a bad scare, but you've nothing to fear from me."

"Pack! I know that. Are you going to leave?"

"Do you want me to? I'll not stay if you want me to go."

"I know you married me because of Papa, and I won't hold you to it. I never thought that it would cause someone to want to kill you."

"Let me worry about that. Do you want me to go?"

"And . . . leave me by myself?"

"I'll never leave you here by yourself. I intend to stay

here, in this house, whether or not we live together as man and wife. If you want me to leave your bed I'll go. I'm a man, Mara Shannon, with the natural needs God gave me. I promised myself that I'd just hold you. But, God help me, I want more! It's been torture to have you in my arms and not kiss you and caress your sweet body.''

"I'm sorry you've suffered. I don't know much about the needs you're talking about. Miss Fillamore said God made men lustful in order to populate the world. She said it was a wife's duty to satisfy the needs of her husband, and if a woman lay still it would be over in a hurry. If that's what you want me to do . . . I can do it. I owe you so much."

"Jesus, my God!" The words exploded from Pack. "Deliver me from stupid, blatherin' old-maid schoolmarms!" He threw back the covers and sat up on the side of the bed. "That isn't what I want! And you don't owe me a goddamn thing." Anger raised his voice to a near shout. He propped his elbows on his knees and buried his face in his hands.

"I'm sorry if I made you angry," she whispered fearfully. He felt her hand on the small of his back.

"You didn't make me angry. That idiot of a woman did! She doesn't have the brains of a goose."

"All I know of life is what I've been taught. I'm sorry I don't know more about what goes on between a man and . . . a woman." There was a break in her voice.

He turned and his fingers found the tears on her cheeks. "Don't cry. It tears me up when you cry!"

"I can't help it. I don't want you to go. There! I've said it, and you can laugh."

"Why would I laugh? Mara Shannon, those are the sweetest words you've ever said to me." He slipped back into the bed and gathered her close in his arms. "I don't want to go back to that lonely bed downstairs. I want to sleep with you in my arms every night for the rest of my life."

"You just want to hold me?"

"Hold you, kiss you, make you mine forever."

"But . . . I am yours."

"Not the way I want you to be," he whispered hoarsely. "I want us to be man and wife in all the ways there are. I want to share my life and my dreams with you. If I stay now, there'll be no going back. It'll be this way from now on.''

Her lovely, curving form nestled close against him; a warm soft thigh snug between his, an arm flung out across his chest. For a brief haunting moment he wondered if this were all a dream. She had brought something to his life that he hadn't realized was so all-consuming, a love that went beyond gratifying his physical needs. She filled his heart. He wanted to love and be loved by her. He wanted to put all his thoughts, toil and love into building a future with her.

His skin was warm, the hair on his chest soft and silky, his breath ragged and uneven. She reveled in a happiness that was new to her, but frightening too. Lying against his great trembling body she felt secure, loved. She wanted with all her heart to give him what he wanted, to take away the lust that Miss Fillamore said tormented a man.

"I don't want to be alone. I've been alone for a long, long time. That's why I came home." She realized that she was saying things to him here in the dark with the rain pounding down on the roof, things she could never say to him in the light of day for fear of seeing mockery in his eyes. "Pack . . . I'm not worldly, but I'll try to be a good wife to you."

"Ah, darlin' girl."

He raised her chin with his forefinger and placed his lips against hers. The kiss began gently without pressure. His mouth lightly caressed her softly parted lips. He took great care not to crush the feeling from her lips but to teach them, second by second, to respond and vibrate to the warm caressing movement of his. The arms that held her to him were loose so that she wouldn't feel threatened. After a long, delicious moment, he lifted his mouth and put his lips to her ear.

"Kiss me back. Please, sweetheart. . . . "

Her lips were sweetly hesitant as they searched for his. And although his lips were soft and gentle, they entrapped hers with a fiery heat that created strange sensations inside her. She opened her mouth beneath his; the tip of his tongue entered and swirled gently over her inner lips, then withdrew. He moved his mouth away, then back.

He murmured in her ear, "Do you like that?"

"Oh, yes! Pack?"

"Yes, love."

"Does it hurt when you get hard?" Her mind whirled giddily, for although she had never seen a man aroused, she knew what was pressing against her thigh.

"Sometimes."

"I don't want you to hurt— ever!" She cupped his cheek with her palm.

Pack smoothed her hair and drew his mouth along the line of his jaw. His parted lips touched hers briefly. She felt the thunderous beating of his heart against her near-naked breasts and the trembling in his arms.

"I don't want to hurt you, but I will when I go inside you . . . for the first time."

She pressed against him as innocently as any young female animal that responded by instinct to the male. She lifted her face to meet his kiss, her lips parting as his mouth possessed hers. His hand slid down her back, pressing her hips tighter against him.

"We'll not have a baby if you don't."

"Do you want to make babies with me?"

"Of course! You're my husband, but even if you weren't I'd still want you to do it. I've . . . never even wanted a man to kiss me before. The ones that did had wet, slobbering mouths. Yours is sweet, Pack. Am I shameful? Miss Fillamore says only depraved women like a man to do *that* to them."

"Forget Miss Fillamore. She didn't know what she was talking about. What we do, we'll do together. I never want you to accept me as a duty. Understand? You'll want me as much as I want you or I'll not touch you."

She pressed warm lips to his cheek. "I want you to touch me."

"We'll love each other, enjoy each other, and when you're ready for me, take me in your hand and guide me to you." His voice was thick with emotion.

He caressed her with his lips and stroked her with his rough palms. He forced himself to go slowly and was rewarded-when a warmth flowed over her and she relaxed. Only then did he dare to slip his hand up beneath her nightdress and cup her firm buttocks. Gradually she responded to his touch. Her hand found its way along his body. With something like wonder, her fingertips moved along his lean ribs to his muscled waist and down his side to hair-roughened thighs. They explored the muscles of his back and shoulders before combing through the soft hair on his chest and resting at the base of his throat. Their breaths merged and became one as his parted lips sought and found hers.

The naked hunger that caught and held them was both sweet and violent. She felt his hand sweep away her nightdress and then her nipples were buried in the soft hair on his chest. Her world careened crazily beneath the urgency of his kisses, and she was swept along in a violent storm of passion. When he lifted her legs over his thighs, her hand moved down to close around him. She felt the jolt that passed through him at her touch. Thinking she had hurt him, she jerked her hand away, only to have him grab it, bring it back and close her fingers around him. A low growl came from his throat. His hand moved over the flat plane of her stomach and into the curly down at the top of her legs. Gradually his fingers slipped into the dark, wet cavern. She almost cried out at the intense pleasure his sliding fingers evoked.

For a long moment they held each other. When he took his fingers away she knew an empty ache that only he could fill. He gently turned her on to her back, came between her legs, and settled his hips into the cradle formed by her thighs. He kissed her without hurry.

''I may hurt you a little—''

Her answer was little jerking movements of her hips. He entered a little way into her. There he stayed and kissed her swollen lips, licked them, nibbled. Every stroke of his tongue sent fire running wildly along her nerves from her nipples to her loins, and she was helpless to do anything but feel and lift her hips and move her hands down his back to his taut buttocks and hold them to her.

Pack had never been nearer to heaven. He lay mouth-to-mouth with his love, feeling the most wonderful of all touches—his throbbing phallus against the membrane guarding her virginity. How had it happened that this wondrous gift was his?

"Pack! Oh, Pack." When she murmured his name, he lost his last remnant of control and thrust. She arched to meet him. The membrane thinned and yielded to his invasion. Mara made a small whimpering sound. A low, rough groan burst from Pack's throat as her hot, moist flesh closed tightly around him and they were locked in love.

"Darlin', darlin', darlin'," he whispered in taut agony, pulled back and then desperately sank deeper into her.

"I love you," she breathed against his mouth. "Oh, I love you."

Her words cut through Pack like a thin-bladed knife. Words he'd longed to hear, even though he knew she was unaware of what she had said. His hips jerked in response. There was no way he could keep them still. A love so intense flowed over him that it reduced everything else to insignificance. Mind-blanking pleasure washed over him in great waves as his life-giving fluid pumped into her.

When he could think and feel again, he realized she was still moving beneath him. He groaned and cursed himself silently. He had not been able to wait long enough! He began to move again when he became aware that he was still hard and needed to satisfy his own hunger again as well as hers. He whispered her name in a raw, shaky voice. He was slow and tender and determined to bring her gently to the mindless level where he and that part of his body that was inside her were the only things in the world.

A purr came out of her throat. "Pack . . . it feels so good," she whispered and sought his mouth.

"For me too." His tongue laved her lips while the velvety tip of his stiffened manhood moved deliciously up and over the hard nub hidden in the soft folds of her flesh. His movements were slow and precise, stroking to bring her to completion. He ignored the desire to bury himself deeply inside her and concentrated only on bringing joy to her.

Her feelings reached such heights that she forgot her shyness and slipped her hand down between them where they were joined.

"Oh . . . I didn't think you'd get all of it inside me."

"Yes, darlin' girl. We fit like we were made for each other."

"I don't care . . . I like what we're doing!"

"Ma said it was one of God's greatest gifts."

"Brita said that?" she whispered.

"She said I could hold a woman closer to me with gentle words and deeds than I could with a strong rope."

"You are a gentle man. Oh, Pack, now I know what you meant when you said a man would hurt me if he forced himself on me."

"I knew you were ready for me when you became wet. It's nature's way of letting me go inside without hurting you. I'll never, never hurt you that way."

"I know you won't," she whispered against his lips. "I feel so safe with you. I'm glad I married you. Pack. . . ."

He had never known such a flood of tenderness and love as when his name came from her lips in a groaning appeal. Her hips tilted to take all of him; her fingers dug into his buttocks as little spasms inside her pulled him, hugged him, caressed him. He knew she was slipping into that sublime oblivion where he had been only moments before.

His breath faltered and he, gasped. "Oh, my sweet." He moved his lips and tongue over her mouth, instinctively seeking the inside of her lower lip. He shivered with pleasure when her teeth parted and allowed his tongue to play over hers. It was beyond his endurance to hold back now.

She was giving herself to him freely and fervently. When she gasped and cried out he tensed and shuddered as his love poured into her.

Mara fell into a deep sleep almost immediately after Pack withdrew from her and turned on his side. She lay on her back, her bent knees over his firm thighs that were snug against her bottom. He lay quietly for a long while, his splayed hand covering the surface of her belly.

She was his now, warm and weak from their mating. She would get used to his possession, learn to trust him, cling to him, and tell him her innermost thoughts. Thank God she had responded to his passion. This part of their life would not be repulsive to her. She had never known the touch of another man. He alone had possessed her. The thought awed him. He hoped that he had given her enough pleasure so that she would never again think of what that prissy old maid had told her.

Each time they mated he would see that she was brought to completion. He would take care of her, pamper her up to a point. She was strong-willed and would soon grow tired of a man who indulged her every whim. She was a fighter, but once she realized that she didn't have to fight him she might even come to love him. When she had whispered the words earlier, she hadn't even known what she was saying.

Pack tried not to think about Cullen. There was time enough for that tomorrow. Mara Shannon would tell him what had happened. He had to swallow the black rage that threatened to consume him when he thought of her cowering in the privy.

She rolled her head toward him and pressed her cheek against his shoulder. He moved his hand up to cup her breast, pressed his nose against her face to smell the freshness of her skin, then tenderly kissed her forehead again and again.

"Little, sweet darlin'," he murmured. "At last you are mine."

Pack awakened suddenly, lifted his head off the pillow and listened. Through the window on the east he could see the light of dawn. His ears were trained to listen for normal sounds and for the lack of them. This morning the birds were not chirping in the trees above the house. Something had scared them away.

He looked down at his wife. She lay with her hand beneath her cheek, her hair spread in a tangle over the pillow. Pack realized suddenly that never before had he slept a full night with a woman in his arms. Never before had he wanted to. Now he wanted to spend every night for the rest of his life with this sweet woman in his arms.

A loud knock on the back door roused him quickly out of

bed. It took only moments for him to slip into his britches, grab a shirt and leave the room. By then someone was shouting his name. He took the steps two at a time to reach the bottom before they knocked again and woke Mara Shannon.

"Pack! Pack!" The voice belonged to one of the twins.

Pack yanked open the door. Trellis stood with hand raised to knock again.

"What the hell are you—" He stopped when he saw the scared look on the boy's face.

"Sam said to come. Steamboat shot the marshal."

"Shot the marshal? Good God! What for?" Pack was momentarily stunned. Then he pulled his shirt on over his head, grabbed his boots and backed into a chair to put them on.

Trellis had started back down the path to the bunkhouse by the time Pack reached the porch. He hurried along the path, poking his shirttail down into the waistband of his britches. The sky was clear. The rain had washed the air, leaving it clean and fresh. The mares he had brought from town ran alongside the fence as he approached. Pack scarcely noticed any of this. He followed Trellis around to the back of the cookshack and out through a thick stand of knee-high grass to where Steamboat had planted his garden. On the far side he saw several men gathered about something lying on the ground.

"He's still alive," Travor called.

Pack looked over Sam's shoulder and saw Ace January lying on his back, his blood-soaked hands pressed against his stomach. His hat was under his head. Pack's eyes darted to where Steamboat sat on the wet grass holding a blood-soaked cloth to his face.

Ace looked up when Pack bent over him. "Ya gawdamned Irish bastard," he snarled. "Ya muck-crawlin' son of a bitchin' mick! If I had a clear shot I'd a blowed you to hell."

Pack was taken aback by the hatred on the man's face. His voice was thick with rage.

"What did I ever do to you, Ace, to make you want to kill me?"

"You took my woman, damn your rotten soul to hell!"

"Your woman? You mean Mara Shannon?"

"You ain't fit to lick her boots!"

"It was you she was hiding from? Damn you! You scared the daylights out of her."

"I wouldn't a hurt her. She got scared 'n ran off. I went lookin' for her 'n saw you coming. I'd a killed you then, but I didn't know which one . . . was you."

"Yo're done for," Sam said bluntly. "Ya know that, don't ya?"

"Me 'n Mara would a seen the world if I'd a got my hands on that gold."

"Well, ya didn't. The only thin' ya can do now is make thin's as right as ya can. Ya been roamin' round here nights lookin' for it, ain't ya?"

The face of the dying man had turned a bluish gray. Blood oozed from the corner of his mouth. He looked old, broken, but he was lucid and spoke clearly.

"Give the gold . . . to Mara. Hear? I was goin' to buy her everythin' she ever . . ." His weak voice trailed away, then returned. "Prisoner . . . in my jail said . . . he was to meet a feller." He paused, then spoke between rasping breaths. "With all the gold he could carry. I let him out and he brung me here."

"What happened to the prisoner?" Sam asked.

"I killed him cause he was a blabberin' fool. They told him his partner come here sick, then up and died. I figured he told somebody about the gold. I been waitin', night after night, for him to try and haul it out." He chuckled, then winced.

"How did ya know it was still here?"

"As marshal I'd a known if it was found. Wasn't even thinkin' about the gold last night. Just waitin' to get a shot at Pack when . . . I saw the old man dig up *my* gold."

Pack glanced over his shoulder at the hole in the middle of the garden, then back at Ace. His eyes were as vacant as a blind man's eyes.

"That old man . . . I never saw a draw as fast. Hang the dried-up old . . . bastard!" Ace reared up. His head dropped back and blood gushed from his mouth. "Hang 'em for killin' me—'' After gasping the words, Ace rolled accusing eyes toward Pack. His jaw hung down. The eyes that remained open and staring were the eyes of a dead man.

Pack stood and shook his head in disbelief. "It was him Mara Shannon was hiding from. I thought it was Cullen."

"He was goin' ta kill ya, Pack."

"I guess he was. Mara Shannon was carrying on that someone was after me last night, but she was in such a state that I didn't pay much mind. I thought it was just more of Cullen's threats." Pack looked over to where the twins were helping Steamboat get to his feet. "What's he got to say?"

"I've not talked to him yet. I woke up when he left his bunk. He was mighty sneaky 'bout it. I got to thinkin' it was a mite early for him to be startin' breakfast. When he didn't go in the cookshack, I got up and was 'bout to slip out the door when I heard the shots."

"You hurt bad, Steamboat?" Pack asked.

"Not much."

Pack pulled the cook's hand away from his face. "Looks like the bullet sliced through your cheek. You're damn lucky."

Sam reached out and lifted a Colt .44 revolver from the holster on Steamboat's hip. "Ya've got some talkin' to do, but it can wait till yo're patched up."

"Sam, is there really gold in them sacks?" Travor asked, his voice shaking with youthful excitement.

"I haven't looked at it, but I'm thinkin' it is." Sam walked over to the cloth sacks piled beside the hole. He looked at the face of each of the men. "It's government gold. I'll be turnin' it in 'n collectin' a reward. I been huntin' it for nigh on two years. After I collect, I'll pay each a ya fifty silver dollars."

In the stillness after Sam's words, Pack looked at Aubrey, then Riley. He knew Willy like the back of his hand. The gold would be only a bother to Willy. Riley wasn't a threat. Aubrey was the only one to worry about.

"Aubrey, if Cullen or any of his bunch came back and

found out about what's here in these sacks, they'd move heaven and earth to get it. They'd kill the boys, Mara Shannon, all of us without batting an eye.''

"I be knowin' that, Pack. And I be knowin', too, that ye ain't havin' much use fer me.''

"And you're knowing why.''

"Aye. 'Tis me fondness fer good Irish whiskey what made me the drunk that I am.''

"I'm hoping that's all in the past. For my mother's sake and for my brothers, I'm willing to lay it to rest, if you are.''

"It's decent a ya . . . considerin'. I want ya to know that I ain't got ter be so low that I be puttin' my lads up ter be killed by robbers 'n thieves.''

Trellis and Travor watched and listened to the exchange between Pack and their father. The hope that the contention between the two men could be settled so they could all live on the ranch peacefully was plain on their young faces.

"I was sure you'd see it that way. We better get Steamboat patched up and take care of the marshal. We've got a canvas in the wagon, don't we, Willy?''

"Ya know durn good 'n well we do. I don't go noplace without a tarp or two. Guess ya want me ta get it 'n wrap that buzzard in it. A pure-dee old waste of a good tarp, if ya ask me.''

"It's got to be done, so get it. What do you want to do about the sacks, Sam?''

"Leave them here for the time bein'." Sam dropped the heavy canvas bags back into the hole one by one, and shoveled a few spadefuls of dirt over them. When he finished, he was breathing hard.

"Do you think Ace shot first?''

" 'Pears so. Shape he was in he couldn't a lifted a gun ta shoot after Steamboat got him. 'N he couldn't a got as close without a gun on the old man. There wasn't a split second atween the shots. I want to hear what Steamboat's got to say. I'd hate to see that old man hang for defendin' himself against a crooked lawman. If he comes outta this, I'll see that he gets a cut a the reward money.''

"That's up to you, Sam. But how do you know he meant to turn it in?"

"How do I know he didn't?"

"It'll take a wagon to take that gold to town."

"Yeah, it will. Ace can ride to town with what he give up his life for," Sam said dryly.

Chapter
SEVENTEEN

Sounds coming from the kitchen awakened Mara.

A slight discomfort when she drew her legs together and stretched brought her thoughts to the night before. She had spent the night in the arms of her husband, naked as the day she was born. They had mated not once, but twice, and she had loved every minute of their union. She felt . . . new, as if this was the first day of her life. For a moment she wondered why she didn't feel disgracefully wanton. Instead of shame she felt a glorious fulfillment. What she had been taught to fear and dread had been the most beautiful experience of her life.

Mara smiled recalling the passion, the power and the tenderness of the man who had introduced her to the joy of uniting. She had felt the thunderous beat of his heart against her naked breast and heard his hoarse, murmured cries in her ear. Later, as she drifted off to sleep, there had been a silent claim of possession in the way he had held her.

He was hers and she was his. Someday he would love her.

Her smiled broadened, then she winced. Her fingertips

sought the soreness along her jaw. All her fears came rushing back. *She had to tell Pack that Ace January had threatened to kill him!* She flipped back the covers and sat up on the side of the bed.

The sun was coming in through the open window. In the distance she could hear mourning doves cooing. Hens were clucking in the yard below and robins were singing. The creaking sound of the pulley told her someone was drawing fresh water from the well. Everything was so normal this morning. How could that be when she was so different?

The loud clang of the iron lid on the cookstove galvanized her into action. She grabbed up her nightdress and held it in front of her while she hurried to close the bedroom door. She stood with her back against it. Her knees were weak. Then she remembered she'd had nothing to eat but a couple of biscuits at noon the day before.

Mara washed her face and hands and between her legs with the wet cloth. It felt so good. She rinsed the cloth in the bowl to apply it again. The bloody water shocked her. At first she thought she had started her monthly flow but decided that couldn't be the case because she had finished it only the week before.

Pack had not hurt her! He had been so gentle, so sweet. She dressed, brushed the tangles out of her hair, rolled it into a soft bun, and pinned it to the back of her head. While she was straightening the bed, she saw the stains on the bed-clothes and remembered reading that centuries ago the blood-stained sheets were hung out the castle window to proclaim the bride had been a virgin on her wedding night. Mara quickly stripped the bed. The bedclothes would not be washed today, not in the middle of the week. She rolled the sheets in a ball, shoved them under the bed and opened her trunk for clean linens.

Her heart was fluttering in the pit of her stomach when she went to the head of the stairs and started down. This morning she was filled with boundless happiness. She longed to see Pack, yet she didn't know how she should act. She nervously smoothed her apron down over her skirt and went lightly down the stairs.

Pack stood bare-chested beside the wash bench with his shaving mug in one hand, the soft, round brush in the other. He had spread a layer of soapy foam over his dark whiskers. His wet, black curls were already rebelling against the brush he had used trying to control them and had curled over his forehead. The skin on his wide shoulders and his upper arms was satiny smooth, the hair on his chest thick and as soft as silk. Mara's heart jumped out of time as she thought of how gently she had been possessed by his powerful body. Her eyes met his and her pulse accelerated even more. The blush on her cheeks made her emerald eyes seem all the brighter.

"Morning." Her mind groped for something else to say, but all thought left her.

"Mornin'." Something warm and affectionate flashed in his eyes.

"I . . . I overslept."

"You were tired." He put the brush back into the mug and set it on the wash bench. "Come here. Let me see your face."

Automatically, she obeyed. The fingers on her chin turned her face to the light coming in through the open doorway. He had feared his whiskers had scratched her soft skin, but there was only a faint redness around her mouth. The dark bruise on her cheek infuriated him. He spat out several vicious oaths before he could hold them back.

"Pack—" She grasped his wrist and pulled his fingers from her chin.

"That goddamn, worthless son of a bitch hit you!"

"It doesn't matter. He's going to try to kill you. He told me he was. I think he was out of his mind," she whispered fearfully.

"He's dead. Steamboat shot him early this morning."

"The marshal is dead? Oh, my goodness." Her eyes were pools of bewilderment. "Why? Oh, poor Steamboat. Is he all right?"

"He has a slice on his cheek. Sam's sewing it up. Fix some breakfast, honey, while I get this soap off my face. I've got a lot to tell you."

Pack honed his razor on the strap that hung at the end of the wash bench and quickly shaved the two days' growth of beard from his cheeks and chin. After he had finished, he swished the blade in the water and dried it carefully. With his two cupped hands he splashed water on his face to rid it of the remaining suds. He smiled into the clean towel as he dried his face. Mara Shannon was as nervous about meeting him this morning as he was about meeting her.

Mara's eyes wandered to him again and again. She was acutely aware of every move he made. While he shaved, she made batter for flapjacks, her mind skittering over the news that Ace January was dead and that it had been Steamboat, the gentle old cook, who had killed him. She moved the heavy spider over the flame and poured in the batter. Pack put on his shirt, and flipped the flapjacks over when they were ready while she set out a crock of butter and the maple syrup.

After pouring coffee, Mara turned to find Pack close behind her. His hands on her shoulders drew her close. He only had time to notice the color that seeped into her cheeks and the way her mouth parted in surprise before he lowered his head and placed a gentle kiss on her lips.

"I never want to go to sleep without kissing you good night, and I never want to start a day without kissing you good morning."

"That's a lovely idea." A quiver of pure pleasure went through her. "You're a little late this morning." Her smile was beautiful, her shining eyes magnificent.

"I didn't want to get soap on your face."

"I wouldn't have minded. But . . . I'll have to have another to make up for it." Her hands moved up his chest, her fingers cupped over his ears. She reached for his lips and placed hers firmly against them.

Feeling almost giddy with happiness, Pack kissed her, slowly, savoring the moment of sweetness. When he lifted his head they stood for a long moment smiling into each other's eyes.

"Sit down and eat, honey. Then you can tell me about Ace."

Honey! Maybe he did love her a little.

Mara told him in detail everything that happened from the time the marshal arrived to the time Pack found her in the privy, leaving out only the part about his fondling her breast and grinding his arousal against her.

"He had just found out that we were married and was very angry. He acted as if he and I had an understanding of sorts. It isn't true. I never encouraged him."

"I noticed him trying to corner you the day of the burial."

"Even then there was something about him that made me uneasy. When he came last night, I thought he was going to tell me that you had had an accident or something worse. When he didn't, I was so relieved that I laughed. That's when he slapped me."

"The rotten, double-dealing bastard!" Pure rage was mirrored in his eyes.

Mara reached across the table to touch his hand. "It didn't hurt at the time. I'd been so . . . afraid." She could feel his wild anger through the hand that gripped hers so tightly. It shone from his eyes in a strange and frightening radiance. She stroked his knuckles with the fingertips of her other hand and he loosened his grip slightly. "It's over now." Her voice was scarcely more than a whisper. "It made me realize how . . . important you are to me and how much I depend on you."

Pack's heart was beating so high in his throat that he felt it would choke him. That was the closest she had come to saying she even *liked* him. He wanted to be more to her, much more. She smiled as she looked at him, and suddenly Pack knew that he had waited all his life for that sweet smile. Nothing else in the world mattered to him at that moment, and gradually the heat of his rage cooled.

"You said you had a lot to tell me and I've been doing all the talking." There was silence for a moment. "Pack Gallagher, are you going to be one of those husbands . . ." Her voice faded as she looked into radiantly clear eyes that held nothing but tenderness for her. "You have beautiful eyes," she said impulsively. "Will our children have eyes like yours? Blue, but dark as midnight?"

"I hope they're as green as new oak leaves in the spring,"

he said quietly, "and have hair like maple leaves in the fall."

A small laugh quivered on her lips. "Something for all seasons, huh?" She withdrew her hand. "You've stalled long enough. Tell me what happened."

Pack continued to look at her for a moment. She was as radiant as the sun. He had never seen her more beautiful. Had his loving put that bloom in her cheeks and the sparkle in her eyes? He reached for the coffeepot with an unsteady hand and refilled their cups.

Her eyes never left his face while he was telling her about Sam looking for the gold bars and about the sick stranger who had come to the bunkhouse months before.

"Cullen collected his money, then paid no more attention to him. Steamboat did what he could. Before the man died, he told Steamboat about the gold and where it was hidden. Steamboat and old Riley buried him up on the hill. They didn't even know his name. He had refused to tell it. Later Steamboat buried the gold in the garden, knowing that it meant his life if Cullen or any of his outlaw cronies found out about it."

"Well, for goodness sake! Didn't Cullen or Aubrey send for a doctor?"

"I guess not. Now that Cullen is gone, Steamboat decided it was safe to dig up the bars, stash them in the barn and turn them over to the army at Fort Laramie on his next trip to town."

Pack told Mara everything except for the part about Ace waiting for him to come out onto the back porch so he could kill him. A quirk of fate had caused Ace to pick a spot from where he could also see the garden. Ace was a good shot. Pack didn't want to think about what would have happened if Steamboat had not gone to the garden that morning.

"Steamboat said Ace came roaring down out of the trees shouting like a madman that he was taking *his* gold. Steamboat said he tried to reason with him but knew that Ace had in mind to kill him. He waited until Ace drew his gun before he drew his. Ace's shot was off by a couple of inches. Steamboat's was on target. As Ace lay dying he told Sam that he'd never seen a faster draw. Sam asked the old man about it, and Steamboat admitted to being George Couch, a gun-fighter of a few years back who was known for his fast draw. He told Sam he had given up the life of a gunfighter, had gone to Ohio and married, but he'd soon discovered that wasn't the life for him either. He'd been staying on here as cook for bed and board in order to stay near the gold."

"Oh, my goodness!" Mara drew in a shuddering breath. "What will happen to him now? Do you have to turn him in to the law?"

"Yes. We'll have to turn him in. You don't just kill a marshal without questions being asked even if the marshal is trying to steal from the government. Sam has an influential friend in town. He's reasonably sure that he'll help Steamboat. After all, Ace shot first. The old man was just protecting himself."

"What about the gold bars?"

"Sam was assigned as a special agent to look for them. He's been looking for two years. He trailed the man here, then he seemed to drop out of sight. The reward will give him enough money to buy that herd of longhorns he's been wanting. He wants to settle down here and marry Emily."

"That's grand! They'll be our neighbors."

"Maybe. He'll need land. Charlie seems interested in long-horns. Maybe they can form a partnership."

"They can put their money in smelly old longhorns if they want to. We can make more money with turkeys and not have to chase them on horseback."

"Turkeys? Mara Shannon—"

"At first I thought you and Emily were sweethearts." Mara rushed into speech when she saw the frown on Pack's face. Now wasn't the time to push for turkeys, she admitted silently.

"We never thought of each other that way."

"I know. She told me."

"Mara Shannon, I'm going into town with Sam this morning. On the way we'll take you over to stay with Emily while I'm gone. We'll leave in half an hour."

"Oh, but—" Tongue-tied by surprise, it was all she could say. She felt the joy drain out of her.

"But what?"

"I'd rather go with you. I'll not be in the way."

"You can't go. This is rough business."

"All right. I'll stay here," she said with admirable calm, even though her hands were clenched into tight fists and she felt as if a rug had been pulled out from under her.

"I said I wasn't leaving you here alone and I meant it."

"I'm not a child who needs minding when left alone!" she spat out, hiding her heartbreak with anger.

She sat stiffly, furious and weary and completely confused. It was happening again. He was determined to keep her out of sight. Was he ashamed to take her to town? Her pain was all the more acute because of what had happened between them only a few short hours earlier.

"Don't argue, Mara Shannon." He didn't raise his voice, didn't change the calm inflection of his tone, but it was a command.

Mara watched his jaw tighten and realized how useless it was to pit her will against his. Nevertheless, her stubborn Irish pride forced her to try. She waited in silence long enough for him to drain his coffee cup.

"This conversation is strangely familiar. Isn't it the same one we had a day or so ago?"

"It is not the same at all. I should not have left you here. This time you will spend the day with Emily. That's my final word." He spoke in a tone that brooked no argument. His jawline tight, his eyes hard and oddly evasive of her face, he got to his feet.

"That's very generous of you." Mara stood, picked up the dishes, and carried them to the dishpan. She flipped back the lid on the reservoir and ladled warm water over them.

"Can you be ready in a half an hour?"

Mara threw the bar of yellow soap into the dishwater so hard that water splashed out onto the hot stovetop, sizzled, and burned off. She turned, her face frozen with anger. She brushed her hair back with a wet hand, yanked off her apron and threw it on the table.

"I'm ready now." Her slim shoulders were still, two

bright spots of color burned in her cheeks, and her eyes looked defiantly into his.

Pack lifted black brows. "Then get your bonnet." He moved away from the table, his throat working as he struggled to control some indefinable emotion.

Mara went past him to the pegs beside the door and took down the dirty felt hat she used when she worked outside. She pulled it down over her head to her eyebrows. The brim was floppy and hung over her ears. She kicked opened the screen door and slammed it behind her after she stomped out.

"Mara Shannon!" Pack roared. "You're acting like a spoiled little snip. I'll not tolerate it."

"You'll not tolerate it? Ha!" She stepped off the porch and looked up at him. "What are you going to do about it? Send me to bed without my supper?"

"A swat on the butt is what you need!"

"A wife beater too! It's no more than I expected of you."

"I'm asking you to be reasonable. I'll not leave you here and I can't take you with me. The only thing to do is to take you over to Charlie's."

"You decided without as much as a by-your-leave to me. Let me tell you something, Mr. Pack Takeover Gallagher, I'm just as capable of making a decision as you are, and although I may have to do as you say—this time—I don't have to *like* it!"

"I don't give a damn if you like it or not, Mara *Stubborn* McCall Gallagher! You're my wife, by God, and if I think it's best that you go to Charlie's, you'll go!"

"Your wish is my command, *master*. Rule number one: Obey your husband. Rule number two: Put your husband's comfort and peace of mind before your own. Rule number three: Never question your husband's commands—his intellect, in his opinion, is far superior to that of the female." Mara had worked up a full head of steam. She spoke faster and louder as her speech progressed. "Furthermore, Miss Fillamore's Book of Rules states: A wife is the sole and exclusive property of her husband. He may beat her and fornicate with whores if he chooses. He may go and come as he pleases, but his wife goes only when it is convenient for him. In return a husband must be thoughtful and considerate of his wife's wishes—''

"I like the part about the beating and the fornicating best." Pack bit back a smile. "What rule did you say that was?"

She was holding her chin high, though a touch of vulnerability shadowed her eyes as she met his gaze squarely. She was so brittle inside that she was sure she would crumble and break apart if she didn't get away from him. The amused glint in his eyes made her anger escalate out of control.

"I'll obey this time, but I don't like it one *damn* bit!" she shouted. She was beyond caring—for the moment—that the men standing on the bunkhouse porch could hear every word she said.

"And I don't care one *damn* bit if you like it or not. You will do as I say!" he bellowed.

"I have only one humble request, sir. May I please use the privy before I go?" She turned, and with her back very stiff walked down the path to the privy.

"To hell with that sour old maid's rule book!" Pack shouted. He looked toward the bunkhouse and saw Willy standing with his hands on his hips. He could tell by his stance that he was shaking with laughter. "If that old fool says one word," he muttered, "I'll break every bone in his body."

When Mara returned to tne house, the wagon was waiting. A stranger was on the seat. Sam and Steamboat were mounted, and Pack stood waiting to help her climb up over the wheel to the seat. She accepted his hand but refused to look at him, nor did she look at the man sitting on the seat next to her, although she was aware that he stared at her curiously.

"Howdy." They were on the road when the man spoke.

Mara turned to look at him. Her neck was stiff, her eyes frosty. It was impossible to tell his age. His face was weathered, whiskered, and he had the brightest blue eyes she had ever seen.

"Howdy," she answered and turned to look intently at the backs of the horses.

"Ya ain't a'tall what I thought ya'd be."

"What was that?" Her eyes, still frosty, stared at him. "You expected me to be some *strumpet* from a saloon or a *lady* from a tonsorial parlor?" she asked haughtily, but her mind was wondering how things between her and Pack could have gone so wrong so fast.

"Ya know 'bout that?" the old man chuckled. "Lot of 'em tried ta catch him."

"Well, they didn't have two thousand acres of land free and clear. I did."

"Haw! Haw! Haw!" The old man laughed and slapped his palm against his thigh. He held the reins in one hand and turned sideways on the seat so he could get a better look at her. "Name's Willy Farragut."

"How do you do?"

"Fine. Jist fine. Ya be givin' ole Pack the what for, ain't ya?"

"I don't exactly know what you mean, but regardless, it's none of your business." Mara's pride held her rigid on the low-backed wagon seat.

Willy cackled loud and long. "Give 'em hell, sister."

"That's exactly what I intend to do." She looked at him with new interest. "Who are you and what are you doing here?"

"Said my name's Willy. I go where Pack does. I been keepin' him on the straight 'n narrow since he was ass-high to a duck. Don't figure he can do without me now." Willy leaned over the side of the wagon and spit a yellow stream of tobacco juice in the dust.

"Well! All I can say to that is you've done a mighty poor job." Her tone was cool, her eyes cooler.

"That so? I was thinkin' I'd not done so bad. He could a been a robber, a horse thief or a rustler."

"If you had done your job *right*, he would've been an

honest, straightforward, hard-working settling kind of man. He'd have built something permanent instead of consorting with whores and traipsing all over the mountains selling cats to miners.''

"Ya know 'bout that, do ye? It was the smartest damn thing he ever done. Why, I remember the time we was in Cripple Creek. This here whore—beggin' your pardon, dance hall woman—real nice lady she was. Well, she—''

"Real nice lady? Ha!'' Mara spat. "I'm not interested in hearing the sordid details of Mr. Gallagher's life. You were hired to drive, so drive.'' She waved her hand toward the horses and turned her back on him.

This was her first trip away from the ranch since she arrived and she was perfectly miserable. Her pride was in tatters, her face was bruised, her hair dirty. She wore the dirty old hat she had carried water in the day she found Pack along the trail out of pure spite, but she had only spited herself. Hope that Pack would come to love her lay like a rock in her tired heart.

Her eyes burned with unshed tears. She loved him! The admission was so painful that she thought she'd scream. How could she love a man who had so little consideration for her feelings? Was this the pattern of her future? Would he order her around without bothering to give her any explanation, expecting her to blindly obey those orders? Of course, he couldn't explain that the reason he didn't want her with him was because he wanted to visit Miss Candy Camp, the whore at the Diamond Saloon, or the other whore. Ace had said there were two.

Mara looked at the old man sitting beside her and opened her mouth to ask him about them but closed it and looked away. *She didn't want to know!*

It was a shorter distance to Charlie and Emily's place than she had thought. Or, she asked herself, had she been so miserable that the time had gone fast? Sam had ridden on ahead of the wagon; Pack and Steamboat were behind. Mara had glanced into the back of the wagon one time and had seen the canvas-wrapped bundle that had to be Ace January's body. It gave her a strange feeling to know that he had come to the ranch and met his death out of his misguided desire for her.

"Emily Rose!" Sam called out as soon as he came out of the trees and saw Emily at the clothesline.

"Sam!" Her voice was eager. She followed the clothesline toward the sound of his voice.

"Hello, Emily Rose." He dismounted quickly and went to her. Just looking at her warmed his heart.

"Hello, Sam. Somehow I thought you'd come today."

He pulled her behind the sheets she had spread on the line. "Pack 'n Mara are comin'. I want to kiss ya, got to kiss ya before they get here."

The wind blew the wet sheets against her. She laughed. "Then what are you waiting for?"

"I just wanted ta look at ya. I love ya, Emily Rose. I got a whole heart full of love for ya."

"And I love you." Her palms caressed his cheeks. "It seems like a year since—"

"For me too."

His hands moved up to cup her face, then his fingers slid into her thick hair. He lowered his lips to hers and kissed her softly and reverently, and then his hands moved down, his arms wrapped around her and he held her tightly to him. His mouth was both hard and soft as she remembered it, hungry as her own was hungry. He kissed her with slow, hot precision, his tongue on her parted lips, the roughness of his face scraping her softer skin. At last he muttered a frustrated curse and lifted his head.

"It's hard to wait, sweet love."

"Dear, darling Sam. I want you to be very sure—"

He put his fingers on her lips. "Don't ya say anythin' like that anymore. If ya'll have me, I'll spend my life takin' care a ya, lovin' ya."

"I never dreamed I'd meet a man like you. You're everything that's good."

Sam grinned. "Ya don't know me a'tall, honey. I can be meaner than a cornered polecat at times."

She nuzzled his cheek with her nose. "You'll never make me believe that!"

"Pack's bringin' Mara to stay with you while we go to town. When we get back, I'll tell Charlie I'm takin' ya to be my wife."

"Oh, Sam, it's a big step. Think about what it would mean to be married to a woman who can barely see her hand in front of her."

"Shh . . . don't ya mention it again." His arms fell away from her and he reached into his pocket. "I brought ya somethin'. I don't want ya to be disappointed if it don't do much good." He unwrapped the eyeglasses and held them by the thin piece of wire between the two lens.

"A surprise! Oh, what is it?"

Sam wiped each thick oval lens with the end of his neckerchief. His heart was pumping like a steam engine as he spread out the ear pieces. Why in the hell had he done such a stupid thing? he asked himself. She would think he wanted her only if she could see.

"Shut yore eyes, sweetheart," he ordered gently. "I want ya to know that this is only a shot in the dark. It ain't worth a second thought if it don't work."

"You've brought me eyeglasses," she said when she felt the scrape of the wire earpieces on her temples.

"Keep yore eyes shut till I get them set." He curled the thin wire around her ears and settled the nosepiece on the bridge of her nose. "Too tight?" he asked in a breathless whisper. His heart was racing as if he had run five miles.

"No." Her lower lip was caught firmly between her teeth in an effort to stop its trembling.

"Now, honey, open your eyes."

Emily gripped his arms tightly and opened her eyes. Sam's face was close and large and . . . distorted. Startled, she drew back and his features came into focus.

"Oh my gosh," she whispered. She stepped back away from him until she could extend her arm full-length and touch him. He was an arm's length away and she could still see his dear face clearly! "Oh, my love. I can see you from here." She put the back of her hand to her mouth to still her trembling lips.

Behind the thick lenses her eyes filled with tears. Sam reached for her arm and pulled her from behind the clothes on the line and out into the middle of the yard.

"Can you see my horse?" he asked urgently.

"Yes . . . and I can see the trees! Oh, there's the washpot and the well. And . . . I can see all of you at once. I'm going to cry and I don't want to."

Sam's heart jumped like a wild thing. Relief made him weak. He took her by the shoulders and turned her toward the house. It was a good fifty feet from where they stood.

"I can see it. It's not clear, but I can see it." She took a few steps toward it and stumbled. Sam grabbed her arm. "Oh, the ground comes up so . . . quick."

"You'll have to be careful at first."

She turned and put her arms around his neck. The wire frames of the glasses scraped his chin. She drew back and laughed.

"I see what you mean. I thank you for them. Oh, I do thank you! Where did you get them?"

"A friend was comin' out from Saint Louis. I wired him 'n asked him to go by a place I'd heard of 'n bring a pair of glasses for someone who was very nearsighted."

"I'd like to meet your friend and thank him."

"I want him to meet you too, sweetheart. Is Charlie here?"

"He's somewhere near. I suspect he saw you coming and gave us some time to be alone."

"Then he isn't dead set against me as a brother-in-law?"

Emily smiled up at him. "No. He likes you, but he also knows it wouldn't do him any good if he was dead set against you. Did you say Pack was bringing Mara for a visit?"

"He's bringin' her to stay while we go to town. He's not easy 'bout leavin' her alone with just the boys 'n their pa."

"I can see something moving along the edge of the trees.

I couldn't even see the trees before. Now I see a wagon and two men on horseback. Sam, it's so wonderful!''

To Mara's surprise the day was not as miserable as she thought it would be. Sam and Pack stayed for only a short while to talk with Charlie. She ignored Pack, keeping her back to him when it was at all possible. She had pushed his hands away when he had come to help her down from the wagon seat and had climbed down by herself. It was a clear, silent statement that she wanted as little to do with him as possible. When Pack and Sam were ready to leave, she deliberately went to the well for a drink of water. If Emily noticed the coolness between them she didn't comment on it.

Mara shared in Emily's joy of the new eyeglasses. She was with her when she stood in the doorway and saw for the first time a panoramic view of her home. She had seen it only one small piece at a time. Charlie was almost as delighted with the eyeglasses as Emily. He brought books down from the shelves and showed her the ones he had been reading to her. Mara stood by as helpless as Charlie when Emily removed the eyeglasses, placed them carefully on the table, hid her face in her arms and cried.

Sam and Pack had told Charlie the highlights of the events leading to the death of the marshal. A good part of the afternoon was spent discussing it. Mara filled in the gaps with as much as she knew about what had happened. She carefully refrained from mentioning anything personal regarding herself and Pack.

At sundown Sam and Pack returned. Mara stood on the porch beside Charlie and watched Emily go to greet Sam.

She loved him and she didn't care who knew it. Lucky Emily.

Mara's anger at Pack was still simmering. In the back of her mind she knew that she was being a shrew. Pack had not agreed to love her, only to marry her. Oh, but it hurt to think of him with that woman! Was he trying to keep his marriage a secret from the whore at the Diamond Saloon? Or was he ashamed of Mara? Mara was confident that she could hold her own in any company. She loved the big, bullheaded Irishman, she admitted begrudgingly. It was not something she had chosen to do, but she did. But she'd be damned if she'd ever let him know it. She'd die with the knowledge locked inside her!

Pack's face darkened and his jaw tightened with anger when he looked at Mara, thinking her temper had cooled enough for her to be civil. She looked at him and nodded as if he were a stranger. She was being civil, but barely. She came to the porch and sat down as far from him as possible. He knew that if he said one word to her his temper, and hers, would break free like a herd of wild horses in a brush corral. So Pack sat silently, holding onto his temper, while Sam, holding Emily's hand, told the news.

Sam's friend had spoken to the judge on Steamboat's behalf. He had explained that the cook had not tried to dispose of the gold and that, because of the outlaws staying at the ranch, he had been afraid to turn it in. He also convinced the judge that Steamboat had killed the marshal in self-defense. The judge ruled that there would be no charges filed, and Steamboat was free to go.

Pack looked directly at Mara. "Steamboat and Willy have gone back to the ranch. We'll go when you're ready."

Before she could answer, Emily jumped to her feet.

"You're staying for supper." Her voice was rich with happiness. "Mara Shannon and I have got it ready."

Mara followed Emily into the house. She washed her hands and began setting the table. Emily talked and Mara added a few comments when it was absolutely necessary. She had suddenly realized that Pack expected her to ride back with him on that big gray horse. The thought of that long ride, sitting behind him like a "baggage" was so demoralizing it almost made her ill. She considered asking Charlie if he had a horse she could borrow. Then the thought came to her that it would be humiliating if Pack vetoed her request. She discarded the idea.

The time spent at the supper table passed slowly, but it passed. Mara had taken a seat beside Pack so that she didn't have to look at him. But watching Sam and Emily made jealousy clutch at her heart. Their eyes strayed to each other often. His right hand and her left were hidden beneath the table much of the time. She hoped that they were so engrossed in each other that they wouldn't notice that the only words between Pack and herself were "pass the butter" and "thank you."

When they finished eating, the men went to the porch to smoke and continue their discussion about cattle, land and the best way to get a herd up from Texas. Mara helped Emily with the cleanup even though she protested.

"You'll be wanting to get home before dark. It's been a wonderful day, Mara Shannon. I'm so glad you came."

"I've been wanting to see your home. I'm happy for you and Sam. Have you decided on a date for the wedding?"

"Sam is going to stay here tonight and talk to Charlie. He'll not ask Charlie's permission to marry me, he'll tell him." She laughed. "Thank goodness Charlie likes Sam. I'd hate for the two men I love to butt heads."

"Will you live here?"

"I'll live wherever Sam wants to live. He wants to get settled on some land now that he has the reward money coming. Sam hasn't had much happiness in his life. I intend to remedy that."

"Mara Shannon," Pack called from the porch, "we'd better be going. It'll be dark soon."

Mara picked up her old felt hat and walked to the porch as if she were going to her hanging. She felt Emily's arm go around her.

"Things will work out for you and Pack. Just give it a little time," she whispered.

"Is it so obvious—that we can't stand each other?"

"No. That's not obvious at all." Emily dropped her arm to allow Mara to go out the door ahead of her. Her whisper just barely reached Mara's ears. "What is obvious to me is that you're a couple of foolishly proud people who love each other but are too stubborn to admit it."

Chapter
EIGHTEEN

"Good-bye, Emily. Thank you for a lovely day. Charlie, Sam, it was nice seeing you again."

Mara offered her hand to each and said all the right things according to Miss Fillamore's ideas of etiquette. Then, with her back as straight as a board, she went down the steps to where Pack was waiting beside his horse. The animal's back was so high she couldn't see over it. It tossed its head, blew and pawed the earth. Inside she was quivering with fear: fear of the horse and fear of Pack. On the outside she appeared to be as calm as if riding this gigantic animal with a husband who had just returned from a visit with his whore was an everyday occurrence.

Pack spoke a stern word to the horse who stood perfectly still. He swung easily into the saddle, reached down and grasped Mara beneath her armpits, hauled her up and plunked her down on his lap. He lifted her leg over the pommel so that she sat astride in front of him, wedged between the pommel and his open thighs. A small cry of surprise escaped her. Her hat, scraping his shoulder, tilted down over her eyes so that she couldn't see; her skirts were up to her knees and her hands grabbed at the horse's mane. Tight fingers on her wrist pulled her hands loose and flattened them on the pommel. Several distinct swear words were hissed in her ear. His arm across her midriff held her in a steel grip as the big gray's powerful hooves dug into the ground and its haunches propelled it forward. Pack's booted heels jabbed into the sides of his mount and urged it into a reckless, bone-jarring pace that covered a quarter of a mile before he allowed it to slow down.

Mara dared to free a hand long enough to push her hat back when the stride of the horse relaxed to an easy gait. This was not the road they had used that morning but a trail that ran alongside a fast-moving creek. It was dusk. Light was fading fast. Already a few bright stars shone in the sky, and a crescent moon rode over the treetops.

Pack's hand on her stomach pulled her back even farther and settled her more snugly against him. In a lightning quick move, he yanked the felt hat off her head and sent it sailing into the creek.

"You look like a potato digger in that damn hat."

"Ohh . . ." Rage came boiling up out of her along with wild, reckless words. "You're an ignorant, uncouth bore without a smidgen of respect for other people's property."

"You're not other people," he shouted so loud that she forgot her fear, let go of the pommel and cupped her hands over her ears. "You're my wife!"

"To my everlasting sorrow!" she shouted back. "I'll never make a bigger mistake if I live to be a thousand."

"Hush up and sit still or I'll put you behind me and you can ride on the horse's rump."

"Don't shout!"

"I'll shout if I want to, and don't be quoting me any rules from that prissy ass old maid's rule book."

Mara barely managed to check the urge to hit him. Her next impulse was to weep. She chose to do neither. Damn, damn, damn him!

"All right. We'll engage in a *civil* conversation. That is, if you're capable of such," she announced.

"Try me."

She drew in a deep breath, held it, then let it out slowly. She did this when she wished to remain calm.

"Did you have a lovely day of debauchery in town, *dear?*" Her voice was heavy with sarcasm.

"Oh, yes, a lovely day." What the hell was she talking about?

"I'm glad. And how was your paramour? I trust she was in good form."

"Her form is always good, the best." Paramour? He'd have to ask Charlie what that was.

"We must have tea together sometime so that I can express my appreciation."

"Appreciation for what, *dear heart?*"

"Why, for taking care of my husband's physical needs, of course."

Pack began to grin and the smile was in his voice. "She does that all right."

"It's her job, *dear.*"

"Ah, yes. Her job while I'm in town. Yours, when I'm at home."

He felt her stiffen even more if that was possible. She was already sitting as straight as a church pew, her breasts riding on the arm he held across her midriff. Her heart was pounding so hard he could feel it against his arm. *The little vixen was jealous!* She thought he had spent the day with Candy. He felt a surge of elation and blessed Travor, although at first he could have swatted the boy for talking about his friendship with the lady from the Diamond Saloon. Aware that Mara's temper was on the verge of accelerating, an imp in him made him provoke her more. He nuzzled his nose into the hair above her ear and his lips nipped at her earlobe.

"Stop that! Go back to your strumpet in town if you're feeling so . . . amorous."

"Which one?" he asked softly.

"Ohh. . . ."

"The sweet-tempered blonde? Or the passionate one with hair as black as coal and eyes as blue as the sky?"

"Either one as long as you stay away from me."

"Oh, but that's not possible. I'll be with you forever and

ever. You promised, with your hand on the Bible, to love and obey me. There was nothing in the ceremony that said I couldn't go to town without you. I promised to provide for you and our children for as long as we both shall live.''

"Which may not be long for one of us if you don't stop what you're doing.''

"You don't like me to kiss your ear? The ladies in town like it. They say, 'Pack, you're the best ear-kisser.' Ouch!''

Pushed beyond endurance, Mara jabbed him in the ribs with her elbow. "Lout! Reprobate! Degenerate! Lecher! Polecat!'' she shouted.

"Sweetheart! Darling! Lover! My sweet-tempered, little Irish potato!'' he whispered seductively.

Mara bent her head until her chin touched her chest. It had been foolish to exchange insults with him. She was no match for him verbally any more than she was physically. It only provided him with a means to hurt her more. She prayed that he would not know of the tears that had come to her eyes. Like an avenging monster, he was so close she could feel his heart pounding against her back and her own pounding in her throat. She caught her bottom lip in an agitated nip and forced the tears from her eyes. *Which one?* he'd asked. In the stillness that enclosed them a statement the marshal had made moved sluggishly through her mind. *He has two whores in town.*

They rode in silence. It was dark. The moon, dim behind a wayward cloud, shed a pale light on the hard-packed trail. The evening was cool, but with her back snug against Pack and his arms wrapped around her, Mara was warm. Yet she was so heartsick she wouldn't have noticed had she been frostbitten.

They came up the trail to the homestead. Maggie, Trellis' old dog, came out from under the cookshack porch, barked once, then went back to her bed. A lamp burned in the bunkhouse. As they passed, one of the twins came to the door, yelled a greeting and went back inside.

Pack stopped the horse beside the back porch and lifted Mara down. After the lengthy horseback ride her legs quivered under her. He dismounted stiffly, wincing with soreness that still troubled him from the gunshot wound. He followed her into the house, lit the lamp, and carried it through the rooms. When he was sure there were no unpleasant surprises waiting for them, he set the lamp back on the table and went out to take his horse to the barn.

Mara stood in stupefied silence and gazed at the boxes, bags and wrapped bundles that took up a good part of the kitchen. Two large sheets of window glass leaned against the wall behind six high-back chairs with solid wood seats. A tin-framed oval mirror and a matching comb and brush rack lay on one of the chairs. A gray graniteware bucket and washpan sat on the table alongside a small glass churn, a caster set with four bottles with glass stoppers, and a stack of mail-order catalogs.

Somehow knowing that there was more, Mara picked up the lamp and went into the parlor. There she found a loveseat upholstered in a deep rose fabric, a rocking chair, a footstool, another mirror, this one ornate, a brass-based lamp with a painted shade, and several more unopened boxes.

Mara was about to cry and desperately choked back the tears. She went back to the kitchen, left the lamp on the table and hurried up the stairs to her room. With trembling fingers, she lit a candle. After she closed the door, she leaned against it. What did it mean? Had Pack chosen the things for her home? Did it not occur to him that *she* should have had that privilege?

Mara washed, removed the pins from her hair and plaited it into one long, thick braid. Her pride had been dealt a blow and the pain was immense. She gritted her teeth against it, slipped the nightdress over her head, blew out the candle and got into the bed. Then and only then did she allow the tears to come. She cried silently and agonizingly, unable to control the turmoil that filled her mind.

The Lord never puts more burdens on a person than he is able to bear. Brita had said that once when she was in pain and Mara had stood helplessly by watching her suffer. How long would it be, she asked herself, before her pain and humiliation eased? And this other thing . . . this awful attraction she felt for him. He was insufferably arrogant and bossy and it brought out a childish side of her own nature that she hadn't known existed. Their relationship had deteriorated to a point where it was beyond redemption.

Mara didn't even wonder if he would come to sleep with her. She *knew* he would. How was she going to cope with it? She moved to the far side of the bed, turned to face the wall and prayed for sleep. At the first sound of his footsteps on the stairs, she began to quiver. He opened the door quietly and pushed it back against the wall. Several minutes passed while she lay tense, listening to him remove his clothes. By the time he was in the bed, she was hanging onto the far edge.

"Mara Shannon, I know you're not asleep. Come here, honey."

He reached for her. She hit at his hands.

"No! I don't want you here. Get out of my bed!"

Strong hands flipped her over. Strong arms pulled her to him. "I told you last night what to expect. I'm holding you in my arms every night. We may fight during the day, but when night comes, I'm holding you."

"But I don't want you here."

She placed her fists against his muscled chest and pushed with all her strength, but he didn't budge. She could feel his breath on her face. He pulled her closer until her breasts were flattened against his chest. His skin smelled cool, soapy, and was damp from washing. She stopped resisting his superior strength. She was too confused and too weak to cope with all the anger and disappointment inside her.

"It's going to take time for us to get used to living with each other."

"A lifetime won't be long enough."

"If you're not going to try, we'll just have to be miserable."

"I've never been more miserable in my life."

"It's not been a very happy day for me, either."

"Oh, wasn't Miss Candy Camp nice to you today?" She pushed with all her strength and kicked his shins.

"Mara Shannon! Stop it!" He captured her thighs between his and held her so tightly she could scarcely move even though she had wedged her arm between them in an effort to hold herself away from him. When she stopped struggling, he began to cover her face with soft kisses. "Are you ready to listen to me? I'm only going to say this one time. I've not been unfaithful to you. Like my mother, I'll honor my marriage vows. Candy and I were friends, more than friends. We were lovers. But that's all over now. She's a mature, understanding woman—"

"And I'm not!"

"When I was in town yesterday, I told her that I was married and that I would not be calling on her again."

"I bet that was a shock."

"She understood."

"Poor Miss Camp lost her lover!" Mara said scathingly. "I bet she wishes she had two thousand acres of land instead of a saloon." Mara knew, even before Pack went suddenly still, that she had gone too far, that what she had said was childish and hateful. Tears of regret tightened her throat. "Pack, I'm sorry," she whispered.

He said nothing at all. The arms holding her loosened. He gently moved her thighs from between his and rolled onto his back.

"That was a mean and hateful thing to say." Words tumbled out of her. "You didn't deserve it. It's my fault. All of it. You didn't want to be tied down to this place . . . to me . . . but I pushed you into it."

He remained quiet. Desperately she pressed herself to his side, her hand caressing his chest, combing through the hair. Unknowingly her nails scraped his male nipples, causing him to stop breathing. Her hand moved up to his throat, and higher to cup his cheek with her palm. She turned his head toward her. Their noses collided. Her wet eyelashes scraped his face. Misery choked her.

"I'm sorry."

"Don't carry on about it." His voice held no anger, only resignation.

"I don't want you to be hurt!" In a fever to make up for her cruel words, she trailed her lips along his jaw. "I don't know what gets into me. I never said mean, hateful things until I met you."

"Forget it and go to sleep."

Tears made her voice ragged, but there were things she wanted to say before she broke into sobs.

"I can't forget it! These feelings are new to me, Pack. I . . . feel things I've never felt before. It's like I'm groping in the dark. I'm edgy and weepy and I'm . . . jealous." She couldn't hold back the sobs any longer.

Pack would never know what it cost her to make that admission, and she would never know the joy that flowed through him on hearing her words. Love, pure, shining and forgiving, shattered his determination to put space between them. His arms reached for her, enclosed her gently, and his tongue licked her tears.

"It's all right."

"No. I've turned into something I don't like. I'm ornery, waspish, sharp-tongued and hateful."

"You're also sweet and honest. Hush, hush, little love, don't cry."

She moved her head and found his mouth waiting for hers. She kissed him deeply, opening her lips, tasting the heat, the hunger and the sweetness of his mouth. She hadn't expected this wild hunger in herself and was powerless to stop it. Her arms strained him to her, her senses spun wildly when she felt the shudder that went through him when her tongue boldly entered his mouth. She loved him, and nothing else mattered.

"Love me like you did last night," she whispered anxiously, tearing her mouth from his.

"Ah, love, kiss me."

She did. She moved her lips lovingly over his mouth and felt his body shift, tighten, tremble. She kissed his mouth, his chin, his eyes. Feverishly, she kissed him with her mouth closed and with it open. She slid her tongue along his lower lip as he had done to her the night before. Hands, soft and sure, moved over his back and down to caress his buttocks. She didn't care if he thought she was bold; all she wanted was to be closer to him, to erase the bitterness that had been between them. Inside her a writhing, burning desire sent messages of an emptiness that begged to be filled.

A ragged, raspy breath broke from him. He turned her onto her back and impatiently flipped her nightdress up and over her head because he couldn't bear for anything to be closer to her than he was. He ran his hands over her naked flesh, from her smooth shoulders to her knees, as if he had to make sure that all of her was there. His features were strained. He was a man on the verge of agony. She was a woman wild with hunger for her man.

He hung over her, then moved into the cradle between her thighs. Her hands glided over his upper body, feeling the power of his shoulders and back. He groaned deeply in his chest, his lips sought her breast, found it, and pulled the nipple into his mouth. His nose nuzzled the soft mound, his lips greedily sucking on the small bud. His tongue was rough and strong and pulled at her inner being. He was no longer gentle; she no longer wanted him to be.

A thin whimper broke from her lips, not a cry of protest, but of intense pleasure. His mouth on her breast intensified the sexual hunger that throbbed at the core of her femininity. And then his hand was there, in that place, cupping, touching, stroking, probing. His fingers slipped inside and were doing things to her that made her roll her hips toward him, cease to exist as a person; she was only want and need and aching emptiness. His mouth moved up to her mouth, leaving her wet nipple to nestle in the rough hair on his chest. His hands cupped her buttocks and ground her soft mound against the elongated sex that had sprung up, hard and ready, tortured with the desire to be home inside her soft body.

Mara felt the pressure and the aching need inside her was almost more than she could stand. Her fingers dug into his tight buttocks. She feared she would shatter if he did not fill her soon.

"Pack, please," she whimpered.

"Please what?"

"You . . . know. I can't . . . bear it."

One of his hands came up and tightened almost savagely in her hair. She was completely helpless against his strength. He stared down at her, his face hard and taut.

"I told you last night," he growled in a raspy voice, "that when you want me, take me in your hand and bring me to you. That's the only way I'll ever go inside you."

Her hands left his buttocks, worked their way between their tightly pressed bodies and grasped him. He lifted his hips. For a long moment her two hands held him cradled between them. The loving gesture sent his heart into an odd little dance that left him gasping. And then, in a movement that was almost more than he could endure, she rubbed the tip of him back and forth across the taut skin of her belly before she guided him to the entrance between her thighs. He entered fully, with one quick thrust, into the mysterious, dark, tight haven.

"Ahhh," he sighed in pleasure.

"Ohh . . . yes, yes!" She gasped at the exquisite pain as her body stretched to accept him.

He withdrew and stroked, seeking to be planted deeper. She caught her breath and held it.

They clung together like two lost souls floating above the clouds. He delved deeper and deeper, seeking more and more gratification. Her pleasure mounted until she thought it had surely reached its heights. They rocked together, consumed by the demand for fulfillment. He held her tightly, slid in and out of her slowly, deeply, sweetly, using all his strength to hold back his own release, because he wanted it to go on and on, because he wanted always to be deep inside her, because he wanted to feel the ecstasy ripple though her body.

Mara's body stiffened with pleasure so intense that she had to bite her lips to hold back a scream. Even then small, fragmented cries rode out on uneven breaths. Pack felt the tiny tremors deep inside her. It had started for her.

"I . . . love . . . I love you," she cried, trying to control the words that burst from her mouth.

Dimly he heard her words. His control burst into a shattering release. *I love you, I love you, I love you.* The words beat against his mind as his body shook with wave after wave of pleasure. With all his strength he locked himself so deeply within her that his pleasure and hers were like one.

"You're mine, mine, mine, mine," he whispered savagely.

They lay silently for long moments, simply holding each other, awed into silence by the bliss they had found together. Pack rolled onto his side, bringing her with him. When he spoke, he placed the tip of his nose against her.

"I give a part of myself to you each time. I am yours and you are mine."

A long sigh escaped her. "I know. I could feel you all through me. You touched my very soul."

His fingers brushed the tangled curls around her ears. His mouth played with tender warmth upon hers.

"Sweetheart, I'm not a polished, educated man. At times I think I've done you an injustice by marrying you. But I'm a selfish lout! I wanted you. I only hope that in the days, months, years ahead you'll not come to be ashamed of the man you married."

"Oh, Pack! You must never think that. Polished and educated isn't everything. Papa once said you had plenty of common sense. You have principles or you'd not have felt responsible for me." The words came shivering and sweet from her throat. Her lips caught his and clung, released and caught again. Her kiss spoke not of passion, but of newly discovered love. "And . . . I love you," her whispered words came haltingly.

"Mara Shannon, sweetheart, ye dinna be knowin' what ye're sayin'." What common sense he had left him. He lapsed into the Irish brogue without being aware of it.

"I do be knowin', Pack Gallagher. Ye dinna need to be tellin' me what's in me own heart," she mocked him gently.

"Don't tease me, love!" he warned.

"I'm not teasing," she murmured between quick breaths. Tears glistened in the corners of her eyes. "I've known for some time that I had a special feeling for you . . . I'll not burden you with it."

"Oh, God! Oh, sweetheart!" With his face buried in the softness of her auburn hair, his words tumbled over each other. "I couldn't believe it when you said it before. I was sure you didn't know what you were saying. I love you so much, I've not been able to think of anything else. Do you really love *me?*'' His mind was empty of everything but her. His lips covered her face, stopping at each closed eye to feel the flutter of it, moved down her nose to lips that waited, warm and eager. "Say it again, sweetheart. Say it again."

"I love you."

"And I love you."

They talked, laughed, kissed. He held her wrapped in his arms while they whispered nonsense to each other.

"Who picked out the things downstairs?" she asked, as if suddenly remembering them. She felt now that she could ask him anything.

"I did. If there's anything there you don't want, we can take it back."

"You picked out all those things?"

"I had to have something to do while Sam was with his friend and Judge Moore."

"Pack?" She leaned over him and rested her chin on his chest. Her hair spilled over onto his shoulders. "Do you think Sam and Emily are as happy as we are?"

His hand moved up to the back of her head and pulled her lips up to his. "Nope. No one could be as happy as I am right this minute . . . or as horny," he said between kisses. He lifted her and settled her on top of him, cradled her between his thighs, trapping his hardness between his firm belly and her soft one.

"What's horny?"

"Me. This." He grasped her buttocks and slid her up and down over his arousal.

"Oh!" She giggled softly. "Will we wear it out?"

"I'm going to do my best to try."

Mara and Pack were having breakfast when the twins, grinning like a couple of cats, came through the back door.

"What a ya think 'bout all this stuff, Mara Shannon? Ain't

Pack just the limit? We had to help unload it.'' Travor helped himself to a flapjack, rolled it in his fingers, and straddled one of the new chairs. ''Goldurn, Pack. Ya must a bought out ole Baker's store.'' He shoved the rolled flapjack in his mouth.

Pack grinned. Mara could not help but notice that when he did, it spread a warm light into his eyes. She found herself beaming with pleasure.

''He's that all right. Help yourself, Trell. There's another flapjack.'' Mara was pleased the boys were so comfortable with her that they made themselves at home.

''Willy said we'd better get our butts on up here 'n help scatter all this stuff out cause he wasn't goin' to.''

''You tell Willy that I'm cooking doughnuts today, and unless he helps he can't have any. Travor, you rapscallion!'' Mara reached to swat the hand that was grabbing another flapjack. ''Save one of those for Trellis. I'll swear! Filling you up is like pouring sand down a rat hole.''

''He ate six down at the cookshack,'' Trellis grumbled.

''Steamboat's ain't as good as Mara Shannon's.''

''How is Steamboat?'' Mara rose to get the coffeepot.

''All right. Just like nothin' ever happened. Pack, is Sam goin' to give me 'n Trav fifty silver dollars?''

''That's what he said. I'm thinking Sam isn't a man to go back on his word.''

Pack wrapped his arm about Mara's thighs when she came to fill his cup. She leaned against him. Trellis watched as his brother patted his wife's leg.

''Lordy! I'm sure glad you two made up. Willy said Mara Shannon was mad as a cow with her tit caught in the fence. He said she was red-eyed and spittin' nails on the way to Charlie's. He said—''

''Willy's got a big mouth,'' Pack said and watched Mara move away from him. ''What are you boys going to do with your money?''

''That's what we want to talk to ya about. Me 'n Trav are wonderin' if we'd have enough to buy us a mare. We figure we could put her to your big gray 'n start us a horse herd. Whata ya think, Pack?''

Pack looked directly at Mara and caught her smiling eyes before he looked back at his brother's expectant face.

"I can't find anything wrong with that. You know those three mares I brought in are going to foal. I've been wondering if you fellows would want to partner up with me. You take on the care of the horses, and one of the foals will be yours. In a few years you'll have a herd of good, blooded horses."

Disbelieving, Trellis and Travor sat with their mouths open. Travor came out of his trance first. "Ya mean it?"

"Well, for the love of Pete and the sake of Pud!" Trellis shouted, then echoed his brother. "Ya mean it?"

"Of course I mean it. We'll need help running this ranch, won't we, honey?" He grabbed Mara's hand as she passed and pulled her down onto his lap.

"Sure. And you know what else? I know two young men who are going to have to learn to read, write, and cipher. Else they'll not be able to do business at the bank, read bills of sale or write out money orders. If they can't do those things they'll be cheated blind."

Travor got to his feet. "You're right, Mara Shannon. When can we start?"

Mara slid off Pack's lap. "Not until all this stuff is sorted out, put away, or stacked in a pile to go back to the store." She reached to jerk a strand of Pack's hair and smiled lovingly into his eyes. He pulled her back down on his lap and kissed her.

"Ahh . . . mush! Come on, Trell. When they get done slobberin' all over each other we'll come back 'n help."

The back screen door slammed. "In a year or two they'll find out that kissing can be a very pleasant pastime." Mara giggled happily.

"So pleasant that I might spend the entire day doing it." Pack looked at her with a consuming tenderness in his dark eyes. She gazed back at him, the ache of love in hers, and shook her head slowly. He stilled her head between his two hands. "What does that mean, Mrs. Gallagher?"

"It means that you're not going to charm me into sitting on

your lap all day and dallying with you. We've got work to do. I'm dying to see what's in all those bundles.''

He kissed her quick and hard. "All right, but as soon as night comes you're going to get it, my girl," he threatened.

She ran a finger over his hard mouth. "I hope so." Her eyes sparkled at him though thick lashes.

Their laughter mingled.

The days slipped past in a flurry of work as Mara arranged the new furnishings, put away the new dishes and cooking pans, hung the mirrors and comb case, filled the new lamps, spread a beautiful new cloth and placed the caster set in the center of the table. Pack and the boys tore the boards from the windows and put in the new glass, letting more light and sunshine into the house. Riley and Aubrey put the new screening on the front and back doors. The new bedsheets, blankets and towels were stacked neatly in the bureau drawers.

It was a busy time. Mara spent two hours each afternoon teaching the boys. Travor was especially bright when it came to reading. His inquisitive mind absorbed the printed word. Trellis, the methodical one, took to ciphering, and in a week's time was far ahead of his brother. Penmanship came hard for both boys, but they tried.

The boys were a joy to work with, and Mara couldn't have loved them more if they were her own flesh and blood. At times she couldn't help but think how different they were from Cullen. Pack and Mara had heard nothing of his whereabouts, nor was he mentioned by Aubrey or the twins.

Mara loved working in her house, and with the twins, but each day she looked forward to the time after supper. This was her special time with her husband. They usually went to the creek and bathed together. Afterward they sat on the porch, fingers entwined, and Pack told her tales of this trips into the mining camps. She told him little anecdotes about her life at the school. They retired early to the room upstairs, made love and slept in each other's arms.

Mara had not thought there was so much happiness in the whole world. She felt laughter bubbling inside her at the most unexpected times. The joy of living flowed in her blood and smiles of pure delight curved her mouth. It was so wonderful to love and be loved. Pack filled every corner of her heart. She felt she knew him as well as she knew herself.

The warm afternoon breeze was drying the clothes Mara had hung on the line. Humming a tune, she checked the meat she had boiling in the pot, covered the fresh loaves of bread with a clean cloth, and wandered out onto the back porch. She saw Aubrey come out of the tack house carrying a harness on his shoulder and go into the shed. Pack had said Aubrey was not drinking, that he had taken an interest in the horses and in keeping the bridles and harnesses repaired.

She stepped off the porch and strolled down the path toward the barn, something she wouldn't have dared do when Cullen was around. The heavy double doors of the barn were closed, but as she neared, she could hear Willy's voice. The words were inaudible, but the tone was complaining. Mara smiled. The old man would die before he admitted it, but he loved Pack. And because of that Mara had become fond of him.

Mara reached for the heavy hasp to pull open the door. "Plop, plop, plop." The sound came at regular intervals. She paused to listen. "Plop, plop, plop."

"Spread yore feet, duck left, duck right, duck right," Willy sang in a monotonous tone.

"Plop. Plop."

"Ah, hell, ya'll get knocked on yore ass if ya stand flat-footed."

She swung the door open a crack and slipped inside. It was stifling hot in the barn. The only breeze and the only light came in through the small door at the back. Pack, stripped to the waist and wearing old britches cut off above the knee, was pounding at something in a gunnysack that hung from the rafters. Sweat was rolling down his face like he'd been in a heavy downpour. His arms, shoulders and back were wet and glistening. He pounded at the heavy sack with his fists, bobbing to the left, to the right. Willy sat on an overturned barrel with a straw in his mouth.

Pack stopped pounding on the gunnysack, opened his hands and flexed his fingers.

"How be that thumb?" Willy asked.

"It's all right."

Holding his arms together chest-high, Pack squatted down. He must have done fifty squats before he jumped up and caught hold of a bar suspended on two ropes. The muscles in his shoulders and arms rippled as he lifted his weight until his chin was even with the bar. He did this until it was harder and harder for his arms to lift him.

"This place is hotter than a two-bit whore," he exclaimed breathlessly when he dropped to his feet and wiped the sweat off his forehead with his forefinger.

"Yore own fault fer keepin' the doors shut." Willy got off the barrel mumbling something about Pack not having any backbone anymore and threw him a towel. "Ya ain't got—" He turned to see Mara standing beside the door. "Ah shit-fire!" he muttered.

Pack wiped his face on the towel and threw it back at Willy. The old man jerked his head in the direction where Mara was standing. Pack turned his head and his eyes came to rest on Mara's white face. He went toward her.

"Hello, sweetheart. It's too hot for you to be in here."

"What are you doing, Pack? What in the world are you doing?"

"Oh, I'm just trying to get some of my strength back. I've been idle for a long time."

"But why were you fighting that sack?"

"It's a good way to build muscles, sweetheart. Go on back to the house. I'll be up soon and we'll go down to the creek." Pack pushed open the heavy barn door.

Mara walked back to the house. A puzzled frown drew her brows together. Pack hadn't wanted her to know what he was doing or he wouldn't have been in the barn with the doors closed.

In a corner of her mind, a little uneasiness began to grow.

Chapter
NINETEEN

Arms entwined, Sam and Emily walked along the path beside the creek. Ahead of them something scuttled in a thicket. An owl glided between the branches searching for a meal. A crescent moon rode high in the sky, but they didn't notice it. They came to a grassy clearing where fireflies flitted their brief lives away. Far away a night bird called. Sam tilted his head to listen. The call came again and he relaxed.

"Pack and Mara Shannon were so angry at each other the day they were here that they hardly spoke," Emily said thoughtfully.

"Pack wouldn't take her to town because we wasn't sure what was waitin' for us. They've straightened it out by now."

"Oh, I don't think so. I'm afraid there's trouble ahead for them. Pack's afraid to take her to town knowing that she'll be snubbed because of him."

"He ain't the most popular man in town. I got to admit it. Ole Piedmont let me know what he thought 'bout him when I went to fetch him for the buryin'. He said a man who fought in a prize ring was a spawn of the devil, or somethin' like that. Pious old bastard! I never wanted to punch anybody so bad.''

"The Laramie Ladies, as they are called, are feeling pretty proud of themselves because for the first time in history some of them served on a jury. They marched in protest against the last fight. Reverend Piedmont's wife was one of the leaders.''

"That'll not keep their men at home. They'll pay to see the fight and they'll bet on it.''

"The last time they carried signs saying gambling was as evil as demon rum. And that Pack was taking the bread from the mouths of innocent babes.''

Sam chuckled. "I bet that was some parade.''

"Oh, it was. They had a band and everything. Charlie said they sang hymns and carried a little girl whose father had gambled away the family home, causing the mother to turn to drink and wander into the mountains never to return for the child.''

"They really get carried away, don't they?''

"They'll give Mara Shannon the cold shoulder. I feel bad about it. I wish I hadn't heard you and Charlie talking about the fight.''

"Pack agreed to it because it's a sure, quick way of earnin' some money. He wants to buy in with me 'n Charlie. He's confident he can win. Even if he don't win he'll get a sizable purse.''

"I wonder if he's told Mara Shannon.''

"Honey, she'll either stand by her man or she won't. There's nothin' we can do. I talked to a young preacher today. His church isn't big or fancy as ole Piedmont's, but I think you'll like him.''

"I will if you do.''

"Tomorrow we'll go in 'n talk to him. Then about this time next week we'll be wed. I'd like to do it afore my friend goes back to Saint Louis.''

"I'd like Mara Shannon and Pack to be there.''

"After we talk to the preacher and make the date, I'll ride over and tell them.''

They heard a plop as a frog jumped from the bank into the water.

"We'll have to come down here sometime 'n throw out a line." Sam's arm across her shoulders pulled her to him. "Right now fishin' isn't on my mind."

"I'm glad." She lifted her lips for his kiss.

Her mouth was warm, sweet. She parted her lips, yielded and accepted the wanderings of his. He raised his head and looked down at her, his lips just inches from hers.

"I've been so damn lucky, I'm scared, Emily Rose. I found you 'n I'll have the means of takin' care of ya."

"No more lucky than I am, Sam darling. The dearest, most wonderful man in the world loves me in spite of what happened to me. I'll have the family I always dreamed of having."

Their lips met in joint seeking. She rose on her toes to press her mouth hungrily to his. His hands roamed over her, caressing every inch of her back and sides. One hand shaped itself over her breast, the other flattened against her buttocks and held her to him.

"I sure like kissin' you, holdin' you. It's goin' to be hard waitin' to make you mine." Sam lowered his eyes and found hers, sparkling like twin stars.

"You don't have to wait," she whispered.

"Godamighty! Sweetheart!" A great swell of joy washed over him. He felt a tremor run through him as if the earth they were standing on was shaking.

"I don't want to wait."

"Emily Rose. Oh, sweet Emily Rose." The words came from his tight throat in a tormenting whisper.

"I've shocked you." Her mouth sought his in a soul-searching kiss as an insidious, primitive desire grew in both of them.

"We can't . . . I can't. . . ." His voice trembled.

She hugged him to her. "I've thought about it." Her words were muffled against his neck. "I'm afraid. At the last minute I may remember what it was like . . . and scream." She pressed herself against the hardened evidence of his aroused body. "I want to know before we're wed. I love you too much to saddle you with a woman who cannot be a wife."

It was Sam who drew back and held her away from him. He felt a strange bittersweet warmth. She was a dream. He was sure her soft, feminine body would respond to the mating instincts of his. He had not thought about her fear.

"We can't, sweetheart. Not here in the grass." There was gentle firmness in his voice.

"I know of no better place for a man and a woman to lie down together than here on God's earth with a blanket of stars overhead." She stroked his cheek with her fingertips. "The other . . . time I was on a soft, clean bed, my hands tied over my head, my legs spread . . . and tied. I've got to know if the nightmare will come back." Her hands cupped his cheeks, and she brought his lips to hers.

After the kiss she stood within his embrace and unhooked her skirt at the waist. As it fell, she stepped out of it and spread it on the ground. Her fingers pulled at the drawstring on her petticoat. It dropped and she spread it alongside her skirt. She stood there in knee-length bloomers and her shirt-waist.

Sam's head was spinning, reality was slipping farther and farther away, but before it was completely gone, the thought came to him that she had planned this and had come prepared. Dear God, he prayed, he wanted to be gentle with her, to show her that mating between two people who loved each other could be beautiful.

He reached for her hands and brought them to the buttons on his shirt. He stood very still while her nimble fingers worked at baring his chest. He pulled the shirt from his britches, slipped it off, and dropped it on the ground. With her hands in his, he pressed them to his bare flesh, inviting her to feel his body. He dropped his own hands to his side and stood still as her soft palms roamed over his shoulders, down under his muscular arms, around his ribs to his flat, quivering belly. He closed his eyes when her fingers found the nipples amid the growth of down on his chest.

When she sank down on the clothing she had spread he unbuckled his gun belt and dropped it down beside her. He sat down and kicked off his boots.

"Shall I take off my shirtwaist?" Her voice was a mere breath in the night.

"Only if you want to." He leaned his head toward her and kissed her reverently on the forehead.

"I want to. I *do* love you," she said as if she had to give a reason for what she was doing.

He watched as she took off her shirtwaist. Beneath it she wore a chemise, tied above her breast with a ribbon. Her shoulders gleamed in the moonlight. He studied her white face, her mane of thick hair, her trembling mouth.

"Emily Rose," he whispered. "Yo're the purtiest woman I ever saw."

In reply, her arms slid up to encircle his neck and she pressed her breast to his chest. Her mouth was soft and sweet against his. He lay down on his back, bringing her with him, careful not to hold her too tight. She bent over him. While they kissed, his hands softly stroked her back and hips.

"I love you," he whispered against her mouth. "I'll never force you or hurt you. You lead the way."

"I don't know what to do."

"Do what you want, love." His arms fell to his sides.

"I want to touch you . . . all over. Aren't you going to take off your britches?"

"Darlin'," he croaked, "what's in there might scare the hell out a ya."

"I know what it is. You were big and hard the night we kissed at Mara Shannon's. I felt it against me. And I felt it tonight even though you were trying to hold it away from me."

He pushed his britches down over his hips. His male member stood stiff and proud out of a nest of dark hair. He knew that she couldn't see it, and prayed that when she touched it, he would be able to control himself. He sank back to see her lift the chemise over her head. He drew in a ragged breath and a small sound came from his throat at the sight of her round, firm breasts.

"What is it? Sam?" Her hand came to rest on the flat plane of his stomach.

"Yore breasts are so purty."

She stretched out beside him and lifted his arm over her head so she could rest her cheek on his shoulder. She brought his hand around and placed it on her breast. His rough, calloused fingers found her nipple and stroked it to a hard peak. He felt a tremor go through her.

"That feels good, so good." Her voice was soft, urgent. She reached for his lips and kissed him with a hunger that surprised him. Her mound was pressed tightly to his thigh. He could feel the heat through her bloomers. His hand traveled from her breast to the waistband, slipped carefully inside, and flattened against her buttocks. She moved her palm down over his stomach and slid it beneath his extended sex. He caught his breath sharply and waited as it settled on the back of her hand.

"Emily Rose, I swear I'll never use it as a weapon."

"I know you won't."

Her hand turned and her fingers closed around him. He ground his teeth and tightened his buttocks. His desire for her was a deep pain gnawing his vitals, but he was determined not to show any aggression.

"Be . . . careful, love. I'm so hungry for you. I want to touch you everywhere. Emily Rose, oh, Emily Rose. Tell me if I hurt you and I'll stop."

She brought his arm around over her head, placed it beside him and turned so that her breast and belly were against it. His hand worked its way into the slit in her drawers. His fingers combed the springy hair at her crotch and slid into dampness. For a long minute she was still. He was still. Then she rocked slightly on his hand and relief flooded through him.

"You're so different from me." She leaned over him. Her mouth moved slowly over his chest. Her lips found a flat nipple. She licked it with her tongue and felt the quiver that passed through him. When she caught it with her teeth, his breath came out sharply. She worried it, then asked, "Does that feel good?"

"Oh, God, yes! Turn over, darlin'."

She turned on her back and spread her legs. "I'm not afraid, Sam. I'm not afraid."

"Give me a little time, love. Let me show you how good I can make you feel."

His mouth, firm yet gentle, fastened on her trembling lips, stealing her breath away. The kiss was filled with sweetness. He put his head on her breast and rubbed his cheek against the soft globe. Then he took her nipple into his mouth, sucking it with lips and tongue while his fingers moved down to the sweet haven between her thighs and slipped inside, stroking, coaxing. She began to squirm, to arch her hips toward his hand.

"Sam!" Something warm and powerful throbbed in the area below her stomach. She whimpered when his mouth left her breast to kiss her mouth and run his tongue over her lips. She moved restlessly against the urgent hardness pressing against her thigh. His fingers worked magic.

"Tell me."

"Yes! Yes!" Her whispered words were like thunder in his ears. "Please. I need you to." Her arms clutched him, her hips thrust up in joyous offering.

"You're sure?" The blood swam in his head, burned his body, pounded in his veins, but the fear of harming something so precious clutched at his heart.

With a breathless laugh her hand searched for him. There was no room for fear as her desire peaked. He lifted her thigh over his and, using all his strength of will to hold back, he slipped into her. She was warm, moist. He was so filled with love for her that he thought he would burst.

Fleetingly, Emily remembered the relentless attack upon her, remembered the pawing, leering, probing into the most secret and vulnerable strongholds of her body. That had been a dreadful and obscene experience; this was heaven.

Love for this gentle, understanding man swept over Emily like a warm wind when he entered her, filled her. She called his name and heard him call hers. With a flurry of softly muttered words of love, he moved within her in a rhythm of loving that increased in speed and intensity. It was like drowning as she was swept along in the turbulence of their desire. Through the bursting darkness sudden joy, like a great flashing light, exploded within her.

The climax of their mating left them gasping. She curled up in Sam's arms, wet tears on her face. She rested her cheek on the smooth hardness of his shoulder, feeling the peace of being loved and cherished. His ardent loving seemed to have opened wide every door in her mind and emotions.

"Sam, Sam, it was . . . wonderful!"

Unable to speak, he kissed her tenderly, lovingly, again and again. Tears he had not shed since he was a child filled his eyes, then rolled down his cheeks onto hers.

Emily, sitting between Charlie and Sam on the wagon seat, saw the train coming up the grade. She had seen it before as only a dim image moving across her vision. Now, with her glasses, she could see the windows and the smoke rolling from the great locomotive as it puffed and wheezed into the Laramie station. She clutched Sam's arm.

"Oh! Charlie said some of the cars were painted yellow, but I didn't dream they were so colorful. It's beautiful! The steam engine is like a dragon and the cars its tail."

"A tail with windows for eyes." Charlie laughed.

Charlie had at first been skeptical about what he considered Emily's sudden infatuation with the Texan. But now that he'd had time to observe them together and to get to know Sam, he realized they had truly fallen in love.

Charlie prided himself on being able to read a man's character. During the war he'd had to choose those who were to lead and those who were to follow. Sam Sparks was not a man to trail along behind other men. Charlie liked what he had seen and heard about him, but it was going to be hard for him to let another man take over the responsibility for his sister.

Emily had been urging Charlie to talk to Sam. She had already told Sam what had happened to force them to leave Indiana and come west, but she hadn't told him all of it. He was not the kind of man to ask questions. Yet there was something he should know, something he would have to know before he and Emily were married. Charlie wished to hell he'd told him before things had gone so far.

"That's the church I tole ya 'bout." Sam motioned toward a small unpainted building at the end of a side street, set off by itself in a grassy field.

Charlie turned down the rutted road and pulled the horses to a stop in front of the church. Sam got down and reached for Emily. He would have liked to hold her there for endless moments looking at her. Her dress was a light gray, her bonnet blue. A continuous smile curved her sweet mouth. He wanted desperately to kiss her.

"What denomination is it?" She looked over Sam's shoulder at the church.

"I didn't ask. Will it matter?"

"Not in the least. Are you coming in, Charlie?"

"No. I'll stay here."

Charlie swung his wooden peg up on the sideboard of the wagon and reached for his pipe. While he lit it, he watched his sister, the only person in the world whom he loved, walk into the church on the arm of the man to whom she had given her heart. He thought of their parents and the love they had shared. Their father had been a rough Scots riverman, their mother a petite southern belle.

Charlie's mind spun back to the first year of the war. He had returned home on a short leave to find that first his father and then his mother had died of a lung sickness that spread through Evansville during one of the coldest winters they had known. Emily, nearly blind even then, and two old colored servants had nursed them, been with them when they died, and had buried them.

The next time he came home it was a month before the war ended. He was weak from losing a leg and lying in a hospital bed. Emily had been brutally raped by three men from prominent Evansville families; one of them was wed and the father of three children. Charlie, teetering on one good leg and his peg, had sought them out and made sure that each of the men admitted his crime before he killed him. Afterward he and

Emily had fled to Missouri and later taken a boat up the river to Wyoming.

The thought of what would happen to Emily if he were caught and sent to prison had weighed heavily on Charlie's mind. His worry had been eased when at last he had taken Pack into his confidence and Pack had assured him that he would see to it that Emily was taken care of if she were left alone. Now Sam Sparks, the Texan, would be the one to take responsibility for his sister.

Charlie was tired. The strain of constantly looking over his shoulder, of having to change his and Emily's name, of being cut loose from everything that had been dear and familiar to them, was taking its toll. It didn't matter so much now if someone called his name and he turned to see someone from his past—Emily had Sam.

An hour later someone did call his name, and Charlie turned to see someone from his past.

"He was very nice. Not at all like the pompous Reverend Piedmont. He asked us if we were aware that the commitment we made to each other was for life. He came here from Kansas and his congregation isn't very big, but it will be, because he's very understanding. We set the date for a week from today, Charlie. He's Presbyterian. Can you believe it?" She turned to Sam. "That's the church we went to back home." She turned back to Charlie. "Mama would be pleased to know that I'm going to be married by a Presbyterian minister."

Emily chatted happily while they drove back down the road toward the main part of town. Both Charlie and Sam chuckled at her enthusiasm.

"See what you're going to have to put up with, Sam? She'll talk your arm off," Charlie teased.

"Do ya reckon a gag would help?" Sam asked. His usually serious face was creased with smiles.

"Don't know, but I'd be tempted to try it."

"Oh, you! Just for that I'm going to the mercantile to buy

some dress goods. Thanks to you, Sam, I can see all the things in the store." She hugged his arm.

"Charlie, I'm thinkin' I might a made a mistake gettin' those glasses," Sam said seriously as Charlie pulled the team to a stop alongside a building.

"And I'm thinking I ought to make her wait until she's wed to you before I turn her loose in that store," Charlie growled.

Emily laughed happily. Sam helped her down and went to fasten the team to the post with an iron ring. He took Emily's hand and drew it into the crook of his arm. They waited for Charlie, and the three of them stepped up onto the boardwalk that fronted the Railroad Hotel. The walk was crowded with loafers and travelers who had come in on the train. They edged their way through the crowd and went on down the street past the barbershop. Emily walked with her head up, looking at everyone and everything. Sam held her proudly and securely to his side.

Zachary Quill came out of the Diamond Saloon and paused to light his cigar. The thump of Charlie's peg leg on the boardwalk drew his attention. Then he saw Sam walking with a peg-legged man and a slim, blond woman.

"Sam," he called and hurried after them.

After glancing over his shoulder, Sam pulled Emily to the side of the walk next to a building.

"Just a minute, honey. Here's someone I want you and Charlie to meet."

Charlie moved over beside Sam before he looked back to see the tall, distinguished looking man approaching them. It took less than a dozen heartbeats for Charlie to recognize him. By then the sharp blue eyes had honed in on his face and every nightmare Charlie had ever had came rushing back at him.

"My God! Charlie! Charlie McCourtney!" Zack smiled broadly, but Charlie didn't. "Why, this is wonderful! Imagine seeing you way out here." He shook Charlie's hand and slapped him on the back.

Sam noticed immediately that Charlie's face had gone

chalk white and Emily's a pale pink. Her fingers on his arm tightened as if she were about to fall off a cliff.

"Hello, Zack. It's been a long time," Charlie said.

"It sure has." Zack turned to Sam. "I've known Charlie since he was knee-high. And is this Emily? Why, of course it is."

"This is Emily, my intended," Sam said. "If you know Charlie you must know his sister."

"Little Emily McCourtney! You're the one Sam wanted the glasses for? Well, can you beat that?"

Emily glanced at Sam's expressionless face and held out her hand. "Zachary Quill. I've heard all about the Quills from Mama and Papa."

"My parents and Uncle Rain and Aunt Amy thought the world of Eleanor and Gavin McCourtney. I sure was sorry to hear that they had passed on."

"Mama just seemed to wither away after Papa died."

"Charlie, you look more and more like your pa." Zack stepped back to allow a woman with a small child to pass. "It's almost dinner time. Come be my guests for dinner at the hotel. Meeting someone from home is almost as good as Christmas."

"Sam and Emily were on their way to the mercantile, Zack," Charlie said evenly. "But I'd like to buy you a drink and find out about the folks back at Quill's Station." Charlie's eyes sent Sam's a silent message.

"Sounds good to me. We can meet Sam and Emily in the lobby of the hotel. Is that all right with you, Sam?"

"Why sure. Emily and I will be back in about an hour."

"Charlie—" Emily reached out and clasped her brother's arm. An almost desperate look came over her face. Charlie patted her hand and smiled with his mouth around the pipe stem.

"Run along with Sam. I promise to tell you all the news I get out of Zack." He turned abruptly and walked away, his peg making a hollow thumping sound on the boardwalk.

Emily stood for a moment looking after him. When she looked at Sam there were tears in her eyes.

"I never thought it'd be like this," she murmured.

"Come on, honey. Let's get off the street."

"Charlie was going to tell you before the wedding."

Sam took her arm and they walked around the corner, past the livery and on out past the wagon yard. They stopped beneath a shade tree. Tears were on Emily's cheeks.

"What's wrong, honey? I'll fix it if I can."

"You can't fix this, Sam. They'll take Charlie back and . . . and hang him for killing those men who—"

"Zack won't turn him in."

"There's a reward. A big reward. If Zack doesn't, someone else will. Charlie said it was just a matter of time. There are bounty hunters all over the country."

"He was worried 'bout me?"

"At first."

"I can't blame him for that."

"It hurt Charlie to have to deny Papa's name. McCourtney is our name."

"Does Pack know this?"

"He knows."

"It must have been a load for Charlie, but he don't have to go it alone now."

"Sam, I'm so afraid. It was all because of me!"

The hour passed quickly. When Sam and Emily walked down the street toward the hotel, she kept her eyes down. Her bonnet hung from one arm while the other was held tightly against Sam's side. Her face was sad, but her eyes were dry. The joy she had felt when they arrived in town had turned to a cold lump of dread that hung on her heart like a stone. Sam could think of no words to say to comfort her.

The hotel lobby was cool and quiet. The builder had taken pains to make it as elegant as possible with limited supplies and unskilled labor. The plank floor had a large square of carpet in the center and runners that led from the desk to the stairway. Deep leather couches forming an L were placed in the two corners. Charlie and Zack sat on the couch at the back of the lobby, deep in conversation.

Both men got to their feet as Sam and Emily approached.

Charlie was smiling, a genuine smile. He stumbled in his haste to get to his sister and put his arms around her.

"It's all right, Sister!" Relief boiled out of Charlie; his voice vibrated with it. "Zack says there are no charges against me. No reward posted!"

"What?" Emily didn't dare believe her own ears. "What?" she stammered again.

"No charges were filed!"

"Not two weeks after you left there was a secret meeting between the sheriff, the judge and an undisclosed number of men and their wives," Zack explained. "It seems the three who attacked you had also attacked other women in town. It had become a game for the wealthy, idle scoundrels. They wore masks each time except the time they attacked you. They didn't think you could see well enough to identify them."

"But I can see up close. I knew who they were, and when Charlie came home he made me tell him."

"There were never any charges filed against Charlie. Folks were rather grateful that he had saved the families the shame of a trial. They decided you had left because it was too painful for you to stay and face folks." Zack turned and put his hand on Charlie's shoulder. "I sent out a few feelers when I discovered you'd had your things shipped to Kansas City. If I had only known you thought you were a hunted man, Charlie, I would have scoured the country looking for you and Emily."

"Oh, dear! I'm going to cry."

"You'll get spots on your glasses," Sam teased.

"It's such a relief. We don't have to worry that every man that comes to the house is . . . looking for Charlie."

"Emily, I'm going to work on the new penitentiary. Zack wants me to work with a Mr. Brown who is the Superintendent of Construction. Later he thinks there'll be a permanent position for me. This is, if he can convince the governor."

"I don't think we'll have any trouble convincing the governor, Charlie. You're the most qualified man I know."

Charlie was so excited he stuck his pipe in his mouth with the bowl upside down.

"Charlie, you're spilling your tobacco!" Emily exclaimed happily. "Sam, Charlie has a degree in engineering. This is something he's always wanted to do."

"Looks like you and Emily can take over the Rivers' place, if you want it, Sam."

"If it's what Emily wants, we'll settle on a price."

"If we don't get in that dining room it's going to fill up." Zack placed a hand on Emily's back and on Charlie's shoulder and urged them toward the door. "When's the wedding going to take place, Sam? By God, I'm going to be there."

Chapter
TWENTY

Mara moved the heavy spider skillet to cover the round hole after she lifted the lid from the top of the cookstove. The hot flames licked at the bottom of the skillet and soon the strips of meat were bubbling and shrinking.

"It's going to be a nice day for the wedding." Pack came into the kitchen. The screen door slammed behind him.

Mara remained facing the stove. "I'm glad. Will you fill the reservoir, Pack? It's almost empty." Moving the meat aside with a two-tined fork, she broke an egg in the pan.

"How come I'm getting eggs this morning, Mrs. Gallagher?"

"Because we have a surplus at the moment."

Pack emptied the water bucket in the tank at the side of the stove and went out to the well. Mara dished up the meat and eggs. She was taking bread from the oven when Pack returned.

It was hard to act normal this morning. She took a deep breath, put the hot biscuits on the table, and filled the coffee

319

cups, giving that chore her full attention. She could feel the tension in Pack. It had been growing steadily since she had discovered him in the barn pounding on that damn gunnysack. Then it accelerated after Sam came to tell them that he and Emily were being married in Laramie and invite them to come to the wedding.

Pack was the same gentle lover, but at times he held her so tightly she could scarcely breathe. Last night his loving had been intense and he became almost desperate in his attempt to hold back his release to make their joining last. Mara had searched her mind for a reason for his unease and came up with only one: He didn't want her to go to town. But why? Her mind worked overtime for an answer. She was sure that Pack loved her, and so it couldn't be because of the woman at the Diamond Saloon.

As Mara moved the caster set so that she could place the butter crock within his reach, she waited for her mind to empty and her nerves to calm. She had worked on being serene; it was what she relied on.

"I ironed your good shirt. You really need another one. While we're in town today we should buy one."

"They usually don't have any big enough, honey."

"If they don't we'll get some material and I'll make you one."

"Did Miss Fillamore teach you to sew too?"

"She couldn't even thread a needle," Mara scoffed. "She hired a woman to give sewing lessons. They cost extra, of course, but Cousin Aubrey came up with the money."

"I told the boys to be ready in about an hour. They've never been to a wedding, and when Sam said they were welcome, you'd a thought he'd given them a silver dollar."

"I should have cut their hair, but I couldn't corral them long enough."

Even normal conversation was somehow strained. Mara picked at her food and drank her coffee. When they had finished eating, she filled the dishpan with the dishes and poured water from the teakettle over them.

Pack was in the bedroom when she went upstairs to change her dress. He was standing beside the bureau with her ivory-handled brush in his hand. He placed it beside the matching mirror and grinned at her sheepishly.

"A Christmas present from Miss Fillamore, or rather, from the funds she kept to buy gifts for those who would otherwise not receive anything. Regardless, they're my treasures." She opened a small box and took out a brooch. "I got this when I graduated. Isn't it beautiful? I don't get to wear it very often."

"Are you going to wear it today?"

"I'll wear it to Emily's wedding. I didn't—" She paused and looked up at him.

"You didn't get to wear it to yours," he finished for her and drew her to him. "Honey, you got cheated. You should have had a pretty dress so you could have worn your treasure. Instead you wore that ugly old black thing and was married after a funeral by a preacher who was less than willing."

"You don't hear me complaining, do you?" She wound her arms about his neck and kissed him firmly on the mouth. "Besides, it will be something to tell our children and our grandchildren. You were so mad at me you could have bitten a nail in two, and I wanted to kick you for being so bull-headed. But, darling, I wouldn't change one thing! *You* are my treasure."

The kiss they exchanged was long and sweet. She felt the trembling in him and wanted to reassure him. But reassure him about what?

Mara, on the wagon seat beside Pack, held her parasol over her head to keep the sun off her face.

"You look mighty pretty, Mrs. Gallagher." Pack's eyes swept admiringly over her from the perky straw hat trimmed in wide ribbon that matched her light blue dress to where soft kid shoes peeked from beneath the hem. The neckline of her dress was low, and nestled between her breasts was one of her treasures, the brooch.

"This is the first time you've seen me dressed up."

"Keep the parasol up, honey. I don't want you getting a

sunburn.'' His eyes lingered on the neckline of her dress and he made a growling sound deep in his throat.

"Behave yourself, sir, and pay attention to your driving. This is not the time for you to get amorous," she said with mock hauteur.

Behind them the boys were scuffling.

"If you boys get your shirts dirty before we get to town I'll box your ears," Mara threatened.

"Ahh . . . you wouldn't do that." Travor gave his brother another push. " 'Sides, you couldn't catch us."

"You're right about that. But Pack could. He'll hold you while I slap you good."

The twins hooted with laughter. They were in good spirits. They had a little money in their pockets and they were headed for town.

"Ya'd better watch out, Trav," his twin warned. "Mara Shannon'll get ya!"

Mara shook her head hopelessly.

"You're about to scare those boys out of ten years' growth, honey," Pack scolded gently, then laughed as she wrinkled her nose at him.

"You're not helping matters by laughing at them," she said sassily, trying to hold back her own smiles.

Pack had forced himself to laugh. He had never felt less like laughing in his life. He felt as if he were sliding down a slippery chute, powerless to stop himself, and at the end was a yawning black pit. He loved this woman sitting beside him more than life. The fact that she loved him in return was a miracle almost beyond belief. She touched off something inside him that was like music. During the last few weeks he'd had more contentment, the kind that didn't require anything but being near her, than he'd had in his entire life. Dozens of questions filled his mind and demanded answers. One stood out above them all. Was it all to end with this trip to town?

Mara knew that Laramie was a new town, but she was not prepared for the rawness of it. Wooden buildings, most of them unpainted, lined the dusty main street that led to the railroad tracks. Compared to Denver, Laramie was a primitive outpost, and yet Mara could see nicely dressed women going in and out of the stores with baskets on their arms. The street was clogged with vehicles of every kind. A freight wagon with a six-mule hitch came toward them. Pack pulled the team to the far side of the road to give it room to pass.

In front of the Diamond Saloon a man in a black serge suit and derby hat was helping a woman into a handsome buggy. The woman was lovely and her clothes the latest style even by Denver standards. She was dressed all in gray from the soles of her soft, high-button shoes to the wide-brimmed hat set atop piled blond curls. As they passed the buggy, she lifted gloved hands and deftly folded back a gauze of gray veil up and over her hat brim. She looked directly at Pack. He tipped his hat and the woman nodded.

Mara didn't need to ask the woman's name. Somehow she knew that she was Miss Candace Camp, the woman who had slept with her husband, the woman whom he had said was so understanding when he told her he was married and wouldn't be calling on her again. Mara glanced at her husband. He was handsome, very handsome, despite his rough, uneven features. How could she hold him when a woman as beautiful as Miss Camp wanted him?

"We're going to be right on time," Pack said as he turned the corner and slapped the reins against the rumps of the horses. "Sam said eleven o'clock and it's that now."

Mara closed her parasol. Her eyes sought Pack's face. His straight heavy brows were slightly wrinkled and his lids were lowered to shade his eyes. Was it nerves that caused the small muscle beside his mouth to jump? A little chill raced down her spine and up again. She placed her hand in loving possession on his thigh. He dropped his over it. The hand over hers was huge, hard as a rock and incredibly gentle. She turned her palm up so that her fingers could entwine with his.

A slight breeze kicked up little eddies of dust along the road but did little to dissipate the late morning heat. Ahead, beside a single giant cedar tree, was the church. Charlie's wagon was there, and a small knot of people stood in the shade beside the church door.

Emily's dress was eggshell white, high-necked, with a

tight, tucked bodice and sleeves that were puffed over her upper arms. The skirt was trimmed with heavy ivory colored lace. A blue ribbon wound its way through the rolls of shining hair she had fastened to the top of her head. Her small wire-rimmed glasses did nothing to dim the beauty of the bride.

The bridegroom, with a fresh haircut revealing the places in front of and behind his ears that had been shaded from the summer sun, wore a new black suit, white shirt and black tie. He stood beside Emily, his hand resting possessively at her waist.

Charlie stepped to the head of the team as soon as Pack pulled them to a stop and tied them to the hitching rail. Pack jumped down, reached to encircle Mara's narrow waist with both hands, and lifted her gently to the ground. He handled her as if she were a piece of priceless china. His face and his smile were the same, but Mara could feel his anxiety. It prevented her from wholeheartedly enjoying the occasion.

Greetings were exchanged. Mara kissed Emily's cheek and exclaimed over her dress. Emily proudly showed her the bouquet of flowers that had come in on the train that morning. Mara and the twins were introduced to Zachary Quill and the young minister. Mara liked both men immediately. The twins were awed by Zachary Quill's distinguished appearance and courtly manner and the fact that he treated them as if they were adults.

After Charlie gave his sister in marriage, he stepped back and placed her hand in Sam's. Tears came to his eyes. He held his head high and blinked rapidly. Sam was uncharacteristically nervous while speaking his vows; Emily was relaxed and smiling. Sam's fingers shook as he slipped the wide gold band on Emily's finger. Hers were steady as she gripped his hand. When they were pronounced man and wife, Sam's shoulders drooped with relief while Emily smiled joyously into his face.

"You may kiss your bride, Mr. Sparks."

Sam bent and reverently kissed Emily's lips. "Hello, Mrs. Sparks," he whispered in her ear.

Charlie cleared his throat to get their attention. He kissed his sister's cheek and shook Sam's hand. Everyone seemed to laugh and talk at the same time. The twins kissed the bride after Pack told them that no brother of his would miss the opportunity to kiss a pretty woman. Zachary Quill was as much at home with the group as if he were a member of the family. He had made arrangements at the hotel for a wedding dinner and invited the young minister to join them.

Zack led the way through the main dining room and into a reception room where a long table had been set up for the wedding party. A three-tiered, white-frosted cake sat in the center of the table and at one end, a bottle of champagne in a bucket of ice. No expense had been spared to make Emily and Sam's wedding day a day to be remembered.

Mara and Pack waited on the boardwalk in front of the hotel with Emily, Charlie and Zack while Sam went to get the wagon. Charlie would be staying in town with Zack and meeting with the superintendent of construction to work over the plans for the new penitentiary. Years had slipped from Charlie's face along with the relief that he was not a hunted man. He laughed at Emily when she cautioned him to eat three good meals a day and get a good night's sleep. He told her to go home with her husband and that he expected to be an uncle before this time next year.

After the bride and groom departed, Zack and Charlie said good-bye to Mara and Pack and turned back into the hotel. The minister had left earlier for another appointment.

Mara stood beside Pack, holding onto his arm. This was the first time they had been in public together, and she was proud of him. He stood head and shoulders above the majority of the men that passed them. A few men spoke to him, eyed Mara and walked on.

"Where did the twins go?" Pack asked.

"They didn't say." Her eyes met his and she smiled, slowly, questioningly. "Let's not go home yet. I'd like to walk up and down the street, see the town, and go into the mercantile."

"All right." Pack felt a quick sliver of panic. Mara seemed pale, unsure of herself. He had never noticed that in her before.

Mara sensed his reluctance. His hand as it covered hers in the crook of his arm was cold. She wondered about it as they started down the boardwalk. Mara looked into the window as they passed the millinery. She saw herself and Pack reflected in the glass. It seemed unreal to her that she was there and that the big, handsome man beside her was a permanent part of her life.

They moved on. A woman came down the walk toward them dragging a small child in her wake. Her eyes were on Pack and the look on her face could only be pure hatred. She paused for only an instant as her bright, almost feverish eyes shifted to Mara. With a toss of her head she squeezed her nose with her thumb and forefinger as if she were offended by a terrible odor, and went on down the street.

"Well, for the love of Pete!" Mara exclaimed. "What was that about? I've never seen her before. Do you know her, Pack?"

"No. I've never seen her before either," he muttered.

"Well, she probably thought that we were someone else, but that's no excuse for rude behavior." Another part of the joy was gone from Mara's day.

They crossed the dusty side street and continued on down the walk that fronted the stores. A woman in a stiff, black bonnet came hurrying through the door of the apothecary store and ran into Mara.

"I'm sorry, dear."

"It's all right."

The woman looked past her to Pack. Instantly the smile was wiped from her face and replaced with a tight-lipped look of disapproval. Pack tipped his hat and urged Mara on down the street. His stride not only lengthened but quickened until Mara was almost running alongside him.

"Slow down, Pack. These shoes were not made for running," she said breathlessly.

"I'm sorry, honey."

Mara had no time to wonder about the second hostile

encounter or to catch her breath before a screech came through the doorway of the barbershop.

"Pack! Pack, darlin'!"

Pack murmured a string of obscenities under his breath. With a firm grasp on Mara's elbow, he steered her inside, knowing that if he didn't, Nan would come barreling out of the building.

"Darlin', darlin', darlin'!"

Mara blinked her eyes to adjust them to the shade after being in the bright sunlight. A small woman with a mop of dark curls came hurling up out of the barber chair and threw herself into Pack's arms. She completely disregarded Mara, and the impact sent her staggering. To Mara's utter amazement the woman wrapped her arms around Pack's neck and her legs around his waist. She clung there, kissing him on the mouth.

"Nan! Behave yourself!" Pack said sternly. He grasped her beneath her arms and pealed her from him. She was thin, but her breasts were rounded and bounced with unrestricted buoyancy beneath the thin material of a dress that came to just below her knees. Black curls tumbled around a small, childlike face.

" 'Behave yourself, Nan,' " she mimicked. "You always say that." She giggled and tried to wrap her arms about him again. He held her away from him. Then and only then did she acknowledge Mara's presence. She backed off and looked her up and down. "Is this *her*?"

Pack saw Mara's face, white with shock, turn red as shock receded and anger took its place.

"This is my wife. Mara Shannon, Nan Neal is a friend of mine."

"Friend?" Nan turned big, brown, accusing eyes up at Pack. Her head didn't even reach his shoulder. "Hell's bells, Pack! We ain't just friends. Ya know I love ya more 'n anythin' in the world, darlin'." Her wide, red mouth was turned down at the corners.

"I know you do, honey. But—"

"Ya love me a little. I know ya do."

"Of course, I do."

"Then why'd ya marry a prissy, namby-pamby like her? Hell, ya need a woman with guts! She don't look like she's got no more guts than a pile a cow shit." Nan moved close to Pack and snuggled her head against his shoulder.

Mara barely recovered from the nightmare of hearing her husband call another woman "honey" and confessing that he loved her "a little" before the soaring heat of her temper loosened her tongue and defrosted her muscles. She clamped her hand around the handle of the parasol that hung from her wrist, drew it back, and whacked Nan sharply on her rear. The girl jumped as if she had been shot.

"Sheeit!" she yelled, grabbing her buttocks with both hands.

"I'm not so namby-pamby that I'll take sass from a two-bit whore," Mara yelled equally as loud. "Keep your hands off my husband or I'll show you enough guts to string from here to Denver."

Nan's fists knotted on her hips, her lips open with surprise. "Well, I do declare! The *lady's* got some piss and vinegar after all."

Pack stood in openmouthed amazement.

"And as for you, Pack Gallagher," Mara continued shrilly, "your whoring days are over as of this minute! If this is whore number two that Ace was telling me about, tell her that you'll not be calling on her again."

"Mara Shannon, honey, Nan's not—" Pack ran his hand over his face, striving to remain calm.

"I am too a whore!" Nan shouted belligerently. "I'm a damn good whore. Ask any man in town. If'n he's not been here, he's heard about me. I'm better than Miss Piss Queen at the Diamond Saloon." She turned a spiteful gaze up at Pack.

"You must be very proud of your accomplishments," Mara retorted sarcastically.

"I am. What have you got ta be proud of, honey?"

"I'm Mrs. Pack Gallagher, something you'll never be."

"Stop it!" Pack shouted. "I've looked out for Nan, and I care for her like she was my little sister. I've never slept with her."

"Ha!" Mara snorted. "Do you take me for a complete fool?"

"Tell her, Nan."

"I won't!" Nan crossed her arms over her chest and stared at Mara.

"Tell her, Nan, or I'll beat your butt," Pack threatened.

Nan turned big, sorrowful eyes up at Pack, took a deep breath that lifted her shoulders and released it.

"Oh, all right. But she makes me so mad—"

"Nan!" Pack roared.

"He's not been in my bed, but it wasn't because I didn't want him there. I'd a give him a hell of a time, wrung ever' drop outta him 'n not charged him a dime." Nan tossed her dark curls back over her thin shoulders and looked lovingly up at Pack before she turned eyes filled with dislike on Mara. "I bet your *wife* sleeps in a sack with a drawstring on the bottom."

"I want to go home, Pack," Mara said in a voice that would brook no argument.

She turned away because it hurt too much to look at him and started for the door. She had taken only a few steps when she saw the poster on the barbershop wall. The big, dark block letters jumped out at her.

PACK GALLAGHER vs. MOOSE KILKENNY.
In the fight of the century, Pack Gallagher,
Wyoming Territory champion, will be pitted
against Moose Kilkenny, Kansas City pugilist
who recently defeated the Union Pacific champion.
London Prize Ring Rules will be observed.
August 28. Tickets: $2.00.

Mara felt as if her feet were glued to the floor. She had not been so isolated at the school in Denver that she had not heard about the barbaric sport called bareknuckle boxing, where two men got into a roped-off square ring and hit each other with bare knuckles until one of them could no longer stand. She was numb and sick and shocked that Pack would participate in such a savage contest. Her husband was a prizefighter, a man considered a tough and who associated with gamblers and all manner of low people. She stared at the poster, unaware of the silence behind her until she heard Nan laugh.

"Are ya goin' to the fight, *Mrs*. Gallagher? Or do ya swoon at the sight a blood? I'll sure as hell be there rootin' for my man. Moose Kilkenny'll think he's been run through a meat grinder when Pack gets through with him! Have ya been soakin' them hands in salt water, darlin'?"

"Shut up, Nan, or I'll—"

Mara didn't hear the last of what Pack threatened. She walked swiftly out the door and down the walk toward where they had left the wagon. She had almost reached the intersection when Pack caught up with her, silently and forcefully took her elbow in his hand, and walked beside her.

The twins were sitting in the back of the wagon sucking on peppermint sticks when Mara and Pack reached it. The boys had decided to wait there and hit Pack for the loan of a dollar, but when they saw the looks on the faces of both Pack and Mara, they instinctively knew that this was not the time to ask a favor. Without speaking a word, Pack helped Mara up to the wagon seat, untied the team and drove out of town.

The ride was one of the longest, most miserable of Mara's life. Pack said one sentence to her all the way home.

"Put up your parasol."

Mara obeyed automatically. Out of the confusion in her mind, certain things were becoming clear. The man she married had not been eager for her to go to town because he had not wanted her to know that he was a pugilist and that he was not considered "respectable" by the ladies of Laramie. Pugilists were not the cream of society in Denver either. How long did he think he could keep that knowledge from her? Of course, there had to have been a conspiracy between him and the twins, for surely they knew.

The sessions in the barn with Willy were to get him ready for a prizefight with the person called Moose Kilkenny. How could she have been so stupid as not to realize that there had to be something more to pounding on a gunnysack than getting his strength back?

And the girl, Nan, who admitted to being whore. She loved Pack, and Pack had some fondness for the girl. He had been firm with her, yet gentle. Mara glanced at him. He sat with his brows drawn together, staring straight ahead. What other surprises awaited her? Through sheer will she controlled the desire to cry.

Pack stopped at the house. Trellis came around to help Mara down, and the wagon moved on down the lane to the barn. Inside the house she went slowly up the stairs to the bedroom, took off her hat, placed it carefully in her trunk, and changed into a work dress. Her good shoes had a little mud on the toes which she wiped off before she put them away. Afterward she went downstairs, sat down on the loveseat in the parlor, and stared at the clock on the mantel. She heard Pack come in, go upstairs and then go out again.

When the clock struck seven, Mara was surprised time had gone by so fast. She went to the kitchen and lit the lamp. A fresh bucket of water sat on the wash bench. She ladled water into the washpan, washed her hands, and began peeling the skins off the new potatoes she had boiled that morning.

Pack came in and stood behind her where she was stirring the potatoes in the spider. He put his hands on her shoulders, kissed the hair above her ear, and then took his place at the table without a word. They ate a silent meal. When they had finished and she rose to put the dishes in the pan, he caught her wrist.

"Mara Shannon, this is killing me. We've got to talk about it."

"Not now, please. It's too new," she whispered raggedly.

He let go of her wrist, got to his feet and went out. He didn't come back to the house until after Mara had gone to bed. He came to the room, undressed, and got into bed beside her. He reached for her, and she didn't resist.

"Good night, sweetheart," he whispered. With her chin in the palm of his hand, he kissed her softly before he wrapped his arms about her as he did each night, her back firmly against his chest.

Mara was sure she would never sleep, but she did and awoke to the rhythmic sound of someone chopping wood.

She knew Pack was not beside her even before she turned and spread her palm over the bedsheet. It was cool. He had not been beside her for some time. Mara went to the window and looked down. Pack was in the yard, stripped to the waist. Piled beside him was a stack of freshly cut wood. Mara knew that because Pack never left wood in a pile. He stacked it neatly, either against the side of the porch where it would be handy for the cookstove, or between the two elm trees beside the house.

She went to the kitchen and prepared breakfast before she stepped out onto the porch and called him. Pack dunked his head in the trough beside the well and washed his shoulders and arms before he came to the house.

"Morning," Mara said. "From the looks of that pile you've been up a long time."

"Morning." He put his arms around her, hugged her close, and kissed her. His lips were smooth and soft against hers. "That coffee smells good."

They sat across from each other. Pack ate a hearty breakfast while Mara picked at hers. He refilled the coffee cups, and when he sat down again, he reached over and covered her hand with his.

"I want to tell you about Nan."

"You don't have to. What you did before you married me is none of my business," Mara said, a tremor in her voice.

"I think it is. I'm what I am, Mara Shannon. I know that you're disappointed and hurt. Nan is hard to take all at once. I should have prepared you for meeting her and for the less than cordial reception from the women in town."

"Don't f-fight that man," she blurted, her voice shrill.

"It wouldn't make a speck of difference in their attitude if I backed out of the fight, which I won't do because I've given my word."

"Your word? For all that's holy! Do you think more of your word than you do of me?" Anger made her unreasonable.

"You mean more to me than anything in the world." He spoke quietly but firmly, his dark eyes holding hers. "I'd lie, cheat, kill, or die to keep you safe. This is another matter.

I've given my word that I'll fight Moose Kilkenny and I will. I agreed to the match because it will give us the money we need to start ranching.''

"We don't need money so badly that you have to debase yourself in such a manner." Tears sprang to her eyes and she lowered her lids. She would not cry! She couldn't talk or think straight if she did.

Pack's hand slid from hers when he sat back in the chair, but his eyes never left her face.

"What does debase mean?"

"It means to . . . to lower or degrade one's self."

"By whose standards, Mara Shannon? Yours?"

"Everybody's. It's what it says in the dictionary."

"I don't feel that I'm doing that by fighting in the ring. Your father told me to be my own man, make my own path. I consider this fight a job. I hold no grudge against Moose Kilkenny, and I don't believe he holds one against me. We'll be paid for a boxing exhibition."

"A sideshow, you mean." She couldn't keep the hurt out of her voice. "It's not civilized."

"It isn't civilized to push the Indians off their land, but we do it. Most people think it's all right because there are more of us than there are of them."

"But the gambling—"

"People have been gambling since the beginning of time. They bet on horses, dogs, cockfights, footraces, anything that's a contest. That's the reason why the women were so hostile to us in town yesterday. Their men will be gambling on the results of the fight."

"Why do they blame you? Why don't they blame their men?"

Pack lifted his shoulders. "It's easier to blame me."

Wildly, she said, "I don't want you to do it!"

"I can understand that, and I'm sorry if you feel humiliated because of it. But I'm going to fight this one last time. After that I promise you, sweetheart, I'll not get in the ring again."

"Why is it always the Irish that do these things?" she demanded.

"It isn't only the Irish, Mara Shannon. It's true that we Irish love a good scrap now and then, but not all prizefighters are Irish."

"I hate when they call us shanty Irish micks!"

Her pain went deep. Pack could feel it. He wished to hell Shannon had never put her in that fancy school where she'd never really been accepted because she was Irish. In spite of the rift between them, Pack was relieved to get everything out in the open. There was one more thing that she would have to be told sooner or later, but he couldn't bring himself to tell her now.

"Do you want to hear about Nan or not?" Pack asked.

Mara looked down at her tightly laced fingers resting on the table in front of her. The vacant feeling in the pit of her stomach expanded. A man like Pack would not allow a woman, even if he loved her, to press him into doing something he didn't want to do. But, Lord! She'd not planned on loving him so desperately.

Pack watched her but said nothing.

She lifted her lids and looked at him. "You can tell me if you want to."

The sadness he saw in her eyes was almost more than he could endure. He wanted to pick her up in his arms and take her to the highest mountain where she would never be hurt again. He wished he could think of something comforting to say, but the right words wouldn't come. Instead, as calmly and as honestly as he could, he told her about finding Nan in the mining camp. He told her that he had given the girl money to buy the barbershop and that she was repaying him.

"I must have been the first man who was kind to her without wanting her body as payment. The man I took her from was a mean bastard who had beaten her every day for months. When I first saw her she was a pitiful little bag of skin and bones. She's grateful, and I think she loves me like she would a brother."

Mara sat quietly looking at her hands. After awhile she heard Pack's chair scrape on the floor when he got up. He went to the water bucket for a drink, then went out the door.

That evening after supper Mara set a pan of warm saltwater on the table.

"You'd better soak your hands."

Pack looked up at her, but she had turned back to the dishpan. When she was ready to go upstairs, she rested her hand briefly on his shoulder as she passed behind him. He sighed deeply. He recognized her touch for what it was. It was not a loving caress, but a gesture of resignation.

Chapter
TWENTY-ONE

The thought that pounded in Mara's head while she went through the motions of cleaning, cooking, sewing, washing and ironing was that she had married a modern-day gladiator. On August 28 her husband would enter an arena much as they had in ancient Rome. He was one of a class of men who fought other men in public for the entertainment of spectators. How could it be called a sport? It was barbaric and uncivilized.

Pack and Willy spent several hours each day getting ready for the boxing match. Mara never went to the barn or the bunkhouse, but occasionally she went to the garden to pick beans or dig a few potatoes. When she came downstairs in the morning Pack would be gone. He appeared for the noon meal and again for supper. The twins, excited about the coming contest between their brother and the unknown Moose Kilkenny, kept their distance.

Mara had retreated behind a wall of polite silence that was not conducive to teasing or laughter or light conversation. She took little notice of things outside the house with the exception of the flowers she had planted along the walk the day Ace January had come to the house. She tended then carefully.

Every day or so a man would ride out from town and spend several hours with Pack either in the barn or the bunkhouse. He never brought the visitors to the house. Mara wondered if the visits had something to do with the boxing match, but she didn't ask.

Most evenings Pack sat on the porch with her while daylight faded. They stared off toward the mountains and occasionally talked about nothing that was important to either of them. The only time the barriers between them were down, and even then not completely, was in the dark of the night while they were in bed. He held her, kissed her, loved her and made sure that she enjoyed the union as much as he. Their bodies communicated in a way their minds could not. But when morning came, they were again polite strangers.

The last week of August arrived and with it the blistering heat of late summer.

"I'm going into town tomorrow and I'll spend the night there," Pack said one evening while they were watching the sky darken. He waited for Mara to comment on that announcement and when she didn't he said, "On the way, I'll take you over to stay with Emily."

"I'd rather stay here."

"You know I don't want to leave you here alone, Mara Shannon."

"For heaven's sake! Do we have to go through that again? I'll be all right here with Steamboat if he's as good with a gun as the twins say he is. And to hear Willy tell it, he's no slouch either."

"Willy's boast is true. That old man can hold his own, but he'll be in town with me. Emily will be at home. I thought it would give you a chance to get away from the house for awhile."

"That's very thoughtful of you, but I've things to do here."

"The boys want to go."

"I'm not surprised. They're at an age where a barbaric, bloody contest between two *gladiators* is exciting to them."

"Mara Shannon, it's not—"

"No?" She threw up her hands. "I don't want to talk about it! I'm going to wash the quilts and blankets if it's a good drying day."

"You're wearing yourself out, Mara Shannon. You've lost weight these last few weeks. Pretty soon I'll not be able to find you in the bed." Pack attempted humor because he didn't know what else to say.

"I'm going to pickle some string beans, make chow chow and start a barrel of vinegar." She spoke absently, as if her mind were a million miles away.

Pack watched her. Her head was tilted back against the porch post, her profile and the arch of her neck clearly defined. Of late her cheekbones were a little more prominent, her eyes less bright. Those things came with hard work and sleepless nights. Her face was the same, but it seldom changed expressions.

It was killing him to be with her and not have the intimacy they had shared those few short weeks in early summer. At that time he had been as near to heaven as he ever hoped to be. Each day now the distance between them seemed to widen. She didn't nag, question or demand. She didn't laugh or smile or make unnecessary conversation either. She was sick with disappointment. He could see it in her eyes.

"It's cooler now. I think I'll go to bed."

Pack didn't reply. It was the same each night. He sat alone, dealing with his own misery while she got ready for bed. After awhile he would follow, slip into the bed like an anonymous, faceless lover, and take her in his arms. No matter how tired he was or how determined he was not to give way to his desire, his body would leap in response to the touch of hers, and he would love her until they were both drained and exhausted.

It all boiled down to one thing, Pack concluded as he

looked up at the stars. Mara Shannon's love didn't include Pack, the bareknuckle boxer who was going to debase himself and humiliate her by climbing into the ring in two days' time. It didn't include the man who had a sisterly love for a little whore who had never known kindness, and her love wasn't for Pack, the man who was held in contempt by the "Laramie Ladies."

How in the hell was he going to make it through the next thirty years living with her, but without her? She was his life.

With a long stick Mara punched the quilts down into the soapy water again and again, going from one washtub to the other. It was an hour after sunup and she had two quilts in each tub and four blankets hung on the line. She was wet from her bosom to her knees. The twins had helped her fill the washtubs and now they were getting ready to leave for town.

Already she was exhausted by the heat and the labor. She poked the quilts down in the water one last time, left the stick in the washtub, and went to the well to draw up a fresh bucket of water. She carried the bucket to the shade of the back porch, wiped her face on her already wet apron, and drank a dipperful of water.

A lone rider was coming up the lane from the road. At first Mara didn't pay much attention, thinking the man was just passing through. She opened the screen door to go into the kitchen. She wasn't frightened, but she didn't like being caught looking so untidy.

"Cousin Mara."

The call stopped her. She squinted her eyes to get a better look at the rider and recognized him just seconds before he rode into the yard. Cullen removed his hat and wiped his forehead with his shirt sleeve. He had grown a mustache since she had seen him last, and he looked leaner, harder. When he smiled, his teeth showed white against his deeply tanned face. The smile was not meant to be friendly, and Mara knew it for what it was: a lecherous leer.

"You're lookin' mighty purty today, Cousin Mara." His voice was heavy with sarcasm. "To see you like this was worth every hot, dusty mile I rode to get here."

"What do you want, Cullen?"

"Do I have to be wantin' somethin'? Ain't I welcome to see my pa 'n brothers 'n my purty cousin?"

"Your father and the boys are down at the bunkhouse."

Even as she spoke Cullen was stepping down from his horse. He dropped the reins, and the ground-tied trained animal stood motionless, his nostrils flaring at the smell of the water. Cullen took the dipper from the bucket, his eyes still on Mara, and drank.

"Your horse needs water."

"I'm hungry. Fix me somethin' to eat, Cousin Mara."

"You can get something at the cookshack."

"I want to eat here." He walked into the house.

"I didn't invite you into my house, Cullen," Mara said, following him.

Cullen stood in the kitchen and looked around. "My, ya got it fixed up purty fancy, ain't ya?"

"Leave. I don't want you here."

"Chairs 'n' a oilcloth for the table," he mused as he grasped the round knob on the back of one of the chairs and rocked it.

"Steamboat will feed you before you leave," Mara said pointedly.

Cullen threw his hat into the corner and sat down at the table. "You fix me somethin'."

"Pack will be back soon. He'll tear you up if he catches you here."

"That's a pile a shit, Cousin Mara. He spent the night in town with the little whore from the barbershop. And today Moose Kilkenny will tear him up, scramble his brains and cripple him for life."

"You're lying."

"About what? The whore or the fight?"

"Both."

Cullen lifted his shoulders and grinned. "If that's what you want to think, it's all right with me. Fix me a meal 'n I just might tell ya what I found out 'bout yore dear papa while I was in Denver."

"I don't want to hear anything you have to say, but I'll fix you a meal to get rid of you."

"You'll want to hear this. Yes, sirree bobtail, you'll want to hear how you got passed over by your old man."

Mara set out the meat she had cooked the day before, bread, butter and boiled eggs.

"Miss High-and-Mighty McCall ain't got a pot to piss in," Cullen remarked and laughed at the way she clamped her jaws together and glared at him. "Chaw on that news while I eat, Cousin Mara."

Travor came bounding in the door. "I thought that was your horse."

"Howdy, little brother. Sit down. Cousin Mara invited me to breakfast." Cullen cut off a portion of meat and took a big bite. "Get me some coffee, Mara."

"I'll not fire up the cookstove. You can drink what is left." She poured the lukewarm coffee in a cup and set it on the table within his reach.

"Purty persnickety for a poor relation, ain't she, Trav?"

"Are you here to cause trouble, Cullen?"

"Naw, Trav. I just wanted ta see my pa 'n my brothers afore I head out for Californy."

"Pa's in the shed working on the harnesses."

"Then switch yore tail down there 'n tell him I'm here."

"Leave Mara Shannon alone, Cullen. Pack'll stomp you in the ground if you don't."

"Pack's in town gettin' stomped, little brother. I'll stomp yore ass in the ground if you don't do what I tell you."

"Go on, Travor," Mara said calmly.

Travor stood hesitantly in the doorway for a moment. Then he went out, slamming the screen door behind him. Cullen laughed with his mouth full. Mara turned away in disgust.

"Sit down, Cousin. I'll tell ya all about my trip to Denver. I got a whole parcel a news." Mara sat down at the far end of the table. Cullen laughed again. "Yo're just dyin' to know what I found out. Ain't that right? Yo're so nosey, I almost think yore kin to ole Brita instead a Pa."

"Say what you've come to say and stop playing your stupid games." Mara's temper flared as she spoke.

"Now, now, now," he said soothingly. "Don't get upset. I need what money ya got on hand, Cousin Mara, afore I set about rememberin' anythin' 'bout that trip to Denver."

"What?" Mara rose up out of her seat.

"I'm headin' for Californy, like I said. I need money."

"Then go. I'll be glad to see the last of you."

"I jist couldn't believe yore fine, upstandin' papa would go through all that money he got from sellin' his claim."

As Cullen's eyes bored into Mara's, she felt a numbness in her chest. He was mean and evil, and he cared for no one but himself. But he was smart enough to come here when he was certain Pack would be away.

"I'll give you what I have and I want you to leave. I don't want to hear anything you've got to say." His laughter followed her up the stairs. Mara opened her trunk and took out the twenty-two dollars she had brought with her from the school. She dropped four dollars back in the trunk, took the rest downstairs and threw it down on the table. "This is all I have. Take it and go."

"Jesus Christ! Eighteen pukin' dollars! Ole Pack holdin' out on ya, Cousin? If I find yo're holdin' out on me—" His voice carried a threat.

The door opened and Aubrey stood there. Travor crowded in behind him.

"Howdy, Pa. The family black sheep's come home."

"How be ye, son?" Aubrey's eyes went to the money Cullen was stuffing in his pocket, but he didn't comment on it.

"Fair to middlin', Pa. Where's Trell?"

"Waterin' yore horse. The poor beastie was fair in need. 'Tis no way to be treatin' a good horse."

"Sit down, Pa. Have ya ate? Mara Shannon'll fix ya somethin'. Fix my pa some breakfast, cousin."

"Cousin Aubrey ate breakfast hours ago. I want you out of here, Cullen. You can talk to your father and the boys outside."

"Ain't she the limit, Pa? Ya'd think she was queen a the roost. I come to tell her 'bout ole Shannon's will, but she don't want to hear it.'' Cullen laughed in a boastful way that made Mara detest him all the more.

"Ye best be shuttin' yer mouth 'bout it 'n bein' on yer way, son.'' Aubrey's voice was stronger and more positive than Mara had heard it before.

"Ya givin' me the push-off, Pa?''

"I dinna want ye to be makin' trouble for Mara Shannon. Me 'n the boys has a good place here, 'n we be treated fair.''

Cullen's eyes narrowed as his lips curled downward. ''You willin' to kiss Pack's ass to have a roof over yore head? What happened to yore pride, Pa?''

"I'm thinkin' I finally found it. Say what ye've come to say, Cullen.''

"I was down in Denver 'n went to see a lawyer feller named Randolph. I seen his name on a letter that come here to ya. 'Course I know ya can't read a line,'' Cullen said with a sneer in his voice. ''Ole Brita'd only tell ya what she wanted ya to know. I got to thinkin' Shannon might a left somethin' to us 'n the spiteful ole bitch didn't tell us.''

"Brita dinna lie!''

"Ah, shit, Pa. She'd spit on Christ if it'd helped that bastard!''

"Hush yer mouth, Cullen,'' Aubrey commanded harshly.

"Whata ya know, boys? Our pa's gettin' guts!'' Cullen's eyes darted to Mara. ''I ain't hushin', cause I want this prissy ass woman with her nose in the air, who come here a stirrin' things up, to know that her pa didn't think she was so much. He cut her outta his will 'n left this land 'n everythin' on it to Pack Gallagher! Her name ain't on the papers a'tall!''

Mara, standing behind a chair, held onto the knobs on the back. It took a few seconds for the import of Cullen's words to penetrate her mind. The smile on his lips and in his eyes was spiteful. She tore her eyes away from his gloating face and looked at Aubrey. She waited for him to deny what his son had said. He was shaking his head sadly and looking at Cullen as if he were seeing him for the first time.

"Ye've got a mean streak in ye, son.''

"Papa wouldn't do that!'' Mara said stoutly. ''Cousin Aubrey, you know Papa wouldn't do that.''

"Aye, lass. 'Tis true. I dinna know till after ye left the school 'n come here. Brita told me the land 'n all was Pack's and he'd a put us out long ago if not fer her 'n the boys."

Mara pulled the chair out and sat down.

"You got all that school learnin', cousin, but yore just *poor* shanty Irish like the rest a us. This house 'n everythin' in it ain't yores. Yo're payin' to stay here by sleepin' with a *prizefighter*. Them high mucks in town call him Irish trash. How's he in bed, cousin? Whores say he's hung like a bull 'n can outlast a two-peckered stallion."

"Shut up, Cullen!" Travor shouted. "You've done your dirt. Why don't you just shut up?"

Cullen turned a mean gaze on the young boy. "Ain't you forgettin' who yo're talkin' to, boy? Watch yore mouth or ya'll be spittin' teeth."

Mara jumped to her feet. "Get out!" she shouted.

"What're ya all up in the air for, Cousin Mara?" Cullen stood, his hands palms down on the table.

"I want you out of my house!"

"Yore house?" He cocked his head to one side. "I've been ponderin' on why yore papa cut ya out 'n left it all to Pack. There ain't but one reason I can think of. Ya warn't old Shannon's kid. I'm thinkin' Pack was. Him 'n Pack was mighty thick. Shannon McCall could a had the hards for crippled ole Brita." His lips curled in a travesty of a smile. "Now that'll give ya somethin' to think about for awhile."

Fury rippled through Mara, turning her emerald eyes dark, loosening the violence that had seethed just below the surface since he had arrived. She took two long strides and swung. Her palm connected sharply with Cullen's cheek.

He grabbed her wrist and bent her arm backward.

"Ya damn uppity bitch, I'll show what a real man—"

"Let go of her!" Travor yelled.

The young boy made a flying leap and landed on Cullen's back. Trellis, from beside the door, tackled Cullen from the front. Beneath the weight of the two boys, Cullen let go of Mara's arm and went down. Chairs went crashing to the floor. The oilcloth slipped and Mara grabbed the lamp before it fell from the table.

"Here now! Here now! Stop! Ye hear?" Aubrey pulled first at Travor and then Trellis.

Eyes wide with the horror, Mara knew that if she'd had the strength she would have killed Cullen. She stood with her back against the cookstove, her hands on her cheeks. Fighting back waves of nausea and tears, she watched as the boys were pulled off their older brother. Cullen got to his feet. For a long moment he stared at Mara with pure hatred in his eyes before he picked up his hat and stomped out of the house. Aubrey and the twins followed close behind him.

Watching from the window, it seemed certain to Mara that Cullen was going to attack the boys. He went as far as to shove one boy against the other, but the twins stood their ground shoulder to shoulder, and if Mara hadn't been so upset over all that had taken place she would have been terribly proud of them. Cullen shouted something and shook his finger in his father's face. After a few minutes of hot exchange, Cullen mounted his horse. He pointed the animal down the lane and kicked him into a run.

Mara was sitting at the kitchen table with her head on her arms when she heard the screen door open. She looked up to see Aubrey standing there.

"He's gone, lass. 'Tis sorry I am that he come."

"Come sit down, Aubrey. I just can't believe that Papa would do this to me."

"He had his reasons, to be sure, lass. I just not be knowin' the meanness in Cullen." Aubrey sat down at the table and clasped his hands in front of him. "What he said 'bout Shannon 'n Brita be lies to hurt you. Shannon be lovin' Colleen to his dyin' day."

"I know that. It made me so angry the way he talked about Brita. Cousin Aubrey, why did you and Brita come to the school and tell me you were my guardians and let me think you were going to take care of my property until I could manage it myself?"

" 'Twas Pack's plan. He said it was a way for his mother 'n the boys to have a home. Ye see, lass, we be down 'n out. Pack come to say Shannon had passed on 'n his place in the

Wyoming Territory would go to wrack 'n ruin without folks on it. I was to bring Brita 'n the boys 'n Cullen too. Cullen was not so wild then.''

"But you and Cullen hate Pack."

"Not so much hate, lass, as resent. He come from time to time, tellin' us do this, do that. I not be knowin' he be the rightful owner, just be thinkin' he be puttin' his bill in. Brita had sworn not to tell.''

Wave after wave of humiliation washed over Mara. She had come here thinking this was *her* home. She had even offered half of the land to Pack if he would marry her. How was she going to face him?

"Cullen said everything. Papa had to leave me enough to pay for my schooling. How else could I have stayed there?''

"I not be knowin' 'bout that. There be no cash money here to be payin' fer a fancy school. 'Twas Cullen's idea to board men on the run, lass. 'Tis hard to say, but I not be man enough to stand agin him, whiskey bein' me best friend. Brita be knowin' it, God bless her soul.''

"Being able to admit it shows that you're more of a man than you think you are. Could it all be a mistake, Cousin Aubrey?'' she asked hopefully.

" 'Tis true as I know it, Mara Shannon. There be a way to know if yer not wantin' to ask Pack. In Brita's box under the bed ye would be findin' letters.''

"The wooden box Pack said his father made while still in Ireland?''

"Aye. That be the one. The key is on a nail behind the bureau, or else it was. Brita did the readin', me not bein' able to read a line. Sure 'n 'tis glad I am the boys be learnin'.'' Aubrey got up from the table. "Pack be a fair man, lass. He took a hard hand to me at first, but 'twas needed. I be sober now 'n lookin' after me boys. 'Twas what Brita always wanted.''

"They're good boys. Not at all like Cullen."

"Aye. They want to be off to town. Steamboat and meself will be keepin' a eye out here, lassie. Yer not to worry. Cullen won't be back.''

"Tell the boys I don't want Pack to know he was here.''

"Aye. He be havin' enough on his mind this day."

When she was alone, Mara dropped her head down on her arms that rested on the table. She felt betrayed. She began to shake as if she had a chill, and then numbness settled over her. It was an effort to swallow, to blink her eyes, and especially to think beyond one thought. She had come here thinking this was her home and that she had every right to be there. She had refused to leave when Pack ordered her to go, and had bullied and shamed him into marrying her by offering him one half of his own property. She moaned aloud as if she were in great pain.

In the early dawn the streets of Laramie were empty of horses and wagons. No one was about except for a couple of drunks sleeping beneath a stairway that hugged the side of a building. The air was crisp and cool. Pack breathed deeply and moved his shoulders in a circular motion to loosen the muscles. His thoughts were not of the fight that would take place in less than six hours, but of his wife at home. He wondered if she was awake, if she was thinking of him, and if she had missed him during the night as much as he had missed her. The twins would be in this morning; he wondered if she would send a message with them.

The weeks had passed slowly while he trained for the fight. Mara Shannon had not come to the barn to watch him work out, nor had she nagged at him about the coming match. She had ignored him except at the times when they ate a meal together or at night when she responded to his loving. When he left her the day before, she had returned his kiss with a little more fervor than he had expected, but he could read nothing of consequence in that.

He no longer had to dread that she would find out he was a prizefighter, but he did worry about what would happen when he told her about Shannon's will.

Pack and Willy had arrived in Laramie at dusk, had supper with Charlie and Zack, and had spent the night at the Railroad Hotel. Sam and Zack would keep an eye on the crowd that could become unruly and try to get to the fighters if they were not pleased with a decision. Pack had gone by the Rivers' place on his way to town. It was a pleasure to watch Emily's face when she looked at her husband. And Pack was surprised to see Sam's usually grim face so relaxed and smiling. Both of them had found together what they needed to make them happy.

The clear sky promised a fine day. Pack didn't care what kind of day it was. He wanted the match over. He wanted to go home with the money it would take to give him and Mara Shannon a good start at ranching. In order to do that, he had to win the fight. He didn't dare be overconfident. Moose Kilkenny was a fighting man and strong as a bull. His weakness was good Irish whiskey. Pack had seen Moose fight. He was what Pack considered a wrestling type of fighter. He would try to hold a man with one arm while hitting him with the other if he got the chance. Moose was experienced, but so was he. He would pace himself and make Moose do most of the work in the early rounds. He would save himself, wait for his chance, and be careful not to be caught flat-footed. If he did that he was confident he would win. He had bet one-half of his money in Flagg's bank on himself. It was his last fight, and the first bet he had ever placed on himself to win.

He walked past the field where the ring had been set up next to the Kosy Kitty Saloon. Plank seats had been tiered against the building on one side and against the corral fence on the other. Along the back and the front, lengths of canvas had been stretched to keep the freeloaders from watching the fight without paying. Herman Flagg expected a standing-room-only crowd. Pack hoped he was right. The larger the crowd, the more money for him.

Pack walked back toward the hotel, his footsteps echoing hollowly on the boardwalk. Later in the day the Laramie Ladies would be marching and singing and protesting the match. They had posted signs calling for a vote to outlaw boxing because it was a savage, primitive custom.

Good luck, ladies, Pack mused silently. Contests of strength and fighting skills had been going on for centuries. Boxing was becoming a popular spectator sport back East where the fighters wore gloves. Pack didn't think the ladies had much of a chance outlawing it if a vote were taken. Although women were allowed a vote, here in the territory men outnumbered them two to one.

The bartender at the Diamond Saloon came out and stood on the walk waiting for Pack.

"Mornin', Pack. How do you feel?"

"I feel fine. I'm stretching my legs before breakfast."

"Have you seen Kilkenny?"

"No. I'll see him soon enough."

"I hear he's turned mean lately. His last fight ended nasty when he tried to gouge a man's eyes out. Watch him. He'll do it if he gets a chance. There's a lot ridin' on this fight for him."

"I'll watch it. Thanks."

"One more thing. There's a gang of toughs in town betting on Moose. If I were you I'd stay off the street until fight time."

"I intend to do just that." Pack grinned. "Thanks again, Boston."

Pack walked on. Many of his teamster friends had come to town to see him fight. It was only natural that Moose had a following too. News of this match had brought men in from all over the territory. Zachary Quill had said that even a newspaper man had come up from the *Denver Post*.

Back at the hotel, Pack went directly to the kitchen for his breakfast, an arrangement Herman Flagg had made with the management. Willy was waiting for him. They ate steak and eggs, then went to the room to wait until fight time.

A loud, boisterous crowd had gathered when Pack, Charlie and Willy ducked into the canvas-enclosed dressing room that had been assigned to them. Pack wore flat-soled shoes made of soft black leather laced up above his ankles. His blue tights fit his legs and muscled thighs like a second skin and ended at his waist, leaving the rest of him bare when he removed his shirt.

"Odds are three to one cause a the beatin' ya took by them toughs," Willy said. "They ain't thinkin' ya've had time to get in shape."

"They're going to get a surprise, huh, Willy?"

The old man grinned. "I'd a not bet a hundred on ya if I thought different." He began to rub Pack's shoulders.

"Don't let Moose get a bear hug on you," Charlie cautioned. "A fellow told me and Zack that he'll get up close so the referee can't see his hand and he'll grab your balls."

"He used to be a pretty square boxer. What's happened to him?"

"He's slipping and knows it. He's desperate to stay in the ring."

"And I'm desperate to get out."

The sound of a bell sent Willy to the peekhole in the canvas. "Big crowd. Lots of soldiers from the fort," he commented before the bell rang again.

"May I have your attention, please! Gentlemen!" The crowd gradually quieted so they could hear.

"It's the sergeant that refereed before." Willy looked over his shoulder at Pack.

"Flagg said he'd be the one. He's a fair man."

"Take a look at what's on the roof of the Kitty Saloon," the referee shouted, and the crowd turned to look. Four men stood on the roof with rifles in their hands, Sam and Zack among them. "These men have been instructed to shoot any man who attempts to lay hands on either of the fighters." The referee stopped speaking when his voice was drowned out by jeering from the crowd.

"There's a tough crowd here," Charlie said softly. "Railroad workers, soldiers, gamblers and town toughs. I see some townsmen and even a few women."

"This boxing match," the referee yelled, "is sanctioned by the Midwest Boxing Association, headquartered in Kansas City. London Prize Ring rules will apply. Any part of a man's body, other than the soles of his feet, that touches the floor of the ring will be considered a knockdown and ends the round. A thirty-second rest will follow with an additional eight seconds to allow the fighters to come to the center of the ring. Butting, gouging, hitting below the belt and kicking will result in a forfeit. A winner will be declared when one man fails to come to scratch within ten seconds of time called for the next round."

"Are ya ready, Pack?" Willy was always more nervous than Pack before a match.

"I'm ready. I'm anxious to get it over."

The referee was shouting through a roughly made megaphone.

"Moose Kilkenny, winner of fifteen fights, loser of three, will be wearing black tights."

Wild yells from Kilkenny's backers and jeers from Pack's announced Kilkenny's entry into the ring.

"Pack Gallagher, the challenger, recently defeated Black Bob Mason in a match that lasted three rounds. He has won ten fights and lost none. He'll be wearing blue tights."

A deafening roar erupted from the crowd. Pack deliberately waited a few seconds before he walked out to the ring. Friends shouted encouragement, foes shouted insults. He vaulted up onto the platform and ducked under the rope.

The referee brought both men to the center of the ring. Moose Kilkenny's body was thick, hairy and powerful. Pack, a good five or six years younger than his opponent, stood slightly taller, slimmer in the waist and even more muscled in the shoulders and biceps.

In a loud voice the referee announced that Pack's nails were too long and would have to be trimmed. An angry hiss came from Kilkenny's backers. Moose grinned and waved. His grin changed to a scowl, however, when the referee called for a bucket of water after he examined Moose's hands and ran his fingers over knuckles that were as hard and rough as gravel. Amid loud, obscene complaints from the crowd, the referee scrubbed Moose's hands with a brush, removing a film of hard, dried dirt mixed with glue. When he finished he said a few loud, uncomplimentary words about a man who would take unfair advantage, gave Moose time to dry his hands and sent him to his corner.

The tough old sergeant held up his hands for silence, his eyes on the timekeeper who sat at ringside. At a signal from him, the referee lowered his arms and yelled, "Time!"

Chapter
TWENTY-TWO

When Mara got up from the chair, it was so fast that the chair rocked back on two legs before it righted itself. She hurried to the bedroom before she had a chance to change her mind and shoved the bureau out from the wall. The iron key was there on a nail just as Aubrey had said. She dropped to her knees beside the bed and pulled out the wooden box. Without pause, she fitted the key into the keyhole, turned it and lifted the lid.

One part of her said it was wrong to read the letters. The other part of her said she couldn't live if she didn't. She closed her mind to what was right or wrong about it and lifted out a packet of letters tied with a ribbon. They were addressed to Brita. She laid them aside and took out another packet. The first one was addressed to Mr. Jack Gallagher. She pulled the letter from the envelope and quickly scanned it. One paragraph caught her eye and she read it slowly.

> Jack Gallagher, also known as Pack Gallagher:
> This is to inform you that you are the sole

beneficiary of the estate of Shannon McCall.
Please call at my office at your earliest
convenience.
James Randolph, Attorney at Law.

Feeling sick inside, Mara held the envelope close to her mouth, blew into the end to open it and slipped the folded paper back inside. *It was true. Her father had left everything to Pack.* Because of her disappointment, she almost didn't read the next letter, but she opened it because it was also from the attorney and addressed to Pack in care of Mrs. Aubrey McCall.

The funds in the account for Miss Mara Shannon
McCall are depleted. Unless payment is made to Miss
Fillamore by November 12, Miss McCall will be
asked to leave the school. Please advise.

Slowly, like someone in a trance, she picked up the next letter and began to read.

Angus Long, the fight promoter, sent the prize
money directly to me as per your instructions.
The amount will cover Miss McCall's tuition until
January 10.

Mara felt as if the breath were being squeezed from her lungs. She feverishly scanned the next six letters from the attorney. The contents were similar. The fight promoters had sent money. The last letter from the attorney was different.

Miss Fillamore has informed me that Miss McCall
will be teaching at the school immediately upon
graduation. She will receive room and board and
a small remuneration. Please advise if the money I
am holding for her personal expenses is to be put
into her personal account as in the past.

Tears began to slide down Mara's cheeks as the events of the past few years fell into place. Pack had been the one who had paid for her schooling. He had earned the money by fighting in the prize ring.

Miss Fillamore's neat, familiar handwriting was on several small envelopes. Tears fell on Mara's hands as she opened each of the letters and scanned them one by one.

> . . .Miss McCall was pleased with your generous
> gift. She is the only girl here who owns an
> ivory-handled hairbrush.

Each of the following letters was to acknowledge a gift; the mirror, the comb, the hair saver, the shawl, the coat. The last letter was dated a few days after she had graduated.

> The brooch was greatly appreciated. I must
> congratulate you on the selection. It is a
> beautiful piece. It was considerate of you
> to attend the graduation ceremony even though
> Miss McCall was unaware of your presence.

Mara's eyes were so blurred with tears that she could no longer read. She returned the letters to the box, locked it and slipped it under the bed. And then slowly, like an old and feeble woman, she crawled upon the bed, the key clutched in her hand. Sobs tore from her throat. Locked in her misery, she cried for a long time.

All of her treasures were gifts from Pack. He was the one who had seen to it that she had a gift at Christmas, not Miss Fillamore. How many times had he stood and taken the punishment of another man's fists in order to pay for them? How many times had he been hurt as he was the day she found him lying along the road? To think of what he must have suffered was almost more than she could bear.

She continued to cry even after she had no more tears.

*   *   *

It was the golden time of the day. The sun had gone down behind the mountains to the west and the light was fading from the sky. The first thing Pack saw when he and the twins rode up the lane toward the house was Aubrey at the washtubs wringing out the quilts and putting them on the line. A pressure began to build in his chest as his eyes searched for Mara Shannon and didn't find her. His instincts told him that something was wrong. Mara Shannon wouldn't leave her washing unless she couldn't do it herself. He kicked his tired horse into a trot and swung down as soon as he reached the yard.

"Where's Mara Shannon?" he demanded.

"In the house." Aubrey looked at Trellis and the boy shook his head.

"Is she sick?"

"Not that I be knowin'. "

Pack started for the house.

"Hold fer just a minute," Aubrey said. "There's somethin' ye should be knowin'."

"Well?" Pack swung around. His face was bruised, one of his eyes was almost swollen shut. He was bone weary and short of patience.

"Cullen was here."

"Cullen? Goddamn it! If he hurt her I'll kill him."

"He didn't hurt her," Trellis said quickly. "He had come and gone before we left for town."

"Why didn't you tell me?" Pack turned his fury on his young brothers.

"It wouldn't a done no good. You'd a just worried."

"Who decided that? Don't ever hold back anything from me when it concerns my wife."

"Dinna be layin' it to the lads, Pack. The lassie be sayin' that ye had enough on yer mind wid the fight 'n all. She dinna want yer to be worryin'."

"Why, all of a sudden, is everyone so concerned about worrying me?"

"There be more, Pack. Cullen be tellin' the lass about her pa's will."

"Jesus, my God! How did he find out about that?"

"He was in Denver 'n looked up a man named Randolph."
Trellis spoke hastily, not wanting his father to stand the brunt
of Pack's anger alone.

"James wouldn't have told him anything. Cullen probably
went to the public records."

"The lass is hurtin'." Aubrey stood holding the wet quilt,
water running down and making a puddle at his feet.

"Cullen's gone to Californy. He won't be back." Travor
led his horse and Pack's to the water troughs. "I'll take care
of your horse, Pack."

"Thanks, Trav. Keep an eye out for Willy. He'll be along
as soon as he sobers up enough to get on his horse." Pack's
hand was on the screen door; his eyes snared Aubrey's. "If
Cullen comes back, he'll wish to hell he had never set eyes
on me!"

The older man nodded.

The table was set for supper. Pack dropped his hat on a
kitchen chair and went through to the parlor. The lamp on the
mantel cast a glow over Mara where she sat as still as a statue
on the loveseat, her hands clasped in her lap. Her face was
pale and strained, with dark shadows beneath her eyes.
Against her almost colorless skin her hair glowed in the
lamplight like dying embers.

"Mara Shannon? Are you sick?" He sat beside her on the
loveseat. She remained motionless, her eyes fastened to his
face. Her skin was almost cold to his touch. "What's wrong,
honey?" He put a finger against her cheek.

"Is it ov—" Her voice broke. She swallowed and tried
again. "Is it over?"

"It's over."

"Are you all right?"

"Bruised and a little tired. Nothing that being here with
you won't cure."

"Your poor face," she whispered. "Let me see your
hands." She took one of his hands in both of hers and ran
her fingers over his cut and swollen knuckles. "I warmed
the ointment—" She bent her head and brought his hand to
her lips. When she looked up, her eyes were filled with
tears.

Deeply touched, Pack lifted her up in his arms and pulled her onto his lap. She wrapped her arms about him and buried her face in his shoulder.

"I'm so ashamed," she managed to say without giving way to the sobs welling up inside her.

"About what, sweetheart? Aubrey said Cullen was here. What did he say that upset you so much? Was it about your papa's will?"

"He said that Papa left everything to you. I don't really care about that, but—" She had to swallow before she could go on.

"Honey, Shannon wanted to make sure you'd not be cheated out of what was yours if something happened to him before you were of legal age. Aubrey was your next of kin, and Shannon was afraid he'd fiddle everything away before you were old enough to take charge of it."

"And he would have, or he'd have let Cullen."

"By leaving it in my name, your father made sure Aubrey couldn't touch it. I've been keeping it for you. It's all yours anytime you want to go to Denver to sign the papers."

"I don't want it. I just want to be here, with you. Pack—" She opened her hand and showed him the key to the box under the bed. She wound her arms around him and held him as tight as she could. He could feel her lips move against his neck when she spoke. "I read the letters."

He didn't know what to say. He held her for a long time, hoping to quiet his pounding heart, wanting and loving her in silence. After awhile she moved her face so her lips were near his ear and they were cheek to cheek.

"I love you." Her voice was merely a breath in his ear.

Deep down inside Pack something warm began to blossom and grow. He felt as if he had been given the world. She lay soft and relaxed against him, her breasts pressed to his chest. With his eyes closed he bowed his head and buried his cut and bruised face in her hair.

"And I love you," he whispered. "I can't remember a time when I didn't love you. Shannon knew it. I think he was hoping that someday you'd love me back."

She moved her lips away from his ear and he could feel

them against his cheek. Her sensitive fingertips moved along the line of his jaw, stroking gently.

"I do love you, and I've been so . . . awful. I don't know how you can still love me."

He was overwhelmed with a feeling of love that went far beyond physical desire. Her lips were indescribably sweet as they searched for his. The kisses they exchanged were soft, gentle and full of sweetness. When she pulled her mouth away, he kissed her eyes, nose and temples, then tantalized the corners of her mouth.

"You're easy to love, sweetheart."

"If you've loved me for a long time, why didn't you want to marry me?" Her palms held his cheeks while she moved her head back to look at him.

He looked at her for a long while, loving the shape of her face, her mouth, loving and wanting all of her, and trying to think of the right words to say. His fingers smoothed the hair back from her wet forehead and then moved to behind her ear to stroke gently.

"Because I didn't want you to be ashamed of your husband, and looked down on because you were my wife."

She drew in a great trembling breath. "I shamed myself by behaving the way I did. Can you ever forgive me?" She gazed at him with big, solemn eyes that slowly filled with tears.

He pulled her close again. "Sweetheart, you don't need my forgiveness. I should have told you about the will and about me being a prizefighter before we were wed. I should have given you a chance to change your mind, but it all happened so quickly, I hardly had time to think. I wanted you so bad—"

"I loved you even then, but I was too stubborn to admit it." She leaned back so that she could see his face. "Why did you want me to leave after Brita died?"

"I wanted you to have a taste of town life while I got rid of Cullen. Then I was going to explain things to you and you could have decided what you wanted to do."

She ran a finger over his puffed mouth and kissed his bruised cheekbone.

"Thank you for paying Miss Fillamore so I could stay in

school. Thank you for my Christmas presents.'' She swallowed, afraid she'd not be able to say all she wanted to say. "Thank you for coming to see me graduate. I wish I had known you were there. I thought I was the only one who didn't . . . have someone.'' Tears she could hold back no longer flowed freely.

"You were as pretty as a picture in your white dress,'' he whispered. "I couldn't keep my eyes off you.''

"Why did you come?''

"To look at my girl,'' he said simply.

"I love you.'' Her hand stroked the bruised flesh of his cheek gently. "I can't bear the thought of you being hurt, of that man . . . hitting you.''

"I hurt him more than he hurt me, sweetheart.''

"Please don't do it again.''

"I won't. I've already promised you that.'' He smoothed the hair back from her face. "Don't you want to know if I won?''

"I knew you'd win. I never doubted it for a minute.'' Her brows drew together in a worried frown. "It was the longest day of my life,'' she whispered.

"Honey, let's go to bed.''

Her emerald eyes searched his face. "Your supper is ready, and I made your favorite—everyday cake.''

"I'm not hungry for supper. I want to go to bed . . . with you.''

At first there was nothing; then a smile that started at the corners of her lips spread into an impish grin.

"We've had some pretty good fights, haven't we?''

"Aye. And I'm thinking we'll have more, Mara *Stubborn* Gallagher.'' His laugh was a soft purr of pure happiness. "Willy says you're just what I need to take me down a notch or two.''

"I think I like Willy.''

She slid off his lap and took his hand. They walked up the stairs with his arm across her shoulders.

"I forgot about the quilts in the washtub.'' She stood in her chemise, digging in the drawer for her nightdress.

"Aubrey hung them on the line.'' Pack, stiff and sore in

places he had forgotten about, grunted as he tugged down his britches and stepped out of them.

"Aubrey felt bad about Cullen coming here. I could tell that he was ashamed. He's a different man since he stopped drinking. Oh, I don't want to forget to tell you about how the twins stood up to Cullen. You would have been so proud."

"Forget Aubrey, forget the twins, forget the nightdress, Mrs. Gallagher. Forget that other thing you've got on too." Pack lay down on the bed, stretched out, and groaned with contentment. "Come here, wife. I need to hold you."

Mara slipped into bed beside him and fit into his arms as if she had been made with him in mind. He closed his eyes and drank in her nearness, her softness, the elusive sweet scent of her.

"You're hurting more than you let on," she accused between pecking kisses on his shoulder.

"I'm hurting in only one place right now," he murmured, rolling her gently over onto her back and hovering over her. "Ye're eyes be all swollen from bawlin', Mrs. Gallagher. Ye be lookin' like somethin' the cat dragged in," he teased in a lazy Irish brogue. His eyes were swollen and surrounded by blue bruises, but they shone with happiness.

"Aye. 'N to be sure ye be knowin' about cats, would ye not, Mr. Gallagher?" Her soft happy laughter was accompanied by his low chuckle. His eyes devoured her face.

"Aye, me beauty. But 'tis not cats I be thinkin' of." He placed soft kisses on her smiling lips. "I be thinkin' on what I want to be doin' when I be findin' a naked lassie in me bed."

"What about yer wife, sir?" she demanded with mock horror.

He lowered his head and nuzzled at her breast with his mouth. "She be cruel 'n cold. She dinna be understandin' me."

"Alas! Poor man!"

With effortless strength he rolled onto his back and lifted her to lie on top of him, her thighs cradled between his, her breasts loving the rough texture of the hair on his chest.

"Bein' a true Irish gentleman, I'll be lettin' ye love me, if ye be so determined 'n all."

"Letting?" Mara almost choked on laughter. "But sir, I don't be knowin' what to do."

He pulled her up until his lips could reach her ear. His whispered words produced cries of alarm.

"Oh! 'Tis indecent what ye're proposin', sir!"

Their laughter filled the room and spilled out of the window and into the yard below. Aubrey McCall paused, listened, smiled, and continued to empty the washtubs. He wished that Brita could know how things turned out between Pack and Mara Shannon. He looked up at the heavens.

"Maybe ye do be knowin', me love," he murmured. "For if ever there be an angel it is ye, Brita Gallagher McCall."

In the bed upstairs, Mara was tangled in Pack's arms as they rolled to their sides, her soft belly against the flat muscles of his. His strong body quivered as hands, softer than silk, glided over his bruised flesh. For a long moment they lay with lips barely touching while she whispered her love over and over, hearing the words returned in a hoarse whisper. Her tongue licked at the cuts on his lips, his sore and swollen hands caressed the smooth skin of her back and buttocks.

"Ah, love, love," he sighed blissfully.

"Lie still, my gladiator, let me love you."

Her heart was filled to overflowing with love for him. He had given her so much. He had asked for nothing in return, not even her love. As her hands and her lips moved over him she tried to tell him all that was in her heart.

And when the time was right, she took him in her hand and guided him to her as he had told her she would always have to do.

"Come in, darling," she whispered. "Please, come in."

EVERYDAY CAKE—Modern measurements
⅔ cup of butter
1½ cups sugar
2 beaten eggs
1 teaspoon vanilla
2½ cups flour
2 teaspoons baking powder
⅔ cup milk.
Mix butter, sugar, eggs and vanilla. Mix baking powder and
flour in separate bowl. Add to the butter and eggs mixture
alternately with the milk, beating after each addition. Bake
25 minutes at 350°.

EVERYDAY CAKE—Brita's measurements
Lard the size of an egg
A teacup and a little more of sugar
Two eggs
Grate a little nutmeg for flavor
Two teacups and a little more of flour
Baking powder to fill the palm of your hand
Milk enough to make batter spread in a pan.

Mix all together and bake in an iron skillet until a straw
comes out clean when poked into the middle of the cake.

AUTHOR'S NOTE

The earliest evidence of boxing as a sport is found in Crete from about 1500 BC. The sport was introduced by the Greeks into the Olympic Games in the late seventh century. Boxing for the Greeks was a part of physical training for the military as well as a sport, with the emphasis on courage, strength and endurance rather than agility and defensive skill.

The first set of rules governing bare knuckle boxing were drawn up by Jack Broughton, known as the father of English boxing, in 1743. The rules were revised in 1838 and again in 1853. Under the new rules, called the London Prize Ring Rules, bouts were held in a 24-foot square ring enclosed by ropes. Butting with the head, gouging, hitting below the waist and kicking were banned, although in some areas back-heeling to trip an opponent was permitted. In 1889 under these rules, John L. Sullivan beat Jake Kilrain in a seventy-five-round fight in defense of his heavyweight championship. He was the last of the bare knuckle fighters.

Beginning with the Irish immigration from the late 1840's, following the potato famines, the Irish provided a constantly renewed pool of boxers in the United States.

Reaction to bare knuckle boxing from the law and from religious groups was persistently hostile in the 1800's, more in some areas than in others.

The Marquess of Queensberry Rules, which called for gloved matches, appeared in 1867. The first champion under these rules was James (Gentleman Jim) Corbett, who defeated John L. Sullivan in 1892.